Guardians of the Time Stream

Book Two

Sanctuary

By

Michelle L. Levigne

Ye Olde Dragon Books
6909 Ackley Rd.
Parma, OH 44129

www.YeOldeDragonBooks.com

2OldeDragons@gmail.com

ISBN 13: 978-1-961129-16-0

Published in the United States of America
Publication Date: November 15, 2023

Chapter One

San Francisco, 1877

"What are you going to do first?" Ess Fremont asked.

She stood with Athena Latymer on the observation deck of the airship, *Golden Nile*, looking out over San Francisco on one side and the ocean on the other.

"As I told your Mr. Fitch, we are going to clean house."

Ess snorted, the best she could do to keep from responding to "your Mr. Fitch." The idea of Allistair Fitch being attached to her emotionally was laughable. Granted, he was clever, a good leader, and good-looking, but she didn't have time for such considerations. She had her heritage to reclaim.

"We are obviously not protected enough by separating the many divisions of the Originators," Athena continued. "It is only by the grace of God that the *Golden Nile* and the Blue Lotus Society have been shielded as well as we have. Perhaps keeping one hand from knowing what the other is doing has worked against us. We need to regroup. Close ranks. We will stay here until Stryker's life as Seth Judson, Pinkerton agent, has been thoroughly excavated and we have some idea of the depths of his treachery." She gripped the rail and looked down on the waves creating frothy white lines along the coast. "Then we go to Sanctuary."

"To do what?"

Granted, the idea of Sanctuary conjured up all sorts of images of vast rooms filled with Originator records, and hundreds of people who could fill in the missing pieces of her life, and perhaps someone among all of them who could help her find out what happened to her grandparents. Still, going to Sanctuary equated with jumping feet-first into a dark pit with no idea of where the bottom lay or what waited for her in that darkness.

Ess hadn't survived seven years, effectively on her own, by taking ridiculous risks like that.

"Enroll you in lessons, of course, to catch up on all that schooling you missed."

"But—but don't you think that's dangerous? If the Revisionists have spies and traitors among us, won't they be at Sanctuary?"

"Most definitely. You, my dear, are our best bet to infiltrate and listen and observe, because you are an unknown quantity."

"Won't that make me your weakest link? I don't know anything."

Yes, and whose fault was that? Ess couldn't help feeling that someone had been playing games with her mind and her memory, just as they had blocked her brother's memories, to keep him under control. It simply did not make sense that she could have grown to the age of fourteen in the household of Ernest and Matilda Freemont, acknowledged leaders of the Originators, and *not known* what the organization did, not even suspected all the resources at their disposal.

"That will be your protection," Athena said, sounding entirely too calm. "No preconceived notions, no sense of how things should be, clouding your judgment. You will question everything you see, and you will see what those of us who are familiar with Sanctuary and the operations and rules of the Originators could miss."

"You can't take me to Sanctuary. If the treachery is there like you fear, we can't let the traitors know you are head of the Blue Lotus Society. The people who know you can hear and use the lotus will make the connection. It will be like blowing a trumpet or hiring a carnival barker to tell the world you are the custodian. Plus, we need to keep the existence of the *Nile* a secret, our ace in the hole."

"True." Athena's lips twitched as if she fought not to smile.

Ess gripped the rail in front of her and tried not to grind her teeth as understanding crashed through her. She muffled a groan.

"You already thought of that problem, didn't you?"

"We did. I'm glad to see we are on the same page."

"The problem is figuring out who else is available to turn me over to higher authorities. Who has the power to —"

Ess caught her breath and pressed her lips flat as the answer burst into her mind. It was the perfect opportunity, the perfect tool, the perfect opening. Even more important, it would give her a chance to vent her ire at those who had helped her grandparents keep her in the dark about her heritage. Her family line for generations, on both side, were leaders of a group of people descended from time travelers. They were engaged in a battle with another group of descendants of time travelers, which had lasted for centuries, trying to influence or corrupt or protect the fate of Humanity.

"All we need is a good excuse for running to them," Ess murmured, and turned to look out over the ocean again. "Some reason for a self-reliant, independent young woman to suddenly need advice and shelter and go running to the other side of the country."

"To whom?"

"To the family lawyers. Endicott, Lewis and MacDonald. Someone did say they were all three Originators, or was I mistaken?"

"You were most certainly not mistaken." Athena rested a hand on Ess's shoulder. "Yes, quite logical. Who else but lawyers entrusted with delicate Originator business would be expected to take you under their wing and set you back on the track of claiming your heritage?" She sighed and nodded with a smile. "Yes, our enemies will never suspect a thing when you turn up and settle in for some long-overdue schooling."

~~~~~

"One problem solved usually leads to several more," Fordyce Chamberlain announced cheerfully, as Ess stepped through the door of the council room Athena used as her office. He and her brother, Ulysses, were the only ones present, but that would soon change, with a council meeting in the offing now that Athena had picked up another task and problem to resolve.

She met Uly's eyes and they both shook their heads and exchanged grins. Ess slid into the chair at the table next to him and waited for him to continue. Just in the short time she had known Ford, she had learned that was the best way to deal with the big man when he was in his odd, mischief-making moods. Something was up, if he could sound and look cheerful when making what should have been a depressing statement.

"Are you sure you want to face down our intrepid family lawyers so soon?" Uly reached to catch hold of her hand under the table. He did that quite often, ever since they had been reunited, and Ess hoped his habit never grew irritating. She had missed her older brother intensely over the last seven years. Half the reason she had joined the Pinkertons was to have the resources to try to find and follow his trail.

"It has to be done sooner or later." She writhed a little in her seat and gave an absent nod of thanks to Ford when he set a bottle of sarsaparilla in front of her. Knowing what she knew now, Ess admitted the smart course of action should have been to turn herself in to Endicott, Lewis and MacDonald when her grandparents vanished and she discovered the headmistress of her boarding school was involved in another Southern plot to restart the Civil War.

"Never pays to hurry, no matter how important the errand," Ford said as he settled into the seat opposite her and Uly. He winked and took a sip from his own bottle.

Ess wished the atmosphere were lighter, so she could tease him about how long it had taken to ask Athena to marry him.

"I still say the sooner we're clear of the Pinkertons and all their questions, the better off we'll be," Uly said. "While I'm grateful for their help, I can't help feeling they're also to blame for some of the Stryker problem."

"I am still a Pinkerton," she reminded her brother.

"Not if I have anything to do with it," he muttered, scowling, then ruined the effect by winking at her.

"You don't," Ford said. "If Stryker hadn't been playing with the Pinkertons, for whatever ends, Ess never would have been assigned to the exhibition and we wouldn't have found her and you wouldn't have been reunited and we wouldn't know that Stryker was a Revisionist. All to the good, I say." He saluted her with the bottle before taking a small sip. "Go at the problem from the other side. The Pinkerton connection may dig up
~~~~~

information identifying who among our leadership knew Stryker was masquerading as Judson, and how many other names he used. Who knew of the plan to use Pinkerton connections and information sources, ostensibly for Originator business, but ultimately for the Revisionists? We need to get some idea of who are traitors, or what's even more troubling, who are Revisionists who snuck their way into our ranks over the years, before we walk into Sanctuary."

"It's all the dratted compartmentalization and secrecy," Ess said. "It has protected us through the generations, but I think it's more a hindrance than a help now. We don't know what anyone is doing, making it easy for the enemy to infiltrate and for trusted members to turn traitor."

"True," Athena said, coming into the room. "Before we discovered Stryker's treachery, I was quite looking forward to taking the *Nile* to the very gates of Sanctuary, and sharing some of the burden we've been carrying since the Blue Lotus was established."

"You wanted to see the astonishment on the faces of those hide-bound fools who have decried airships since they first appeared in the sky." Ford hurried to get up and hold her chair for her.

Ess was as delighted with the kiss he brushed across Athena's cheek as she was with the brilliant, rosy blush that threatened to cover her mentor from head to toe.

"True." Athena winked at Ess and rested her hand on his for a moment when he sat down next to her. "I have also felt that while our divisions protected us, they also handicapped us. I can't help feeling that the Revisionists are all one mind, working in unity, and while our resources tell us their numbers and tools are much smaller than ours—"

"Can we trust those resources?" Uly said.

"Exactly," Ford said. "Unity of mind sounds lovely on the surface, but smacks of a hive mind like various insect species. My team and I ran into too many of those in our travels. Horrific things, all swarming in one huge carpet across the ground, chewing up everything that had the misfortune of being in their way, or great black clouds in the sky, moving in perfect synchronization, as if one mind did all their thinking." He shuddered, and Ess suspected only a small part of that revulsion was foolery.

"There is that," Athena said. "However, I can't help feeling that sometimes they have an advantage over us."

"Well, they don't have to worry about traitors in their midst," Uly said. "Unless that's what you mean by the advantage? They would have detected treachery much sooner?"

"We didn't detect it at all," Ford said, his tone mournful.

"Question. Who among the leadership in Sanctuary knows about the society and the *Nile* as an academic disguise for our activities? Are any of them among the traitors? If no, we're safe. If yes, then we're wasting our time taking these precautions."

"If we continue with our precautions, they won't suspect that we know the truth," the older man said with a thoughtful frown.

"Here's something else to consider." He tightened his grip on Ess's hand. "The longer we take delivering Ess to Sanctuary for training, the more suspicious they will be. Especially if there was a leak somewhere, and someone heard she's been found, and reported to the higher-ups. Yet how do we explain how we found her without revealing the society's activities?"

"That is what this meeting is about," Athena said. "Ess and I have come up with the general idea, but we need to work out the details carefully. We need to delay long enough so Ess goes in with some training and preparation, and yet not so long that no one believes she knows nothing. I still find it difficult to believe Ernest and Matilda kept her in ignorance. We are quite caught between a rock and an even harder place."

"The problem is determining who has heard the news, and how they heard it," Ford said. "If even the slightest hint escapes that we were involved, using the lawyers as the cover story won't do us a speck of good."

"I trust all our people, everyone who reports directly to me," Athena said. "In this instance, our compartmentalization works for us."

"Can you be absolutely sure?" Uly muttered, as the door to the council room opened and Theo walked in, the first to arrive for the meeting.

~~~~~

Endicott, Lewis and MacDonald visited their various offices in a set rotation, sometimes going as a group, and other times individually, to cover as much territory and deal with as many clients as possible. As Ess realized now, they also dealt with Originator business under cover of their ordinary legal activities. The three lawyers would be all present at their Cleveland office in three weeks. That gave the crew time to clear up the last few questions, make arrangements for regular check-ins with the Pinkertons, and take care of necessary repairs, maintenance and supplying chores. Then they would set off across the country at a leisurely pace, heading for Cleveland. The airship had several stops to make as it crossed the country, picking up supplies and dropping off people who had assignments to complete, and carrying messages from one Originator outpost to another.

Ess knew she couldn't justify changing the set route and schedule just to suit her impatience to have questions settled, but that didn't help her deal with what Hilda, her grandparents' cook, had called a bad case of the grumbles. She couldn't help wishing to speed up the process. Until they had settled the problem at Sanctuary, she had no hope of finding the information or the resources to search for and hopefully rescue her grandparents. Her best way of dealing with her prickly spirits was to get away from everyone and dive headfirst into catching up on her Originator education. The best place for that, despite the chill air, was the observation deck. Ford found her there on the third day after making their plans, when they were still docked in San Francisco.
~~~~~

"You need a distraction," Ford announced.

He had to shout, because at this altitude, the wind whistled past the many bracing wires that turned the open observation deck into a birdcage. Most people tended to find the constant whistling and moaning irritating. Ess couldn't understand why. She liked the background sounds. Something about it held a promise of turning into music, maybe even words. Maybe it was just her imagination, but the sensation of memories poised on the brink of bursting into consciousness confirmed her aching suspicion that her memory had been tampered with just as her brother's had been.

Besides, she found the song of the guy wires and the wind actually helped her remember more clearly what she had just read. The song seemed to open up deeper recesses of her mind and assisted in subconsciously sorting the information. Athena wore a thoughtful expression just last night over dinner, when Ess told her why she preferred studying in the chilly observation deck, rather than the forward lounge. When that tiny vertical line formed between Athena's elegant brows and her eyes took on a distant look, Ess had learned she could expect something interesting.

"I don't need a distraction," she said, scooting around to find a more comfortable nest among the pile of seat cushions and five blankets she had brought up with her. The gray clouds threatened rain, and she looked forward to discovering just what changes rain would make to the song of the air. "I'm up here to avoid distractions."

"Let me rephrase that. You need guidance." He braced himself on the thickest of the vertical struts.

"In what? I'm working my way through all the books Athena has assigned me. I've written down everything I can remember from when we cleared out Granny's and Grandfather's offices and the archives in our house, and all the visitors we had around the time Uly vanished." For punctuation, she slapped the journal sitting next to her. "Do you know how depressing it is, to consider that some of the people they welcomed into our home were using that welcome to plot treachery against them?"

"Yes, Odessa, I know exactly." Ford's usual cheerful expression went unusually somber. "It's been eating at me since my team ran into trouble on our last expedition. Hindsight made us realize we were given just enough contradictory pieces of information to guarantee we would meet with disaster. Just like Uly was sent after us, with false information, to get him out of the way. Some clues found in our treacherous Mr. Stryker's personal effects... well, they suggest the plot had a specific focus on your family. We're in a tangled position, needing to move quickly to reduce the damage, when we would prefer several years to prepare for this battle."

"My family." The back of her head ached as thoughts swirled through so fast she thought she might get dizzy. "You mean my parents might not have died in an accident on their last expedition, but they were murdered?"

"The hands that built the trap that killed your parents have been dust for centuries. However, I fear someone knew about those traps and dangers, and they made sure your parents got the information that sent them, specifically, into the tunnels."

"Why would someone want to kill them? I know the Revisionists want to wipe us out, to try again to rewrite history. But why does it seem my family, specifically, is in the rifle crosshairs?"

"Blood and crystal, my dear." He bent and offered her his hand to raise her to her feet. "Your bloodline has an unusual affinity for the crystal at the core of the Machine."

"So does Athena. So do a dozen or more people." Ess put her books and the stoppered inkwell and pens away in her satchel before she stood. Ford gathered up the blankets, and pushed the cushions tightly enough into the gaps in the wires that it would take hurricane-force winds to pull them out.

"Yes, but you get it from your mother's bloodline *and* your father's. Ernest and Matilda both came from those bloodlines, so it's possible you and Uly would have a strength of affinity for the crystal that hasn't been seen since the original six women dismantled the Great Machine."

"If we don't continue our family line, then chances are better the Revisionists will have the only people able to fully reassemble and awaken it." She tried not to hunch her shoulders against a chill that had nothing to do with the rising wind, and let Ford guide her down the winding path through the wires, to the door back into the airship.

"Revisionists are constantly trying to control everything," he said, once the door was shut and warm air and comparable silence surrounded them. "Every few years, someone crosses over from their side to ours, thoroughly disgusted by the tactics they employ. And that reminds me. I have something of your mother's that I put aside in one of my caches. You should have it. She was friends with a woman who left the Revisionists, and they made friendship tokens for each other." He gestured at his neck, and Ess could only assume he meant a necklace or pendant of some kind. "Over the years, I've wondered if your parents were killed in an attempt to find the woman... Be that as it may. What was I talking about?"

"Revisionists controlling everything."

"Yes. The Revisionists have been breeding themselves since before the War for Independence, to have the strongest crystal affinity bloodlines."

"I thought the race to find the parts of the Machine was only a recent development."

"Oh, yes, the race. However, the determination to be ready for when the pieces came out of hiding has been going on since the Machine was disassembled. Our ancestors learned then it was impossible to destroy a single fragment of crystal. Only the strongest minds can re-shape it." He winked at her. "Which is why that intriguing box of dust you delivered to us has been driving Vulcan and her team to distraction."

"Theo thought it might be lubrication or something like that," she said, as she led the way down the corkscrew stairs, two levels, to the main deck.

"Lubrication for what? The emerging theory is that there are really no moving parts."

"How can a machine not have moving parts? How can it do anything if it doesn't move? What kind of energy does it need, to do what it's supposed to do? I just assumed it used the same kind of energy that made the Zeus guns work, or the lights, or all the incredible devices that make the light bulb and steam engine seem rather clunky and filthy by comparison."

"That's just it. Energy. The crystal doesn't require energy, so much as it *generates* energy, and that energy opens the way, moves the material of space and time, to allow travel through time. The more the Machine comes together, the bigger the clumps of it, the more frustrating the whole conglomeration becomes. Because it defies what we know and understand of science and engineering."

"Vulcan must be thoroughly delighted with the puzzle," Ess murmured, pausing at the doorway into the main deck area.

"We're taking bets on how long it takes for her to pull out all her hair, and how she will do it, a strand at a time or in great clumps." He reached around her for the latch. "Care to place a wager?"

Ess stuck her tongue out at him. Ford just chuckled and thumped her on the shoulder as she pushed open the door.

They didn't go to Vulcan's workshop, as Ess had half-expected, or to the conference room, or even Athena's office. Ford took her as far forward in the airship as they could go without standing outside. As soon as he opened the door and bowed her through, she felt the difference in the air, the subliminal humming of the ship as it hovered in the heights. Ess pressed her fingertips to the bones around the openings of her ears, confused by the sensation that her ears had been plugged. It was something like the temporary blockage she got when she rode in the basket, either rapid ascent or descent, a change in atmospheric pressure that required a corresponding change in pressure inside her ears.

"Ah," Dr. Sylvia said, stepping into the pool of light from the lantern hanging from the middle of the ceiling. "You were right."

"Right about what?" Ess flinched as she caught the oddly dead sound of her voice and the doctor's.

Chapter Two

This room had several windows across the front, for a spectacular view of the sky and landscape. They were covered now. Why? How had the acoustics been changed so their voices didn't bounce off of anything?

Athena stepped into the light and reached up to the lantern, turning a knob to adjust the wick, increasing the size of the flame. Why a lantern, when every room in the airship had the crystal-based lighting in the joins of walls and ceiling?

The light didn't reflect off anything but the two women and a table draped in dark cloth. Ess decided whatever covered the walls muffled sound as well as absorbed light.

Ford closed the door behind her. Ess heard the soft swishing of heavy cloth and surmised he had covered the door. She wanted to make an acerbic comment about secret societies and initiation rituals, just to release some of the pressure filling the room, trying to squeeze the air from her chest.

"Your comment about hearing singing in the guy wires got us thinking," Dr. Sylvia said, as Athena bent and reached under the heavy cloth draping the table. "Some of the oldest journals of the ancestors mentioned music and the song of creation as being the inspiration and guide for their stewardship. We thought they were simply waxing poetic, building themselves up as romantic heroes and martyrs for the good of mankind."

"Not to mention the fact that they wrote in a language few can read," Ford commented, settling down into a bench tucked into the corner furthest from the door.

"There is that." Athena set a bundle wrapped in more of that cloth on the table.

"What if music, or singing, or some combination, isn't just a clue, but the key itself?" Dr. Sylvia said. "What if it takes someone who can hear a song no one else can hear, to sing along with it?"

"I'd like to read some of those ancient journals." Ess clasped her hands behind her back to still the shiver deep inside.

"You'd have to get access to the legend to decipher them, although I doubt you'd have any trouble picking up the trick of the language and the alphabet," Ford said, a hint of laughter in his voice.

"Let me guess, Grandfather was the one who cracked the code?"

"Your great-great-grandfather," Athena said. "Then Ernest and his father translated all the journals, when he was younger than you. Our scholars have been arguing about the meaning ever since."

"It would help if they had access to the original legend and the original journals," Dr. Sylvia said. "That could be why Stryker wanted to get access to you, and perhaps recruit you."

"We're frightening her." She rested a hand on Ess's shoulder. Her touch did soothe. "One step at a time. Determining if you can learn to read the journals as easily as Edward and Vivian did is a strong reason to take you to Sanctuary. Everything is stored in your grandparents' vault in Sanctuary, and it takes a blood-and-crystal key to open the vault. Uly was never keyed to it, but you were. When you were a babe in arms," she added, before Ess could ask why she couldn't remember.

"The Revisionists get me to open the vault, maybe translate, and they gain a big lead in the race to find all the pieces." Ess shuddered. "Athena, what if... well, you've shown me how the lotus can control the pieces, make them adhere when the ones that fit together are close... I'm botching this. Does it make any sense that if enough pieces come together and generate this energy that Ford mentioned, maybe the big piece can find the other, smaller pieces? Maybe even... I don't know... draw them? Like a magnet draws iron filings?"

"That is what we hope, and what we fear." She stepped back over to lift the cloth from around the cube-shaped object she had put on the table. "That is part of why we have worked in separate, smaller units for so long, keeping the disparate pieces apart. Not just to prevent the Revisionists from finding and annihilating us, but to keep from generating energy and mass. The Blue Lotus Society hides behind the mask of the Consortium of Antiquities, while operating fully in the public eye. Hiding in plain sight."

"Poe's *Purloined Letter*, the principle illustrated there." Ess stiffened as the familiar shimmering of crystal went through her bones. "The dust is in there," she whispered, frowning at the slightly giddy sensation that accompanied the sound. "Why is it reacting like that—why am I reacting like this? It didn't happen before."

"The resonances of the outside world are muffled by the acoustic fabric," Dr. Sylvia said. "They don't interfere with the energy cohesion and sub-resonances of the dust. We have determined by exhaustive tests the dust resonances are just different enough from most of the crystal we have recovered so far... well, we theorize it was never part of the Great Machine to begin with."

"Then what is it for, and why was it preserved in the canopic jar?"

"Are you familiar with Blake?" Ford chuckled when Athena gave him a thoroughly disgusted look. Her lips twitched into a smile a moment later. "Your father's favorite wild goose chase was some elusive communication device of the ancients. He also loved to speak in riddles and hide his notes inside cyphers." His amused expression faded. "Served us well when we picked up clues to traitors moving among us. Not that we suspected anyone was selling us out to the Revisionists, just self-interested parties, trying to profit from the knowledge of the ancestors."

"Ford." Athena gathered up the cloth swaddling the box. Ess estimated it held only a cup of the dust she had found in the canopic jar in Kansas City.

"Sorry, my dear. The signal that he had found something relating to the device was a quote from Blake, 'The world in a grain of sand.' Well, what if it wasn't just whimsy, but a clue? What if we could see the world, speak to the world, or more accurately, people elsewhere in the world, not through a grain of sand..."

"But through a speck of crystal dust," Ess whispered, fascinated by the theories and possibilities unfolding in her head.

"You've already proven sensitive to the crystal. Your comment about the vibrations in the wires got us thinking last night," Dr. Sylvia said.

"Very late into the night. Into the morning," Ford added cheerfully.

"We don't want you to try anything specific." Athena held out one of the helix-shaped crystal rods. "For now, for today, we want you to just... play. Listen to the crystal, sing to it, if you want. Let it speak to you. It might take days of listening and perhaps even dreaming. Vivian often made her greatest healing advances after she had studied and experimented and worked herself into headaches, and then everything came together in her sleep. In her dreams. She often said she had a friend who visited in her dreams, and then you had an imaginary friend very young..."

"Carmen." The image of a little girl her own age at the time seemed to pop into Ess's mind, like stepping from behind a thick screen. She had a momentary sensation of having been spun around, or the room had suddenly expanded in size.

More proof, perhaps, that memories had been blocked just like Uly's had been? She made a note to confer with her brother, to find out how he felt when memories and bits of his life returned to him.

"Yes." Athena blinked away a sheen that hinted at tears. "Vivian wrote to me of your friend, how glad she was that you... well, that is neither here nor there. Yet it does rather reinforce my theory. Your mind works enough like your mother's, I'm hopeful you inherited that gift as well."

Ess took the rod and pressed it between her hands, to keep it from picking up the deliciously fearful shivers vibrating in her breastbone. Ford stood and opened the door, then waited until Athena and Dr. Sylvia stepped outside.

"How long?" She wasn't quite sure herself what she was asking.

"As long as it takes," Dr. Sylvia said. "As long as you feel comfortable working on it. I highly recommend regular breaks for fresh air and food, exercise and rest. Especially rest."

"Take as long as you want," Ford said. "But try to finish before we reach Cleveland." He chuckled when Athena sighed loudly. "Once those lawyers get hold of you, I doubt you'll have any room in your head for experiments."

"He's right, in a way." Athena made a shooing gesture. Ford grinned, bowed, then sauntered away. "Take your time. Expecting miracles in a matter of days will simply put up a barrier. This secret has waited for centuries. Your family has been working on it for generations. It would be ridiculous to expect you to unlock it in a few days. And it would be equally ridiculous not to try, while we have time and opportunity."

With a smile, she stepped out and closed the door.

Ess inhaled, raising her fingertips again to press, to relieve the sensation of increased pressure in the bones around her ears. When that dissipated, she put the crystal rod down on the table, wrapped it in a fold of the acoustic cloth, and reached to open the box of dust.

The shimmer of sound wasn't as strong as the first time she encountered the dust in the canopic jar. Likely an effect resulting from both the acoustic cloth and the reduced amount of dust. Ess played with the amounts, spreading a little on the table, then tapping the rod, listening to the sound that resulted, gauging the reaction in her sinus bones, then adding more dust. She repeated the process until all the dust lay on the table. Then she experimented with arranging the dust, drawing furrows, piling it as high as she could get it, then spreading it out as thin as she could.

She discovered that while the crystal rod vibrated, the dust clung together, so she could guide it into shapes. She had fun with that for a while.

When her thoughts wandered, she created a three-dimensional copy of the lotus, without quite knowing how she had done it.

"I think it's time to get some fresh air," she whispered, and set down the rod with as much care as possible, with her shaking fingers. Watching the lotus, she wrapped the acoustic cloth around the rod, and backed away from the table, then out of the room. She expected the construction to fall apart at any moment, but it still shimmered softly in the lantern light as she closed the door.

Uly stepped into the corridor at the far end when she was only a few steps away from the room. She signaled him to be quiet before he opened his mouth, and beckoned for him to approach. Frowning, he obeyed. She pressed one finger to her lips as she reached for the doorknob with the other hand. He rolled his eyes.

His mouth dropped open when he followed her into the room and saw the lotus. He walked around the table twice, with his hands clasped behind his back. Then he stepped out into the passageway.

"How did you do that?" he whispered, once the door had closed.

"The door is soundproofed," Ess said at normal volume. "I have no idea. I was—well, I wasn't concentrating on the dust. I was daydreaming, wondering about all the things the lotus could do, and I was playing with the helix rod and... it just came out of my mind, I suppose."

"You are amazing." He crossed his arms and leaned back against the wall. "Granny will explode when she finally comes back and sees all she's been missing. I know they tried not to pin all their expectations on us, but you are the answer to generations of prayers and hopes."

"I wish they had told me about some of those expectations, our whole family heritage." She leaned against the wall next to him. "I would have made so many different decisions the last few years."

"Hmm, true, but I think part of you wouldn't have missed all your adventures for any price."

Ess tried not to, but she returned his grin, and then they laughed together.

"I'm almost relieved we're not going to Sanctuary just yet," she admitted. "Ford mentioned the family vault, and something about a crystal and blood lock. It sounds rather... gruesome."

"The crystal of the Great Machine is miraculous stuff. We have the potential for technology our world will not achieve for another century or two. Think how much damage, how much change we could inflict on the world if we push technological and scientific developments faster than they are meant to go in the original schedule of history. Even more than frustrating the dreams of the Revisionists, we must protect the stream of time itself." He tipped his head to one side. "What's that look for?"

"What look?"

"Trying to decide if you're impressed or amused."

"You sound unusually responsible and philosophical."

"Wretched child!" He reached for her, started to shake her, then before Ess could do more than squeak and laugh, he drew her tight against his chest. "There's nothing more horrid than regaining all my blocked memories and realizing that for nearly four years, you didn't exist in my head and heart. It was like I had somehow killed you."

"Athena wouldn't have suggested it if she didn't think it was necessary."

"That's a polite way of saying I was a reckless, irresponsible mess."

"Hmm... true."

"Wretch!" He tugged on her braid. "Speaking of Athena, she needs to see what you did."

"I'm not sure what I did."

"At the very least, gave us an idea just how the women who dismantled the Great Machine managed it. If you can recreate the lotus while you're daydreaming, imagine what you could do when you're trained and your thoughts are focused." Uly turned her to face down the corridor.

"Did you ever go to Sanctuary?" she asked as he linked their arms and they headed for the far door.

"Once. Before you were born." Uly frowned, and his gaze didn't seem to be on the door only a dozen steps away. "I remember we didn't stay very long. Father argued with someone, and it was severe enough that we left immediately. I was supposed to be keyed to the family vault, but it didn't happen. Then after you were born, Father took me on an expedition with our grandparents, while Mother was recovering. You took far too long making your entrance into the world," he added, tapping her nose before reaching to open the door.

"Uly!" Ess laughed, despite the sudden ache of longing in her chest.

"While we were away, Mother visited Sanctuary with you, so you've actually spent more time there than I have."

"I can't imagine it did me any good, since I certainly can't remember."

"Well, you were keyed to the door. That's the important thing."

"What exactly does that mean?"

"There's a special panel, it's the lock and the key together. It's somehow locked into the special..." He threw his free arm up in the air. "Mendel? The monk who worked with peas. The things in the blood." Uly paused as they went through another door. "The recessive... something."

"Are you talking about genetics?"

"Yes. Genetics. You're the scientist, I'm the soldier."

"So the panel in the door somehow can look into our genetics?"

"It's keyed to our family's bloodline, and only someone of the bloodline can add an outsider to the lock. Touch a drop of our blood to the panel and press our fingertips into the indentations in the proper order. Then, when we want to open the vault door, we just touch those spots again and offer a drop of our blood. Crystal and blood."

"As I said before, gruesome."

Uly chuckled, and released her arm so they could go up the corkscrew stairs to the next level, on their way to Athena's workroom.

The lotus had collapsed back to dust by the time she and Uly led Athena, Theo, and Ford back to the acoustic cloth-draped room. She tried to duplicate what she had achieved, but thinking about how she had done it blocked the daydreaming state that had brought about the lotus in the first place.

That night at dinner, Ford presented her with one of her father's journals, which had been among a large stock of items Athena had kept with her, for reference and guidance. Ess couldn't help feeling it was on the order of a stick of candy to console a sulking child. Then Ford explained why he had chosen that particular journal, and promised when he had a chance, he would retrieve a dozen more just like it. This journal contained some of her father's research into the legendary communication device of the ancients that let them speak and hear and see each other. According to Ford, it had references to crystal, specifically crystal dust, mirrors, and blood links.

"Here's one of the most fascinating and frustrating passages," Ford said, flipping open the book to about two-thirds of the way to the back, and tugged on a strip of lacy blue cloth. "He meanders, quoting all sorts of sources that talk about crystal resonance, without actually saying what those sources are, so we could go back and read the entire passage. Probably because Edward made those notes just to remind himself what he had read. He lists all these resources, hints at theories that he agrees with and disagrees with, then here—" He tapped his finger on the bottom of the right-hand page. "Here he starts weaving together his own theory."

"The resonance," she said, reading aloud, "is not in the crystal itself, but inside the brain that is linked with the crystal. It is inside the perceptions attained through the extra energy, the power afforded through the crystal. Just as it is theorized that some animals can see colors that we humans cannot, and humans can see some colors that animals cannot, and many animals hear sounds and in ranges that humans cannot, the crystal that is properly linked—perhaps in the same method as the crystal-and-blood lock—with the human brain can speak and give images directly into the brain."

"Oh, yes, of course," Uly said. "Entirely clear and perfectly logical."

"You clown," Vulcan said, clouting him on the shoulder. He snorted and grinned.

"Father theorized..." Ess closed her eyes, trying to hold onto the idea that felt as elusive as mist. "Am I wrong, or was he theorizing that the crystal would put images and sounds directly into our brains, so that those who aren't linked with the crystal wouldn't hear or see... through the communication device?"

"You realize she's going to stay up until all hours reading, and thinking, until she figures it out?" Dr. Sylvia said.

"She is her father's daughter," Athena said.

They were right. Ess stayed up to read the journal from cover to cover. She didn't understand the entirety of it, because so much seemed to be mere jottings of notes, a gathering place of research results, with no theorizing until more than halfway through the book. Edward changed his theories multiple times as he learned more and either proved or disproved earlier theories. She found it fascinating to witness how her father's mind worked. Still, there was too much for her to comprehend in the first read-through.

She wasn't at all surprised when her dreams were full of broken mirrors, the pieces flying through the air, or crystal dust swirling about and taking on shapes she could never clearly identify before they swirled back into dust clouds and dust devils. She woke up several times, feeling as if she had been yanked out of the dream just a few heartbeats before an image solidified in her mind. Shortly before dawn, she fell into a deeper, more solid, yet no more restful sleep and dreamed of a mirror formed of the crystal dust. It swirled in a flat whirlpool, yet even as it retained its shimmering, granular texture, she could see herself in it. Behind her, other images spun and bounced from one side of the invisible frame to the other.

The mirror shattered and she cut her hand on a shard that exploded into dust and reformed into the mirror. Several drops of blood from her cut hand fell into the center of the spinning dust surface, and it turned smooth and glistening as pure glass. Ess gasped as her parents appeared in the new, liquid surface. They smiled and spoke to her, but she couldn't hear them.

She was waking. She knew she was waking, and knew that fighting to stay asleep, stay dreaming, would only wake her more. She absolutely hated that sensation.

Focus on the dream, think about it, not sleep, she scolded herself.

She saw her parents in the dream. They were looking at her, but outside the mirror. The dreamer. Her parents could see her.

Did the mirror allow her to speak to the dead?

Somehow that felt wrong. She had no time to think about the theological implications, but Ess was fairly positive that God didn't permit communication between Heaven and Earth. She knew her parents were in Heaven. The fact that she didn't see her grandparents in the mirror was some comfort.

Not that she could use that as proof that Matilda and Ernest weren't dead. Yet.

Ess sat up, sweating so she felt drenched and sticky. She picked up her father's journal, clutched it close for a moment, then rolled over, untangled her legs from her sheets, and put the journal down on the small table that extended out from the wall. She stripped off her nightshirt and washed in the water remaining in the pitcher and basin.

In that time, her head cleared enough to play with the images that remained sharp from her dreams. Ess stripped the sweaty sheets from her bed, curled up on the mattress with her one dry blanket, and scribbled semi-coherent notes to herself in the new journal Athena had given her.

Once she got all the fragments of ideas and bits of her dreams down on paper, Ess knew she wouldn't be able to go back to sleep. She dressed, scribbled a few more ideas that came up from the depths of her still-churning mind, then made her way to the forward kitchen that served the upper decks. When the morning cook showed up, Ess already had the coffee water boiling and was mixing up a bowl of hotcake batter.

Gustav had emigrated from Bavaria when he needed to retire from active service and evade enemies among the Revisionists in Europe. He had stories to tell her about her grandparents. By the time Uly walked in, the first to arrive, Ess learned how Matilda and Ernest had met on a mad scramble through England to retrieve several fragments of a map to a major deposit of crystal pieces. The map had been broken up by grave robbers and sold to tourists in Egypt. Matilda and Ernest had been working for different divisions of the Originators, and according to Gustav had nearly come to blows before they realized they were on the same side.

Chapter Three

"We really do need to bring all the different divisions together," Ess told Uly after she repeated the story to him. Her belly ached slightly, watching him load his plate with his third stack of four hotcakes and proceed to drown them in syrup.

"Don't take that as your new mission in life," he said, setting down the syrup pitcher with a *thunk*. "First priority is to find Granny and Grandfather."

"Did you ever consider that there might be allies among other divisions, the ones we don't speak to, who might have vital clues to what happened to them?"

"And they might have left notes in the vault detailing where they were going and what they were going to try to do when they were in South America. Sometimes," he said, putting down his fork instead of attacking the hotcakes, "I swear people were frantic to find you just to get access to the vault, and not because you were a helpless little girl, lost in the cruel, cold world."

Ess snorted, knowing he was joking even though his face and voice were perfectly serious. She had rarely been helpless, and she most certainly had never been lost. Yet her brother had a point. As far as everyone else knew, Matilda and Ernest Fremont's granddaughter was still lost. The blame for that lay in the secrecy they maintained among their own people.

"I was thinking about that puzzle Athena has given you," he continued, reaching for the cream pitcher to doctor his third cup of coffee. "It would have given us an enormous advantage if we could have had some kind of instantaneous communication that didn't require being tethered to wires, or waiting for couriers to arrive. I was thinking about Father's notes. If only there was some way to make a piece of crystal split without destroying it, and then those who held the halves, even hundreds of miles away, could talk to each other." He shrugged and picked up his cup. "I don't know if I dreamed it or I just remembered something I overheard when our parents were theorizing. They always had such great fun, talking and throwing wild ideas around and arguing just for the sake of turning an idea upside down to see if it would still work."

"Dream," Ess murmured.

"What did you do?" Uly laughed when she grinned.

The laughter turned to a groan when she pulled the journal out of the satchel she carried, holding paper, pencils, and books. The teasing light in his eyes turned to sparks of interest as she talked, first outlining her dreams and then the ideas that had come from them.

"What if that's the key piece Father was missing, or that no one ever mentioned or even thought about recording? It was just a given, so thoroughly understood no one ever thought it would be lost?" she said, scribbling down the new idea Uly had given her.

"Did you ever think that the ancients *wanted* that knowledge lost, so the Revisionists couldn't regain it and use it against us? Maybe our people needed to be scattered to prevent the rechanneling of the time stream, just as much as we needed to keep the enemy from trying again."

"You're so depressing in the morning. Have you had enough coffee? Or perhaps you've had too much?" She snickered and ducked when he pretended to slap at her head. "Just think. It's so obvious."

"What is?" Ford said, strolling through the door. "Ah, blessed child. Gustav informed me you took over the kitchen. He has some ridiculous idea that meat is better morning food than hotcakes." He paused at the end of the table where the covered server of hotcakes sat in a long steam tray sitting on short, lit candles. "Enlighten me on your discussion?"

"You don't want to hear it all again," Ess said. "Here's the most important point of all my dreams and thinking this morning. There are two sides to communication, or else it is not communication. Maybe that is what has always ensured failure on the part of those trying to recreate the instantaneous communication devices. Sender and receiver need to exist at the same time."

"So maybe... the crystal has to be locked to a sender and receiver at the time the crystal is split," Uly mused, gaze unfocused.

"What's this about splitting crystals?" Ford set his full plate down opposite them at the table. "Can't be done. At least, can't be done with the technology available today. Even those clever blades they use to shape diamonds in the jewelers' trade can't cut crystal."

"We don't have to split any crystal." Ess shivered as insight caught hold of her. "We have dust that, as I proved entirely by accident yesterday, we can shape to suit the need."

"What good does it do if it doesn't hold the shape?" her brother immediately responded.

"We only need it to hold the shape while we're using it. We certainly don't want it to stay open and active as a communication receiver if, say, some Revisionists got their hands on it."

Ford dropped his fork onto his plate and got up so quickly he toppled his chair backward. He muttered under his breath as he dashed from the room. Athena arrived a few minutes later, as they were clearing their dishes from the table and trying to decide what to do with his cooling food. She looked at his abandoned plate and smiled, shaking her head.

"I wondered what got his brain working at such a high velocity so early in the morning," she said, stepping over to the sealed pitcher of coffee at the far end of the table. "What were you talking about that had him muttering about mesmerism and mind readers and the twin phenomena?"

Ess and Uly looked at each other, shook their heads, and laughed.

"We could explain, but I'd like to save some time and wait until we see which ideas work." Ess tucked her journal back into the satchel. "If I'm right—if we're right—I'm going to need Uly's help."

"Ah," her brother said. "Of course. Two sides. And maybe that's what the mention of blood and crystal was referring to. Genetics, perhaps?"

"Oh, I hadn't thought of..." Ess frowned, trying to bring up the fading fragments of the dream where blood had made the crystal into a mirror. The problem with trying to remember dreams was that the effort of remembering seemed to shred them even more. "Oh, botheration."

"What?" He gripped her shoulder.

"Say my—our—theories are right, and the communication link requires a blood link, or more accurately a key made of blood. Similar blood. We won't be able to work together, travel together, because what good is a telegraph that only reaches to the next room, rather than the next state or even country?"

"Please don't tell me you've solved the problem of the communication device already?" Athena said, settling down next to Ford's abandoned plate.

"Hardly," Ess said with a snort. That earned a chuckle from her. She caught hold of her brother's hand. "We're off to play with crystal dust. Pray hard for us, Auntie Eena."

~~~~~

Ess was pleased, and Uly amused as well as pleased, to discover his sensitivity to crystal dust increased inside the room lined with acoustic cloth. They determined the resonance from machinery interfered with his ability to hear the nearly subliminal shimmering of crystal when she struck the helix rod. Yet when Ess moved the rod closer to her brother, and he stepped closer to the table, a piercing dissonance joined the crystal song. It faded when he stepped away. When Ess waved the rod along his body, listening as the harshness of the sound increased, the source of the dissonance turned out to be a dagger and the pistol that he carried hidden under his coat. She theorized refined, forged metal reacted badly to crystal. Something to keep in mind in the future.

"Seriously, Uly? What do you need weapons for on board the *Nile*?" Ess wrapped her hand around the rod to stop the humming and folded a corner of the cloth over it to shield the sound. The dissonance made the roots of her teeth itch.

"I don't need them, but... well, Granny gave me the gun when I turned thirteen, and the dagger was Father's." He studied the two weapons, with the side of his coat pulled back to reveal them. "I suppose they'll be safe enough out in the passage. Hardly anyone comes to this part of the ship."
~~~~~

She sighed, knowing exactly why he carried them and why he hated to take them off. She felt the same way about the derringer their grandfather had given her. Holding out her hand, she waited until Uly thought a few moments more, then gave them over. She wrapped blade and gun in several layers of the acoustic cloth, and his relieved smile made her want to laugh.

The laughter faded into awe and amazement when, without those two sources of dissonance, the shimmering chimes from the rod grew stronger. Over the next several days, they experimented, identifying the sources of interference with his sensitivity. He also learned to shape the crystal dust by holding the helix rod and concentrating. If Ess's theory were to work, they had to be able to shape the crystal dust outside of the cloth-lined room. Neither of them could do anything with it the first day. They kept trying, moving throughout the ship and first checking for signs of dissonance, then trying to mask it with the chime-hum of the rod.

Their experiments led to interesting discussions over meals with various members of the team. Dr. Sylvia was fascinated by the idea that manufactured items, rather than just machinery, interfered with sensitivity to crystal. She busied herself creating a testing protocol for everyone on the *Nile*. If she could find a way to block out the dissonance, especially if it was undetected and beyond the range of human hearing, then conceivably all members of the Originators should sense the presence of crystal. That would aid enormously in their search and their mission.

Focusing on the puzzle of the crystal dust occupied them so thoroughly that Ess barely noticed when the airship could finally leave the docking tower and head east for Cleveland.

Another result of working with the crystal dust, and the discussions that followed, lay in the realm of Ess's dreams. Her sleep was often broken by awakening with the sensation of being torn so abruptly from sleep that she couldn't remember her dream. That made no sense to her at first, until she thought about the dream that inspired her breakthrough, and how she had awakened sweating. What if the dreams were so disturbing that she awoke as a way to escape them?

She mulled over the idea for two days, working up the courage to ask Dr. Sylvia what she thought of the theory. Maybe an infusion to drink, or perhaps even a treatment with the blue lotus, could either stop the dreams or help her remember them so she could untangle them. Ess did recall her grandmother was a great one for obtaining all sorts of results in the mind and body with her herbal potions and infusions.

Another of Edward Fremont's journals had been the object of Ford's quest when he abandoned his breakfast so abruptly that first morning. He didn't have anything of Edward's with him, which would have been foolhardy, considering the expedition he had been lost on for years. Even without knowing Stryker had sent him off to become lost and perish, it would have been reckless to take any keepsakes of his boyhood friend with him. Ford had needed to refer to his own much-battered journal to recall where he had stored many of Edward's possessions, left in his care in multiple caches across the country.

The theory their group formed, after several evenings of discussion, was that Edward and Vivian already had some suspicions about the leadership of the Originators, dating from before the fierce argument Uly only vaguely recalled. Athena agreed with Ford's theory that part of the trouble might have resulted from Anna, the Revisionist woman who had come over to join the Originators, whom Vivian had befriended. They needed to hide the woman's location from whomever in the leadership Edward and Vivian didn't thoroughly trust. Athena recalled that the keepsakes the two women had made and exchanged, when Anna went away to her new identity and life, were two roses formed of crystal. It spoke to the combined power of their minds that they had been able to shape crystal into the roses. Ess thought that rather spoke to the value the mysterious Anna likely had for the Revisionists, and how crippled they had to be when she turned her back on their cause.

Vivian and Edward had hidden many of their notes and reference materials, and the results of expeditions with trusted friends, rather than making regular deposits in the family vault. Whether Ernest and Matilda knew what their son and his wife had done, no one could be certain. Ford insisted they make a detour over the border into Canada, to raid one of the caches he and Edward had set up before they docked in Cleveland. He was sure Vivian's crystal rose was in that particular cache.

The location was still ahead of the *Golden Nile*, so they didn't need to backtrack, and the detour only added half a day to their journey. If the winds remained with them, they could ride the air currents around the Great Lakes instead of having to fight them.

Ess decided she had built up too great an expectation, when she finally could read the journal and it disappointed her. It held more of the same disjointed, fragmented tangle of notes making references to sources that Edward wanted to remember. Obviously, her father never expected anyone else to read his journal, since he made no effort to be clearer, allowing other people to follow his train of thought. This journal was all research on mental powers, people who claimed to be able to read minds and tell the future, to interpret dreams and charm wild animals docile and even heal illnesses and wounds with a touch. Edward seemed focused on determining if they were charlatans, tools of the devil, or servants of God Almighty. Ess found it somewhat fascinating to untangle some of her father's ramblings and theorizing and realize he had wanted to believe in supernatural powers, gifts that came in the blood and were inborn, like other people had a talent for music or woodworking or navigation or invention. He was especially fascinated with the allegations that many sets of twins could communicate over long distances, either by images or mere impressions, sharing physical sensations, or hearing each other's thoughts.

Reading the journal brought her a little closer to the father she could only remember in bits and pieces of images. Since the first journal was put in her hands, she had experienced oddly vivid fragments of dreams that she increasingly suspected were not dreams at all, but actual memories. She wasn't sure if she should be pleased or amused or a little saddened to realize that the great man of science and adventure wanted almost desperately, like a child, to believe in magic and wonder and miracles.

Vivian's crystal rose was indeed in that particular cache, and Ess was pleased and relieved when Athena and Dr. Sylvia and Vulcan all agreed that she should have it and wear it. She half-feared that they would insist the rose should be added to the growing collection of pieces of the Great Machine. From the moment she strung the rose, the size of the end of her thumb, on a new silver chain and hung it around her neck, she felt a little closer to her mother.

She remembered coming upon her mother, sitting perfectly still, eyes closed, with two fingers of her right hand pressed against the rose. Vivian hadn't heard when Ess called her. A toddler at the time, she hadn't hesitated to climb up into her mother's lap. Ess had felt a humming-chiming sound when she touched her mother. It grew stronger when she reached up for the rose. Vivian stopped her just before she touched it, and seemed pleased when Ess said she heard the rose sing.

That night, Ess didn't dream of her parents, as she half-expected, with all her thoughts focused on them. Instead, she walked through a vast camp meeting tent, dark with shadows, moonlight spilling through thin spots in the canvass and the doorways on the sides. A young woman stepped up onto the platform at the far end and sat down at the upright piano. She wore a nightgown under a man's mud-colored duster, and her dark auburn hair hung loose, spilling past her waist. When she lit an oil lamp sitting on a stool next to the piano, the light glistened on something hanging around her throat.

Focusing on the shiny spot drew Ess from the far end of the tent. She felt rather breathless as she landed on the end of the platform. The young woman turned around and smiled at her, as if she was expected. Then her smile melted into a confused little frown. Her eyes flicked downward and then her hand raised to touch the sparkling spot at her throat. Ess mimicked her movement and found her mother's crystal rose at her throat. The other girl pushed the duster aside to reveal a matching rose, set in the center of a cross, hanging on a short chain at her throat.

"Essie?" the girl said. Her frown softened into a smile. "I haven't thought about you in years."

"Hello, Carmen. Why are you grown up?"

"I grew up." She laughed and put her hand down on the keyboard. The muted clash of several notes threw Ess out of the dream.

She sat up, shivering, again drenched with sweat.

"Botheration," Ess muttered. She climbed out of bed and peeled out of her nightgown. Then she froze, the damp cloth in her hands.

She only sweated like that when she had memory dreams. Yet she could have sworn she had never seen Carmen before in her...

"We grew up," Ess whispered. She shivered more as she dug her other nightgown out of a drawer and quickly washed the sticky sweat off her body, dressed, and climbed back in bed. Her mind raced the entire time, spinning together theories and discarding them.

What could explain her make-believe friend growing up with her?

Was it possible her make-believe friend had never been make-believe? If Carmen wore a crystal rose, and Ess had worn her crystal rose to bed, was it possible that their roses helped their minds meet—fitting one of her father's many theories of using crystal to communicate?

Where did Carmen get her rose? More importantly, who was Carmen? If she had been a little girl when Ess was a little girl, and they hadn't spoken since around the time of her parents' deaths...

"How in the world do I find out if Carmen is Anna's daughter?" Ess asked the night quiet of her cabin.

Easy enough: ask.

Falling asleep again and being aware enough in her dream to ask those questions when next they met was not that easy.

Ess resolved not to tell anyone what she had experienced and theorized until she had made contact with Carmen again. First she would have to convince her childhood friend that "Essie" was real. She likely would have to explain the years of silence, and then convince Carmen to trust her.

Yes, best to keep silent until she had some answers, and some concrete proof.

~~~~~

The markings in the margins of Edward's journal brought back memories to Ess of her grandfather drawing similar images in the margins of his own journals. She puzzled through them, wondering if perhaps they were a code of some kind, repetitive and yet tiny details making each one individual. Ford laughed when Ess showed him several pages she had filled with the little images, in an effort to make sense of them.

"I haven't thought of that cypher of his in... years," he finished on a sigh. Something in his expression sent a tiny shiver over her scalp.

"None of this is decorative, is it?" she asked, already knowing the answer.

"Ernest was a friend of my father's when they were young. They had a game, a sort of competition, to create a code for secret communication." He gestured at the journal she had brought with her to his office. She picked it up from the far end of the table and handed it to him. He opened it at random and ran his finger down the edge of the page, studying each image
~~~~~

in turn. "Along the way, they came up with a series of symbols for basic sounds. The more a symbol looked like the actual sound or rather the source of the sound, the better."

"A wolf for a howl, a pig for a squeal, that sort of thing?" She took the journal from his hands and bent her head over the images. "None of these look anything like animals, nor any of the images I have studied so far."

"That's because these were my father's invention specifically. He was something of a musician, and constantly bemoaned the bulky necessity of using a staff to record music." He chuckled as Ess's mouth dropped open. "Ernest recorded music visually. Don't ask me to interpret, please, because it has been nearly thirty years since my father taught me the cypher, but the first few symbols in each line of communication indicated the key, and I know there was a specific formation to indicate if the notes were half, quarter, whole, sharp, flat, as well as how many octaves above middle C."

"All in an image the size of the tip of my pinky," Ess murmured.

"I'm sure you're clever enough to decipher what it all means, and do it much faster than if you relied on me to dig through memories I haven't touched in decades." He chuckled when she bent and brushed a kiss across his cheek.

Ess shared the code with Uly, and he agreed. If that trip to South America hadn't interfered, she would probably know how to play the music from the journals by now. Ess was positive the music itself would provide a key or code to unlocking something else within the journal. Fortunately, Athena had replaced the flute that Miss Van Hastings had taken from her when she was a virtual prisoner in that wretched boarding school. Ess put the task of deciphering the musical code further down on her list of mysteries to investigate, something to help her relax at night before bed. Figuring out the use for the crystal dust and Athena's theory of a long-distance communication device was a far higher priority for the siblings.

Chapter Four

The *Golden Nile* headed south back into the United States, following the western shore of Lake Michigan. It left Chicago behind just before Ess and Uly decided the time had come to put all their theorizing, refining, study and experimenting into practice. By this time, Uly could tap the helix rod and hold the bottom to the bridge of his nose, so the humming filled his sinus cavities until the dissonance faded from the background environment. Then he would tap another rod and use it to shape a tablespoon-size pile of crystal dust into whatever shape he envisioned. His concentration was sketchy, but for their purposes, the flat plate of crystal dust was the easiest shape to create and hold, even with distractions. Ess didn't need to clear away dissonance, and she had learned to manipulate the dust by humming to it, no need for the rod after the initial tap.

Halfway across Indiana, they returned to the shielded room at the nose of the airship to bring all their work and dreaming and hoping to the final test.

Athena, Vulcan, and Ford had shared everything they knew about the lock plates on the vaults in Sanctuary. There was precious little recorded detailing the process of creating the lock plates, which had taken place more than a century ago. Their mentors agreed the information was recorded and locked away in one of the vaults, perhaps one of many vaults that no longer could be opened because everyone keyed by blood to the lock had died. Any explosive powerful enough to break the crystal embedded in the lock would destroy everything in the vault, and vaults on either side. Perhaps in another century, scientific knowledge would develop to the point that someone could break through, or even persuade the lock to open. Not now.

Ess could only hope she had inherited her grandmother Matilda's ability to make intuitive leaps of genius, so the theories and ideas that came to her in her dreams were workable. Now was the time to try.

Uly held her hands and they whispered a prayer together that their dreams and theories were correct. Then he rolled up his sleeve and handed her the lancet Dr. Sylvia had loaned them. Ess wrinkled up her nose at him, knowing he had deliberately skipped a step. She picked up the leather strap and tied it around his biceps and handed him the India rubber ball to squeeze. When his veins stood out in his arm, she nicked the largest vein, then held up the small collection cup to where the blood welled up. It trickled into the pointed spout and they counted down together for the agreed fifteen seconds. She loosened the strap and pressed a wad of gauze into the bleeding point, then wrapped gauze around it to hold it tight. Repeating the process for her went just as smoothly. Uly finished wrapping the gauze around her arm, then handed her the cup, to swirl their mixed blood together.

In the lantern light, the wet gloss of their collected blood had dimmed. Ess rolled her sleeve back down, then stepped to the other side of the table where two small piles of crystal dust waited. She uncovered the helix rods and handed one to Uly. He mouthed the countdown from three. On one, they tapped the rods against an exposed edge of the table, then swirled the rods over their respective piles of dust. As the round plates formed, Ess picked up the cup of blood and turned it around to spill out their mixed blood equally in the center of each surface. The blood shot across the surface of each plate in a symmetrical wave, then darkened.

"Great jumping Jehoshaphat," Uly whispered. He met her gaze and they exchanged grins.

Despite her hopes, despite the dream that made the process so clear, Ess took a step backward as the dark surfaces of both plates shimmered and turned silver, to reflect the lantern light. Holding the rod, she gestured as practiced, though her hand noticeably shook. Her plate lifted off the surface of the table, turning to hang vertical. It hovered in the air, following her as she stepped backward.

Uly repeated her actions, putting the width of the room between them. As his plate turned vertical, hers shimmered. She saw his face staring out of the plate at her. Uly's eyes widened and his mouth dropped open, then he let out a whoop.

"Don't let it drop!" she blurted, when Uly took a couple steps toward her and lowered the rod.

Just in time, he raised it, and kept the plate from dropping to the floor. They held their breaths as they guided their plates back over to the table, and down onto the squares of silk prepared for the next step. In unison, they set the ends of their rods down on the table with a gentle thump, stopping the shimmering chime. The mirrored surfaces darkened, then turned back to dust. Carefully, holding their breaths, because this would be the absolutely worst time for a sneeze, they tugged on the drawstrings sewn into the edges of the silk squares, creating pouches. The helix rods went into little pockets sewn on the outside.

"It works," she whispered.

Uly let out another whoop and wrapped his arms around her, swinging her off her feet in a full circle.

Their celebration turned out to be premature. While the plates re-formed with ease and they repeated the sequence without need for another dose of blood, the transfer of sound was beyond them. Communication was still possible, though, by writing notes and holding them up to the plate for the person on the other side to read. They demonstrated what they had accomplished at dinner that night, as the *Golden Nile* approached the docking tower in Cleveland. The astonishment on the faces of those gathered around the table was reward enough for all their hard work.

As Ess had feared, however, only she and Uly could activate the communication plates. Athena and Vulcan both learned easily enough how to use the rods to create shapes in the dust and form the plates. However, the crystal dust infused with Ess and Uly's blood no longer responded to anyone else. To use the communication device they had rediscovered, they would have to separate.

"That's all right," Uly said, once the celebration over dinner wound down and Ess finally confessed the one dark spot in their triumph. "I didn't really want to have you travel to South America with me, when I go look for our grandparents. I'd much rather you stay safely up north and provide communication with our allies up here."

"Safe?" Her voice nearly cracked. "With traitors and Revisionists hiding behind masks, pretending to be Originators and our friends? You have an odd definition of safe."

~~~~~

Endicott, Lewis and MacDonald had their offices in a building on the corner of Superior and East 6th. Ess paused to admire the pavilion on Public Square as she passed it that morning, on her way from the newest docking tower just off of West 6th. The wind tearing up Ontario from off of Lake Erie yanked on her hat. She fought the inclination to press her gloved hand against the crown to hold it on. She had to trust in the long pins holding her hat firmly to her braided hair, just as she had to trust Athena and Dr. Sylvia that the outfit she wore would have the proper effect on her family lawyers. She had wanted to have one more laugh, strolling into their offices dressed as a boy, and wheedle her way past the secretary. Or better yet, sneak past the secretary, maybe cause a little bit of an uproar. Then, when she had the attention of all three men, reveal herself.

Instead, she had let them talk her into dressing as a lady of consequence. She presented a very different picture from the girl she had been the last time she talked with the three men, just a few weeks before her grandparents' departure for South America. Would they recognize her? Would they doubt her, perhaps subject her to some questions? Perhaps she would need to describe the letters she had written to them just before the axe fell on the Van Hastings and their Resurrectionist friends, courtesy of the Secret Service. She imagined stunning them as she recounted Mr. Endicott's visit to the academy, searching for her, and some of the conversation she had overheard between him and the Van Hastings.

"Yes, I admit it," she murmured, "I'm still something of a child. Considering how I was deprived of a normal childhood..." Ess chuckled. She had no real idea of what a "normal" childhood was supposed to be. She had loved the academic challenges and the adventures her grandparents
~~~~~

had provided her. Other than retaining her parents, she wouldn't have changed anything.

Her steps slowed as a new thought filled her mind.

If they managed to find all the pieces of the Great Machine someday... was it possible to go back in time to the right moment to stop her parents from going into that booby-trapped ruin? Theo had theorized that it was indeed impossible to change history. The Great Machine didn't take the ancestors of the Revisionists and Originators back in time in their own world, but to a parallel world, a copy of Earth, where their presence didn't violate laws of nature and science.

"Think about it later," she scolded herself, and slowed as she neared the door of the lawyers' building. "One step at a time. Convince them I'm me. Then find out if they know where Hilda and the others are. Then find out how much they know about Granny and Grandfather's mission."

"Excuse me, Miss?" A man who had stepped around her and reached for the door of the grand, ten-story building, paused and looked over his shoulder at her. "Are you in need of assistance?"

"Bolstering my courage, sir." Ess summoned up the smile she had learned to use with officious Pinkerton clients with an inflated sense of their importance in the grand scheme of the world order.

"Are you seeking a lawyer?" He glanced upward at the building. Many of the lawyers in the city had offices in this particular edifice.

"I have several, and am in need of... shall we say, reconciliation?" She thanked him with a nod when he opened the door for her and tipped his hat as she stepped through.

"If you don't reconcile, I hope you'll keep my firm in mind." He reached into his vest pocket as they walked down the long, marble-lined lobby with brass fittings and inlaid tiles in the ceiling, and withdrew a business card. "Is something amusing?" he asked, when she had to muffle a chuckle at seeing Endicott, Lewis, and MacDonald printed in large, dignified letters, with his name in print half that size underneath: Mr. R.D. Wallace, Investigator.

"If I fail to reconcile with my lawyers, who are family friends, I will find it difficult to turn to your firm, Mr. Wallace, as you seem to work for my lawyers."

"Ah." He seemed to consider the conundrum for a moment, then grinned with some mischief and offered her his bent arm. "I can't imagine a charming lady such as yourself earning the wrath of any of the senior partners of our firm."

"That is the hazard of retaining old family friends. They believe they have the right to scold. And I must confess," she said, pressing the back of her hand against her forehead, which earned a rumbling chuckle from him, "I have not acted with the dignity they expect of me. Thank you," she added, as he bowed her into the brass cage of the lift.

Mr. Wallace's eyes sparkled, and Ess imagined the questions he wanted to ask, following up on that admission. However, two more people hurried across the lobby from the door that opened onto East 6th, and stepped into the lift before the bell clanged, signaling the doors were about to close. The four of them said nothing as the brass cage rose to the third floor, the first man stepped out, then they went to the fourth floor, her destination. The doublewide doors of the waiting room for Endicott, Lewis and MacDonald opened off the lobby where the lift deposited them. Wallace hurried ahead of her to open the door, and tipped his hat again to her as she stepped through.

"May I help you?" A balding gentleman, with muttonchop whiskers and a high, stiff collar, addressed Ess as she turned to the reception desk.

"This lady is a client," Wallace said. "If you'll excuse me for a moment, to check messages, I would be delighted to attend to your concerns."

"Thank you, Mr. Wallace, but I do need to speak to Mr. Endicott — in point of fact, I need to speak with all three partners, as soon as possible," Ess said, turning back to the receptionist.

"I'm sorry, Miss, but that is nearly impossible. It's very rare when the partners are all three in town at the same time, and they're very busy." The muttonchop man looked like he truly regretted giving her such news.

"Peterkin," Wallace began.

"Thank you for trying to help," Ess interrupted, laying a hand on his arm. "I'm sure Mr. Peterkin wants to help. I'm willing to wait, and I would hate to interfere with whatever appointments or duties are waiting on you." She barely restrained herself from fluttering her eyelashes.

Wallace hesitated, shook her hand, promised to check on her in half an hour, reminded Peterkin to take good care of her, and finally strode down the hallway and out of sight.

"Mr. Peterkin, if you could be so kind as to pass my card on to each of the partners, I would be more than willing to wait through the afternoon, if necessary."

"Are you sure, Miss?" He looked like he might just weep with relief. Ess wondered what sort of abuse he earned from impatient people.

"I look forward to the opportunity to catch up on my reading while I wait." She lifted her very large handbag, which in point of fact held a small journal, several pencils, the next book on the history and practices of the Originators, and her derringer.

"That's very gracious of you, Miss..." He turned the card over to read the front.

"Miss Evangeline Peabody, lately of the Pinkerton Agency, but now attached to the Blue Lotus Society."

"May I ask what the Society does? Gathering clothes and funds for war widows and orphans?" His smile seemed to freeze, just a little bit, and his gaze went over her shoulder.

Ess guessed that someone had come down the hallway from the back offices. She pretended not to notice, even though she could almost feel the eyes focused on the nape of her neck. She clenched her fist to resist the urge to stroke the hairs back up into place, which had been tugged loose by the wind off the lake, and make sure the blue lotus tattoo at the nape of her neck was clear to be seen. The entire purpose of wearing this dress was because the low collar would expose the tattoo and catch the right sort of attention.

"Goodness, no." Ess settled on the spindle-backed bench nearest the reception desk. "We are historians and archeologists, specializing in ancient civilizations. While our name might indicate we focus on Ancient Egypt, we divide our efforts equally among Egypt, Rome, Greece, and the South American empires."

"Do tell," a raspy baritone voice said, from over her shoulder. "Archeologists, you say?"

Mr. Stanton Lewis, the youngest of the three partners, stepped around the end of the bench and faced her, his hands clasped behind his back. He tipped his head slightly to one side and regarded her through narrowed eyes. His pursed lips were barely visible under his full moustache — which, Ess was slightly dismayed to note, had silver threads of hair woven through it. She held still as Peterkin handed Lewis her business card.

"Pinkertons?" Lewis raised his left eyebrow. "I think we need to talk, Miss Peabody. Peterkin... when MacDonald returns from lunch, hopefully soon, could you ask him to join me in my chambers immediately?" He held out his hand to Ess. She complied and let him raise her to her feet.

"Sir, you have an appointment in —" Peterkin began.

"Cancel it." He tugged Ess's hand into the curve of his arm and kept a tight grip on it. "I have to deal with this conniving little fraud who has invaded our office."

"Fraud, sir?" Peterkin's eyes went wide.

"Keep it quiet, and send MacDonald as soon as he arrives," Lewis shot back over his shoulder. He tugged Ess down the hall at a fast trot.

Her heart raced from more than the pace, and she wished Athena hadn't insisted on such a wide brim for her hat. Held this close to him, she couldn't see his face, couldn't even guess what was going through his mind right that moment.

He slowed at a door with a large brass "E" in place of a nameplate, thumped four times in an odd rhythm, and hurried into the next office down the hallway. Ess stumbled when he gave her a little shove into the room, and a moment later the door slammed behind them.

"You rascal. You scoundrel," he said, the rasp deepening, threatening to crack his voice. He caught hold of her again, shook her once, then held her out to arm's length, his fingers digging into her shoulders deep enough to bruise. His eyes flicked back and forth, studying her features. A rap sounded on his door, and a moment later it opened.

"Stanton?" Mr. Randall Endicott said, stepping in.

"Look what the tide dropped on our doorstep." Lewis turned Ess around so quickly she nearly lost her balance. It was a good thing he kept his tight grip on her shoulders.

"Odessa," the elder partner whispered. He took two jerky steps forward. For a few seconds, she thought he might collapse—or lunge forward and shake her until her neck snapped.

Then Endicott tipped his head back and laughed, until he staggered back a step and had to catch his breath. Lewis let go of her and hurried to fetch a chair for the older man to sit down.

She complied when Endicott held out his hand and gave hers into his grasp.

"Shades of Matilda and Ernest," Lewis said, bringing over another chair for Ess. He settled on the edge of the massive desk, shaking his head and grinning. "You wouldn't believe the story this scapegrace told, coming in here. A false name, a Pinkerton agent, and working for one of the premier historical consortiums in the world. Girl—no, *young lady*—what have you been up to?"

"Actually, the only lie I told was my name, which I used on my most recent assignment with the Pinkertons," Ess said.

"Indeed," Endicott murmured. He released her hand and sat back in his chair, folding his arms across his chest.

"I canceled my next appointment," Lewis said. "I have the feeling I should cancel the entirety of the afternoon. Shall I have Peterkin send out for a tray of something to sustain us while we debrief the prodigal?"

"Oh, no, please," Ess said. "I didn't intend to disrupt your day. I know how busy you are. In fact, we were hoping you three would join us on the *Golden Nile* for dinner tonight. Something of a war council."

"A war council?" Endicott nodded, his gaze still searching her face. "And just who might be included in this 'we' you mentioned?"

"Miss Athena Latymer, Dr. Fordyce Chamberlain, and various members of their cell of the Originators."

"Ah," Lewis said, and his eyes seemed rather sad for a moment. "So you found all that out, did you?"

"If you had told me—if Granny and Grandfather had told me something of my heritage, maybe I wouldn't have felt compelled to handle the Resurrectionists on my own and gone haring off across the country, looking for Uly and determined to stay free of more intolerable boarding schools."

That earned a snort and a crooked smile from Endicott. "I imagine you had a great deal of fun turning those terrible people over to the Secret Service. The people I talked to showed me some of the letters they received, and I recognized your handwriting."

"You didn't identify me to them, though."

"No, I didn't." He sat up a little. "How do you know that?"

"I ran into Agent Sutter several months later. In fact, I worked for the Secret Service for a short time, until I found it more... entertaining to join up with the Pinkertons."

"Until you met up with Miss Latymer and Dr. Chamberlain," Lewis said. "Fancy that, some of our own, operating in broad daylight, in the guise of historians. The name itself is a dead giveaway, yet I never would have suspected. It's rather cheeky."

"Yes, and all the secrecy and divisions and keeping the left hand from knowing what the right hand is doing has got to stop. We're shooting ourselves in the foot, keeping secrets, hiding our heritage from the next generation. Keeping me in the dark is totally in keeping with Granny and Grandfather's practices, but I am a little miffed that you would agree to it," Ess added.

"Yes, well, considering some of the troubles Ernest and Matilda suspected, since your parents were killed, it was all for your protection." Endicott sighed. "And theirs, when you come right down to it. After Ulysses got the attention of the wrong people on his first assignment, we felt it best to—"

"You were part of keeping me in the dark?"

"My dear girl, William MacDonald is a talented mesmerist, but Matilda trained him. They created the mental locks for your clever little mind. Do you think when you and the household staff emptied the house—a very wise and mature tactic, I might add—do you think when you moved all that material that you were protecting the greatest treasures and secrets of our organization?" He sat forward and tapped her forehead right between her eyebrows. "The information hidden here, the memories locked away so you wouldn't find the treasure map for yourself, that is the greatest wealth and the most perilous duty among all your grandparents' responsibilities and guardianship."

"So... you're saying I actually knew... about the Originators and our battle with the Revisionists and... our whole history... and the Great Machine?" she finished on a whisper.

Chapter Five

"Hard to keep a clever little spy like you from knowing," Lewis muttered. He winked when Ess glanced sharply at him. A chuckle escaped the tight bands wrapping around her throat.

"So you... you blocked my memories, hid them, just like Athena did with Uly?"

"How do you know..." Endicott sat up more. "Yes, you did say Ford was on the airship, so he's been rescued from whatever God-forsaken wilderness he got himself lost in, and I did hear Ulysses was sent to find him. Nasty business. I rather suspected for a while it was a trap or a plot."

"It was." Ess got no satisfaction from how his eyes widened.

"You have a great deal to tell us." Lewis slid off the front of the desk. "Not another word out of you until I return, with an afternoon's worth of refreshments, and once I find William. He should have returned from his luncheon appointment by now."

"We'll need someone to record the debriefing," Endicott said. "None of our own people are here. High time we let Ransom in on the secret, do you think?"

"If he hasn't already figured it out yet," he said, nodding, as he pulled the door open and slipped out.

"Who is Ransom?" Ess had to ask, though she was tempted to follow the order of "not another word," just to tease them both.

"We ran into a very clever, very honorable young detective while we were dealing with the whole ugly mess of that boarding school. I must confess, we chose it just because no one would expect such exceptional people to subject their granddaughter to the guardianship of Miss Van Hastings. Matilda wasn't sure if she should be amused, anticipating all the tricks you would pull, or if she should feel guilty for caging you."

"Deceptions within plots within schemes within masks," Ess murmured.

"Exactly. As I was about to say, we feared for a time that wretched woman had actually sold you into marriage in some deplorable benighted country. We encountered this detective and found him so useful, we decided each of our offices should have one on staff. Ransom Wallace just transferred here to help us begin preparations for a massive expansion project."

"I have already met your Mr. Wallace." Ess slipped the business card out of her purse and turned it so he could see.

"Good man, Ransom. He has proven himself intensely loyal, and as I mentioned to Stanton, it might be time to reveal our true purpose to him. It's rather awkward keeping secrets from people you hire to find out secrets. If we trust him enough to handle the sensitive nature of our project, why cannot we trust him with the existence of the Originators?"

"Surely not everything? The time stream? The Great Machine?" Ess said, softening her voice.

"Oh, of course not. If I haven't seen pieces of crystal and the... well, the keystone, shall we say, in action, I would sometimes think we were mad." He winked. "This project of ours is vital for the convenience and safety of our cause. We need the right location, and the right people to design our building, and the right people to build it."

He asked her to fetch him paper and pencils and set about sketching out for her the preliminary design and idea for a building owned entirely by the Originators. Cleveland was growing as a port city, with access to all the Great Lakes, the expanding trade routes through the Midwest, and the hub of several railroad lines to be established in the area. Several airship companies devoted solely to shipping were talking of building docking towers and warehouses in the surrounding countryside. All the traffic soon to fill Cleveland and spread around the shores of Lake Erie would be good cover for Originator activity. Endicott had just asked Ess to think of anything the firm might have missed when there was a sharp rap on the door. It swung open and Mr. William MacDonald leaned in. When his gaze landed on Ess, he seemed to fall into the room.

"Well," he said, shutting the door with enough force to be punctuation, "both of you have stolen all my thunder."

"Excuse me?" Ess had to laugh, as he bent down to capture her cheeks between his hands and press a kiss into the center of her forehead, nearly knocking her hat askew.

"I don't doubt our esteemed leader has scolded you within an inch of your life." He winked at her when Endicott just snorted. "I came hurrying back with some amazing news that I suspect you brought. That's just the way things work out with you Fremonts."

"Hurrying back, my Aunt Fanny," Endicott said. "You were supposed to be back from lunch more than half an hour ago."

"Yes, but Mrs. Parsifal was all atwitter over the arrival of the *Golden Nile* and the Blue Lotus Society. She wants my help in persuading them to conduct a symposium on Egyptology. I reached the airship dock, to go up and request an appointment, when who should I see leaving the ship?"

"Miss Latymer and Dr. Chamberlain, arm-in-arm, most likely."

"By the way, he finally asked her to marry him, and she said yes," Ess offered.

MacDonald dragged over another chair from the other side of the room. "There, you see, you've stolen all my thunder. May I assume that somehow those two sweethearts took their eyes off each other long enough to discover wherever you've been hiding, and drag you back to civilization? And if I know you, forced you back into petticoats?"

Ess wrinkled up her nose at him, prompting laughter from both men. Before they quieted, there was another rap on the door. Endicott said to come. Wallace stepped into the room, carrying a huge tray with a sealed pot of coffee, cups, plates and utensils, and a thick stack of papers and a handful of pencils tucked in among the dishware.

"Ah, Miss Odessa Fremont, I presume?" He set the tray on Lewis' desk, then crossed the room to bring a table over. "You quite piqued my interest, and your face looked familiar, so I did some digging."

"And that is why we snatched him up before the Secret Service realized he wasn't a pest and an inconvenience, and shanghaied him," Endicott said.

"We're in luck," Lewis said as he came in with another equally large tray, this one loaded with sandwiches and cakes. "Marguerite was just putting the raspberry creams out into the display case."

"One of the benefits of this location. And I confess, the reason we took this building," MacDonald said, moving aside so he could put the tray down on the table, while Wallace retrieved the first tray. "The most incredible bakery and café off the lobby. Quite convenient when we work late or have breakfast meetings. We made a rule that whoever fetches mid-afternoon snacks must take the stairs, to work off all the sweets."

"Might I suggest, sir, that the new building offer a restaurant?" Wallace said.

"Hmm. On the surface a good idea," Endicott said. "What do you think, Odessa?"

"What about... security?" she said, with a sideways glance at Wallace as he snatched up his paper and pencils and settled in at the desk. She guessed he was used to acting as secretary for sensitive conversations. "Oh, I know—I was going to ask if you were in touch with Hilda. And with Peggety and the others from home. Perhaps Hilda would want to run a restaurant in your new building? She always said she enjoyed cooking at a restaurant in San Francisco and would like to have her own someday."

"Yes, in fact, we are in touch with Hilda." Lewis exchanged a strangely somber glance with MacDonald. "Ess, we know her side of the story, how you protected the house from the Resurrectionist plot, but... well, did you know—"

"Giles was killed, and Mr. Darius, who was waiting for him in Parkerton?" She sat up a little straighter, to fight the shiver that ran through her. "Yes. I managed to talk to Mr. Darius before he... succumbed to his injuries. When Giles didn't show up for our meeting, I went home and learned what happened."

"No wonder you hightailed it for parts unknown," Endicott said, patting her hand.

Ess gave them her story, but only the bare bones. It wasn't just the presence of Wallace or the knowledge someone was writing down her words that made her reticent. She preferred not to go into details unless someone asked for them. No need to give the names of the friends she had made. What good would it do her to confess her silly mistakes, the changes in plans, the near-misses and infuriating characters she had encountered? Starting with the headmistress acting contrary to habit, Ess glossed over how exactly she had climbed into Miss Van Hastings' office and discovered the letters kept from her, the instructions from the odious woman's even more odious brother, and the plans to control Ess's life and her family estate. She gave few details of how she had escaped the school. She glossed over the sabotage she had done to the tunnel system under the school, used by the Resurrectionist rebels. She told how she had traveled to Springfield, working at the airship docking tower that brought Mr. Lincoln to town for the dedication. Then she related how she recognized some Resurrectionists and then Agent Sutter, and how her attempt to warn him led to her capture by the Secret Service detail. Lewis muttered into his coffee cup, while MacDonald didn't even try to restrain his dismayed oaths.

She regaled them with stories of her life among the circus folk, the riding and shooting and sleight of hand tricks she had learned, but Ess knew better than to reveal Stockwell's past and the price on his head. Why confess she had been assigned as a guard for the man and had nearly been killed in a train wreck? She merely told them that when her assignment ended, Sutter employed her as a courier, until she foiled some inept thieves under the very nose of Horace Winslow, Pinkerton agent, and then was offered a job. No need to tell these friends how a gang of train robbers had nearly kidnapped her before she was shot in the hip and spent a week in bed.

"Since then, I have been working in various guises and roles for the Pinkertons, with Horace as my team leader and mentor. Last winter, his granddaughter fell through river ice, and he lost his life saving hers. I moved among several teams until I was assigned to guard the traveling exhibition courtesy of the British and Cairo museums. I encountered Athena Latymer of the Antiquities Coalition when they came to help protect the artifacts. She saw enough of my parents' features in me, she investigated beneath my *nom de guerr*, and proved she was acquainted with them. My assignment ended, I resigned my position to join the Blue Lotus Society. As a bonus, they were able to reunite me with Uly."

"Excuse me," Wallace said, interrupting for the first time in more than two hours of talk and minor detours into reminiscing, and laughter. "Who is Uly?"

"Her scapegrace adventurer older brother, Ulysses Joshua Fremont," Lewis said. "If he hadn't been out gallivanting around the country when their grandparents vanished, Ess never would have..." He sighed and smiled wearily. "Well, you wouldn't have had all your fascinating adventures, would you?"

"While I enjoyed hearing of your adventures, Odessa," Endicott added, "I shudder to think what your grandparents will say, when they finally return to civilization. I feel we failed in our duty to them."

"Granny might scold, but only about where I acted the ninny or took foolish risks," Ess retorted. "She'll laugh louder than all of you put together, and you know it."

"She's right," MacDonald said.

"I envy you," Wallace said. "I had the honor of training for a short time under Horace Winslow. You can take my word for it, gentlemen, Miss Fremont had no greater guardian and mentor while she was under his leadership."

Ess employed the next hour going over Wallace's record of what she had related. She filled in a few places where he had questions and made corrections in a few spots where she had transposed a name or date or detail for another. That gave Mssrs. Endicott, Lewis and MacDonald time to deal with the business they had set aside to interrogate her. There was still some time remaining until they had to walk to the *Golden Nile's* dock, so she left word with Peterkin that she would be on the square, doing some sightseeing. She could barely restrain her laughter until she was safely in the brass cage of the lift, heading down to the lobby. Poor Peterkin still regarded her with some trepidation, even when Lewis confessed that he had been jesting when he accused her of perpetrating fraud.

"You don't look quite as bruised and beleaguered as I expected." Uly came up from behind her as she started a slow circuit of the square, studying the handsome edifices.

"Don't crow so quickly. I'm sure you'll come in for your share of scolding at dinner. Or on the walk to the *Nile*, if you're brave enough to wait and walk with us." Ess laughed as he twisted his face into an exaggerated mask of dismay.

"I need some bolstering for that. Would you care for a glass of lemonade, Miss Peabody?" He offered her his bent arm.

"There is no more Miss Peabody. No more... no, that isn't true." A sensation of weight pressed down on her shoulders, and her head ached slightly. "I still have to wear a mask, don't I? At least until the problem with Sanctuary is dealt with."

"If you think about it, this is our heritage. Constantly wearing masks, pretending to be what we aren't. What would our lives be like if our ancestors hadn't leaped through the doorway created by the Great Machine and followed the Revisionists to this world, to protect the time stream?" Uly led her across Ontario, toward the cart selling lemonade.

"I should hope we would be the same people, but how can we know? Would our grandparents have even been born? If they had, in the far distant future, would they have met and married? Would our parents? Thinking about all the possible worlds and futures makes my head ache."

"Ess, I know I'm not the best sort of example to follow, but I hope you'll consider this bit of advice." He slowed them as they approached the short line of people out enjoying the bright afternoon, waiting to be served. "Don't tie your brain into knots over things you can't change or you have no chance of influencing. I think it's enough to expend our energy and worry and headaches on what we're capable of fixing. If that makes any sense."

"Quite a bit of sense. And don't be too hard on yourself, Uly. I was always proud of you when we were children. I was quite ready to get into fisticuffs with anyone who mocked my big brother."

"You're lucky I never knew that. I might have instigated more quarrels, just to see you shred the little fools."

"You, sir, are incorrigible." Ess muffled a chuckle when a couple standing ahead of them in the line turned to look briefly at them.

They never had much privacy as they strolled around the four quarters of Public Square, divided by the intersection of Ontario and Superior. Ess could only give him a general idea of what had occurred when she walked in on their family lawyers. All in all, she was pleased. They were more happy to see her than angry at the admittedly immature and selfish choices she had made, running off in search of adventure. Their lemonade was gone and they turned to take the wooden cups back to the cart when she got to the subject of Wallace. Uly's smile faded when he learned the man was a detective. His expression turned to a worried scowl when she repeated Endicott's words, that it was time Wallace was included in the secrets behind the law firm.

"Ordinarily, I wouldn't doubt his judgment in anything, but..." Uly shook his head.

"Telling an outsider all the sticky, nearly impossible to prove details?"

"Not even that. Endicott and company have such stalwart, sensible, respectable reputations. What could anyone do to them if, say, Wallace decides they're insane and tells authorities or perhaps even the newspapers? No, what worries me is the possibility that Wallace isn't what he seems."

"As in?"

"A Revisionist spy?"

"Ah. Yes." She fell silent until they had returned the cups, then crossed Ontario and strolled down Superior to meet up with the three lawyers. "I'm sure they've considered the possibility. After all, they are used to dealing with all sorts of unsavory characters."

She had even more reason now to be glad that Wallace had errands to run this evening and wouldn't have been able to come to dinner if Endicott had wanted to include him. They needed to discuss the repercussions of discovering Mr. Judson of the Pinkertons was August Stryker, and a traitor to the Originators. Ess had hoped to share the news of traitors in the

Sanctuary at this afternoon's meeting. She would just have to deal with it on the walk to the airship docks.

The three lawyers emerged from the grand entryway of their building when Ess and Uly were only a dozen or so steps away.

"Ah, the two rascals together, united in mischief," Lewis called.

Laughter and handshakes went around the group, and they started down the sidewalk, heading west toward Public Square again, and the docking towers beyond.

Ess mentioned the law firm's plans to build. Uly offered his opinion of several locations, which led to admitting that he had been in Cleveland several times on various assignments. That earned him a gentle, amused scolding from Endicott for never turning himself in. Uly's sole defense was that none of the three had actually been in town any of the times he had been in the port city. He had had time to familiarize himself with the docks, the law enforcement personnel, the traffic patterns and merchants, and the smugglers' routes, as the Cuyahoga River curved around this part of the city and emptied into Lake Erie.

"Over there would be an ideal location," he said, gesturing at a cluster of older buildings between the southwest quadrant of Public Square and where the land sloped, and in some cases dropped sharply, down to the bend in the river. "It's rumored that there are old Indian tunnels honeycombing this area, and the Underground Railroad put them to good use hiding slaves waiting to be smuggled across the lake to Canada."

"I should hope we never need to make use of smuggler tunnels, no matter how vicious the Revisionists become," MacDonald said.

Everyone fell silent for a minute or two, as they strolled westward, until the buildings in question were blocked from view by closer buildings and the thinning traffic. Ess and Uly exchanged glances. She almost wished he would bring up the unpleasant subject for her.

"I didn't tell you everything that happened when I first met up with Athena," Ess said.

"That's two dollars you owe me," Lewis said, nudging MacDonald with his elbow. The other man made a show of rolling his eyes, but he winked at Ess as he handed over the coins.

"We knew you wouldn't discuss Originator business in front of Ransom," Endicott said, "but we couldn't agree on what exactly you held back."

"Yes, well, the Revisionists played a large part in the whole situation."

"We had our reunion and didn't even know we were passing each other at the time, thanks to the Revisionists," Uly offered. "I was heading down on one of Vulcan's droplines, and Ess was heading up at emergency speed in the retrieval basket, with a poisoned bullet in her shoulder."

"Start from the beginning, please." Endicott caught up Ess's gloved hand in his as they continued walking.

She tried to take everything in chronological order, from receiving the assignment to guard the Egyptian artifacts. Her chase through the rafters of the Smithsonian's warehouse drew chuckles, then sympathetic winces and mutters when she described being shot with the Zeus gun. Ess decided to be entirely forthcoming and admitted her prickly feelings and reluctance to cooperate with the Society, delaying her first lessons about her heritage. She confessed to ignoring attempts to make contact with her along the way, leading up to the tricky situation in Kansas City when she needed to protect the large quantity of crystal dust she had taken from the canopic jar.

"Things just got worse when we reached San Francisco." Uly took over after relating how the tainted bullet fragments in her shoulder made her ill. "Ess had been mystified by how the Pinkertons knew about her knowledge of all things Egypt. Her mentor kept her background hidden. One of the muckety-mucks high in the ranks knew Ess was perfect for the assignment of hostess and curator for the exhibition, putting her in position to guard the artifacts. We learned in San Francisco he wanted to test if she was who he suspected and would be sensitive to the crystal."

"One of us?" Endicott squeezed Ess's hand as he stopped and turned to face her. "Why didn't he just identify himself to you, or at the very least contact us with the news that you had been found?"

"Because he was a traitor," Ess said. "Among the Pinkertons, he was Mr. Judson. When Uly infiltrated the exhibition in San Francisco, we were already suspicious. Something about the man just rubbed me crooked. Uly came in disguise. Mr. Judson wasn't in disguise."

"August Stryker," Uly said.

Ess noted pursed lips, extra wrinkles around eyes or across the forehead, and especially telling, several vertical lines between Endicott's eyebrows. None of them seemed to have favorable impressions of the man.

Uly went on to describe how Stryker had confronted Ess on a foggy night in San Francisco and stepped into the trap laid for him. He gave only the sparsest details of the confrontation when he, Ford, and a handful of soldiers showed up to take Stryker into custody. In the struggle, Stryker fell and hit his head severely enough that he died soon after. Uly then described the double-dealing Stryker had been involved in, specifically the faulty information, bad equipment, and other small details of the missions that he and Ford and their men had been sent on, indicating both groups of men were intended to never return.

Chapter Six

"You're right," Endicott said, nodding to Lewis. "Stanton has complained before how much we trip over our rules of secrecy. No one knows all our leaders, no one knows all our bases of operation, no one knows all our contacts around the world. Stryker's deception proves how easily someone could turn against us and hardly anyone would detect it until too late."

"That's what we need to discuss over dinner tonight," Ess said. "We're still trying to put together a plan to plumb the depths of Sanctuary and lance the boil to cleanse the poison."

"The timing was perfect, a gift from the Almighty, if you really think about it," Uly said. "Athena was ready to fly up to the gates of Sanctuary and reveal all the resources of the Blue Lotus Society and the *Golden Nile*, sort of a visible trumpet blast to rally the troops for a major offensive."

"That would have been suicide," MacDonald said. "You have no indication of who else in Sanctuary might be in the devil's service."

"Exactly." Ess met Uly's gaze again.

"What are you two plotting now?" Endicott swung their joined arms with a little extra force.

"Well, we're somewhat agreed that since I am an unknown, I would be the perfect tool to infiltrate and see what's what."

"The perfect bait and sacrificial lamb, you mean." He squeezed her hand a little tighter.

"My fear exactly," Uly said. "While we're on the subject of who can be trusted," he hurried on, when Ess opened her mouth to argue, "just how much do you know about your man, Wallace? Ess said you're planning on letting him in on the secret?"

"Some of our secrets," Lewis said. "Depending on his reaction to the milder secrets, we'll know whether to reveal more to him."

"Not to change the subject," Endicott said, "but how much time do we have before dinner?"

"More than two hours. Vulcan wants to show off her workshop, and Captain Astrid will want to give you a tour of the *Nile*," Uly said. "We dine late, usually because someone always gets tied up in something fascinating by the end of the day and can't get away. Why?"

"We need to take a slight detour here." He gestured with his cane south, away from the lake. "Ess asked about some old friends." He winked at her. She blinked against sudden tears. He had to mean Hilda.

As they walked three more blocks, and traffic thinned, Uly answered questions from MacDonald and Lewis about the airship. It turned out both were rather mad about airships and took every chance they could to use one for transportation. MacDonald mentioned his dream, to turn their planned office building into an airship docking tower. Now that they knew the Originators actually possessed a ship of their own, it only made sense to have secure docking facilities. Ess rather liked the idea he proposed now, of adding smaller docking facilities for courier craft, or even investing in and building up their own fleet of airships. What could be more secure for rapid transportation, for courier and cargo duties, perhaps even expeditions across the ocean?

"We could expand into shipping as a cover for our activities around the world," MacDonald concluded as they approached a building with people waiting on the steps to get inside. "Nobody pays attention to cargo handlers. They're certainly less likely to be fired on, approaching ports or buildings where situations might be tense."

"I hate to admit it," Lewis said, tone weary but eyes sparkling, "but he does have a point." He winked at Ess, and she was hard put not to laugh.

"Mark this day." MacDonald pressed his hand over his heart. "Stanton actually agrees with me."

"Hush, you two." Endicott gestured at the building, three stories tall, showing signs of recent repair on the brickwork, and evidence of scrubbing away the grime of years in other places.

"What is this place?" Uly asked. "I was here four years ago, and if I recall, this wasn't as..." He glanced at Ess and colored a little. "Well, as respectable as it looks now."

"Three years ago, Hilda came to us with a proposition for the betterment of the neighborhood. That rather started us on our path of investment, and real estate in particular. The top floor is a dormitory where street children can come for shelter, food, medicine, clothes, what have you. The second floor is a school where they learn reading and writing and figuring, and a trade if they are so inclined. Whatever they choose, however much they let her, she gets them presentable, helps them find jobs, and most important, protects them from the Fagan types roaming every big city, looking for prey. The first floor." Endicott chuckled. "Well, the first floor is Hilda's domain. I was hard put not to laugh when you suggested she establish a restaurant in our proposed building."

"Hilda runs a restaurant here?" Ess studied the people waiting to get inside. Yes, they looked hungry. If they had eaten Hilda's creations before, they couldn't help being hungry in anticipation of whatever was on the menu tonight.

"She teaches the children to cook, and they wait tables, wash dishes, and even deliver meals to customers to enjoy at home," Lewis said.

"How successful is she?"

"The children sleep three to a bed and on the floor, and on the floors of the school rooms, as many as she can fit in. Some people who have fallen on hard times bring their children here, instead of accepting help from the state, her reputation is so good. Just in three years." Endicott sighed, with a pleased smile. "There are times when I am not entirely content with the things I must do to protect my clients, but this... this makes up for the more unpleasant aspects of my duties and obligations. We're currently in negotiations to buy the adjoining building to expand the school and dormitory. The owner wants the restaurant expanded as well, and a permanently reserved table."

"Is that a problem?"

"He is nearly thirty stone, and despite warnings from his doctors, he is determined to reach forty stone before he dies."

"I'm surprised he hasn't demanded Hilda marry him," Uly remarked, his tone sour.

"His wife is one of Hilda's dearest friends and supports her efforts to improve the neighborhood. Happily, she is to blame for his girth. Well, shall we go in?"

"Do we dare interrupt?" Ess said. Hilda was a marvel of control and efficiency in her kitchen, but she was rather a stickler for no one being allowed in unless they helped prepare the meal.

"Oh, but we dare not," Lewis said, stepping up and linking his arm through her free arm.

"What he means is, we sent one of our runners with a note when we left the office, saying we would be bringing you for inspection." MacDonald pressed his hand between her shoulder blades and gave her a gentle shove.

"I didn't see any messenger," Uly said, as the five started up the steps.

Ess decided the three lawyers were regular visitors, because the people waiting on the wide stone steps moved aside to make way for them without any resentment on their faces.

"No, we don't use the local messenger services. We employ some of Hilda's students, boys and girls. Very efficient, and in that lovely place between utter devotion to and terror of Hilda," Lewis said.

"Since you're thinking of recruiting Mr. Wallace, have you considered adding these street children to our numbers?" Uly said, as they stepped into the foyer of the building.

They were alone for the moment. Ess guessed that those waiting to be seated had to wait outside. At the back of the foyer, she saw stairs with a chain and a "no admittance" sign strung from one newel post to the other.

"He has a point," MacDonald said. "It's a good bet the Revisionists haven't limited their training to just their own descendants."

"Oh, don't sound so surprised," Uly said with a chuckle. "I have grown up since the last time you saw me, and my job does involve tactical thinking."

Before Ess could even think of a humorous, teasing response, the door at the back of the foyer opened and Hilda bustled out, wiping her eyes on the corner of her massive white apron. How she always managed to create culinary treasures without messing her apron, Ess had never been able to figure out. A boy scurried out behind her and unchained the bottom of the steps. Sniffing, Hilda gestured for them to follow, and climbed the stairs with a surprisingly light step for all her bulk. The boy grinned at them, waiting with the chain in one hand. Ess looked back in time to see MacDonald toss a coin to the boy, and guessed this was the messenger. She quite approved. Children living in poverty or out on the streets were vulnerable to far worse than the criminals portrayed in Mr. Dickens' novels. If they had a job, their employers provided some defense, if only to protect their own interests.

At the top of the stairs, Hilda yanked Ess from Endicott's grip and enfolded her in a tight hug, just like all the embraces they had exchanged in her childhood—except that this time Ess was disconcerted to realize her chin was even with Hilda's ear. She wasn't aware of having grown during her years of travel and adventures. If possible, the woman was even rosier in her cheeks and whiter in her hair. The strength of her grip was the same as she held Ess out at arm's length and inspected her.

"Just look at you. The hoyden is all grown up, and such a lovely lady."

"Oh, I guarantee she's still more comfortable in trousers and cap than skirts," Uly said, stepping up next to Ess and grinning.

"You—you scoundrel!" Hilda boxed his ears before pulling him into a hug and sputtering between laughter and tears.

Ess knew she had softened the blow, because Uly barely flinched. When he was a boy, he would complain that Hilda had fractured his skull after she dispensed the standard punishment for all his tricks and mischief.

"There now, both my ducklings together again. Ah, if only your grandparents could see you now." Hilda stepped back, jamming her fists into her ample hips, and smiling with tear-bright eyes.

"That's our next task," Uly said.

"Hilda, did you see about—" Endicott began.

"I just sent my two fastest bicycle boys for the others." She wiped her eyes again on the corner of her apron and gestured at a nearby circle of chairs. She tucked Ess's arm into hers as she wobbled the few steps necessary to reach the chairs. "The rest will be so delighted to know you've finally showed up. Thomas always insisted you would track down your grandparents and then all of you would come back and avenge Giles." She caught her breath. "You do know about Giles?" She clucked when Ess nodded. "He gave those Resurrectionists what for, that's for certain."

"They might not have all been Resurrectionists," Uly said, as the rest took their seats.

"We are expected at the *Golden Nile*, eventually," Endicott said. "I know you too well, Hilda, to ask you to abandon your kitchen. You will join us there later? Or should we bring the party here?"

"The *Golden Nile*?" Her eyes widened. "You two are tied in with those historical lah-de-dahs who just came to town?" She sniffed. "Your grandfather might enjoy debating their outlandish theories and knock their pins out from under them. After all, our ancestors were there and we have the records to prove it."

"Do you remember Athena Latymer?" Ess said, repressing a smile.

"I looked after that girl when she was your grandmother's student. Just like you, when she was younger, climbing trees and learning to shoot." Hilda gasped. "Don't tell me — she's with those folks, too?"

"Auntie Eena is their leader. It's a cover," Uly said.

"Well, that puts a different color on things. Clever. Who'd expect warriors under the cover of those grave robbers?" She sniffed and nodded. "That's why you asked me to retrieve everything, when you sent word my girl here had finally waltzed through the door."

"Retrieve what?" Ess felt like she was ten again, and coming in on the end of an adult's war council. She always had to piece together what everyone had been discussing, just from cryptic remarks and overheard conversations in the days that followed.

"Why, everything we cleared out of your grandfather's house before that rabble attacked."

"Since there's room on the *Nile*, and quite a bit of what you sent away for safekeeping might just be relevant," the senior lawyer said, "I asked Hilda to send for the others to bring everything together."

"The others, meaning Bridget and Thomas and Peggety and Waldo?" Ess blinked away a threat of tears.

"They've had some fun the last few years, playing the carnival game," Hilda said with a chuckle. "Shuffling all those crates from one place to another."

"Not all fun," Lewis said. "There are some very determined people trying to track down whatever was in your grandparents' archives. Waldo got himself some nasty powder burns, about three years ago, setting up some booby-traps around the newest hiding place. The man would have been in his glory as a pirate on the high seas."

"I'm sorry," Ess said. "I just wanted to save everything from the Resurrectionists — you did hear they tried to burn the house, didn't you?" She flashed back to that horrid moment when she had approached her grandparents' house and saw the evidence of battle and burning, and then read the newspaper account of how Giles had died. "I didn't think there would be more trouble, dogging all of you this whole time."

"Now there, don't you fret. It was our duty, and quite frankly, something of an adventure." Hilda squeezed her hand. "I assume you're finally going to tell our girl here all the things that were kept secret and unlock some of those doors her grandmother built in her head?"

"I already heard about that." She couldn't quite repress a sniff.

"Did you now?" The older woman tipped her head to one side and pursed her lips, gazing at Endicott.

Ess was astonished to see him shift uncomfortably in his seat and actually flush a little.

"Actually, Odessa," Lewis said, reaching to rest a hand on her forearm. A consoling and calming gesture if she had ever seen one used. "There are quite a few things your grandmother locked up inside your head, for safekeeping, so to speak. You were left behind when you would have been quite a useful asset on their latest expedition, simply to protect you."

"And all of us," Endicott said, his voice just above a whisper. Somehow, the words landed in the room with all the force of a bellow.

"Your grandparents feared something might go wrong with their expedition. That's why they left you behind," Hilda said. "You were the key to opening the family vault, and they fiddled with your head so that anyone who got their hands on you would see that it was impossible to retrieve that information by force. In fact..." She sat up straight and her lower lip stuck out just enough to be noticeable.

Ess shivered with an odd kind of eager anticipation. She recognized that protruding lip from the few times Hilda did something tinged with rebellion. The woman had never been so devoted to the elder Fremonts that she had stifled common sense, but it was rare when she outright rebelled against what was expected of her. Each time, Hilda's gut instinct and refusal to comply had turned out to be the more intelligent choice or tactic.

"Well, the truth is, Mr. Endicott and company, Giles and I lied to you, when you informed us of Ernest and Matilda's expedition vanishing like it did. We did in fact get a message from them. They specifically asked us not to tell anyone what they had learned, what they feared, if something untoward happened to them. Not until Odessa turned eighteen. Our friends should have returned Ulysses by that time. We were to reveal the nasty business they had uncovered, assess the current state of affairs, and decide what to do. There's all sorts of secrets and keys and such locked up in your head, my girl. Matilda even said the fate of our people could rest entirely on your shoulders, when you were a woman grown. She said you were the key—a door key and a musical key. Does that make any sense to you?"

"Indeed it does," MacDonald said. "Music is the third side of a triangular key, so to speak, used to dismantle the Great Machine. Blood and crystal and music."

Ess and Uly exchanged glances. She knew her brother was just as eager as she to reveal what they had learned to do with the crystal, recreating the communication plates of their ancestors.

"Your grandparents suspected treachery at the highest levels. Their expedition was meant to force the traitors to act and reveal themselves. They left something important behind in Sanctuary, with clues to lead the traitors into a trap. Trusted folks in Sanctuary discovered that their research had been twisted and gutted, so no one could make any use or sense of it."

"Everyone but those who saw the original reports and made the changes," Uly murmured.

"Your grandparents were sure they would find the doorway into a box—a box of time, if that makes any sense." Hilda shrugged. "Their last message said they were being herded into a trap. Ernest said a trap with a door that opened only one way could be used as a defense, as a hiding place. A trap wasn't a trap if the victims knew it was, and stepped into it deliberately, to hide." She spread her hands. "That's it. I remembered it because it struck me as so strange."

"A box of time," Uly whispered. He caught hold of Ess's other hand. "Do you think..."

"Granny and Grandfather didn't really vanish, so much as step... oh, I don't know, sideways, into a side room, in the stream of time. No, that's the wrong imagery. If time is a river, then they stepped out of the river, not onto shore, but into an inlet, waiting out of the current until the proper time to re-enter it." Ess shook her head. She wished she could contact Ford right that moment and bounce her theories off of him. He loved such mind-stretching theorizing.

"Time?" Lewis said. "Do you mean manipulating time, to travel through it as our ancestors did? How can they do that without the Great Machine fully assembled?"

"The Machine is only necessary to send people backward in time," Endicott said. "If I remember my basic orientation, someone nearly a century before the development of the Machine discovered a way to, shall we say, *skip forward* in time. A one-way trip. A doorway forward. It was originally developed to resist the progression of the horrific diseases of what will be our future, to buy time to find treatments. Someone reasoned it would be less dangerous to jump forward in blocks of time. The patient wouldn't age, the disease wouldn't progress any further, but science and medicine would have had five, ten, twenty years to develop a cure."

"So Granny and Grandfather... they discovered whatever made it possible to enter the time stream... buried in South America?" Ess hazarded.

Uly pursed his lips in thought. "Knowing them, they set up a trap for whoever came to attack them, thinking them stranded."

"Knowing your grandparents, they *chose* to go at that time, counting on the turmoil in that region to hide their tracks and slow down whoever had been sent to either capture or kill them," Endicott said.

"I'll wager, when we open the door and let them out of the box, they'll demand to know what took us so all-fired long," Ess burst out. "Secrets inside of secrets!"

They had already taken too long talking in the classroom. Hilda was needed in her kitchen and the rest were expected at the *Golden Nile* soon. They made arrangements to return to Hilda's headquarters the next day. If Waldo and Thomas couldn't arrive by the next afternoon, they would at least send a message saying when they planned to arrive. Hilda surprised Ess by going a little white when she was invited to the *Golden Nile* for a tour. The woman who had faced down marauders and held off a Rebel raiding party during the Civil War, with a bayonet and an entire kitchen of knives and cleavers, went queasy at the thought of stepping onto a craft hanging high in the air.

They were all rather subdued as they resumed their walk to the docking tower, deep in thought. Ess was grateful she didn't have to keep up a conversation. She shuddered from time to time as she processed all Hilda had revealed. Yet among all the weight of new information, new theories, new puzzles to solve, a sense of relief made her feel rather weightless. Her grandparents had left her behind for a reason. They had entrusted her with the protection of their family's secrets and treasures, heritage and historic duty. The keys were hidden in her mind.

Or rather, the keys to her mind were hidden somewhere, somehow. Perhaps the information was among the crates sent away for safekeeping, or perhaps in the family vault at Sanctuary. That added another reason to the long list of why she needed to go to Sanctuary, no matter how deep and dark the nest of treachery might be.

"Blood and crystal and music," she murmured to Uly, when he caught hold of her hand again. "A three-sided key."

"Do you think..." He grinned and twined his fingers through hers. "Maybe that's the missing piece in making the plates work. We have to find the right musical note to allow us to speak through them?"

"Plates?" MacDonald said, blinking rapidly as he was visibly pulled from his deep thoughts.

By this time, they had reached the door into the docking tower. Uly signaled for them to wait, until they were able to procure a lift car all to themselves. Then he and Ess explained, briefly, what they had managed to do with the crystal dust. All three men were astonished, enough to be nearly comical. That raised all their spirits, so they stepped noticeably lighter as they crossed the gangplank to the *Golden Nile*.

Chapter Seven

Theo waited for them. He knew all three men and greeted them as old friends. They had spent enough time with Hilda that there wasn't time for a tour of the airship before dinner. The three guests went with Theo to cabins where they could freshen up before dinner, while Ess and Uly hurried to their cabins to do the same. Ess was glad to get out of what she still considered a costume rather than day clothes. Dinner tonight wasn't a formal affair, but she knew better than to show up at table in her usual long shirt, loose trousers, and light shipboard boots. She chose a looser dress, one that didn't require a corset, and gladly left her hat behind.

For a moment as she did a quick freshening with a damp washcloth, she considered wearing the crystal rose. She hadn't worn it much because she feared any resonance from it interfering with her work on the communication plates. Ess stared into her eyes in the little mirror over her washbasin, puzzled over her reticence. The rose was a link to her mother — what was wrong with her to fear wearing it? Was that one odd dream enough reason to fear?

Yet what if her theory was correct, and the rose had linked Vivian and the former Revisionist woman, Anna? Was it possible that the make-believe friend, Carmen, was Anna's daughter, and the two girls' minds had touched in their childhood when they wore the crystal roses, just like their mothers? Didn't she have a duty to pursue her theory?

The problem was that Ess had worn the rose to bed several times, and yet nothing had happened. No fun and games and giggling with her make-believe friend like in her childhood. No more visions of Carmen, in her nightgown and duster, practicing playing the piano at night inside the vacated camp meeting tent.

"Botheration," Ess muttered, and snatched the rose off the wall hook where her few pieces of jewelry hung next to her mirror. She clutched the crystal piece in her hand and closed her eyes and focused, calling up the face of the girl and the young woman she had seen since regaining the rose.

Nothing happened. She wasn't surprised. Maybe relieved, if she was being totally honest with herself.

Perhaps the problem was that Carmen wasn't wearing her rose. Ess finally opened her eyes and shook her head at herself in the mirror. She put the necklace on and made a mental note to wear it whenever possible.

Unless, of course, the crystal did interfere with using the communication plates and dealing with more crystal dust.

Ess arrived first in the forward cabin designated as a parlor. She felt no guilt whatsoever taking the first dish of lemon ice from among the various appetizers. Shaved ice concoctions were Dr. Sylvia's new passion, and she had plans to visit local markets with the woman to stock up on all sorts of exotic fruit, no matter how expensive, for experimentation.

Ford was next to reach the parlor, and he laughed when he saw her. Ess knew better than to ask why he laughed. If she kept silent, the pressure of needing to tell whatever odd or amusing thoughts had come to him would build until he burst. Ford was a combination of favorite uncle and younger brother, and better yet, he was full of all sorts of stories about her parents. Through him, she was getting to know them. She knew now, in light of what she had learned today, her own memories of her parents had been locked up inside the vaults her grandmother created in her mind.

"What's that frown for?" Ford settled down on the sofa opposite her. He had a large glass of soda and some garishly green syrup Ess had yet to try from the many pump-topped bottles on the sideboard.

"Granny put locks in my mind. It's rather disconcerting to realize that people have been using my head as a cedar closet."

"Do tell," he murmured, glass paused at his lips. "We're to have an interesting dinner, aren't we?"

Despite Ess's best efforts to get the more unpleasant news over with before dinner, much of the conversation did deal with the questions of how badly Sanctuary was compromised, who were traitors among the leadership, and how to go about unmasking them.

Between dinner and moving back to the parlor for coffee, the three lawyers sent to their hotel for clothes. The war council clearly would go far into the evening, perhaps near to morning. They would catch a few hours of sleep on board the *Nile* and go from there to their offices in the morning.

They settled two vital elements in the plan, somewhere after the second cup of coffee. First, the *Golden Nile* and crew could not go to Sanctuary. Revealing their cover story would put too much power into the hands of the enemy. Instead, the airship and crew would head for South America. They would be far safer there, despite the turmoil among the various countries. Uly would go with the *Golden Nile* with his communication plate.

The second part of the plan made Ess feel a little breathless, a little proud, and a little frustrated—like the time she set off for town on her bicycle for the first time to fetch sugar and peaches for Hilda's baking. She had been so proud at age eight to be allowed to go all that distance by herself. Then she looked around when she reached the steps of the grocer's shop to discover Uly had followed her, sent by Giles and Ernest. At least Granny Matilda had believed she could handle the trip into town by herself. This time, though, she knew she would be a fool to try something so huge by herself. Endicott, Lewis and MacDonald would escort her cross-country, by train, to San Francisco, and then down the coast to the gates of Sanctuary.

They would vouch for her identity and the extremely edited narration of her life since her grandparents' disappearance. They would claim Ess had had most of her memories blocked by her grandparents and had been living under a new identity. She became a Pinkerton, and injuries sustained during the Egyptian exhibition assignment had triggered a cascade of memories, which prompted her to contact the law firm.

They needed to create a letter that had just recently arrived at the New York office of the law firm, after being waylaid, misplaced, and delayed on its journey from South America. The letter would explain how to start the "unlocking" process. Ess volunteered the services of a good friend among the Pinkertons, a dab hand at forgeries, to create the letter and make it convincingly travel-worn and stained.

Hopefully, the ruse would convince the enemy that Ess's ignorance of her heritage made her a golden apple that had figuratively rolled out of the garden of the gods, right into their hands.

"If only we could depend on a war more devastating than Troy to erupt among all those conspirators," Athena remarked.

Ess would put her years of Pinkerton training to use, playing innocent and confused, duping the traitors into revealing themselves and walking into the noose they likely had prepared for her. Her mission would be determining who was friend, who was foe, who was dupe, and who had been foolish enough to make Sanctuary vulnerable to their ancestral enemies. Far easier would be getting into her grandparents' vault and identifying what they had left behind to unlock the time box. Once Ess knew who in Sanctuary could be trusted, she would recruit help in traveling to South America to rejoin the *Golden Nile*. From there, they would figure out how to locate the elder Fremonts and unlock the time box.

William MacDonald proved to be brilliant when the evening turned to the question of the communication link. Athena and Ford both laughed when Ess and Uly brought up the theory that audible communication had to be triggered by the third side of the key: music. MacDonald revealed, after some gentle teasing from Lewis, that he had made a hobby of studying the ancestors' cultural records. Namely, the music passed down through the generations. The evening turned rather entertaining for nearly an hour, as everyone searched their memories for songs and bits of music they had been taught by their parents, or teachers and mentors. MacDonald astounded them, time after time, identifying the name of the melody or correcting the notes of a song or the words themselves, warped or swapped out for something else through the centuries, as language changed.

"Here's a funny bit," he said, after winnowing down a list of the oldest remembered tunes. "This song has been variously called 'Speak to Me,' and 'Hear Me.' The words have changed multiple times, but always harken back to one theme. Communication." He took a breath, pulled back his shoulders, and ah-ah-ahhed through the first dozen notes.

Athena dropped her coffee cup. It didn't break, hitting first her knee and then the carpeted floor, and splashed a last few teaspoons of coffee on her clothes.

"Miss Latymer?" Endicott said, holding out a hand to her in some concern.

"It's the call for help song," Ess said, as Athena's mouth twisted into a rueful smile. Next to her, Uly slapped his knee and tipped his head back and laughed.

"More important than that," Athena said. "Ford, would you fetch my flute?"

Ford frowned just for a moment, then his eyes lit up and he nodded, grinning, as he leaped to his feet and hurried from the room.

"Matilda made sure Vivian and I specifically knew the song," Athena continued, "and that we each had a flute made just like hers; silver of a specific purity, embedded with fragments of crystal. She did this after determining that we had lived up to our heritage as descendants of the women who dismantled the Great Machine."

"Is it possible?" Ess asked. "We've had the key all along, and never knew it?"

"Oh, I'll wager your grandmother knew," Theo said. "She was a great one for keeping her cards so close to the vest, even her allies were surprised to discover she was holding any cards at all."

"I replaced your flute, but I fear departing on our various missions will simply have to delay until Vulcan can replicate a flute for Uly." Athena winked at him. "You can still play, can't you?"

"Not nearly as good as Ess, but yes, I can still play the help song," Uly said.

"Excuse me." Vulcan looked up from the journal where she sketched and made notes. "Help song?"

"It's a sort of request for aid, thrown out to the wind," Ford said, hurrying back through the door. "Ernest and Matilda made sure the children knew it, in case they landed in trouble and weren't sure who to trust. All our traveling agents know it." He held out the flute in its soft leather case to Athena, but she shook her head and gestured for him to give it to Ess.

Ess slid the flute out of the long, padded protective tube and slid her fingertips over the tiny specks of crystal embedded in the dull silver surface.

"No time like the present." Uly stood and held out a hand to her. Ess let him help her and they walked over to the table on the other side of the parlor, where the bags of crystal dust waited, with the helix rods in their swaddling of acoustic cloth.

As they had done earlier that evening, they struck the rods and created the crystal plates. When the surfaces darkened and turned into mirrors, they brought the plates vertical and hung them in the air. Uly took a rod in each hand, keeping the plates floating, while Ess picked up the flute and played slowly through the help song. She nearly stopped when at the twelfth note, a shimmer of blue-tinted light covered the surfaces of both plates. The blue shimmer increased noticeably as she continued playing. When she stopped, it dimmed just a little. Slowly, she put the flute down on the table and took her rod from Uly. He nodded to her, his grin strained. The pressure of all those expectant gazes from the other side of the room froze the words on her tongue for a moment.

"This is rather a historic—"

Ess nearly dropped the rod. Her voice had a slight echo. Sweat instantly coated her forehead. She traded grins with Uly. A glance showed everyone else leaning forward in their seats. Athena and Ford held hands. Only Dr. Sylvia looked relaxed, her expression closer to "it's about time," than wondering astonishment.

Uly gestured at the open door out into the corridor. Before Ess could think and respond, he guided his plate before him across the room. He stepped out the door, then pulled it shut behind him. They waited in silence for nearly a full minute.

"What do you suggest we try next," Theo said, "if this doesn't work?"

"Oh, it works," Uly said, his gleeful face filling the plate and his voice spilling through the room with a slight crystal undertone. "Heard you loud and clear, all the way down at the first intersection."

The cheers that filled the room prompted him to press his hands against his ears. The communication plate spun upside down, reacting to the movement of the rod.

For the next half hour, they were all rather childish, taking turns running back and forth between the parlor and Uly, who moved farther away through the decks of the *Nile*. They sang to each other and told riddles and tested the clarity of transmission by scribbling images no larger than a thumbnail, and having someone on the other side copy what they saw. By the time Uly returned to the parlor, Ess was sure everyone on board the *Golden Nile* knew of the successful activation of the communication plates.

Successful, with limits. Others could use the plates once they were awakened and the link established, but only she and Uly could create and awaken the plates or shut them down and return them to mere piles of dust in a silk-lined leather bag. This convenience of visual and audible communication had its limitations. Ess understood that communication between the two groups with their separate missions was vital to their success and safety. That didn't mean she didn't want to whine a bit over the necessity of separating her from Uly. They had just been reunited. She couldn't shake the awful certainty that if he flew away on the *Golden Nile* without her, she might never see him again.

Ess finally rolled into bed at a slightly headachy three a.m. She wasn't surprised that her dreams were filled with spying on Miss Van Hastings, adventures with Uly in their childhood, and ransacking her grandfather's study, searching book after book after archival box for some mysterious item she couldn't quite recall after she woke. She washed her face and drank some water, and curled up to try to doze and let the fragments of her dreams rise to the surface and form a coherent picture.

At some point, she clutched the crystal rose without thinking. Her dream shifted so she was sitting on the edge of a narrow cot, watching a young woman sitting in a corner of the room. She had her knees drawn up to her shoulders, her face rested on her knees, and she wore all black, with her long, dark auburn hair hanging loose and tangled. Ess watched her for several moments, her thoughts tangled up in that drifting feeling that came often in dreams.

The realization that drifting, hazy sensation meant she was dreaming changed everything. The light lost its misty gray softness, taking on sharper, harder edges of black shadows. The young woman's shoulders shook, and Ess decided she was weeping. If she knew she was dreaming, maybe this was more than just a dream? Were all the theories about communicating through crystal, the link between Vivian and Anna, possibly true and real?

If they were, she shouldn't be wasting time.

"Carmen?" She nearly laughed to hear herself speak. Yes, she did know the girl weeping in the corner. "Are you holding the rose?"

Carmen raised her head, her face a swollen wreck of tears and bloodshot eyes and utter misery. She sniffled and blinked and raised one hand to rake hair out of her eyes, where her tears had plastered it.

The other hand was clutched tight, with a silver chain spilling out between her fingers.

"Rose?" Her voice was thick with tears, hoarse from weeping.

"Yes, like this." Ess held out her hand with the crystal rose in it.

"How odd." Carmen unfolded her hand to reveal a cross of silver, inset with blue enamel, and the crystal rose in the intersection of the two bars. Ess estimated it was perhaps four inches long and two wide.

"Why are you crying?"

"My Papa is dead." She hiccupped. "Everyone is saying such horrid things about him. They aren't true. None of them. Nobody would say anything if he were still alive. Nobody will listen to me." Another hiccup. "Nobody will help me. I have to sell everything. They say Papa owes so much money. How could he, when he never bought anything? Never owned anything but his Bible and our clothes and my piano." Her shoulders shook and she bent her head into her knees again. "My piano. And Mama's cross. They're going to take everything."

"Your mother's cross?" Ess somehow managed to slide off the bed and float across the room.

"It's all I have left of her. I have to give them everything, to pay Papa's debts. He didn't have any debts. You believe me, don't you?"

"Of course I do. Carmen, don't let them have the cross. Or at least, let them have the silver, but don't let them have the rose in the center."

"Why?" She sniffled and sat up a little more.

"That's how we talk. Your mother was named Anna, right?" Ess shuddered, feeling the dream shifting around her, starting to shred at the edges. "If you lose the rose, we won't be able to talk again. Please, Carmen?"

"This is silly." She sniffed and rubbed her eyes with her free hand. "I'm hysterical with grief, that's all. You're... you're not real. This is just a dream." Another sniff. "I have to sell my cross. They're coming for it and my piano. They'd take the tent if it didn't belong to the Bible society. They're taking everything in the morning."

"Don't let them. Run away, if you have to. Please, Carmen? This is important." Ess muffled a snarl as a sensation of being yanked backward washed over her. In moments her childhood friend, her make-believe-but-now-real friend, was a tiny speck of light in a dark, warped landscape.

She was awake, pulled entirely out of the dream. Yet could it be called a dream when, if her theory was right, she had talked to Carmen, the daughter of Anna, through the crystal roses?

Ess took deep breaths and tried to recall the calming litany her grandmother had taught her to bring on sleep. She lay still. She got comfortable. She drifted in and out of sleep for what felt like half the day.

Dreams returned, but they were only fragments of memories, brought on by perhaps some of the songs she had played the night before. She didn't return to the cold, bare room where Carmen wept over the loss of her father. Ess could only speculate that he had been a preacher. From Carmen's words and the setting of that first dream, the dead man had been part of a traveling revival group, running camp meetings, sponsored by some Bible society. Ess wished she had been awake enough to think clearly and ask for Carmen's last name, or even more useful, the name of the town, the address of the boarding house or hotel where she had been weeping.

"Don't be ridiculous," Ess whispered into the darkness of her room. "I can't put aside preparations to storm Sanctuary and bring down judgment on the traitors' heads just to follow my dreams. Even if I could find her location by this afternoon, I certainly can't fly there and drop out of the sky and prove that I'm just as real as she is." She sighed and rolled over and buried her head under her pillows. "But please, Savior, watch over Carmen and help her get away from those horrid people? Keep her safe until I can find her? If she's Anna's daughter, and if she can touch the crystal with her mind like I can..." A gusting sigh escaped her, followed by a shudder. "She is in just as much danger as I would be, if the Revisionists ever got their hands on me. Please, protect her?"

Finally, when the effort to return to sleep and dreams had generated a headache, Ess gave up and got out of bed to wash.

The three lawyers had already had breakfast and left for their offices, by the time she visited the kitchen to scrounge some breakfast. The first task on their list was to send a telegram to their contact in Monterey, a growing city south of the coastal canyon area where Sanctuary lay hidden. They would report that the long-missing Odessa Vivian Fremont had contacted them and was making her way cross-country to meet them in Cleveland. The lawyers wanted instructions from their superiors on the next step to take. Telegrams would criss-cross the continent for a week at minimum, two if they were lucky, giving the crew of the *Nile* plenty of time to prepare for the journey to South America. The responses from the leaders in Sanctuary would also give them some hint of how to proceed when Ess and her escort reached the center of all Originator activity in the Western Hemisphere.

Uly and Ford had gone to see Hilda and obtain the route that Thomas and Waldo were expected to take. Athena was busy responding to requests for consultations and visits from various local historical and scholarly societies. There was the façade of the Blue Lotus Society to maintain, after all. Theo and other friends among the crew were busy with various errands and tasks. That left Ess at loose ends. She was in the mood for a holiday. Just a little adventuring.

Her spirits fell when she put on her trusty shape-changing corset and it felt tighter than the last time she wore it. Surely she hadn't been so sedentary over the last few weeks, with her increasingly scholarly life, that she had gained some unwanted padding on hips and bosom? Pure determination and stubbornness fueled her as she struggled to close up the corset to flatten bosom and hips and affect the way she walked. The bit of discomfort could be ignored and was a small price to pay to spend the day with Hilda.

She left a note for Athena, who was currently having mid-morning tea with a delegation from some of the leading families in Cleveland. Then she stepped into Vulcan's workshop to see the progress on Uly's flute. Theo tipped off a salute to her and gestured for her to run. Vulcan never looked up from some test of the metal in a small smelting pot. The stink of various chemicals in the air, strengthened by the scent of molten metal, made Ess wonder how either of them could breathe in there.

Chapter Eight

The sentry on duty gave Ess a double look as she slid past him, heading for the gangplank to the docking tower. He nodded to her but said nothing. Maybe he thought she was on some secret mission?

Ess detoured a little on her way to Hilda's, to look at the neighborhood Endicott and his partners favored for their building. She had learned some things while she worked as a water boy on the tower in Springfield, and during a few undercover assignments with the Pinkertons. The area along the river was a good location, sitting on a sort of bluff, with a steep drop-off on one side. She could envision a dock down below, for discrete arrivals and deliveries by water, or exits by water. If there were Indian tunnels or natural crevices in the rock below the growing port city, they would be useful for Originator business. Still, lives and businesses and homes and livelihoods would be disrupted when those buildings currently on the site would be torn down. That unpleasant necessity was probably what made Endicott, Lewis and MacDonald hesitate to act. She imagined they were taking their time investigating. She admired them for that and pitied them the choices that could be very unpleasant.

"Please, Savior, is it possible to have what we want without discomfiting anyone?" she whispered as she waited for traffic to cross the intersection so she could step out.

How much time would she have here in Cleveland before they had made all the necessary arrangements? The *Golden Nile* needed to refill its supplies of food, ammunition, fuel, and spare parts. Vulcan and Captain Astrid planned to thoroughly check the massive airship before heading south, to make sure every thin spot was strengthened, every loose joint and nut and bolt tightened, and every chart of weather and wind patterns thoroughly checked. Ess was glad to know she had some clout to contribute to the preparation efforts. She still had some connections among the Secret Service, though she hadn't had contact with Agent Sutter in nearly two years. Investigating developments, political and otherwise in South America was probably the most important step in preparing to head south.

As she approached Hilda's building, a pair of broad shoulders ahead of her looked strangely familiar. A big man with a dusty bowler hat leaned against the railing along a half flight of steps, four doors down from Hilda's doorway. Ess was about to pass the familiarity off as a result of reminiscing about her adventures with Sutter and his team. Then the big man took off his hat to scratch at his dry nest of thinning, ginger-colored hair. The tilted way he shrugged, right shoulder and then left, and the way he slapped his hat back on his head confirmed his identity.

Agent Collins.

Muffling a chuckle, she slipped up the steps behind him, on the other side of the wall that divided the stairs to two separate doorways in the long row of three-story houses. Many of the houses on this street had originally been built to let the owners run a business from the lower floor, with a half-flight of stairs going down from the sidewalk. Tailors, jewelers, book binders, cobblers, and other small craftsmen plied their trade on the lower floor, lived on the second floor, and often rented out the upper floor.

Ess stood two steps higher than Collins, to look over his head. She had never seen the big man standing still except on assignment. She lined herself up with the dome of his hat, wondering who he was watching.

Collins watched Hilda's house. She was sure of it after the fourth person approached or exited the front door, and Collins' head moved to track their movement.

What could he possibly want with Hilda?

One way to find out. Ess slipped her hand between Collins' bent arm and the front of his coat. She leaned as close as she dared, watching over his shoulder, and directing her breath away, so it didn't touch his ear or hair. Patience worked best when the mark was standing still and she had no helpers to create a distraction. The next person through the doorway was an errand boy, carrying a tray. Collins pivoted to watch the departing boy until he turned the corner and went out of sight.

In those few seconds, Collins shifted enough to tug open the front of his coat. Ess slipped out his coin purse and his handkerchief. She tucked the handkerchief into her pocket and hefted the coin purse enough to test the weight. The soft chink of coins got a twitch from Collins, but not enough to make him turn.

"Hey, Mister?" She caught at his left sleeve as she reached the bottom of the steps and came around his left side. "Didja drop this?" Ess tugged her cap low on her forehead as she held out the coin purse.

Collins opened his mouth to say no—she saw the denial in his eyes—then he frowned and pressed a hand against his coat over the now-empty pocket.

"Thank you, lad." Collins tugged open his coat to slide the coin purse back into place and froze. His frown deepened.

"Hot morning, ain't it?" She swiped at her forehead with the handkerchief, arranged to show the monogram with Collins' initials.

"What in tar—" His mouth dropped open as he reached to grasp her wrist, at the same moment she pushed up the brim of her cap with her other hand. A loud bark of laughter escaped him as he lifted her off her feet and into a short, affectionate shake. "Up to your old tricks, are you?"

"So are you. What brings you to town? Is the rest of the team here?" Ess nearly faltered when Collins turned just enough to keep his gaze focused on Hilda's door.

"I'm the first man here. Just checking out a few rumors."

"Rumors? Here? This is the quiet side of town. Millionaire Row is the other direction, down Euclid. These are the small businesses, the elderly, the lower class."

"Makes me wonder how you know all that. We weren't aware the Pinkertons had any jobs nearby." Collins winked. "Ready to stop playing with the amateurs and come back to work with us?"

"Actually..." Ess glanced around, spotted the man at the far end of the street, leaning against a lamppost and slowly rolling a cigarette. Very obviously trying not to watch them. "One of yours?"

"No. One of the jobless. Enjoys it." His eyes narrowed. "Wanders this part of town looking for pity and anybody who'll listen to him complain, but won't sit still long enough to take a job."

"You'd like to give him a real job, eh?" she guessed. That earned a grin from the big man. "No, actually, I've left the Pinkertons. I found my brother, at long last."

"Glad for you, Ess. Everybody needs family." He tipped his head to one side, his gaze sliding over her shoulder, again toward Hilda's doorway.

Was someone using Hilda for nefarious purposes? Ess couldn't imagine anyone managing that for long without Hilda detecting and then putting a stop to it. With boxed ears, at the very least.

"We've found some friends and hope to go south and finally locate our grandparents."

"Good for you. And your brother doesn't mind you gallivanting in boy guise?"

"My brother was a bad influence on me—let's leave it at that."

"I think I'd like to meet him."

"You will." She looped her arm through his and took a step down the sidewalk. "Before that, though, I want to know what you're doing watching my friend's doorway."

"Your friend?" Collins tried to stop, but she tugged him off balance, so he had to take a few steps.

"Hilda was my grandparents' cook. I've only just been reunited with her, and I don't appreciate you causing her trouble."

"Me? You have me all wrong, girl. I don't cause anyone trouble."

"Nor does Hilda do anything to warrant the Secret Service sticking their noses into her business." She pulled harder and stepped up the pace when Collins opened his mouth to protest. "She's helping children. Giving them a safe haven, helping them learn a trade, and doing what she does best—feeding them. Why don't you taste her rum cake before you jump to any conclusions?"

"Are you bribing a federal agent?" He pretended to scowl. They stopped on the second step up to Hilda's door. He sighed. "I hope for your sake, your friend really is doing exactly that. The problem is, the local man reads nothing but Dickens. He sees someone getting orphans off the street and can't see anyone doing good for the sake of good."

"Come in and talk to Hilda." She took a step up.

"You did say rum cake?" Collins took a deep breath and followed her through the door.

Hilda came out from the kitchen before Ess could flag down a child to fetch her. She laughed at Ess in her boy clothes and barely waited to be introduced to Collins before beckoning them to follow her.

"It's teaching time, and I'm trying a new recipe for tonight. You're just what I wanted. Test subjects, as Matilda would say, when she was investigating some new tonic," Hilda added with a chuckle.

"Just promise me you won't poison Collins. He's already accused you of being a new Fagan."

"Odessa!" Collins and Hilda said in unison, with the same dismayed tone.

Ess explained, and Hilda got that thoughtful expression that had prompted Matilda to declare she could read the very thoughts in people's heads. She pressed one finger to her lips to signal them to silence, then led them into the kitchen. More than a dozen children swathed in white aprons stood at tables, cutting and measuring and stirring. Hilda made a circuit of the tables, checking the progress of their work, then she gestured at two of the oldest boys, busy washing pots and pans, as Ess had once done for her. The boys followed her over to the doorway where Collins and Ess waited. The four of them followed her to the next room, every surface covered with dishes and utensils and linens.

"These are Tobias and Matthias. Cousins, but they like to tell people they're twins." Hilda winked. "Boys, why don't you tell us about those men who have been trying to hire you and the other children?"

Ess was glad to hear that the men who wandered the lower-class streets of the city, talking to every child who was the least bit ragged, didn't get many takers. Still, they did get some, usually the most desperate. They offered jobs with new homes and adventure, wouldn't tell the children where the jobs were, and showed a preference for utter orphans. No siblings, no relatives looking out for them, however badly.

"Well, Saunders had the right idea. He figured out something was going on, just not in the right area," Collins said.

"It's a sad state the world has fallen into, when the first people you suspect of preying on helpless children are the ones trying to help them." Hilda sniffed, then turned her head enough only Ess could see her wink. "What are you going to do about this problem? Eventually, they're not going to be satisfied with the willing children. They'll start taking everyone who can't resist."

"We need to set a trap." Ess nodded at the boys who, from the way they gaped and nudged each other, had just figured out she was a girl.

Collins smiled, very slowly, with a hint of threat that made her feel very good. "Ma'am, would you mind if I borrowed your boys for a while?"

"To do what?" Hilda crossed her arms over her ample bosom.

"Boys, how would you like to be of help to the Secret Service?"

Tobias and Matthias went perfectly still. Their mouths dropped open as they looked Collins over, head to foot.

"Who's going to wash the dishes, then?" Hilda said with a chuckle. The boys whooped, and gladly followed Collins outside to talk and plot.

Ess rolled up her sleeves and took care of the dishes. She and Hilda chatted while she supervised the cooking class, mostly filling her in on what Peggety and Waldo, Thomas and Bridget had been doing since they all separated. Then when the children went upstairs for their school time, she felt free to fill Hilda in on her adventures. They had a relaxing day, chuckling and interrupting, and reminding each other of people who had visited her grandparents when she was a child.

"I was hoping we'd have some time alone," Hilda said, as they settled down at the long, cleared table with tea and scones. She winked and unbuttoned the front of her shirtwaist and pulled a folded packet of what looked like old, worn oilcloth from the front of her corset, to hand to Ess. "This came in that last letter from your grandparents, and I completely forgot about it until oh, around midnight. Matilda said this was specifically for you when you were grown and ready to hunt the dragons in their lair." She sniffed as Ess unfolded the packet. "Considering some folks refer to Sanctuary as a dragon's lair, I thought... Well, no matter."

Inside the oilcloth was a yellowed piece of paper with three figures drawn in such precise, neat lines, Ess would have believed they were woodblocks for printed illustrations of a mantle clock, a padlock and key, and a deer with a wide rack of antlers. A neat loop had been drawn around the clock and the padlock, and a second loop drawn around the padlock and the deer.

"What is it?"

"Matilda said you'd know what they meant once everything started falling into place. Specifically, she said you'd know when you played the right tune and someone convinced you she once broke hearts."

Ess snorted. "Granny was more likely to break heads than hearts."

"Yes, well, you didn't know her when she was a hard-headed young adventuress. Ernest tamed her, that was for certain." Hilda winked and settled back in her seat, and finally buttoned up her shirtwaist. "Believe it or not, she had a number of suitors, when she was a student at Sanctuary."

"So whatever I need to help me figure this out, it's there. Or rather, *someone* is there. More and more reason to go." Ess wondered what Hilda would say once she heard about the discussion last night, the plans they had made, the speculations on who could be a traitor to the Originators. The woman had been a second mother to her, providing all the cossetting Matilda simply didn't have time for, giving Ess a chance to be a little girl.

~~~~~

"I didn't realize until just now how much I missed Hilda," Uly said, sighing in satisfaction.

The basket sitting on the floorboard of the steam-powered cart, borrowed from friends of the law firm, had been greatly depleted of its contents, and it wasn't quite noon yet. Hilda had outdone herself with provisions for him and Ford. Enormous, rolled up concoctions, the bread light, almost requiring two hands to eat, and bursting with thin-sliced cold meats, cheeses, pickles, and a spicy condiment that made Uly's eyes water and his nose run at the first bite. Hilda definitely remembered what he liked. He suspected she had spread the spicy sauce a little thicker than necessary as an extra slap for worrying her and Ess all these years.

Ford sighed and swallowed the last of his lemon cream cake, more cream and lemon curd than cake. "What I want to know is why such a talented woman isn't married. Any sensible man would be beating down her door. Doesn't matter her age or the size of her waist, when she can cook like that and command an army of children as she does and run a sensible business."

"She was supposed to be." Uly nodded at the steering rod. Ford took over, and he bent to tug the thick, insulated oilcloth cover over the basket, to protect the remains of what Hilda claimed was "just little picnic lunch, a snack to hold you until you meet up with Peggety and her provisions."

"Supposed to be?" Ford prompted, when Uly sat up and checked the road behind them and ahead, as he did regularly every ten or fifteen minutes.

At this point, the road curved enough that the roadside bushes and short trees, and piles of moss-covered rocks pushed there during the initial construction of the road, blocked the view more than two or three hundred yards in any direction. The constant battle for funding at the state and federal level, between accommodations for airships and providing more and wider and smoother roads for the gradually increasing numbers of steam-powered vehicles, sometimes led to visual disparities as this. A four-lane highway of awe-inspiring smoothness, some offshoot development of the oil industry, surrounded by debris that should have been cleared at the time of construction. Funding for building the roads, but not for cleaning up after the effort. Uly had seen the same situations with railroad tracks that went off in all directions, sometimes to towns that were nothing more than a station, a fueling dump, and a dozen or so houses with a general store. Airship docking towers fared a little better, mostly because people saw some profit in the buildings themselves and made sure the surroundings were cleaned up.
~~~~~

"Supposed to be married," he said, as Ford opened his mouth to ask again. "She was engaged to a cousin of Granny Matilda. Then a great ruckus rose up, all sorts of accusations against his father. It turns out that the father had stolen the identity of one of our agents, who had been on assignment way north where even Canada has no authority. He was a Revisionist, sent long-term to infiltrate us. He courted Great-Granny at one time, but she disliked him from the get-go. We suspect he went after her sister, just to... I don't know, what's the term for stealing a bloodline?"

"Ah," Ford said with a nod. "Thought he'd try to get himself some daughters with the same talents for commanding crystal." He shook his head. "Hilda's swain must have been devastated."

"Granny was furious. Like to have torn the man to shreds when she found out. It just added to her grudge against her uncle, for creating the rift between her mother and aunt, who chose him against Great-Granny's advice. Anyway..."

Uly sighed, trying to remember the details. His grandmother hadn't wanted to discuss it, but Grandfather Ernest had told him, in as sparse detail as possible, as a warning tale. Uly understood that he had been told, not to explain why loving, warm Hilda didn't marry, but to impress on him his duty to protect his little sister from just such heartache in the future.

"Well, Granny's cousin was a good man, but one of those brilliant inventor types. All the common sense of a rock when it came to people and politics and philosophy. His father tried to recruit him, and when he failed, resorted to stealing some of his inventions to hand over to the Revisionists. Everyone believed the cousin didn't know what was happening. Everything just passed over his head. He was devastated when the truth about his father came out. He broke off the engagement, and promised Hilda that as soon as he had cleared his name and retrieved his inventions, he'd return for her."

"Never did, eh?"

"He was a dreamer, a poet. Loved all the tales of old-time heroes, Robin Hood and the Knights of the Round Table and such. He had the sense to ask the young men he had grown up with to help on his quest for redemption. They were all idealistic idiots too," Uly added, wanting suddenly to spit.

"Not many made it back?"

"A little more than half, a lot sadder and wiser. Hilda's swain was one of the first lost."

"She's a good woman. The world lost out. Turned out good for you and Ess, though. I greatly admire your grandparents, but they were not suited at all to the more mundane details of raising children."

"Hilda raised our father, as well as us. At least until our minds could take in everything Granny and Grandfather wanted to pour into them," Uly added with a chuckle.

They both fell silent after that, more from the shadows of the forest closing around them than from the somber topic. Uly took over the steering again, which made Ford chuckle. He had teased him several times about how he loved to push the speed limits of the steam-cart.

The trees along the road thinned after another ten minutes, and Uly asked Ford to check the map and written instructions from Hilda. He couldn't recall all of them, but he felt certain the turning point, and possible meeting point with Thomas, Waldo, Peggety and Bridget, would be close. Hilda had chuckled when she told him that if he missed the turning point, he would soon see the lake, and if he did, he should make sure he didn't race the steam-cart off the road and into the water.

"Looks like another half-mile or so, actually," Ford said, after he squinted through the dappled shadows to study the map and Hilda's instructions. As he spoke, the road turned and the trees fell away, revealing a wide expanse of sunny meadows on either side of the ash-black surface of the road. Four wagons loaded with tarpaulin-covered freight had been pulled off the road, and a number of people appeared to be having a picnic.

Uly was surprised by the haze that filled his eyes the moment he recognized Bridget and Peggety strolling away from the picnic toward the roadside. He thanked Ford with a nod when the older man took the steering bar from his hand. That gave him enough time to knuckle his eyes clear before they got close enough for the two women to start waving and calling his name. He waited until Ford brought the steam-cart to a stop before he jumped out. Both serving women hit him with hugs at the same time, sandwiching him between them. Uly lost his breath from how the years showed on their faces, rather than the impact. The three spun around together, and he managed to get enough breath to laugh with them before Waldo and Thomas caught up with them. Everything was chaos for several minutes as they shook hands and hugged and thumped each other on the back. Bridget threatened to box his ears a dozen times to make up for all the times he probably deserved it and no one did.

Chapter Nine

By the time their happy, slightly teary knot separated, Ford had settled down on the edge of the picnic and helped himself to a bottle of root beer and a sandwich. Two teenage boys hadn't moved from their lounging position on the opposite side of the picnic blanket during the entire reunion. Hilda had said she would send her fastest messengers to meet up with the two couples and let them know Uly and Ford were on their way to meet them. He looked around as Bridget hooked her arm through his and tugged him toward the food. Then he saw the oversized balloon tires on the tandem bicycle frame. One of Hilda's graduates was an apprentice with a machine shop and had built a series of gears that increased the pedaling power. The boys had already won several races and accompanying fat purses. She trusted them with speedy errands. Uly made a mental note to see about adding these boys to the proposed recruitment and training plan. No one would notice bicycle messengers when they were looking for men in steam-powered carts or airships.

The problem would be convincing Hilda to encourage her orphans and street children to join up. Uly had enjoyed catching up with her while they waited for Ford to show up with the steam-cart. He had learned that she had custody of less than a third of the children in her care. The other children had parents who had fallen on hard times and couldn't feed or clothe or shelter them, or any combination of the three. Their parents visited as often as their constant battle to find steady work or a new home allowed. Several children had been brought to her by officials who preferred Hilda's methods over the accommodations provided by the state. Some were waiting for missing relatives to take custody of them. While Hilda could encourage the children to join the Originators, she wouldn't until she could talk to the parents.

Uly was glad he had stuffed himself early with Hilda's bounty, because he didn't have much chance to eat. The two couples kept him busy answering questions about what both he and Ess had been doing. He managed to get more details from them of that hectic time right after his grandparents vanished, and what Ess had done to frustrate a Resurrectionist cell. Uly and Ford traded glances, both impressed by Ess's clear thinking at age fourteen. The suspicion that had formed at the back of his mind since being reunited with his sister solidified that afternoon. Ess was the more logical and devious thinker. While he was a good soldier and hunter—after all, he had found Ford when others had given him and his team up for lost—Ess was going to be the shining star of their family history and heritage.

He didn't mind at all. Ess had been the brains in their childhood adventures. While he had had the ideas that launched their fun, his sister, even as young as five years old, had the foresight to predict problems and figure out how to avoid them. Uly had learned early that he could be forgiven a great deal of mischief as long as Ess was safe from harm. Protecting her was his primary mission in life. Even now.

However, soon he would be leaving Cleveland. Without Ess. How could he protect her when they would be separated not just by a few states, but by a continent? How could he face his grandparents without Ess standing beside him?

~~~~~

"We should make use of your Secret Service friends," Athena said that evening. "There are too many blind spots, and we don't have the time to investigate them all before we must send you to Sanctuary."

The reunion had continued on board the *Golden Nile*, after the wagons full of crates and files and trunks, and all of Waldo, Thomas, Bridget and Peggety's personal goods, had been loaded on the airship. Ess had stayed at Hilda's all through the dinner hour, helping with serving and washing dishes and putting the younger children to bed under the supervision of the older ones. Then she and Hilda had brought provisions for a late dinner to the airship, and they had a merry evening of eating and reminiscing and plotting in the parlor cabin. Ford and Athena and Vulcan had been visitors often enough at the Fremont house that the household staff was old friends. Ess received several bouts of scolding for her secrecy and choosing to strike out on her own. She chose not to retort that if her memories hadn't been blocked in the first place, she might have acted differently.

"You want me to ask Collins to investigate everyone at Sanctuary." Ess restrained a most unladylike whistle.

"It makes sense to me," Hilda said, glancing up from casting on to begin a new knitting project. "The fewer chances you have to take, the happier I'll be."

"Isn't it taking a chance on giving the names of Originators to the government, and asking them to investigate? I trust my friends among the Secret Service, but they have superiors they have to report to, and fellow agents who will grow curious. When one anomaly catches their eye, they'll follow it until everything unravels."

"We can't ask the Pinkertons to help, as much as Fitch would like to help you." Uly crossed his eyes at Ess. "Chances are good Stryker had other traitors working with him. The Pinkertons are the perfect tool for finding out all they need to trip us up."

"Then common sense says we need to obtain our own 'perfect tools' to match them, and then overstep them," Ford said.
~~~~~

"Ernest would remind us that's what happened to our ancestors, in the distant future," Thomas said from the corner of the room, where he and Waldo looked over the schematics of the *Golden Nile*. Ess suspected they would be very happy to sign on as maintenance men for the rest of their lives, climbing about among all the gears and chains and wheels. "He called it the 'arms race.' Everybody focuses on having bigger and nastier weapons, until we can destroy the world a dozen times over."

"We're not building weapons, we're asking for some very discrete investigative assistance from the people who do it best," Athena said. "Not every member of our organization. Just the ones in the highest positions of power. Besides, Mr. Fitch has initiated his own investigation into everyone who worked with Mr. Stryker."

"Couldn't we use what Allistair finds as a starting point?" Ess asked.

"We should start with anyone who vanished under mysterious circumstances over the years," Bridget said, startling everyone, because she preferred listening rather than participating in such discussions. "Not the ones on assignments. You expect something untoward to happen to them. The little people." She gestured to include Peggety and Hilda beyond her. "The ones who kept house and did shopping and such. We have our own grapevine, you might say. We hear stories about folks who went to fetch a special order of supplies a day or two away, and never made it home. Or the ones who went out to do the washing, and a wall fell on them, never any sign the wall was unsteady. You get my drift?"

"She's meaning the ones who had a chance to talk with or just see the high and mighty who came to visit," Thomas said. "The ones who outstayed their welcome and argued a bit with the mister and missus. People heard what they shouldn't have, and someone got scared."

"Find the common denominator," Athena nodded, "and you find the threat."

"I'm sure Grandfather noted every argument and suspicion in his journals." Uly held up both hands as if to ward off a blow. "Please don't put me in charge of reading through all of them for clues."

That earned a little laughter and some lightening of the atmosphere.

"I'll do it," Ess said. "I read faster than you, and if I'm going to be the bait to bring the jackals from their dens, I need to offer more. Some carefully chosen bits and pieces of our grandparents' archives should do the trick. Especially if I can convince the muckety mucks at Sanctuary that I don't have a very good idea of what I'm handing over."

~~~~~

A telegram came from Mr. Kirkpatrick in Monterey. He would be delayed several days taking the news to Sanctuary and warned them to prepare to put Ess on the fastest available transportation for the west coast. He sent greetings to her, as a friend of her parents. Neither Athena nor Ford nor the three lawyers could verify if Kirkpatrick truly was a friend of
~~~~~

Edward and Vivian, if he had puffed up his importance and connections, or if the passage of years had led him to imagine friendship where there was none. Or, he was playing games, political or otherwise, grasping for power by claiming ties with her parents.

Of greater concern was the knowledge she would be expected to go to Sanctuary with all speed. Nearly as great a concern was the hint that she would be expected to travel alone. The three lawyers were supposedly her only contacts with the Originators, possessors of her missing past, and her guardians. If she was expected to travel without them, was it another ploy to get influence over her, or perhaps to make her vanish, like the people Bridget, Peggety, and Hilda worked to remember?

"Anyone who knows Odessa would scoff at the idea," Dr. Sylvia said, as they discussed the telegram and its implications the afternoon Lewis brought it to the airship. "However... that's the trick. Their reaction could be a bellweather for helping determine their loyalties."

"What trick?" Ess asked. She knew by now that when the ship's doctor got that spark in her eyes, that little twist to one corner of her mouth, she was coming up with some new elixir or powder that would have interesting results, at the very least.

"I've used it in the past, to get people into heavily guarded buildings. No one ever suspects a nurse or a physician or an orderly of carrying a weapon, or concealing documents under the blankets of someone feigning some foul illness."

Ford laughed and bowed to Dr. Sylvia. By the end of the day, they had refined their story so it dovetailed neatly with any information that might slip out about Ess's travels with the Egyptian exhibition, or the dustup in San Francisco. She would claim to have run afoul of someone trying to steal Egyptian artifacts and had been injured and poisoned, the residual effects of which made it impossible to travel by airship because inner ear imbalances gave her altitude sickness. Debilitating headaches, sweats, vertigo and other maladies could strike without warning, or as the situation demanded. Naturally, an ill young lady couldn't travel by herself. The three lawyers, as her guardians, were vital as her escort. In the meantime, Dr. Sylvia promised to come up with potions and powders that Ess could take to support her role of invalid, producing the visible signs without making her suffer the actual symptoms.

~~~~~

Collins was more than willing to help with the investigation, and more than a little curious about Ess's association with the historical consortium. Hilda's work with her street children had earned his respect, so he was willing to contact Sutter. Ess teased him he just wanted to stay in Hilda's good graces so he could be sure of more baked goods. His promise to stay in Cleveland until the problem of the Fagan-esque operators had been ridded out did much to earn Hilda's trust and friendship. Ess sometimes
~~~~~

had the oddest feeling that if they were a few years closer in age, the two might grow sweet on each other.

Sutter arrived four days later. Ess didn't ask how convenient or inconvenient it was for him to sidetrack to Cleveland, but she was grateful. By that time, she had dug through enough files and read enough of her grandfather's journals, and Athena and Bridget had come up with a list of people and disappearances to investigate, they caught the senior agent's interest. Names and dates when visitors to the Fremont house irritated or worried Ernest enough to be mentioned in his journals were the launching point. Bridget had an incredible memory, able to recite dozens of rumors that came to her through the network of support staff, of people who vanished or were injured or killed soon after encounters with high-level members of the Originators. The three of them put together a chart that found the common elements among all the odd instances, unlucky incidents, disappearances and disasters that any of them could remember or had found documents for in the last thirty years. Sutter was impressed with the vast amount of work they had done, and how all the information was organized.

"This is much more than a gang of arguing historians, isn't it?" he said to Ess, when she escorted him down the long corridors of the *Golden Nile* to make his departure.

"That's not a question, is it?"

He snorted and shook his head. "Collins speculated this might have something to do with your grandparents' disappearance, and very little to do with the political unrest in South America, back then and now."

"Academics can be worse than politicians, when it comes to feuds and theories clashing and protecting information."

"Enough said." He clapped her on the shoulder as they came to a stop at a closed doorway. "I think you've finally come into your own."

"Not yet." She glanced at him as she stepped over to a lever in the wall and pulled down on it, opening the door and dropping a short set of stairs at the same time.

This was a shortcut to the outer walkway to the gangplank and the docking tower. The cargo bay, where visitors would normally enter and exit the *Golden Nile*, was currently full of Vulcan's team adapting the baskets for rapid descent, with armor-plating and the new, larger, more powerful Zeus guns Theo had finished designing.

"I can safely say my grandparents sent me away to protect me from some of this nastiness that we're hoping to rid out now. They weren't sure who to trust and believed that I might be in more danger from those people, should something happen to them — more danger than if I had accompanied them to South America."

"And your brother?"

"Uly was sent away for generally the same reasons. He was entrusted with some secrets that made rivals and generally nasty sorts want to destroy anything that doesn't conform to their standards and theories. They hoped to strike back at our grandparents through him. I wasn't told what was going on because I was a child." She snorted. "And they knew I would either want to go adventuring with him, or I would go haring off on a crusade of revenge against the people who threatened my brother."

"It's more than academics, isn't it?" Sutter asked, stopping her with a hand on her shoulder again when she would have led him down the steps.

"Much more," she said on a whisper.

"Mr. Lincoln believed the ancients were far wiser than modern men. He believed their tools and their arts and sciences were advanced beyond all the marvels we are discovering now. Perhaps the proper word is 'rediscovering.' We had rather interesting discussions, on those long nights when his illness and pain wouldn't let him sleep."

"Why are you telling me this?" She breathed a little easier when he released her and she started down the steps with him close behind her.

"He believed the Almighty hasn't so much *sent* all the disasters that have struck the world, the floods and plagues and earthquakes and tornados and such, as much as He has loosened His hold and allowed the devil to have his way. We aren't as good and wise as we need to be. There's a vast difference, Mr. Lincoln always said, between wisdom and intelligence. We aren't wise enough to make proper use of what our intelligence has created. So all the disasters that have destroyed seats of knowledge and the arts and sciences either threw humankind backwards in terms of development, or kept some incredible breakthrough from happening. Imagine where we could be now, if the Library of Alexandria hadn't been incinerated? If invading armies hadn't destroyed centers of philosophy and medicine?"

Ess laughed a little breathlessly as they stepped outside onto the walkway and the breeze whipping in off the lake slapped at their faces.

"You should have been a historian or a philosopher, Agent Sutter."

"I'm just repeating what Mr. Lincoln said." He shrugged.

"You miss him, don't you? Working with him, I mean." She bit her tongue to keep from remarking that it had to feel like a demotion, to no longer be the President's personal bodyguard, now that someone new sat in the White House.

"He gave far more than this country deserved, and served far longer than he or his rivals wanted, but our country needed him during the war and all the rebuilding afterward. His illness forced him to step down when he wouldn't spare himself for other reasons." He sighed and nodded, his smile suddenly weary. "Yes, I miss him. Our country is much poorer without him standing in the breech. But you're wondering why I waxed philosophical, aren't you?"

"Perhaps."

That earned a chuckle from him. He waited until they had crossed the gangplank and stepped into the shelter at the top of the docking tower.

"All right, Miss Odessa Fremont, suppose you tell me why you think I told you all that?"

"You're explaining why you *know* there is far more to this silly academic feud and cloak-and-dagger maneuvering than my associates are willing or able to admit."

"The past holds the keys to the success and the survival of the present, and the future. It also holds the weapons that could destroy us. Best to ensure those who know where those weapons are buried are the right kind of people."

"I think I will take that as a compliment," she said, her words slow and soft.

"In every aspect." Sutter caught hold of her hand and bowed over it, and Ess was hard pressed not to giggle like a child half her age.

His words helped her make a decision, and she didn't feel a bit guilty that she would entrust him with a secret she hadn't divulged to Uly or Athena or even Hilda. She had grown desperate, fearing that her inability to meet with Carmen in her dreams meant her friend had indeed been deprived of the crystal rose. While having no crystal in her possession effectively made her safe from the Revisionists or anyone else who might try to use her inborn gift, that was no comfort for Ess. She had to find her make-believe-turned-real friend.

"Will you help me look for someone?"

"Separate from this investigation?" He patted his coat pocket where the reports and lists Athena had given him were safely stowed.

"That's the problem. I'm not sure. I wish I could explain to you how and why I need to find this young woman, but..." Ess sighed and rubbed at her temples. "I don't know her last name. I don't know where she is right now. I can't tell you how I know the things I do know about her, but it is vital that I find her. She is in danger. Her father was a camp meeting preacher. He has recently died and someone is destroying his reputation and taking everything she owns. She has no one to protect her. Carmen was a friend when we were very small." Ess shrugged. "Will you let me send you a report on what I know, and drawings, to have an idea what she looks like? Will you help me find her? Or at least give me a jumping-off point?"

"Gladly." He winked. "And someday, perhaps when it's safe, you'll explain why?"

"I would like nothing better."

~~~~~

The Presbyterian church on the corner of Ontario and Rockwell was an impressive and beautiful structure of gray sandstone, but Uly couldn't understand why Ford paused to study it every time they passed through the center of the town on errands. The day Agent Sutter visited, he finally
~~~~~

confronted the older man.

"You don't suppose you have to be a Presbyterian to get married there, do you?" Ford asked, gesturing with his chin at the building. A puzzling tide of red began at his collar and rose to his forehead.

His arms, like Uly's, were full of bags and boxes, all sorts of bits and pieces of mechanical items, tools, and spare parts that Vulcan needed. The errands simply went quicker when a man dealt with the various shops and tool-and-die shops. Despite being one of the crossroads of the nation, some of the artisans, mechanics, and even the inventors in Cleveland's back streets had a hard time dealing with a woman of Vulcan's complexion and her mechanical acumen.

Uly stopped, dumbfounded as understanding struck. He returned the grin splitting Ford's face. "All we can do is ask."

"I should ask Athena before I stir up the barrel. But what if they say no, and I've convinced her now's the time?"

"I can't imagine a better wedding trip than a leisurely flight along the coast, all the way down to say... Rio de Janeiro?"

Ford chuckled, took two steps to cross the street, then sighed and looked down at his full arms. "Not a good impression, you think?"

"The minister might think you're hen-pecked already, and refuse."

Ford was still laughing about that remark an hour later, when they returned with another list of items to find at the stationer's shop. A number of people came out the double doors and down the front steps of the church as they approached. Chances were good, Uly reasoned, that someone who could at least answer Ford's questions would still be inside.

"May I help you?" a tenor voice, touched with gravel, called out from the sanctuary, when the two had stepped into the narthex. Only one gaslight remained lit, next to a door likely leading further into the building.

Footsteps rapped on stone, and a figure came from the front of the sanctuary. The man was just taking off his robe. He had a round, unlined face, but streaks of gray at his temples betrayed his age.

"Yes, thank you, I'd like to ask about membership—that is—is membership required?" Ford muffled a groan and belatedly remembered to take off his cap.

"What my uncle wants to ask," Uly said, sternly scolding himself not to laugh, "is if he needs to be Presbyterian and a member of this particular congregation to have a wedding ceremony performed."

Chapter Ten

"My." The minister blinked rapidly a half-dozen times, then smiled. "I'm sure my superior will argue with me. However, since he left not fifteen minutes ago, I am in charge for the next two weeks, and I say... well, let me start over. I believe that it is far more important to be a follower of Christ and to obey what is taught in the Bible, than it is to belong to a particular congregation. If you are indeed a soldier in the army of the Savior, then I would have no hesitation in joining you and your sweetheart in holy matrimony." He glanced around the narthex. "May I ask why she isn't here?"

"The bride is a very busy woman. I don't suppose you've noticed the airship that has been docked for a week now?" Uly pointed in the general direction of the *Golden Nile*.

"Most of our congregation has been talking about it. Rumors are you're going on some incredible expedition overseas. Egypt, is it?"

"Yes, exactly," Ford blurted.

Uly decided not to contradict him. The more lies there were to throw off any enemies spying on them, the better.

"How soon do you need to perform the ceremony?"

"Twenty years ago." Ford grinned and turned even brighter red when the minister tipped his head back and laughed.

Timing, Uly soon discovered, was everything. After Ford had made arrangements to return with Athena, Rev. Berger revealed that if they had come into the church on their first trip, they would have encountered Rev. Styvves, the senior minister. He would have been in a flurry of last-minute details to leave town, and in a bad mood, which had soured the prayer meeting to send him off to the yearly meeting with the Ohio council of Presbyterian ministers. He most definitely would have refused Ford's request to be married in the lovely church, and forbidden Berger to accommodate them.

Athena laughed when Ford told her of his tentative arrangements, and she blushed as she agreed that yes, it was high time they were married.

~~~~~

"What would Granny do?" Ess said, after helping Hilda slide the last layer of the delicate spice cake out of its pan onto the cooling rack.

They were alone in Hilda's kitchen at nearly midnight. All the pieces to assemble an incredible wedding cake had been created, or procured and pronounced satisfactory, and now waited in covered bowls and boxes. The
~~~~~

lemon curd to go between the layers, the sweet, light butter frosting to cover all the tiered layers, the chrysanthemums in yellow, pink, and white, and the sugar figures of a man and woman to stand on the top layer, under an archway made of spice drops and meringues. Hilda agreed to allow one of the more popular bakeries off of Euclid Avenue to provide muffins and other pastries for the wedding breakfast, but only because two of her students now worked there and she could be sure of the freshness and quality. Some unpronounceable French egg dish had been baked already. The aroma lingered tantalizingly in the kitchen even now, competing with the perfume of the cake layers to make Ess's stomach grumble and her mouth water. Before she and Hilda left to ride to the church for the morning wedding, they would have the cake frosted and put the egg dish in the oven to warm. They would add the decorations to the cake when they came back after the wedding. Mr. Endicott had borrowed his friend's steam-cart again to transport the cake and food to the waterside park where the wedding reception and breakfast-picnic would take place.

Hilda shook her head, sighed, rubbed at her temples, and settled down on the wide chair that was her sole domain in her kitchen.

"Those Benedict Arnolds, you mean," the woman said, nodding. "Easy enough in theory. The execution, however... well, from the stories your agent friend told me, I think you can carry off the play-acting well enough."

"Pretending to be something I'm not is easy enough when I don't have the weight of the past, present, and future resting on my shoulders," Ess grumbled. She hitched herself up on the counter and hunched her shoulders, then arched her back to get the stiff ache out of it. Baking was exhausting work. She would almost prefer trick riding on horseback or spending hours practicing marksmanship. "Some games are harder to play than others."

A massive game of intense deceptions and layers of lies waited to begin for her. Just yesterday, the last telegram had come from the leadership of Sanctuary. Endicott, Lewis and MacDonald had agreed to act as escorts for the invalid Miss Odessa Fremont. Besides their insistence that they were responsible for her since her brother and grandparents were still missing, they reminded their leaders that none of them had been to Sanctuary in the last ten years. It was high time they made a personal appearance, talked with the leaders of the various divisions, and checked the contents of their own family vaults. Since they represented more than a dozen other Originator families, this was a logical opportunity to carry out business for all their clients.

Logic had a tendency to blind opponents and dull their suspicions. Or at the very least, send those suspicious thoughts on detours, away from the true reason for the action. Even if that action was also logical.

Two retired doctors, friends of Ernest and Matilda, had come to Cleveland and verified that Ess's last assignment with the Pinkertons had exposed her to some new, lingering, debilitating illness. This documentation was sent by very expensive unmanned courier dirigibles, along with documentation proving that the young lady claiming to be Odessa Fremont was indeed the long-missing heir of an important Originator family. The doctors' reports stated she could not take the air pressure of the higher altitudes at which passenger airships traveled. The other options of transportation would take too much time and inflict too much stress on her nerves and exhausted body. The only workable means of crossing the continent at a reasonable speed and with any comfort was by train. A private railway car would provide her privacy and time to heal and regain her strength. The three lawyers would spend the time teaching Ess everything she might need to know about Sanctuary and Originator history.

"True enough," Hilda said with a sigh. "You learned acrobatics when you were in the circus, didn't you?"

"Some simple trapeze tricks. Nothing fancy. I had a good head for heights, but we never got that far before things sort of fell apart. Why?"

"It's a balancing act, I suppose. You need to trick the traitors into revealing themselves. Convince them you're oblivious to your heritage, or at least the implications. Get them to fight over you. Make them think you're so valuable, they need total control of you to accomplish their aims. At the same time, get them to distrust each other, so they'd willingly sell out their own mothers." She shrugged. "I was never one for scheming, but I know what Matilda would do. She loved puzzles."

"That makes sense, actually. Allistair did mention some contradictory correspondence they found in Stryker's lodgings." She snorted. "The wretched man had lodgings in every major city in the country. Thank goodness the Pinkertons are determined to root out and cut off anyone he was working with. The last packet from Allistair mentioned... indications that Stryker was working with three or four different groups, and they didn't know the others existed." Ess slapped her thigh. "I wish he had sent the letters themselves, instead of just what he deduced from them."

"The Pinkertons have their very valuable reputation to protect and a very nasty spot of sickness to clean out of their organization. I doubt they'll hand over anything until they're satisfied. Certainly not without expecting us to reveal dangerous information in return."

"I wish it were that simple, with different factions among the traitors working at cross-purposes. I could simply turn them against each other and let them self-destruct." Ess sighed and slid down off the counter.

"We can't bring our people together," Hilda said, "until that nest is cleared out."

"Perhaps we should abandon the Sanctuary altogether."

"It would take longer than it took to build Noah's great boat, to empty out the Sanctuary. Originators have been building on it and storing records and bits and pieces since the white man discovered the Pacific coast. King Minos' labyrinth would look pitiful in comparison, all the tunnels and levels dug down into the rock." She heaved herself out of her chair and reached for the cheesecloth that would protect the last layer of cake from drying out while it cooled. "Your grandfather's books should have a history of Sanctuary. Read it before you go. The way I heard the story, some of our ancestors finagled themselves in among the Conquistadores, just to get them to the coast to scout out locations. The first generation recorded enough information to reveal how long it would be until European civilization reached the Pacific. Anyone who volunteered for guard duty was effectively asking for exile, but we needed a safe haven the Revisionists couldn't find too easily. I swear, half the destructive attacks on monasteries and ancient libraries were to make sure we hadn't found safe repositories for our memories and the bits and pieces we couldn't bury with the ancients."

"The lotus," Ess murmured.

"We need a safe hiding place that can't be touched by either side, to stow the lotus and all the pieces of the Great Machine for eternity. That would resolve the problem once and for all."

"Where could we find a place like that? Even if everyone who could hear the crystal died out, eventually, someone would come up with a device that could find it, and then we'd start the whole game all over again."

"Remember your grandfather telling you stories about the bubble people?" Hilda smiled wearily as she finished tucking the cloths around the layers and beckoned for Ess to follow her out of the kitchen.

"Somewhat. People were able to blow bubbles that would hold other people, or things, and..." Ess stumbled, feeling as if her head would burst with memories and ideas. She blindly reached back for the knob that controlled the gas jet for the kitchen lamps and turned it until all was darkness behind her. Hilda's lips had a mischievous twist. "Time seemed to stop inside the bubbles," she finally said on a sigh.

"If only we had those bubble machines or generators or whatever you call them."

"Grandfather said the wands for blowing the bubbles were made of glass, like Cinderella's slippers."

"Crystal." She patted Ess's shoulder as they started up the stairs. "I didn't remember the stories until the other day. Sorry to say, I put quite a few memories away, once we heard about Giles and realized you wouldn't be catching up with us. Some things are too painful to recall."

"Would you mind too much writing down everything you remember?"

"I doubt I'll come up with anything useful." Hilda sighed.

"At this point, I'm convinced everything my grandparents taught us, every silly game, every bedtime story, was preparation for our adult duties. If Grandfather told me about people who could stop time inside bubbles, then there either *was* a machine that controlled bubbles of time, or it was something Granny theorized and hadn't perfected yet. For all we know, the pieces are waiting in our family vault." Ess stopped with her hand on the knob of Hilda's bedroom door. Her cot waited. Until two seconds ago, she had quite looked forward to peeling out of her clothes and diving into it for some well-earned oblivion.

"Child?" Hilda whispered, when she stood perfectly still, not even breathing, as images flashed through her mind's eye and puzzle fragments fell into place.

"That's it." She blinked away totally ridiculous damp heat. "Something they weren't planning on. Granny needed something for the time bubble machine." Muffling a curse, mindful of the children sleeping behind the doors down the long, dimly lit hallway, she turned the knob and stomped into Hilda's bedroom. "I had it, so clear in my head, just a moment ago. Now it's gone."

"You need a good ten hours of sleep, but you're not going to get it. Not Matilda Fremont's granddaughter," the woman said with a chuckle. She gave Ess a solid nudge toward her cot, tucked up against the wall under the low casement window. "You're going to go roaming the planet and a good couple of centuries of history in your sleep, and like as not remember every single bubble people story your grandfather ever told you."

"I wish he... no, he did write them down." Ess bent to untie her boots before she sat on the cot. "I can see it quite clear in my memories. I wish I could call up the stories themselves that clearly."

"Your grandfather was the one for words, while you and your granny were the ones for pictures. You get your drawing talent from her and from your mother. That's why your mother was her student, because of her artistic talent." She settled down on her bed with a weary smile, the dimming light in her eyes a clear indication that she had slipped into memories again.

Ess hoped Hilda was right, and she would remember all the stories in her dreams. More important than that, she hoped she remembered in which journal her grandfather had written the stories he made up, so she could find it quickly when she searched all the crates of his books. If this information was important enough to teach her and Uly through stories, chances were good that more details were recorded with the stories.

~~~~~

The next morning, Uly felt a little sick when he saw Ess coming down the aisle as Athena's sole attendant and realized just how much his little sister had grown up, and how beautiful she was. He could blame part of that on how much she favored their mother when she actually wore a dress and put her hair up. The other part came from the realization that despite all her common sense, his sister might be fatally susceptible to all the tricks and games men played to win women's hearts. How was he going to protect
~~~~~

her when she was on the Pacific coast and he was digging through the jungles of South America?

"Please don't tell me those bruisers on the basket team talked Ford into a night of carousing after all?" Ess whispered when she slid into the bench next to him. Athena and Ford joined hands in front of Rev. Berger. "You look positively green."

"I'm proud to admit — well, maybe not the way I learned it — but I have an incredible capacity for alcohol without losing my balance, my wits, or my stomach," he whispered back. Uly felt he might choke with the force of his love for his little sister. Leave it to her to find the exactly right words to dispel the weight of despair crushing him.

"Scoundrel," she whispered back, and wrinkled up her nose at him when he turned to glance at her profile. She tipped her head, indicating he should be focusing on the ceremony, and he caught hold of her hand in lieu of words.

Uly missed most of the homily and the vows. His brain was too busy trying to come up with the right words to persuade Ess, without infuriating her or making her break down in hilarity, to promise him she wouldn't let anyone at Sanctuary court her until he showed up to protect her interests. Uly had a horrific vision of the worst man in all the world winning his sister's heart. Outwardly, he would be perfect: intelligent, strong, trustworthy, with a wicked sense of humor, who admired her for her escapades rather than horrified at how unladylike she had been. Everyone would agree that he was the perfect match for Matilda and Ernest Fremont's only granddaughter. Until he drugged or mesmerized Ess into joining the Revisionist cause, and they fled with the lotus in their possession.

The ceremony ended, and Uly released some of his anxiety by joining in the loud applause and cheers as Athena and Fordyce Chamberlain turned to face all their friends and loved ones as husband and wife.

Ess drafted him to help with transporting the food to the park via steam-cart. She never gave him a chance to refine his little begging speech, chattering the whole way as they skimmed through morning traffic, with Hilda in the back seat. Uly barely heard what she said for the first block or so, then his brain caught up and he was fascinated by Ess's conversation with Hilda about Grandfather Ernest's bubble people stories, and then her dreams that followed.

"What if they had the bubble machine with them?" he said as they pulled up to the doorway of the lower-level entrance of Hilda's building. "Something that could lock people or things in a moment of time would make an incredible weapon."

"Then what were they sending for, before they vanished?" Hilda said, holding out a hand and gesturing for him to help her down from the cart.

"Oh." Ess went perfectly still, poised with one foot in the air, stepping down from the passenger side of the cart. Uly shuddered, seeing the expression their grandmother wore just before she locked herself in her workshop for days at a time, and all sorts of bizarre smells and sounds emanated from it.

"Child?"

She shook her head and nearly lost her balance. Uly caught hold of her arm, helping her get steady before she stepped down to the pavement. "What they wanted didn't matter. It was a ruse. They identified the traitor or traitors. What they sent for was just to prove they were right, depending on how the traitor responded to the message. The unrest in that area simply intervened and Granny and Grandfather and their teammates had to use the time box to escape trouble."

"You need to get into that vault and find out what they left behind to help us." Uly barked laughter when she stuck the tip of her tongue out at him, picked up her skirts in both hands, and whirled to head down the stairs. They did have the wedding breakfast to transport to the park.

Despite all that, his new worry for Ess stayed uppermost in his mind. He managed to get the gist of it across to Hilda in pieces, every time he stepped into the kitchen to get a basket or crate of food or dishes or linens for the picnic breakfast. Uly could almost laugh at the depth of his relief when Hilda didn't laugh at his fear, and promised she would have a talk with his sister.

They discussed Ess's revised theory as they drove to the waterside park and agreed on a plan. Ess and Uly would divide up their grandparents' records and books to search. Ess needed to clear as many books as possible from her share of the chore before leaving for Sanctuary, so she wouldn't take anything potentially dangerous with her. Uly would implement whatever they found when he reached the long-abandoned archeological camp. Ess would get into their family vault and learn what she could. They planned to speak to each other every night via the communication plates, whether either of them had found something useful during their day's studies or not.

Uly refused to speak, and tried not to even think of the one grim possibility that loomed over them as they climbed out of the steam-cart to haul the food to the picnic site.

What if the time trap had failed? What if it didn't protect their grandparents' archeological party, and the revolutionaries had caught up with them? What if the time trap had failed so spectacularly that it destroyed everyone at the site, archeologists and their attackers together?

Uly hoped Ess hadn't thought of that particular possibility. This was a wedding party, after all, and she deserved to have as much fun as possible before the weight of responsibility caught up with her.

~~~~~

Hours before Ess and her escort-teachers boarded their private train car for the first leg of the journey west, Collins came through with the first
~~~~~

batch of information provided by the Secret Service. All three lawyers got to work, requesting verification of the most sensitive and influential of that information, entrusting telegrams to their assistants. Wallace raced to the train station and spent some time in conference with Endicott in the private car, taking several pages of notes, while Ess supervised the loading of their luggage. The train actually got moving, building up speed as it left the station, before Wallace tipped his hat to Ess and leaped from the back of the car onto the platform. The three lawyers conferred over all the last-minute work they had done, from the time the train departed until the porter brought their luncheon. That was the first chance Ess had to find out what the Secret Service had discovered. She supposed some of what they needed to have done was a little difficult, since less than a quarter of those who worked for the firm were Originators. Secrecy was even more vital now than before, by the simple fact that if they couldn't be sure of the loyalty of those who belonged among them, how could they quite trust those who were outside of their circle? For all they knew, someone in the firm could be a Revisionist spy. Information that meant nothing to outsiders could have a great deal of meaning and be quite valuable to the enemy.

Despite all the activity generated by the first batch of information, nothing had changed or been verified regarding the people under suspicion. Ess found it most aggravating. Especially when the topic of conversation turned to her battle strategy when they reached Sanctuary. She was grateful for the potions and powders Dr. Sylvia had provided, which would mimic the symptoms she complained of without actually making her dizzy, nauseous, and alternately suffering chills and overheating. Still, she disliked having to use the concoctions. The longer she used them, the greater the chances she would fall ill.

Chapter Eleven

They discussed the possible interpretations of the deliberately vague and diplomatic report sent to Sanctuary regarding her mental and emotional condition. Key words they could play to their advantage included "resentful," "confused," and "eager for a steady foundation in her life." Hopefully enough information would come by way of Uly and the communication plates, passing along further reports from Collins and Wallace, for Ess to know how to respond to the overtures of the people waiting for her to arrive in Sanctuary. She knew it would be too easy to hope they would tip their hand and give themselves away the moment she met them, like melodrama villains twirling their moustaches and letting out evil cackles.

The conversation soon switched to other tasks they felt necessary to perform when they reached Sanctuary, in light of the proof of infiltration by the enemy.

"Emptying out our clients' vaults might be a challenge, if we want to do it with as little fuss as possible," Lewis said, his words underscored by the clink of cups settling back into saucers.

"Don't you have all the paperwork and authorizations?" Ess asked.

"Of course we do," Endicott said. "The sticking point is that we don't want anyone to know we distrust the security of Sanctuary. If we are asked, we must answer, and while yes, we do have an answer prepared, we would prefer not to have to use it. The fewer lies and prevarications we must use, the better for everyone."

"Have you brought Mr. Wallace inside?" Ess asked, following that trail of thought.

"Not yet, but we will certainly have to when he joins us. If he joins us."

"That's still up in the air?"

"Everything is." He turned, reaching for the folio of papers sitting on the sideboard. "Much as I dislike spoiling such an excellent meal, we do have work to do. I fear if we continue to receive more such information from our allies, we shall be revising and requesting further research for the duration of our journey."

"It could be much worse." Lewis stood up with Ess to retrieve the serving trays to clear the dishes from the table. "Having everything go through Ulysses and the people on the *Nile* will increase our security and decrease the time spent in transmitting that information." He gave an exaggerated shudder. "And waiting for responses. And having to get off the train to use a telegraph every time we stop for water, or to change engines. To think we used to consider the telegraph a marvel of modern technology."

He winked at Ess as they carried the trays to the shelf by the door where the porter would retrieve them eventually. She had to agree with him, and yet she could almost wish she and Uly hadn't deciphered the riddle of the blood-crystal-music key. The convenience of the communication plates would indeed give them vital security and secrecy, yet it required the *Golden Nile* to stay in Cleveland until Agent Sutter and his people had dug up all the available information on the people who needed investigating. The attempt to find and rescue her grandparents would remain on hold as long as Uly needed to transmit information to the train. He had met the staff at the law office, who had been instructed to give him anything he asked, without question.

"What we need now," Ess said, as she and Lewis returned to the table, "is some device that can take photographs of everything that appears in the communication plate, and develop it rapidly, without all the stink of chemicals and bulky equipment, to save us the time and hand cramps of writing it all down."

"A small, portable printing press that combines with a camera would be useful," MacDonald said, his gaze going distant.

Ess knew he had wanted to be an inventor in his youth. He had laughed when he told her once that he had driven his instructors mad with devices that fell to pieces at the wrong time, or chemical combinations he could never duplicate, to repeat amazing results he produced by accident.

Then the four settled down to go through the reports from the Secret Service, one person at a time. Ess made notes for her own use, against the time she would be separated from the three men. She used the private cypher she had developed, a combination of Egyptian and Aztec symbols, mixed with French, German, and Navajo. She had learned her lesson about ensuring her privacy, when Horace Winslow had so easily decrypted her private journal, the day he recruited her for the Pinkertons.

Just before the porter came to take their order for dinner, they finished disinterring the first batch of reports. Ess retired to her cabinet bedroom to take a short nap as the train pulled into the station for the first stop of the day. She tugged aside enough of the curtain over the narrow window of her bunk to watch the other passengers climbing off the train. The first- and second-class passengers had the benefit of cushioned seats and access to refreshments. Still, more than seven hours of travel without stopping had to be uncomfortable. Especially for the people who sat near the privy booth, no matter how many scent bottles sweetened the air. She hoped the people who had to ride in the third-class carriages had plenty of room so they could stretch out. Her days of travel in disguise as a boy weren't that far behind her that she couldn't sympathize with their discomfort.

~~~~~
~~~~~

After dinner, Ess settled down with her flute in her continuing effort to translate the markings that littered so many of her grandfather's books. Her goal was to identify tunes that struck chords of memory or affected the pieces of crystal Athena had given her for practice and experimentation.

The men had their cases to keep up on and would communicate with their various offices by telegraph and by letter at every stop along the way. This set up their pattern for the duration of the trip. Ess felt somewhat guilty that they had so much work to keep up with business while escorting her.

Just before she went to bed each night, she set up the communication plate to contact Uly. The three lawyers took turns sitting with her, to copy over any information he passed along. In the days to come, that might be pages he had found in his own research, or messages from the various law offices requiring the three lawyers' attention, or new reports from the Secret Service. After sketching a drawing Uly held up to the plate, and taking turns with Lewis to copy over several pages of notes, Ess thought with longing about her proposed machine that would copy images and print them out for her. She mentioned it to Uly and asked him to suggest the idea to Vulcan. He scowled, teasing, and told her not to distract the woman who was busy preparing for any and every eventuality on their trip.

Just before closing communication, Uly winked three times with his left eye, the signal they had agreed on to request private communication later, after everyone had gone to bed. Ess mirrored the signal back to him, to acknowledge the message. She had been tired and looking forward to bed during the last half hour or so of the transmission, but those three little winks made her heart skip a beat and woke her up completely.

An hour later, when the private car was dark and snores came from the cabinet bedrooms on either side of her, she hung blankets over the little alcove under her bunk, to muffle the sound, and activated the communication plate. Uly had a single page of musical notations to show her, and a sketch of the lower levels of Sanctuary he had found in one of their father's journals. Then he commented that Wallace seemed suddenly more interested in her. Perhaps Allistair Fitch had a rival to worry about.

If she didn't have to worry about unexpected sounds penetrating the rattle-click-rumble of the train wheels and waking her three escorts, Ess might have laughed at him, or squealed some denial. The need for quiet helped her control her reactions. She told her brother to go to sleep and raised the crystal rod to shut down the communication panel.

"Be careful, Ess. You know I love, don't you?" Uly hurried to say.

"Of course. And I love you." She wrinkled up her nose at him. "As little as you deserve it."

Uly grinned and laughed a little louder than was wise. Ess hurried to shut down communication. Her heart thumped a little faster for several minutes, even after she put away the packet of crystal dust and climbed up into her bunk and curled up in her blankets. Still, she smiled into the darkness.

<div style="text-align:center">~~~~~</div>

On the third night, Uly remembered Ess's half-joking, half-wistful request for the visual copying machine, and wished he hadn't teased her about it. His hand ached from scrambling to copy the diagrams of a box that seemed to turn itself inside out every time the angle changed. Why his grandmother had drawn so many versions of the box, he had no idea. He would have to leave that up to Vulcan and other mechanical theorists among the crew. All that mattered was copying everything that Ess held up to the communication plate, accurately, and swiftly. He knew how much effort it took, even resting the book on the table, to keep it steady. Then there was the challenge of copying and focusing on what he saw and not letting the discussion filling the room behind him distract him into mistakes.

Ess had been visibly vibrating with excitement when her face appeared on the plate that evening. She insisted that he had to fetch Athena, Ford, and Theo. Vulcan was away for two days, supervising the creation of some delicate, exacting parts at a machine shop in Akron. He fetched the others, and as soon as Ess held the journal up to the plate, Uly understood her excitement. The words "time trap" were clear across the bottom of the right-hand page and looked like they had been written several times in pencil, making the letters dark. Matilda had a very light hand. Their grandfather had joked that she could get three times as much written with one pencil as anyone else, because of how light her touch was. For her to write something over and over again with so much force had great import.

Uly went over each diagram four times. The first time he simply looked over each angle and number and notation. Then he copied it. Then he checked it. Then he came back after he had copied over each of the twenty diagrams, to make sure everything was accurate. He still didn't understand them. Ford and Theo seemed to understand some of the words and numbers, and soon Athena argued with Ford about the translation of some words, whether they were abbreviations or some obscure ancient tongue. One mistake in translation could have a world of difference — some of it disastrous — in deciphering how to make the diagram work. If it really was the time trap.

"Done?" Ess asked, when he had gone over each drawing for the fourth time.

"As done as I think I can manage. Rest your weary hands," he said with a smile.

"No rest for the wicked." She turned the journal around to face her. Now Uly saw several slips of paper tucked into the pages. If that indicated how many more drawings or entries he needed to copy over, they were going to be there until morning.

The groan birthing in his throat caught and died, as Ess turned the journal around again and showed him the map filling both pages. The names on the map didn't make sense, except for one important detail. Those were Incan names. Not the modern names applied to the places by the Spanish colonists and the tribes who lived in the area now, but the ancient Incan Empire names. Uly didn't remember much of that summer Ernest had tried to fill his head with what seemed meaningless information about South America. After all, at that time, they believed all the pieces of the Great Machine lay hidden in Egypt and Italy, Greece and Palestine, and all the battles with the Revisionists had taken place there as well. He did remember enough to recognize those names as Incan. Not Aztec or Mayan or Toltec or even Spanish from antiquity.

"You need to see this!" He waved a hand at the other three, still arguing about one word while they arranged the fresh tray of tea and cinnamon rolls from Hilda's baking students. Uly couldn't take his gaze off the map. He flexed his sore fingers and reached for a fresh sheet of paper and the box of pencils. To his dismay, only two sharpened pencils remained. "Somebody, sharpen these for me?" he added, gesturing blindly at the pencils he had put aside when they became too dull for precise drawing.

"What's that?" Theo rested a hand on Uly's shoulder as he leaned closer to look at the plate. His whistle was loud, but Uly was too caught up in what filled his vision to react.

"There are entries for fifty pages," Ess said, "talking about bizarre occurrences in the mountains in this drawing. There are little spirals in ten places where all these oddities took place. Some are stories about people stepping into shadows and vanishing, to emerge days or weeks later, positive that no time at all had passed."

Ford spilled a stream of what Uly suspected was Arabic and leaned closer to get a good look at the screen.

"Where exactly is that?" Athena had to give Ford a hard nudge in the ribs with her elbow before he shut up, and then another nudge to move him aside so she could see the screen.

"We have no idea. It was rather frustrating," MacDonald said, his voice coming from beyond the communication plate. "We were so sure we had the map for your grandparents' expedition, but we have no atlases here. Of course, obtaining a map of that part of the world when we make a stop will be difficult. The next step is yours, obviously."

"My guess is it's an ancient map, and the landscape could have changed drastically since the Incan empire fell," Uly said.

"We obviously didn't pack enough of the right books from Grandfather's library," Ess said, her voice a teasing wail. "You have a great deal more work to do, Uly. I'm sorry."

"Oh, don't be sorry," Athena said, turning to smile at Uly. He bared his teeth in a grin that made his cheeks hurt. "You've given us an incredible leap forward. Once we find other journals and maps that tie into this drawing, our search will be shortened drastically." She looked down at the blank sheet of paper on the table in front of him.

"Oh. Sorry." Uly picked up a sharp pencil, took a deep breath, flexed his shoulders against the soreness of being hunched over for so long already, and got to work.

He found it hard to draw when Ess and MacDonald, sometimes with help from Endicott, related the stories in the pages that followed the map. This was the breakthrough they had been praying for. Sometimes Uly's hand shook, necessitating a brief rest. Once, he gripped the pencil hard enough that it snapped in two. Before he could even muffle an oath, Theo handed him a freshly sharpened pencil, squeezed his shoulder, and leaned a little closer to study the map. Uly envied Theo's incredible memory and all the fine detail he could retain after a short period of study.

Once, he glanced over and saw Athena making notes. He muffled another oath when he thought of all the pages still to be copied from the journal. Had Ess said fifty pages? Perhaps they could wait for the next evening? He wondered if this was retribution for all the copying she had to do the last three nights.

Finally, the map was finished. He slid it over in front of Theo, gesturing between the image on the plate and the paper, silently asking him to compare the two. Uly looked up and realized several other people had joined them while he was hard at work, and they were all writing. He sighed and massaged his aching hand, relieved that someone else had the task of recording what Ess was saying.

"That's the ticket," he said, when his sister paused at the end of one story. "Should have thought of it before."

"What is?" she said. "Are you done copying?"

"The map, yes. How accurate is it?" he asked Theo.

"Your brother has a brilliant future as a forger and copyist ahead of him," Theo announced.

"Why can't we get a recorder in here, tomorrow night? Instead of taking the time to write down what Ess finds, why can't she read it aloud and record her voice on this end?" Uly said, before anyone could start in on the questions he could almost see shimmering in their eyes. "Then we have it, on those wax cylinders or those new crystal rods Vulcan is so proud of, and we can listen to the recordings over and over again, with no change."

"That would save some time." Ess closed the journal and her face appeared in the communication plate again. "That would make it easier to pass on to you the songs I've translated."

By the time they agreed to wait on the rest of the journal entries until the next evening, Uly felt the effects of the work he had done. Pains shot up his arm whenever he tried to move his fingers, which had cramped into a curve.

"What do you think?" he said, after the communication plate had returned to a pile of crystal dust bound up again in its protective bag. "Can we cast off the mooring lines and head south?"

"We still need to hear from our contacts in the State Department and the Army," Ford said, settling down on the couch closest to the table, his arm automatically curving around Athena's shoulders. "There's always a powder keg ready to go off. Especially as they keep fighting over their borders. We need to know what sort of turmoil we'll be flying over."

"More importantly, we need to know what sort of weaponry advances they've either made or obtained." Theo crossed from Uly's table to the decimated remains of the tea tray. "We can only fly so high before the air isn't any good. What if they have cannons or those new long-range explosives that can rise high enough to hit us no matter how skillful Captain Astrid is with evasive maneuvers?"

"We know how hard it is to wait and wonder, Uly," Athena said. "It's even harder to wait now that we have some answers and a chance of success. Just remember that for Matilda and Ernest, time is standing still."

"But for how long?" he retorted, and stood, arching his back against the aches. "All those stories of people stepping into and out of time whirlpools or whatever you've decided to call them. The time trap finally released them. Sometimes only a few days later, and in one case, more than a year later, did I hear right? And sometimes, people walked into the whirlpool on one road, and came out on another road, on a different mountain, hours away, in only a few minutes' time. What if that's what happened to them, or could happen to them at any time?"

"There is one vast difference between the inhabitants of that area, and your grandparents' team," Ford said. "A device to control when and where the time whirlpool caught them. Since nothing was found—"

"That we know of," Uly couldn't help interjecting.

"Granted, no device was found that we know of. My guess is that Matilda is holding onto it, and the device is keeping them in the time trap."

"That's supposed to be comforting?" In essence, his grandparents and their archeological party were trapped within the very thing they had depended on to protect them from either local threats and dangers, or some attack from the traitors among the Originators.

"I studied with Matilda, remember," Athena said. "She was known for being prepared for any contingency, whether a party or an illness or a proposed experiment. She and Ernest would have made sure to leave behind all the clues and tools we need to rescue them. We still have many crates of pieces and records to go through. I would rather delay our trip until we are sure of what we have and don't have and what we need, than have to fashion something makeshift at the last minute. Wouldn't you?"

Uly nodded. He hated admitting that he hadn't quite thought through all the implications, as Athena obviously had. Yet he did feel better. There was some comfort in not being responsible for having all the answers.

~~~~~
~~~~~

The train arrived in Denver just after dawn. Ess and her escorts should have been asleep, but she woke up early, yanked out of sleep by the same dream that kept repeating itself, most likely triggered by the new tune Uly gave her during their private communication time. She had played it, softly, under her blankets, three times before going to sleep. Soon after she settled down in the main room of the car with her journal and pencils, the other three emerged and admitted to having had restless nights also.

The porter surprised them all in their shirtsleeves and messy hair, and Ess in trousers, when he let himself into their car without knocking. He let out an oath, and nearly dropped the urn of coffee he carried when Ess and Lewis leaped to their feet, drawing the weapons closest at hand. She had her derringer and he whipped out a long hunting knife.

"How did he get in here?" Ess blurted, as Endicott rose from the table. He had sole possession of it, since it was covered with paperwork for a case that he had admitted, with a rueful smile, had been bothering him all night. "That door should be locked. I locked it, since I was the last to retire."

"Yes," Endicott said, stepping between the porter and Ess, who he looked over, head to foot, several times. "Either you're a lockpick, or you have a key. How do you explain yourself?"

The porter held up his hand, from which dangled a ring of braided leather, with a dozen keys hanging from it. Each was wrapped in threads of different colors halfway up the shaft, leaving the teeth of the key free. The threads effectively muffled any clattering.

"The key is passed along," the man finally said, "every time the car is transferred to a different line and engine. For safety reasons. And it's the law." He leaned slightly to the left to look around Endicott. His gaze met Ess's, and she stuck the tip of her tongue out at him. He turned bright red. "And since this is still railroad property, it's our right and responsibility."

Chapter Twelve

"He has a point," MacDonald admitted with a sigh. He stepped forward now and held out his hand for the urn of coffee. "I have to admit, that smells incredibly good, and while your timing leaves something to be desired, it is, ironically, very good timing. I've been up half the night gnawing on that French ambassador's problem." He winked over the porter's head, and Ess was hard pressed not to chuckle. He had no work relating either to an ambassador or anyone French.

"This is a respectable rail line." The porter straightened his shoulders and spread his feet, as if he intended to spend some time in that spot. "May I ask what all of you are doing?"

"You have the paperwork arranging for this car, the stewards' services, transportation into town for errands during prolonged stops, and access to the telegraph system," Endicott said. "You know who we are. We, on the other hand, have no proof that you are indeed an employee of this rail line. You could be someone who assaulted the real porter and stole his uniform, intending to sneak in while passengers with less pressing business to deal with might still be sleeping. Which, as you can see, we were not doing."

Ess decided it was wiser to turn her back on the seesaw interrogation and go back to her seat. She had been sketching a series of images from the dreams that had kept disturbing her sleep.

"The paperwork claims you are lawyers and accompanying a young lady to deal with legal matters. Nothing more." He huffed. "Excuse me, sir, but that—" He gestured at Ess as she settled down, tempting her to stick her tongue out again. "That does not look like my definition of a young lady. That is a hoyden. I have heard that the harlots in the rougher parts of the country wear such costumes."

"And so do young women who put their lives on the line for their country," Ess said, snapping her journal open so the binding crackled. "Since President Lincoln himself expressed approval when, *disguised as a boy*, I identified several Resurrectionists intent on threatening his life, I don't see how your opinion supersedes his."

"The—the President?" The porter went white, then flushed even darker.

"Our client is held in high regard by several members of the Secret Service," Lewis said, as he brought cups out from the cupboard. "We would appreciate it, and so would they, if you didn't indulge in gossip about what you saw here."

"Oh—yes—yes—of course." He bobbed his head a few times, then it visibly dawned on him that he wasn't wanted or needed.

"Porter," Endicott said, as the man shuffled backward to the door, "what was your name again?"

All four waited, grinning and visibly fighting not to laugh, until a good thirty seconds after the porter finished stumbling through his apologies and pulled the door closed. Ess counted. She snatched up the key from the hook on the cabinet that held the dishes and hurried to lock the door again while the others settled down in their previous spots, chuckling.

"You are a wonder," Lewis said, when Ess stopped on her way back to the couch to pour herself a cup of coffee. Not that she needed it, after that bit of excitement. "It reminds me of a social event in New York. Your grandparents had come for the opening of an exhibit they had contributed to, at the natural history museum. Matilda pulled aside the barrier in front of one of the displays to turn a piece of stone carving right side up. Whoever set up the display had it lying on its side. Some self-important museum toady, dripping in hair oil and reeking of the most foul-smelling cigars, came hurrying up and launched into a lecture on how she had violated museum protocol and very rudely repaid the—"

"The great honor the museum had bestowed on her, allowing her, a *mere woman*, to have a sneak preview of the exhibit." Ess couldn't understand why her heart raced and sweat beaded on her forehead. The incident had been highly amusing. "I remember. I was there. Granny took me into the display with her. She had me hold her handbag while she fixed the display. As the museum director and Grandfather and Uly came racing up, she tipped her head back and skewered him with her glare. She lectured him on the dynasty featured in the new exhibit, and how if the tablet was displayed improperly, it could be read entirely wrong. Then she invited him to read it aloud and translate it for her, both in the proper position and the improper one." She chuckled, but the sound caught in her throat. "He fussed and burbled for a few seconds, and then insisted that she was a *mere woman*—why did he love those words?—and even if she had picked up a few details, she had no right to be touching the items, that the great Professor Fremont would be aghast."

"Then Ernest spoke up and said that Professor Fremont always deferred to Professor Fremont in matters where she had made the discovery and wrote up the documentation." Endicott frowned as he studied Ess. "Yes, I remember it clearly. What strikes me as odd is that you do, because you were only, what? Five?"

"Nearly six." Ess gave in and wiped the sweat from her forehead with her shirt cuff. "It's the oddest thing, but I'm sure I didn't remember any of that until just now."

"Are you feeling all right?" He moved over to the couch facing hers and leaned forward, studying her face. "You look like you've had a fright."

"I feel that way, but it makes no sense." She put aside her journal and reached for the cup of coffee. Ess had the awful feeling she needed something more than coffee. If she started drinking whiskey this early in the morning, she would start a bad habit that Horace had always warned his agents to avoid at all costs. "What do we have for nibbling? I think I need something in my stomach before I take a headache powder."

When she came back from refilling her cup and excavating a tin of burnt almonds and another of gingersnaps, she found Endicott looking through her journal. This was actually her third in as many days. Most of them were filled with drawings done in pencil, some mere sketches to help her remember details from her dreams, while others were fully fleshed out, to the point she could almost hear the sounds that accompanied the scene she had captured, smell the leather or flowers or cigar smoke, and could see the colors of the clothes and furniture or trees, even though everything was done in shades of gray.

"Dreams?" he said, holding out the journal, open to a drawing that filled both pages.

"Yes." Ess shuddered and hurried to put down the cup on the side table.

"Memories." He smiled somewhat sadly. "Matilda speculated, with your artistic, your visual tendencies, when you regained the memories she locked away, many of them would come out in dreams. You're drawing important scenes from your life here."

"That should be helpful." Lewis stepped over to join them. MacDonald only glanced up from the sheaf of photographs he was studying in connection with a case. "You won't be going in blind, or at least as blind as we feared."

"The problem is pretending her memories are still as lost as we want our enemies and uncertain allies to believe," Endicott said. "How long have you been having these dreams?"

"That's a good thing, isn't it?" Lewis said, when Ess frowned and tried to think back, to answer his question. "That means whatever is needed to unlock Ess's memories is already at work, it isn't hidden in the vault, so there's no chance of it falling into the enemy's hands."

"Yes, it's good for us, but creates another problem if we don't understand what triggered the unlocking of the doors that were, in the final analysis, closed to protect her."

"The songs. The coded songs in Grandfather's journals," Ess said. "Ever since I started playing them. Some gave me such awful headaches, remember?"

"Maybe that headache was a cascade of memories trying to burst out."

"You do realize this creates another problem." MacDonald put aside the photos. "What's to keep the traitors, if they knew Ernest and Matilda well enough, from trying music to unlock Ess's memories? What's to keep them from trying to use music, since Ess has proven susceptible to that kind of memory and mind control, to in essence *rewrite* her mind?"

That morning's discovery and the conundrum that followed took up most of that evening's communication with the *Golden Nile.*

Ess's head ached, and oddly enough, so did her lips, from playing the flute multiple times to demonstrate the various tunes she had discovered that affected her dreams. Uly promised he would test the tunes on himself, because some did give him a slight throbbing in his temples. The effect didn't last more than a few heartbeats, and they speculated that going through the communication plate might affect the pitch or tone of the flute.

She lay awake in her cozy little cabinet bed, waiting for the headache powder to take effect, long after the men had made the rounds of the car, checking the locks on the windows and doors, and then retired to their beds. The tempo of the wheels on the rails changed, signaling the change in grade and slowing as the train neared the station. Ess calculated it was nearly midnight.

A muffled thump on the roof of the car yanked her up from the first spinning sensation giving a teasing promise of sleep. Ess sat up, eyeing the paneling of the ceiling. Her cabinet room offered a wardrobe on one side, and a desk with a clever little seat that swung out from the wall, tucked up underneath her bunk bed, which put her near the ceiling. She lay still, holding her breath, waiting.

Was that a footstep, or her pulse in her ears? Did her headache make her hallucinate? Was another memory forcing its way into her consciousness? Definitely, she had more items to add to the list of complaints to spill on her grandparents when they finally were reunited.

There—another thump, followed by a scraping sound. Something dragging across the top of the cars as they approached the station? Her imagination? Some hobo taking advantage of the slowing cars to jump on board and get a free ride?

"No," she murmured, and sat up to swing her legs over the side. She slid down to the floor without benefit of the ladder built into the wall.

Hobos or tramps or anyone else sneaking on board the train wouldn't do so as it approached the station, but as it left. So if a person had jumped on board, what did he want?

Ess tugged on her pants, tucked her sleeping shirt in, and pulled on the clever knit vest Dr. Sylvia had given her, for just such emergencies when she didn't have time for more clothes. It provided some padding and the copper threads throughout offered some defense against punches and knife thrusts in a fight.

Barefoot, her derringer in one hand, a knife in a wrist sheath, Ess slipped out of her room and crept through the dark car. She wished she had a Zeus gun, even though a lightning strike in the wrong place might ignite all the papers strewn around the car. Five steps took her to the door.

A louder scrape came from the roof. She tipped her head back, following her ears, and saw strips of starlight in the darkness of the ceiling.

Of course—the square vent. She mentally kicked herself for not thinking of that before, especially since one of her earliest jobs as a Pinkerton was to break into a train car where a kidnapped girl was being taken over the border to Canada.

Metal squeaked and scraped. Now Ess knew the sounds. Someone loosened the screws holding the cover plate in place. Whoever was up there obviously wanted to avoid noise, necessitating moving slowly, so she had some time. She hurried to knock on the first bedroom door. Lewis pulled the panel open almost immediately. She signaled him to silence and pointed up to the roof, then knocked on the other two doors. One thing she greatly admired about her lawyers was that they knew when not to ask foolish questions. By the time the third screw came loose, all of them were ready for whatever or whoever came through the roof. That vent was too small to allow a full-grown man, so either a boy or a young woman was about to enter. Was the person who now pivoted the vent around on the fourth screw working alone, or did someone wait at the door to be allowed in?

All of them stepped back and crouched down, allowing the furniture and deep shadows to hide their presence. A rope slithered down from the roof, the last few feet hitting the floor with a muffled splat. Endicott rested the shielded lantern on the table in front of him, ready to blind the intruder with a beam of light. The plan was simple enough to be flexible, depending on what they faced.

A dark shape blotted out the starlight. Ess played with the idea of trying to sever the rope and make the intruder hit the floor, but she didn't trust her knife throwing skills, especially in the dark, with the car swaying as the train slowed. The fall wouldn't be far enough to even momentarily stun the intruder. The feet appeared, then the legs, then the rest of the slim frame. She couldn't get any more details in the shadows as the figure slid down and landed with a soft thump.

"Halt," Lewis barked, as Endicott snapped open the lantern, hitting the dark figure in the face with a beam of light. The yelp of pain was definitely from a young male throat.

Ess dove in as the boy turned to flee, wrapping her left arm around his legs and using her momentum and weight to yank him sideways. He went down, right into MacDonald's grasp. In seconds, both he and Lewis had the boy face-down on the floor and knelt on his back and knees.

Endicott offered Ess a hand to get back to her feet, and then they moved around the car, lighting lanterns. MacDonald's slow, growled string of curses drew them back when they had only lit two each. Ess was surprised to see him slide off the intruder's back and gesture for Lewis to move. When he picked up the boy by his shoulders and turned him around to face them all, the other man let out a groan.

"Hiram Beech, what in tarnation do you think you're doing?" MacDonald said.

"Hi-yo, Mr. Mac," the boy said. In the light, Ess guessed he was fourteen, with the scratchy voice to support her estimate.

"You know this scallywag?" Endicott settled down on the couch and raked one hand through his tousled hair. "Beech? Not Rupert's brother?"

"One and the same, and scallywag is too kind a word for him." He half-carried the boy over to one of the toppled chairs, bent to right it, and shoved him down into it. "Will any of your brothers and cousins come barreling through the door any minute if you don't signal them?"

"I was just supposed to sneak in and look around." Hiram hunched his shoulders and tugged his cap down lower on his forehead, and then had the audacity to nod to Ess. "Was just supposed to get a look at the lady, maybe listen some, sneak out when you left to take care of a telegram."

"A telegram sent by your brother?" Endicott guessed. Sitting close to him, Ess saw the corners of his mouth twitching as he fought not to smile. "Why did you need to get a look at the lady?"

"Not really sure." He glanced at Lewis and MacDonald, who stood on either side of him, a hand gripping each shoulder. "Lots of talking and whispering and people sending messages. Like a coyote got in the chicken coup, when Rup got word you were heading cross-country with the lady."

"Who is spreading the news?" Lewis said.

"It wasn't really a secret," Ess offered. "But the people Athena had watching out for me knew to be discrete. Sanctuary seemed eager to get me there as fast as possible, correct?"

"Eager enough they argued a little about getting you on an airship despite our claim you were deathly ill."

"My point is that despite who my grandparents are, people shouldn't be talking. They shouldn't have anything to talk about. Or am I wrong with this assessment?"

"Not wrong at all," Endicott said. "Perhaps, though, your grandparents are the explanation."

"Yes, any mention of their names is bound to cause an uproar. I have this growing impression they're somewhat equal to Queen Victoria and Prince Albert."

"So the lady's not a prisoner or something?" Hiram said.

"That depends on your definition of prisoner." Ess got up and stepped over to the chair and held out her hand to the boy. "Pleased to meet you, Hiram Beech. I'm Odessa Fremont."

"Fremont?" The boy's expression lit up. "Like Uly's sister?"

"Exactly like Uly's sister, and twice as much trouble," Lewis muttered, gazing up at the ceiling.

Ess muffled a chuckle. She liked being identified with Uly for a change, instead of their grandparents.

"What do you think?" MacDonald said. "We can't just let him go, and we certainly need to find out what sort of rumors are going around."

"I think we are owed at least a hot breakfast." Endicott beckoned for Hiram. The boy pasted a cocky grin on his face, but Ess noticed his hands trembled just a little bit, as he crossed to stand in front of the older man. "Where might your brother and cousins and their fellow scallywags be hiding right now?"

~~~~~

After they sent Hiram off with a note for the conspirators, the four separated to wash and dress and take advantage of their scheduled five-hour stop. Endicott gestured for Ess to wait while the other two men went into their rooms.

"Those tunes you've been deciphering... how confident are you? Able to play them from memory?"

"I've gone over the fingering every afternoon. Some aren't quite safe to play aloud." She shivered, sensing what he was about to ask her.

"Ah, good. Those not quite safe tunes are exactly what I had in mind." He didn't meet her eyes as he spoke, but gazed at his hands, fingertips pressed together hard enough they were white.

"The memory tunes."

"Yes." He sighed. "While I have the utmost trust in Rupert, these are perilous times. What is to keep the traitors from tricking the trustworthy members of our organization to do their dirty work for them?"

"You think someone sent Hiram here to spy on me. The boy thinks it's just to verify rumors, but there might be other purposes." She settled down on the end of the couch she occupied during the long, pleasantly quiet work hours, and pulled out one of the drawers underneath it. Her journal dedicated just to the songs she had decoded from her grandfather's journals was buried under all the others. "Do we want to search their memories, find out exactly what they heard or were told to do? Or do we want to block their memories so they don't unintentionally betray us?"

"Hmm, I was thinking more of finding out if they are being used, but that is a good question." He let out a weary groan and heaved himself out of the couch. "Let us hope we find nothing but good when we search their memories, so we have no need to implement the other tune." Nodding to her, he went around the table and down the hallway between their cabinet bedrooms.

Ess took the journal with her, and propped it open on her desk. While she dressed, she studied the notes she had made on the effects, or alleged effects, of the tunes she had in mind. Her task slowed her, so the others were waiting for her when she emerged, still pinning her hair up.

"We have plenty of time," Endicott said, gesturing for her to join them at the table. "What have you found?"

Ess went through her notes, listing her preferred songs for the task and
~~~~~

her reasons. Some of the notes in both her grandparents' journals indicated side effects. One especially worried her.

"Granny indicated a pattern she noticed, and she hoped she was mistaken." Ess rolled her flute between her fingers as she spoke, trying to ease the growing discomfort over what she had found. "She hadn't examined enough people, because she hadn't used the songs to manipulate many memories, and she was very clear that she didn't want to build up a large number to be sure of her theory."

"Some residue from using the blocking songs?" Lewis reached over to rest his hand over hers, stopping her nervous motion.

"Not a residue, per se, but more a weakening. Grandfather likened it to opening and closing a door too much when the hinges were badly made or the door wasn't fastened to the wall properly. We don't have the tools of our ancestors, to look inside the brain and measure the effect of the song on the neurological tissue. We can't be totally sure there isn't some inimical effect until it builds up enough to make itself known. Granny feared using the songs to manipulate memories too much would make the affected minds more susceptible, more vulnerable to further manipulation."

"Ah, that is a concern," Endicott murmured. "Since they did perform multiple layers of blocks on your memories, did they find some kind of protection? Something to heal the damage?"

"In theory. Much of the work Granny did on memory manipulation was theory *because* she hesitated to experiment. And of course, much of what she wanted to do was put aside when they went to South America."

"What worries me is that the traitors might know of your grandmother's work and try to take advantage of the vulnerability you might suffer, when we reach Sanctuary," MacDonald said.

"Are you asking if I feel confident enough in Granny's work to use it defensively?" Ess weighed everything she had researched in the last few weeks, as well as what she had read and refreshed her memory on just a short time ago. "Yes."

"How soon do you need to use it?"

"She recommended regular treatment, or perhaps doses would be more accurate, with the frequency depending on how often the subject's memory was affected. Or how deeply."

Chapter Thirteen

A knock on the door stopped the discussion. Temporarily. Ess found some amusement in the intensity of Rupert Beech's scrutiny of her, and the looks he and his companions gave his younger brother. Obviously they hadn't believed what the boy had told them, or they expected her to still be in trousers when they came to escort the travelers to breakfast at a nearby hotel.

The morning traffic of a town that hosted a major train station was just starting to fill the streets. Ess couldn't decide if those numbers guaranteed some privacy in conversation or threatened the security of whatever they said. Either way, it didn't matter, because no one said much of anything, other than to ask about or point out various businesses to meet the travelers' needs, as they walked the three blocks to the hotel.

"One of us. Very nice," Lewis commented, after their party of twelve had been escorted to a small private dining room. "The manager," he added, when Ess looked around, trying to pinpoint who he meant.

"Let us start with that, shall we?" Endicott said, as they settled around the table. "How many of our people are here, in town and the surrounding countryside — say about a twenty-mile radius?"

"Why?" Rupert frowned, caught reaching for the coffee sitting on the sideboard.

"We need to know how many we have to deal with, and how far this breech in security goes."

"Security?" He finished bringing the urn to the table. His glance lingered on Ess a few seconds too long, and she could almost hear his thoughts. This was more than being Ulysses Fremont's long-missing sister. That realization visibly dawned in his eyes. "You're worried because we decided to check you out, make sure of what we heard."

"Did someone *ask* you to investigate us?" Lewis said.

"Maybe someone is claiming I'm not who I say I am?" Ess said.

"Oh, you're definitely Uly's sister." Rupert chuckled as he filled cups and handed them around the table. Ess liked him just for that little bit of thoughtfulness. He was the leader but didn't expect others to wait on him. "Your face. The way you ambushed Hiram." His smile faded as he handed off the last cup and sat down. "Truthfully... yes, there was some chatter."

"There shouldn't have been any chatter," Endicott said.

"Stry—" Ess caught herself in time. What if a traitor was at this meeting? "Our suspect must have notified his co-conspirators."

Rupert wasn't happy but didn't argue about discussing what his team had heard and been told to do. This town was a hub for collecting and disseminating important news, especially warnings of trouble, passing along supplies, and shuttling people from one assignment to another. Rupert's parents and their siblings had specialized in creating new identities for Originators who had run afoul of Revisionists too often and needed to vanish. They altered appearances and taught people how to talk and move to fit their new backgrounds. They also created those new backgrounds, with necessary documents, and sent people to the coast, to take ships to other countries and new lives. Ess kept that bit of information at the back of her mind, gnawing on that niggling sense of impending insight while she listened to the others talk.

At first there had been little more than whispers and speculations. Someone had overheard something, someone had come in on the end of a conversation or saw a letter or telegram, or someone else needed to confirm that something they heard wasn't true. Ess's parents and grandparents had been well-respected among many divisions of the Originators. The contributions both generations had made to the scholarly foundation of the Originators' cause had made their names known, if only in reports. When Edward and Vivian had died, many who had never met them mourned. Ess felt a little uncomfortable, knowing that hundreds of people knew her name and some of her family's history. She felt rather exposed.

When Matilda and Ernest vanished, their entire archeological expedition gone without a trace or explanation, that had created even greater ripples. Ess cringed and feared her face was bright red when Rupert repeated the requests for information and help that had gone around, passed from one group to another, asking for any sign of her, any news of her, when she had fled the boarding school.

"Wait," Lewis said. "Who, *exactly*, was asking for news of Odessa?"

As she listened to the members of Rupert's team talking, trying to prod each other's memories, Ess wished she had brought her flute and her journal, to record what they said and try to help them remember. Of course, she didn't have the ingredients for the tea that her grandmother recommended be ingested before using the music to affect the mind. Asking for the herbs and salts here in the hotel might prompt questions she didn't want to answer.

Several members of Rupert's team agreed that the questions, the requests for information about her, had begun when she fled Miss Van Hastings' academy. That meant someone had been watching her at school since her grandparents went to South America. Could the Revisionists, traitors, or both, have been planning to influence her, kidnap her, or just steal information from her? Her grandparents had feared this happening, and this was why her memories had been blocked.

Breakfast dragged on as they verified dates and attached names to specific requests. Rupert reported several sources had suggested that the young woman who turned herself in to the law firm might not be Odessa Fremont at all, but a Revisionist. She wanted to laugh at the idea that anyone would believe that Endicott, Lewis and MacDonald could be fooled.

What was the purpose for planting doubts about her identity throughout the Originators? To make the leadership doubt? To keep her from getting into Sanctuary at all, and accessing her family's vault? Maybe the enemy wanted justification for putting her through many tests to prove her identity, thereby tapping her memories and finding the information her grandparents had hidden?

The secrecy among the Originators had to end. What had once protected them made them vulnerable. Secrets made them doubt others' truth and trustworthiness and crippled them at crucial times. If imposters and infiltrators could get into the ranks of the Originators, what security was there for anyone?

Then the thought that had been wriggling up to the front of her consciousness finally became clear.

"The identities you create," she said. Her face warmed when everyone turned to look at her. "Who has come to you for help in creating temporary identities? Not to escape trouble, but to infiltrate other places? Anyone in the upper ranks of leadership?"

"Ah, of course," Endicott said, nodding. "Think back to members of the leadership, especially people assigned to Sanctuary, who came to you between ten and five years ago." Then he held up his hand before Rupert could do more than open his mouth. "I think this is something that needs to be discussed in the security of our car. Search your memories. Do you have any records you can retrieve?"

Rupert sent Hiram and another boy in the team to fetch records from a specific trunk, while the rest of them walked back to the train. They were a silent company. Ess was grateful when Endicott looped his arm through hers and clasped her hand as they walked. His small smile of approval for her idea made her feel somewhat better, although she didn't like this evidence of how widespread the blindness among the Originators extended. No wonder her grandparents had been so secretive.

Rupert's office must have been very close to the train station, because the two boys weren't long on their errand. They found enough chairs in the train car for everyone to sit, pushed two tables together, and Ess requested boiling water for tea from the porter. Then the boys rejoined them. She assembled three recipes for memory access, depending on what they might need to do, depending on what they found out in the next hour.

It would have to be less than an hour, because in an hour and three-quarters, the train was scheduled to begin the next leg of the journey.

Lewis volunteered to be the recorder, as Rupert and his right-hand assistant, Violet Beauchamp, read through the records and the names and identities created. Ess was glad she wasn't writing, because she needed to clasp her hands together in her lap, hidden under the table, when they read out loud the records affirming that Stryker had taken the name and identity of Pinkerton Agent Judson. The real Judson had been temporarily detained, dosed with various herbal concoctions to keep him delirious and unaware of the time passing, and fool the physicians who attended him. The intent, according to what Stryker told Rupert's parents, was to infiltrate the agency, gain access to some vital information the Pinkertons had uncovered, and substitute some much-edited information with details of Originator activities deleted. When his mission ended, the real Judson would be released by the doctor, free to go on his way. He would have memories implanted so he wouldn't contradict his encounters with the people Stryker had met. Obviously now, Stryker had retained the identity and the real Judson had been killed. Or worse, in Ess's estimation, he was languishing somewhere in an asylum.

The identity creation and exchange had taken place two whole years before Ess ran away from Miss Van Hastings' academy.

"Excuse me." Van Dorn was a member of the team who had been mostly silent. "Am I mistaken, or are you unusually interested in this particular identity?"

Ess felt almost a sense of relief when he spoke, as if she had been waiting for those particular words, that particular tightness in his tone. Every time she had looked up during the recitation of case files, he had been watching her. Was she imagining it, or did he seem to go pale when he saw her flute lying on the sideboard, as if he knew what it could do?

"We have information on questionable activities. The more questions we ask, the more threads we find attached, leading us to the answer. Or should I say, the more lines of the spider's web we discover." Endicott sat back and exchanged glances with his associates. "Perhaps it is too much to hope that we will find the thread that leads us to the chief spider."

"There is too much information in those files," Ess said. "We're only halfway through, and the porter should be knocking soon to warn of preparation for departure. Would you mind too much if we took them with us? We will return them on the way back through."

"Excellent idea."

Van Dorn, Ess noted, was not pleased with the idea, and looked daggers at Rupert when he agreed with only a moment to think. His expression turned bland a heartbeat later, so she could almost question what she had seen, influenced by her suspicions of him.

"Perhaps we need to investigate newcomers," she said. "Or perhaps someone who has been transferred in recently?"

More than half the members of Rupert's team automatically glanced at Van Dorn. He didn't look around at all. Ess would have looked around, unless she was the guilty party, trying not to look guilty.

"It might interest you to know that Mr. Stryker is dead," she said, watching Van Dorn.

He startled, his gaze locking with hers. It took a visible act of will to tear free, and his face glistened with sudden sweat as he looked around the table, offering a weak chuckle.

"Ess?" Lewis murmured. He tipped his head toward Van Dorn, and she nodded. He got up and moved over to stand behind the man.

"Sir?" Rupert turned to Endicott.

"As a point of fact, Mr. Stryker died while wearing the identity of Mr. Judson of the Pinkertons. He was introduced to Odessa as one of her superiors among the Pinkertons, which is where she has been working for the last four years. One has to wonder where the real Mr. Judson vanished to, if his identity and position were stolen," Endicott said. "Would you happen to know, Mr. Van Dorn?"

"Me?" Van Dorn leaned back in his chair. Ess saw it move out a few inches from the table. He was going to try to run.

"Yes, try to remember your last meeting with him."

"Why would I meet with him? I've never met with him."

"Mr. Van Dorn, you look rather queasy. Perhaps from exercise too soon after breakfast? Odessa, do you have something to offer him to help? Perhaps one of your grandmother's restorative... potions?"

Ess hurried to the sideboard, glad to put her back to the group. She had difficulty not smiling. It would be rather a nasty expression.

Mr. Van Dorn protested that he felt fine, and half-rose from his chair as Ess brought a cup of the potion to make him vulnerable to questioning. Lewis rested a heavy hand on Van Dorn's shoulder, settling him back in the chair with an audible creak of legs sliding on the carpet.

"Rupert?" He gave the man a beseeching look when Ess set the cup of faintly purple-tinged, steaming liquid down in front of him.

"Sir, Van Dorn came to us highly recommended," Rupert said, his eyes hooded. He leaned back in his chair. "By Mr. Stryker. That's enough for me." He crossed his arms over his chest. "Be a gentleman now, Van Dorn, and drink the tea the nice young lady gave you."

Van Dorn's hair and collar looked dark with damp. He glanced around the table. None of his associates showed any sympathy.

"You can't kill a man without a trial, without proof." His voice creaked.

"We're not going to kill you." Ess nudged the cup closer to him. "I can't guarantee that my Granny's potion won't make you wish you were dead, though. Especially if you resist the effects." She waited until he picked up the cup and brought it to his lips, then stepped back to the bench against the wall, sat down, and readied her flute. Several turned curious glances to her. She waited for the signal from Endicott.

"That's a good little traitor," Lewis murmured, and bent to take the cup from Van Dorn's hands when he had emptied it. That remark earned some murmurs from the others.

Ess played. She watched the faces she could see, anticipating some effect on their minds. Without the help of the tea, the influence of the tune could be easily resisted. Or at least, that was the theory. If people didn't know what the tune was doing, how could they resist?

'Tell us what happened to the real Mr. Judson of the Pinkertons," Endicott said.

They were still questioning Van Dorn, his answers leading to more questions, when the train pulled out from the station. Rupert sent Hiram and Violet back to headquarters, but the rest of the team stayed on the train. The next stop was four hours away. They would get off there and take the next train back home. After only ten minutes of questioning Van Dorn, it was evident Rupert's team needed to get to work immediately, dealing with the traitors and information uncovered.

Van Dorn knew few names. The traitors kept their activities hidden, so each member of the group only knew maybe ten other names. Van Dorn, as a messenger and errand boy, had a slightly wider grasp of what was being done, but not by much.

The potion to render him incapable of refusing to answer their questions had an interesting side effect of nausea and drowsiness. Ess supposed it only made sense that weariness lowered inhibitions and self-control and the ability to resist orders. They had to end the questioning when nausea made speaking coherently difficult. They ended the questioning by using the malleable condition of his mind to implant lies. He was ordered to forget the questioning had taken place, then to betray all his contacts in the surrounding area, leading them into the traps Rupert's team would organize.

Most important of all, he was to report to his contacts that Ess was ill, suffering from nerves. Van Dorn had been specifically assigned the task of making sure she was indeed incapacitated. Unfortunately, he had no idea who received his reports. Everything went through a coded communication system and relays. He would be allowed to move about, fulfilling his duties, and enabling Rupert's people to track down traitors within their reach and warn the people they could trust.

As an added layer to the multiple defensive layers of lies, they implanted in Van Dorn's mind the notion that Endicott and his partners feared for Ess's health and hoped to access the lotus for healing. Stryker, to all indications, didn't know Athena Latymer headed the Blue Lotus Society, and therefore couldn't betray her to his co-conspirators. Only the highest levels of the leadership knew she had the lotus and it was not safely hidden away in the deepest vaults of Sanctuary. However, since the leadership of the Originators was under suspicion, there was no way of knowing if the Revisionists had that information.

Ess hoped they hadn't missed some tiny, vital piece of information and made dangerous assumptions. All the lies they were sending to the traitors could turn into a snare for them all, because everything that contradicted what the traitors knew could notify them they were under suspicion.

All this deception, layers upon layers of lies, made Ess tired and her head hurt.

The trip to the next station gave them time to test everyone on Rupert's team, at his insistence. Ess used a different tea, to help them access their own memories, rather than be searched by others. All were dismayed to discover odd little events, cryptic words, things they had seen and hadn't paid any attention to at the time, which now seemed to leap out and form a disturbing pattern.

There was some satisfaction in knowing progress had been made toward identifying and ridding out the traitors from among them. That satisfaction was tempered by the sense that they couldn't be sure what direction they were headed.

~~~~~

Uly hunched his shoulders against the mid-afternoon damp that shifted from mist to drizzle. He considered ducking into the pavilion on Public Square for shelter. The offices of Endicott, Lewis and MacDonald were only another five minutes of walking down Superior. Three if he ran. Would anyone notice him or care, with the drizzle turning to actual rain?

"Mr. Fremont?" Wallace, the lawyers' investigator, stopped short as he nearly came face-to-face with Uly. He touched the brim of his hat. "Just the man I wanted to see."

"Another report to send on?" Uly glanced at the heavy leather satchel bouncing against Wallace's hip with every step, the wide strap slung over his chest.

"That... depends. Could that lovely lady with the incredible scones provide us a place to talk privately?" He shrugged. "Something hot to drink would be a blessing, come to think of it."

"We're more likely to get a scolding from Hilda about using some common sense." He gestured back the way he had come. "Is there a problem?" he asked after they had crossed Ontario.

"Ethics, I suppose. What do you do when someone you respect greatly, who hires you to find out the truth about other men, is revealed as not who he claims to be?" Wallace hunched his shoulders, frowning at the damp pavement ahead of them.

"Unfortunately, that occurs more than I would like." He played with the idea that the investigator was going to confront him with the false fronts the Blue Lotus Society employed to hide the activities of the Originators. Wallace had been specifically put on the trail of uncovering all the people who had gone through Rupert Beech's very clever identity-changing operation, to discern who might not be who they were supposed to be. Athena and Ford had asked him to investigate everyone who crossed their
~~~~~

paths, and the paths of the leadership in Sanctuary, just to ensure no 'i' was left un-dotted or 't' un-crossed. Had he discovered far more than he was supposed to?

That decided him. Whatever worried Wallace, Uly knew better than to try to comprehend on his own what could be filling that satchel.

"I think we need to go to much smarter people, right from the start." He gestured toward the airship docking towers in the distance.

Wallace's silent acquiescence just confirmed what his gut had told him. Then again, maybe the chance to finally come aboard the *Golden Nile* had helped persuade the man.

As they walked, Uly asked where Wallace had been. He wasn't surprised to learn the investigator had just arrived from Washington, where he had been given access to Secret Service records. He remarked that Ess certainly had influence in high places with powerful people.

"She impressed Agent Sutter when she was fourteen and he's tried from time to time to get her to work for him again." Uly grinned, recalling hearing Sutter's version of the events that his sister had downplayed. It didn't take more than a curious look from Wallace to convince him to tell the tale. They were both chuckling as they reached the airship docking tower and stepped into the lift to ride to the top. "Did you try to contact me here when you arrived?"

"I didn't come by courier airship." Wallace grimaced and leaned back against the wall of the lift as the gate across the opening slid closed. "Bullet train. My ears are still aching, and it arrived more than half an hour ago."

"It's as bad as we heard?" Uly winced in sympathy for him.

The bullet train was solely for government use, for cargo that needed guarding and to be transported with great speed. Airships and courier airships were fine for things like documents, but not when it came to people and animals, and heavier objects, such as weapons or gold or artifacts. The bullet train, however, lost in comfort what it gained in speed. For speed, it pulled a maximum of six cars, three of which were solely for fuel and water. Crew went in the fourth, leaving two for passengers and cargo, and supplies to survive the rapid trip without any stops. Besides the noise from the engine and the wind and the thunder of the rails beneath the oversized wheels, there was the constant bouncing and banging, and the smell that collected in the cars, which had no windows, nothing to cause air friction and drag. Remembering that, Uly tried not to take too deep a breath until they had reached the top and stepped out into the open air.

Chapter Fourteen

"Someone experimented with hammocks instead of the usual bunks and bench seats," Wallace said with a grin. "There are huge springs between the hammock knot and the wall, supposed to soften some of the worst of the bouncing. Well, maybe in less bumpy terrain. I spent one year on a whaling ship and didn't get seasick, but this crossed the line for me."

"How fast?"

"Eight hours, instead of the usual two days." He patted the satchel. "Should tell you how... how touchy this all is."

Uly offered Wallace a chance to freshen up and change his clothes, since they were close enough in size. As he expected, the man leaped at the chance, giving Uly time to find Athena, Ford, and Theo. Dr. Sylvia was with Athena, and she came along when they all met in the parlor cabin.

"What do you have for us?" Athena asked, once everyone was settled and greetings exchanged.

"Pictures, reports, some wax disk recordings of testimonials." Wallace gestured at the long table that usually stayed pushed against the wall, until they needed to convene a council of war. "I'm glad I caught you before you headed for South America. This might... well, it might change everything."

Athena nodded her permission and they all gathered around as Wallace spread the contents of the courier bag across the long table. He organized everything into four groups, with three on the table and the fourth set aside on a chair, out of sight. That set off a warning bell in Uly's head. The papers went into one pile in each group, but there were several maps, and at least five, sometimes as many as eight photos with each group. The photos were of one man in each group, so there were reports on three separate men. Why so much material on only three men? Where he stood, only one man was right side up to him.

Uly stepped up as soon as Wallace moved out of the way and studied the photos. They seemed to be a progression of changes in the same man — muttonchop whiskers, graying hair, spectacles, high collar, hunched shoulders. Oddly, in the first two pictures, the left shoulder was higher than the other, but in the last three, his shoulders seemed to have straightened out. Did Uly's eyes deceive him, or was the man's beard darker in the last three? He stepped closer, glanced at Wallace, who watched him now, then bent over the photos, studying smaller details. Dr. Sylvia and Athena did the same. The shape of his nose changed, thinner in the bridge from the first photos to the second. The left corner of his left eye drooped in the first photos, but didn't droop in the last.

Wallace snorted when Uly left the first group and moved to the end of the table to study the second group of photos. Athena took his place, while Dr. Sylvia moved over to study the pile Athena had left. Uly glanced at the maps spread out with the photos. The maps seemed to mark a journey, then a second journey, but what one had to do with the other, he couldn't tell. This time, the first five photos showed the same man, wrinkles appearing around his eyes, then looking thinner, as if some illness made him lose weight quickly. Then in the following photos, he visibly regained at least a stone of weight. He had been gesturing with his right hand in the first five photos, but the left hand seemed dominant in the remainder. Wallace leaned back against the wall and watched Ford step up to study the photos and maps with Athena and Dr. Sylvia. They switched off again.

"Do you know who these men are?" Wallace asked, after everyone had studied the photos and maps and settled down on the couches.

"They're all high-level assistants to some very important people in our organization," Ford said at last. He glanced at Athena, who looked somber and nodded agreement.

"They *were*, apparently," Dr. Sylvia said.

Wallace didn't react, other than a relaxing of the lines around his mouth. Then again, it could be the large tumbler of whiskey Ford had offered him when he learned the investigator had come on the bullet train.

"Are you aware," she continued, "of a medical technique that originated during the Napoleonic wars, when so many men returned from the battlefields with horrible cosmetic damage? It's called plastic surgery, or in other areas cosmetic surgery, but it entails the rebuilding or reshaping of facial features through surgery."

"Ah." Athena nodded. "So you think the differences in all three men came about through—no, not changes in the original men, the real men. Changes to help imposters pass themselves off as them."

"You have friends and connections and access to information that would have helped the North win the war in the first six months." Wallace put his glass down on the floor, tucked under the couch, and sat with his elbows on his knees. "I had some fun, tracking down documentation about these men. What caught my attention was that all three of them simply vanished on a journey east." He gestured at the table of documentation. "One map shows them all leaving some place south of San Francisco. No coincidence that it is my employers' destination? Somewhere around the second day of their journey, they vanished. Then, two, three days later, they reappeared, all deathly ill. Out of their minds. Sweating themselves into skeletons. Each one of them was retrieved from the charity wards of the hospitals where they landed, taken away by friends who were utterly devastated at what had happened to them. And what's interesting, friends whom all three men, according to the doctors, claimed they didn't know. It was assumed the lack of recognition was part of the delirium they suffered."

"When it was actually the truth," Dr. Sylvia murmured. "Why do people always assume that a fever means mental incapacity?"

"Exactly. Then, all three men vanished in the care of these supposed friends. Sometimes as much as two weeks later, they reappeared at their original destinations, still suffering some vestiges of the illness, ashamed of their weakness, unwilling to talk about it. The illness was blamed for whatever mistakes they might have made with their associates." He shrugged. "I wasn't aware of this fascinating trick of plastic surgery until I puzzled my brains raw over the discrepancies in appearance."

"Our enemies are substituting their own people for ours. Somehow, that strikes me as worse than conscious treachery," Athena murmured.

"It poses a threat to all of us," Ford said, slipping an arm around her shoulders. "Once they identify more of us, they could conceivably find our doppelgangers, adjust them to be a better match, then kidnap us and make the substitution. And like Stryker taking Mr. Judson's place, the originals are eventually disposed of."

"My, what fascinating activities you are involved in," Wallace said.

"How did our enemies have enough information to capture those men?" Athena got up to pace. Uly took that as a bad sign. "They should have been traveling with protection, their itinerary should have been arranged at the last minute, just so they couldn't be tracked. Yet they were."

"Meaning someone very high in the ranks, someone with the right and the need to know. Someone they reported to," Uly said. He wished he had taken a larger glass than Wallace had.

"That narrows things down considerably," Ford said. "The most crucial question is if they have any clue that our intrepid Mr. Wallace has been asking such piercing questions."

"We need Ess. She could devour all this paperwork and distill it to the right conclusion in a tenth of the time the three of us would need." He gestured at the cabinet where his bag of crystal dust and the rod and flute were stored. He glanced at the clock and grimaced. They weren't due to communicate for eight more hours.

"I agree," Athena said. "Judging from the thickness of the stacks of papers, it could take several hours to pass on the information. I wish we did indeed have the device she wanted, to record everything in images."

"What are you talking about?" Wallace said, lines forming around his eyes and his smile looking a little strained with every heartbeat.

"We should tell him," Dr. Sylvia said. "Our friends are planning on bringing him into the effort once this is cleared up, so what harm could there be in doing it early?"

"If Mr. Endicott trusts you," Uly began. He frowned when Wallace held up a hand to stop him.

"That might not be wise." He gestured at the photos and papers on the chair, partially hidden by the table. "There's a fourth man who might not be who he says he is. When Agent Sutter saw what I dug up, he practically threw me halfway across Washington to get me on the train in time."

Uly strode over to the table and picked up the whole pile and turned it over on the one corner of the table that was open and empty. He tried to swear as a familiar face looked up at him from a photograph yellowing with age. The sound caught in his throat, so he couldn't even breathe for a few seconds. He shook his head and took a step away, then snatched up the pile of photos to deliver to Athena and Ford. He put them on Ford's lap and stepped back. The wide-eyed look Athena gave him as their eyes met made him want to howl.

"It can't be," Dr. Sylvia whispered, as she stepped over close enough to see the photos of Randall Endicott, showing his face as a young man, the changes in beards and hair and jackets and neckcloths over the course of nearly thirty years.

~~~~~

Uly wished he could leap through the communication plate as he prepared the materials to pass on to Ess that evening. He wanted to pull her back through to the safety of the *Golden Nile*, since he couldn't stay at his sister's side to protect her. The infiltration of Sanctuary to discover the identity of the traitors had changed from a spy mission to war. Simply by being an unknown factor, Ess was the most potent weapon they had. Uly hated the exigency that put her in such a precarious position, especially when someone he trusted to look after his sister in his absence, someone his grandparents had trusted, had now been revealed as a traitor.

Knowing highly placed members of the organization—Graebausch, Whickham, and Polidory—had betrayed their own assistants, handing them over to Revisionists to put substitutes in their places, infuriated him. He hated feeling helpless. The advantage they had been depending on, that the leadership of Sanctuary didn't know that he and Ford and their men had all returned from the expeditions that should have killed them, might not exist. Not if Endicott had betrayed every single secret they had told him in full trust. There were more men involved in the attempt to get rid of him and Ford than just the late, unlamented Stryker. As long as their enemies thought Ess was untrained, her memories still blocked, they would consider her easily manipulated, her many questions perfectly reasonable. That advantage would only last until Endicott revealed the truth to his superiors.

To encourage everyone, Uly revealed the extra communication he and Ess indulged in, sharing the memories they were regaining, and their agreement not to reveal those memories. Hopefully, Endicott might believe Ess truly was ignorant of so many things.

The only hope Uly had now was the plan they had put together while Captain Astrid and her crew scrambled to ready the *Golden Nile* to leave Cleveland and head due west. That plan, and the information he would give
~~~~~

Ess tonight, were her only protection until he and his soldiers could infiltrate Sanctuary and rescue her. She needed to work quickly to determine who she couldn't trust, to be safe, impervious to their lies and flattery and charm.

He wondered if this was how his grandparents had felt when they sent him away for training, and when they set off on their expedition. They knew they were walking into trouble dangerous enough to prompt them to leave Ess behind and hide information inside her head.

~~~~~

Ess fell asleep, waiting for Uly to contact her early that morning. She dreamed, and knew she dreamed. She was young, toddling along in her grandparents' wake, down a slightly curving passageway. They walked in silence, soft blue-tinted light glistening on the curiously smooth, rounded rock walls. Ess couldn't determine if the walls were wet, or just so smooth they were polished glossy. Then her attention caught on the source of the light itself, and there was no sense of wonder. If anything, it felt familiar.

A faceted ball of crystal filled Matilda's gloved hand, spilling out the blue-tinted light in an unwavering puddle. Every dozen steps or so, Matilda hummed a single note, and the light brightened.

"This is the last trip," Ernest said, as the gently downward sloping, curving passageway leveled out, and a long, dark hallway stretched out before them. Matilda stepped aside. Her grandfather pushed a wheeled cart, maybe three feet wide and four or five deep. "You open the door this time, Odessa." He went down on one knee and beckoned for her, holding out one hand.

Ess stepped up and gave her hand into his. Her hand barely stretched from the heel of his hand to the base of his fingers. She felt she was maybe six years old. Yet she could have sworn she had never visited this place.

Ernest led Ess up to an alcove dug into the rock face. Glancing down the dark hallway, she saw other alcoves, all identical, all curiously smooth — she could think of no device that could cut solid stone so smoothly. The alcove was perhaps two feet deep, the shape of a massive, round-topped door cut into the stone, with a silver border perhaps an inch wide. A dull silver-blue oval marked the place where a doorknob would be. As Ess approached it, holding out her hand, a light shimmered softly inside it. She pressed her palm against the bottom third of the oval. A sensation of dozens of tiny needles in her fingers and palm made her hiss. When she pulled her hand away, she saw no blood.

The light in the oval flared red, then shifted to lavender, then blue. The door slid backward into the rock face nearly six inches before sliding aside, vanishing into the rock on the left. Beyond the doorway was darkness.

Matilda sang the same note that lit the crystal ball, and light sprang up from smaller crystal knobs set into the wall just above adult eye-level. The room stretched out in front of Ess, the rock just as smooth as the rock of the
~~~~~

hallway. Seen through her childhood eyes, the dimensions were hard to estimate, but she guessed the room was fifteen feet deep, maybe eight wide. Wooden shelves filled the walls, but other than the bottom shelves on the back wall, they were empty. While Ernest transferred small wooden boxes and crates of books onto the cart, Matilda led Ess to the open wall on the right side of the room. She sang to the crystal in her hand. The light changed from blue to lavender, and rippled out to stroke the wall, drawing a circle. The stone rippled aside, like water, leaving a depression in the stone.

"Do you remember what we taught you on the way here?" Matilda went down on one knee so she was eye-level with Ess.

Ess-at-six nodded, dug in her coat pocket, and brought out a short slide whistle of crystal with a silver ring on the end. At Matilda's nod, Ess put the whistle up to her lips and blew softly. The song sounded like the wind across the eaves on a stormy winter night, and she pulled on the silver ring, adjusting the high-pitched moan. Her grandmother stopped her before she finished the song. Ess could hear the rest of the song, three high-pitched, prolonged notes in her head. She remembered how playing those notes made her skull vibrate and threatened to loosen her teeth.

"Remember that song, my lamb," Matilda whispered. "Remember when you need it most, when time itself hangs in the balance. Never play the last measure until the grave needs to be closed." Then she held out her hand. Ess gave her the whistle, and she put it into the new alcove in the wall. As she and Ess walked away, the stone filled in again, until the wall looked like it had never been disturbed.

"This is very important, Odessa," Ernest said as he gestured for her to help him push the loaded cart out of the room. "If the liars and bullies continue to gain power, as we fear they will, there may come a day when this hiding place of ours must not be allowed to endure. Even if all our friends listen to our warnings and remove their family heirlooms and memories from this place, too much remains here that cannot be allowed to fall into the wrong hands."

"What are you going to do about the bullies, Grandfather?" Ess asked, leaning into the support bar of the cart with all her strength and weight.

"Not I."

Ess saw him exchange a wry smile with Matilda. She couldn't understand how her grandfather could smile and yet look so sad.

"You are of the bloodlines of all the women who dismantled the Great Machine. You have inherited the duty and the authority, and perhaps the right to make that decision. Do you remember my stories about the plates in the ground? The way earthquakes are made?"

"Noah's flood broke the shell of the planet, and the pieces keep moving around, rubbing against each other." She nodded

"Your multi-great grandmother was one of those who chose this spot for our Sanctuary just because a wise man — or woman — knows sometimes you must destroy a great treasure, rather than let it fall into the wrong hands. Our ancestors knew of the unstable ground in this part of the country. Those who built the Sanctuary dug down to find the places where the plates keep moving and banging against each other. They stabilized them, making this a very safe place to build. The day may come when you must decide to remove the stabilizers, and bring this great fortress of ours down on itself into the dust."

"How?" Ess shuddered when the blue-tinted light from the crystal in her grandmother's hand wavered and took on a reddish tint.

A loud bang shook the passageway and the floor heaved up underneath her. She cried out and reached for her grandfather, but Ernest just smiled at her and kept pushing the cart. Another bang brought the ceiling reaching down to slap at them.

With a yelp, Ess banged her head on the ceiling of her cabinet bedroom. She clutched at the side rails of her bunk as the train car rumbled and swayed underneath her and thunder boomed overhead. Shuddering, sweat covering her face, she smiled to know she was awake. The cave-in hadn't happened.

Nausea tightened her throat as her dream flashed through her mind. Not a dream, but another memory. The new song Uly had passed on to her earlier that evening had released this memory. Which was more disturbing? The knowledge she had the ability to destroy Sanctuary, or the proof of imposters at the very heart of Sanctuary? Ess slid down to the floor and snatched up her journal to sketch what she had seen so clearly in the dream and write down the details.

On the trip back from dealing with her parents' deaths, her grandparents had taken a long detour to the Sanctuary. They had crept in through a side entrance and went down into the bowels of the warren of tunnels and caverns. They sidestepped all the alarms and security checkpoints and showed Ess how to do it. Then they had gone to their vault and emptied it.

"Almost everything," Ess murmured, as she closed her eyes and focused on that part of the dream again. She recalled the notes her grandmother had hummed to the crystal that served as a beacon, a lantern, and had guided them through all the crystals that kept watch in the doorways and tunnels. Her grandparents knew how to circumvent the security system the ancestors had installed when they built Sanctuary. They had gone in unseen and unheard. Yet if they had been able to do it, logic said they weren't the only ones who had discovered the way.

"If they could do it, then others did as well," Athena agreed, when Ess shared the details of her dream with her, Ford and Uly just a short time later.

She had been startled to see them on the other side of the communication plate when it shimmered into life. Common sense told her something serious had prompted her brother to include them when he contacted her tonight for their private talk.

"Where are the stabilizers, and how are you supposed to use them to bring down Sanctuary?" Ford murmured.

"We didn't get there in the dream." Ess held up the journal, showing the map of the route she remembered them taking.

What if she hadn't unearthed this particular memory in time? She wondered what Uly would dream, prompted by the same tune he had given her. They already had proof that whenever she had a dream released by a tune, Uly also had a dream, but something different. Then a new thought startled a chuckle out of her.

"The vault is empty. Won't that be a great shock to the traitors, when I open the door and they try to rush in to steal whatever they have been waiting for all these years, and there is nothing to take?"

"Nothing but that slide whistle."

"Could that be the key to unlock the time trap?" Uly said.

"I don't think so, or rather the whistle might be a key to something larger and more sensitive, maybe part of reassembling the Great Machine. Perhaps so sensitive they didn't dare hide it with everything else they had to get out of the enemy's hands." Ess frowned and flipped through the journal to get to her sketch of the whistle. "They weren't working on anything relating to manipulating time, or even the discoveries leading up to Grandfather's theory of time bubbles until several years later. He didn't start telling me the stories of the bubble people until I was ten or so."

"Then what happened, or what did they find out, to prompt them to empty their vault, and warn their trusted allies and friends to do the same with theirs?" Athena murmured. Her eyes widened. "Of course. The deaths of Vivian and Edward. Not an accident at all, but perhaps the first sign of treachery."

Chapter Fifteen

Ford's face wrinkled and he thumped the table edge hard enough to make the communication plate on that end jolt. "Curse this pervasive need for separation and secrecy. Oh, no, I understand completely." He held up his hand to delay interruption. "They were wise not to tell anyone. Just one tiny error could have been disaster. For all the things they told us, I'll wager there is twice as much they didn't."

"We still have a problem." Uly gestured at Ess's journal. "The traitors are waiting to get into our vault, to take whatever they think Granny and Grandfather left behind. As soon as they see it's empty... they'll know the game is up."

"So do I refuse to open the vault?" Ess said.

"Just long enough for us to get there," Ford said.

"You're coming here?"

The grimness in her brother's expression stole her breath.

"Knowing how to take down Sanctuary might be helpful," Athena said. "If our plan fails. If what we discover is too large for us to deal with by simply removing the traitors."

"You didn't tell us everything Mr. Wallace discovered, did you?" She glanced over her shoulder, as if she could see through the muffling blankets to the door of her cabinet bedroom. What if it wasn't enough to keep someone standing outside from hearing everything they said? Ess shivered, fighting the urge to get up and open the door and look out into the darkness and silence of the train car.

They would arrive in San Francisco tomorrow, and the next day take a steam-cart down the coastal road to Sanctuary.

"Let's deal with this question first," Ford said. "Uly, do you remember anything that ties into Ess's dream?"

He met Ess's eyes, and she muffled a sob as she felt the weight resting on her brother's shoulders. How long had he been dealing with this memory?

Slowly, his voice calm but weary, Uly answered. He knew about the stabilizers. Their father had taken him down into the deepest levels of Sanctuary on his one visit to the stronghold. The tunnels had braces everywhere to keep the fissures and crevices of the natural fault lines deep within the ground from collapsing. Ess shivered as Uly described his memories, the impressions so strong on the little boy he had been that the sensations stayed with him all these years later.

Edward had taken Uly down with him into a place where flames were forbidden. They carried crystal shards strapped to their wrists to light their slow path, clambering over boulders and sliding down slopes full of debris and dust, until they came to a cool, dark place, lit by crystal dust scattered over all the surfaces. They didn't go into the cavern. Edward showed Uly the barrier of shimmering light and how a stone thrown at the barrier bounced back. Then he showed him how continued contact ignited the end of his walking stick.

"Nothing can get through that barrier," Uly said. "It holds everything safe from fire and ignition."

"Ignite what?" Ford asked, from somewhere outside of the visual range of the communication plate.

That startled Ess. Such a simple question implied he didn't know about the place Edward had shown Uly, didn't know about the field that protected whatever was inside that cavern. Why wouldn't her father's close friend know about this, when he had showed his young son?

"Barrels and barrels of gunpowder. Sticks of dynamite encased in wax to keep them dry. Everything connected by priming cord. The explosions will unsettle the rock, crack all the places where it's balanced on a feather."

"An earthquake sudden enough, drastic enough, could shatter the coastline of California and plunge hundreds of miles of it into the sea," Athena said. "Matilda insisted all her students study geology, so we could protect the Sanctuary in our turn."

"Father said most of the braces will stay in place. The purpose was to collapse Sanctuary in on itself, bury it in its own grave, without endangering the rest of the coastline. The fault line extends hundreds of miles." Uly rubbed at his eyes, then his temples. Ess felt sorry for him. Did it hurt, remembering those things? Was it as disturbing for him to have pieces of his life ambush him, as it was for her?

"Pray the good Lord we never need to consider the exigencies that would require us to destroy Sanctuary," Athena said.

"Hear, hear," Ford murmured. "We do have far more important concerns to deal with."

"Identifying the traitors," Ess said.

"We need to use the vault as a trap." Athena's smile was slow and thoughtful and sent a pleasant shiver up Ess's back. "Capture their attention. Play with them, Ess. Taunt them, play frivolous and silly and temperamental. Make them earn your friendship. Keep them convinced the vault is filled with treasures of information and technology that will fulfill their wildest dreams. Make them boast to you, make them think you're malleable enough you can be impressed, so they will confide in you. The vault is the prize. Keep them busy, so focused, they don't notice you learning what you need, and they don't notice the noose that they put around their own necks."

"Distract them until we can get there," Uly said.

"To do what?" Ess flinched as her voice rose. "Why? What happened that you couldn't tell the others?"

"We are going to use the songs and the tea, just like you used on Rupert's team," Athena said. "Sylvia is adapting the potion to use it in an atomizer—"

"A huge atomizer," Uly muttered. He winked, making Ess feel a little better.

"We will invade Sanctuary, using those secret entrances you just remembered, and reach the ventilation system, fill the air with soporific, and then investigate every person inside."

"Why?" Ess demanded. She wished she could take the plate and shake it, or perhaps reach through and shake someone.

"First, you should know some details we did not reveal when we talked to all of you earlier." Athena glanced sideways to where Ess thought Ford stood out of sight of the plate. "The three men who were replaced by Revisionist spies are personal assistants to three members of the Council. Evidence is strong that their superiors arranged for them to be taken."

"So who do I need to beware, when I reach Sanctuary?"

"Graebausch, Whickham and Polidory."

"We're investigating where they are right now," Uly said, "if they're at Sanctuary or out causing mischief. Whoever is waiting at Sanctuary is preparing a trap for you. Whoever isn't there..." He shrugged.

"All right. I'll be ready to change the script." She nodded and wrapped her arms tight around herself, feeling chilled despite the enclosed, stifling sensation under all her blankets. "There's something more I need to know?"

"Randall Endicott is not Randall Endicott." Ford stepped into view of the communication plate. His eyes were as hard and bleak as his voice. "We have proof he took the place of the real Randall more than thirty years ago. He was a young man studying in Asia, after his family was wiped out by illness, and there was no one to say he wasn't the original. Who knows how long he has been working among us, trusted by Edward and by Ernest and Matilda, by all of us? How many Originators are clients of his? How many people has he betrayed?"

"And he's there with you, ready to turn you over to the Revisionists," Uly said. "I'm sorry, Ess. I promised Grandfather I would take care of you."

"Well, then hurry and get here. I'm good at delays and distractions." She managed a smile for him, despite the ache that his guilty expression and agonized tone sent through her.

They showed her only a few of the documents Wallace had brought them, tracking Endicott, speculating on who he really was. They identified where and when he had taken the place of the real young man whose family had been assigned to a remote, isolated location to conduct research. Ess took notes in her private cypher and let all the information simply slide through her mind. Maybe tomorrow all the implications would crash through her mind and heart, but right now the shock was too fresh.

~~~~~

"Be safe," Uly whispered, watching the sun rise behind the *Golden Nile*. He braced himself on the guy wires and refused to let the chill of the altitude and early hour drive him indoors.

"Please, Lord Almighty, keep Ess safe. Don't let her be trapped. Keep her alert and strong and help her always think two steps ahead of those Benedict Arnolds, those Judases, those Manassehs who would sacrifice their own children for their profit. You made blind eyes see when You walked on this soil. Now, please, make seeing eyes blind."

He took a deep breath and leaned forward, to see the darkness slipping away, pushed by the silver light of dawn turning golden behind him. Everything that could be done had been done. Today Ess would reach San Francisco. Tonight would be their last chance to communicate, although he would activate his plate every night and keep it open until past midnight, if Ess needed to call him. Once Ess was within Sanctuary, within reach of unidentified traitors, they wouldn't be able to communicate through the plates. The risk of someone among the enemy discovering what Ess could do was too great. Endicott might not reveal the plate to his superiors, since the uses were limited, but if he did or if the traitors had access to technology that let them detect and even control or interfere with crystal energy, it would be safer to maintain silence while inside Sanctuary. She would have to go outside the tunnels to contact him. Better not to take the risk.

Uly didn't like being out of contact, but what could he do? They both had a duty to the ancestors. He knew sitting up here, willing the *Golden Nile* to fly faster westward, really didn't help, but it made him feel better. He could pray. He could think hard and deeply, and he could search his memories for every tunnel and passageway of Sanctuary, to be ready for the day and hour and minute when he would lead the soldiers under his command and join his sister in the duty they had inherited from their parents.

~~~~~

"How do invalids survive?" Ess muttered later the next day.

While the steam carriage they had rented to drive down the coast to the canyon entrance of Sanctuary was luxurious, being forced to recline and essentially ride sideways going down such a bumpy road was inexcusably uncomfortable. Why had she agreed to pretend to not only have a blinding headache, but to be chilled and nauseous? The heat was the worst of the experience, and the weight of her clothes—a woolen skirt and sweater, coat, hat, and gloves. She felt she would start to melt at any moment, thanks to the high humidity after yesterday's torrential downpours.

"That's why invalids stay sick," Lewis said, glancing over his shoulder and not even trying to look sympathetic.

"Hypochondriacs must enjoy misery, which just proves their illnesses are in their heads." She craned her head around, trying to see out the open window that resisted allowing any breeze into the confines of the vehicle. Apparently, just her window was so cruel, because Ess could have sworn that a breeze ruffled the hair of the other passengers.

Maybe they were comfortable because they faced forward, and rode closer to the front. MacDonald drove, with Endicott beside him in the front seat. Lewis sat in the seat behind them, and Ess had the third seat, which she swore was placed directly over the rear axle. Perhaps the rear seat had so little padding because baggage was always expected to ride at the rear of the vehicle.

Heaven help her, she even sounded like an invalid, whining and complaining and thinking of nothing but her own comfort. She would be better employed to pray for the remainder of their journey, and especially ask that no new security and defensive measures had been invented and installed at the front entrance of Sanctuary.

As if thinking that were a signal, a high-pitched tone filled the air. Ess inhaled sharply and pressed her fingertips against her temples, moving back to brace the bones around her ears. She glanced up and found Lewis and Endicott watching her. They didn't seem at all uncomfortable.

"Please don't tell me you didn't hear that," she said, and fought not to gasp aloud in relief when the tone dropped at least an octave and softened.

"For men, it's more felt in the sinuses," Endicott said. "The stronger the reaction, the stronger your sensitivity to the crystal. It's something of a test, I suppose." He opened his door, and Ess realized then that the carriage had come to a halt.

"What is done to those who don't react at all?"

"We pity them," an alto voice responded from behind her, outside the carriage, "and we give them duties where they can be useful, and they don't have to work with crystal."

Ess slid her legs off the bench and sat up. She didn't have to pretend weakness because she felt quite cramped and stiff from reclining. The three lawyers exited the carriage, and Lewis stepped up to offer Ess a hand to help her out.

The woman stood with her hands clasped at her waist, head slightly tipped to one side like an inquisitive bird. She had a pointed chin, high cheekbones, and large gray eyes. Her ebony hair had stark white streaks extending from her temples and caught up high at the back of her head before hanging free in multiple braids. Her eyes had a faint slant, and her skin tone tended toward coffee-and-cream. There was something exotic in her style of dress, though Ess couldn't quite put her finger on it, other than that the material was a muted rainbow, thin and light and suited to the humidity, and the style itself seemed most sensible, with few layers and very little cinching. In contrast to her light clothing, she wore heavy, thick-soled boots. A moment of thought, and Ess decided that was sensible, if one dwelt in an underground complex carved entirely from bedrock.

"Well, Clytie?" Endicott said, stepping around the side of the carriage and bowing to the woman. "What do you think?"

"I'm pleased to see so much of Vivian in her. As much as I loved Matilda and Ernest, I feared the Fremont side of the family would dominate." Clytie chuckled and held out a hand, beckoning for Ess to approach her. "Your mother was a dear friend, though I'll wager she never spoke of me—or at least, you don't remember her speaking of me?"

"No, unfortunately, the Fremonts conducted some of their memory experiments on their own grandchildren." Lewis had his arm looped through Ess's, in pretense of supporting her.

"Yes, so we were told. It makes sense, even as it is regrettable. Ernest and Matilda were wonderful people, self-sacrificing to the point we could never be angry with them, because they always practiced before they preached. However..." The woman sighed, shaking her head slowly.

"We have endeavored to fill in the holes in her education," he continued, as Ess came to a stop within arm's reach of Clytie.

The woman stepped up and gently touched her chin, studying her face with such intensity, Ess could believe this stranger could see right through her.

"However, we thought it best to stick to generalities, and leave the more astonishing revelations and incredulity-straining facts in your capable hands."

In point of fact, they had not expected Clytie to be here at all. Endicott had gone through a list of names and brief backgrounds of all the leaders and authorities and teachers who could be here at Sanctuary and would want authority over Ess. Clytie wasn't on that list.

"Ah, well, I hope I will indeed be permitted that task." Clytie nodded, her expression softening, looking pleased. "No, my dear Odessa, we never met. I took a post in Cairo soon after your parents married and didn't return to this country until just a year ago." Eyes sparkling, she gestured around them. "What do you think, eh?"

Ess couldn't be sure if the woman was testing her or making a joke. They stood in a narrow box canyon, the mouth of it choked with the debris of what looked like a recent landslide, huge boulders surrounded and half-buried by gravel and hard-dried mud, the broken trunks of uprooted trees sticking up here and there. The floor of the canyon looked like it had been scoured clean by recent flooding, most likely last night, and the only vegetation that held on was a tangled, thick, woody vine with leaves so dark they looked purple in the shadows. It cloaked all vertical and semi-vertical surfaces and hung in clumps like Spanish moss. She could make out no opening in the rock face through all the drapery of vines. In fact, she couldn't discern any place where Clytie could have emerged, yet logic said the woman wouldn't have hiked here from some other location to wait for them. She couldn't have been visible from the mouth of the canyon, a good two hundred yards away, partially hidden by the crooked walls.

"I don't know what to think," Ess said, and was glad to press her knuckles to her forehead. "I'm sorry, this ridiculous headache..."

"Hmm, yes, we will get to work on a cure. And if this is some vicious new trick of the Revisionists, hopefully we can adapt it for our own uses, or at least distribute a defense to our forces." Clytie offered her bent arm.

"Vicious trick?" Ess echoed as she complied.

"It's only logical." She patted her hand and led her down the left side of the canyon, toward the largest overhanging clump of vines. "You were working with the Pinkertons, protecting Egyptian artifacts — your grandparents would be so proud — and the Revisionists are pathological about obtaining every artifact they can, in their search to obtain all the pieces of the Great Machine. You do know about the Great Machine?"

"Yes, and if it weren't for vague memories of Grandfather's bedtime stories, I would find it entirely unbelievable. However, since these gentlemen insist it is true..." Ess frowned as they approached the thick wall of vines. The darkness behind them wasn't more vines, but an opening. The angles and shadows created an optical illusion, she decided, then winced as that not-quite-audible tone pierced her head again. She followed the sound downward, and saw Clytie held a faceted crystal ball in her hand, a third of the size of the crystal that had been in Matilda's hand in the dream.

"Quite logical of you, though I daresay, being Vivian's daughter, you want proof, and lots of it." She chuckled and gestured at the darkness behind the vines, which seemed to be moving. Then the vines swayed, though a breeze wasn't blowing. "The long and the short of it is, we suspect the Revisionists are able to breed and change different bacteria and viruses, to create new diseases. Germ warfare, the ancestors called it. From the report Mr. Endicott and his associates passed on to us, we fear you were subjected to some experimental disease to cripple you, when you encountered the Revisionists in protecting the exhibition and artifacts."

"Will you be able to help me? I'm quite sick to death of being ill."

"I am not a doctor, but we have a good number on hand here. One of them should be able to help you." She patted Ess's hand. "Don't you worry. You'll be back to good health in no time at all."

Then she gestured with the hand holding the crystal, and the vines swept aside like a curtain in a theater. Ess couldn't decide if that bit of showmanship was friendly or threatening. Clytie led the way into a tunnel, barely wide enough for the two of them, which widened, doubling in width every ten or fifteen steps they took, and sloped downward, the floor turning into stair steps. Shimmers of crystal resonance washed over Ess's skin when they started down the steps. She watched her feet, not trusting the steps in the darkness only lit in green-blue by the light of the crystal in Clytie's hand.

A shiver washed over her that had nothing to do with the pleasant cool that soaked through her entirely too hot and heavy clothes.

"Just getting out of the heat makes me feel better." Ess glanced back and up, to see her three companions following close behind.

After twenty steps, they reached the bottom. The tunnel widened out into a cavern, the walls vanishing into utter darkness. The mineral here was dark gray, streaked with obsidian and threads of red that glistened when the light from Clytie's crystal brushed against them. Ess tried to remember seeing this entryway into Sanctuary in her most recent dreams. The mineral struck her as different, there was more blue and black in the passageways she had dreamed. It made sense to her that the secret entryway her grandparents had brought her through was far distant from this place she saw now. How distant? What obstacles lay between wherever she would be quartered and that doorway, which she would have to overcome to let Uly and the soldiers from the *Golden Nile* into Sanctuary?

One step at a time, she scolded herself. *For want of a nail, the shoe was lost...*

She decided she hated that particular poem about a war that was lost because a battle was lost because a message was lost because a messenger was lost because a horse was lost because a shoe was lost, all because of a horseshoe nail. While it seemed noble to consider herself willing to do her small part unnoticed or unappreciated, Ess wondered if anyone considered the situation from the nail's perspective, always trod upon and pressed down into the mud and banged on stones.

I must cut back on Dr. Sylvia's compounds. They are making me truly delirious.

A sense of pressure in her ears and the back of her head prompted her to turn enough to see the shimmer spread across the cave opening. The small streaks of sunlight spilling through dimmed.

"Illusion?" she asked, as Clytie paused and looked back as well.

"It seems that is all we specialize in nowadays," the woman said with a tiny shrug. Her glance seemed to linger a moment or two longer on Endicott as she swept her gaze over their small group. "Come. While the others are most eager to speak with you and begin your testing, our physicians have first claim on your time and person."

Chapter Sixteen

"Testing? You don't believe I'm me, do you?" Ess glanced at Endicott, who walked on her other side. "You did warn me. I'm surprised you didn't make a wager with me. These three are constantly making wagers."

"There's very little available to us for entertainment," Endicott responded. "And as a matter of fact, we did wager on whether you would believe our warnings."

"I hope you lost." She wrinkled up her nose and pouted long enough for Clytie to chuckle and tighten her arm looped through Ess's.

The passageway curved downward, making almost a complete circle before widening out into a room large enough that the light from the crystal didn't touch the far walls. Several young men and women waited, each holding a lighting crystal. While they weren't dressed in the same cut and color and cloth, a similarity among their clothes suggested a uniform. Ess's studies about Sanctuary and how things were done and handled answered her questions before she could ask. These would be the advanced students, those who had proved themselves especially talented and intelligent, brought here for specialized training in some aspect of the Originators' centuries-long task. They acted as messengers and assistants throughout Sanctuary as they determined where their true talents and interests lay. They all seemed to be around Ess's age. Clytie introduced them and assigned them various tasks to settle the four visitors.

She assigned Phoebe to Ess as her guide and assistant. Her first task was to take Ess's bags to her guest room and then join them at Dr. Lockhart's workroom. The girl, who looked perhaps a year younger than Ess, slightly rolled her eyes at the mention of the doctor. Her lips twitched, visibly fighting a smile. Maybe, just maybe, Ess thought, she had been blessed with someone who could be a friend?

"No last names?" Ess asked, pitching her voice low, as the group hurried off with baggage and errands and it was just the five of them again.

"We try to avoid the ranking and its attendant problems, while they're students. Then they graduate and get their first assignments, and the political maneuvering sets in with a vengeance." Clytie sighed and looped her arm through Ess's again.

"They know my name. I assumed I would become a student, if just to get me caught up on all the things I missed out on since my grandparents vanished. Or am I a lost cause because of the memory blocks?"

"Knowing your grandparents and your bloodline, once we release your memories, you could likely be years ahead of your peers."

"That's God's own truth," Lewis muttered from behind Ess.

All of them laughed as they headed into the vast darkness.

After another dozen steps, the light from the crystal revealed regular doorways cut into the rock. Ess soon decided they weren't doors but tunnel openings. She supposed this area in the vast ridge running parallel with California's coast, where major tectonic plates met, was honeycombed with tunnels. This was an entire underground city, rivaling New York. How could anyone bear to live most of their lives underground, never seeing sunlight or breathing fresh air? Could this hive-like existence somehow create some mental pressure or malaise, which led to people in positions of power turning traitor? Was it a sickness of the mind and soul, and not simply evil and greed? If it was a mental problem brought about by darkness and damp and the pressure of all that rock hovering overhead, why didn't anyone notice? Not the people who dwelled in this underground city, of course, but the ones who had regularly cycled in and out on errands, making reports, bringing in supplies. Or weren't they important enough to have their words noted and considered, if they even noticed a problem?

Not my problem, she scolded herself. *Focus on all this. I can't afford to get lost.*

Ess knew better than to depend on the maps sketched in her father's and grandfather's journals, and the dream-memories of moving through the tunnels. In the years since those maps were drawn, the routes had likely been altered to serve the needs of the changes in population. Shortcuts from one passageway to another, vertically and horizontally. One wrong turn, when she didn't expect an access tunnel or a stairway, or even a ladder, could throw her completely out of kilter at the worst possible time.

Clytie pointed out the markers carved into the walls of the passageways every time there was an intersection or branching. The code was simple enough to decipher, but Ess knew half the battle was creating a mental map of the place, so she would know where she needed to go, what turn to take, to get from one place to another.

Light spilled down at a little more than a forty-five-degree angle up ahead, and Ess nearly lost a step when she realized that golden-white light was sunlight. Or was it? Did her eyes deceive her, or did it flicker and warp? Another dozen steps and the light grew brighter, the passageway around them widened, and she thought she heard a rushing, spattering sound.

"It's a waterfall," she blurted, as the passageway widened into an irregular room, at the same moment a breeze touched her face, bringing damp cool with it.

"Do they have waterfalls underground?" a gravelly voice asked.

"Obviously," Clytie said. Or rather, Ess decided after a moment, she chirped.

The low voice chuckled, and a series of sharp thuds echoed off the slopes of rock, barely muffled by the soft roar-rush of water, maybe thirty feet wide, falling at least fifty feet through a crevice that she estimated curved a good hundred and twenty feet overhead. Trees and vines draped down the rocks on all sides, creating enough camouflage and blocking vision to keep people on the surface from seeing what lay below. She supposed the sound of the falling water created enough cover to allow conversations down here from being heard above.

"What happens during flood times, when the winter snowmelt comes down from the mountains? Or isn't there enough snowfall in this part of California to be much of a threat?" she asked, as a man emerged from the shadows of the overhang opposite the waterfall.

"Ah, and that is definitely the voice and analytical mind of Edward," he said, gesturing at her with a cane.

The cane only explained half the sharp thuds on the rock. The other half came from an artificial leg that ended in an arrangement that looked more like a bird of prey's foot than a Human foot, with three talons facing forward and one protruding out the back, most likely for balance. It was a simple mechanical leg, with visible springs in the knee, and no sounds of any other gears at work. Ess tried not to stare, but she couldn't imagine why the man coming toward her, old enough to be her grandparents' peer, didn't cover his false leg with his trousers, so it matched his remaining leg. That one was decently dressed and wearing the same kind of heavy boot that Clytie did.

"Are you tired of constantly being compared to your parents?" the man continued, stopping maybe a dozen steps away from them. "Or was that frown for some other reason?"

All right, you're testing me. Do I play squeamish and hide behind my illness? Do I use it to excuse bad manners? Or do I engage in a battle of wits? It might be worth my while to make him laugh. Laugh because he likes me, or laugh because he thinks I'm an idiot and I don't live up to the Fremont reputation and legend?

"Trying to decide if it's rude to indulge my curiosity," she said, when the balding man's eyes narrowed and he tipped his head slightly to one side, visibly studying her. He snorted and nodded, which she took as permission to continue. "Are you conducting maintenance on that leg?"

"Conducting maintenance? Curious wording. Why? Are you offering to help?"

"I had some experience with a mechanical leg, helping to rebuild it after it suffered from a gunshot straight through the most delicate part of the mechanism. Of course, it was an experimental mechanism, with the inventor constantly tweaking and improving, so there is no comparison." She shrugged, then raised a hand to press against her temple. She did have an illness to feign and an illusion to maintain.

"Ha! That is Matilda, through and through. I'm still not sure if I should thank God she refused me, or continue to curse Ernest for stealing her heart." He winked at Ess and gestured for them to head to the left, behind a screen of vines that spilled all the way down to the bottom of the crevice.

As she approached it, Ess realized someone had built a wall, partly of stone, covered with dirt and moss and allowing the ends of the vines to take root. Behind the screen, she saw a living area set up, with several long tables covered in books and papers, dozens of chairs scattered about in groupings, two cabinets against the far wall, with dishes, and even a copper water tank sitting above a six-burner coal stove. She wondered if the hangings on the wall were to keep down the dust, absorb some of the damp, perhaps muffle sound more, or even hide doorways into other chambers cut from the rock. She could imagine with enough furnishings, this would be a pleasant place to conduct daily living, without ever having to go into the tunnels. She decided she would prefer that.

"What? No questions of how I possibly could have been your grandfather?" He waved his cane around. "Make yourselves comfortable, of course. It's been some time, but I'm fairly sure of all your faces and names." His eyes narrowed as he watched Endicott walk past him to take one of the seats at the table that had the least amount of debris covering it.

Ess tried not to react, but she couldn't help holding her breath, just for a moment. This had to be Dr. Lockhart. Since he implied he had courted her grandmother, did that mean he knew the family and their friends from far enough back that, possibly, he would notice something different, something not quite right, and identify Endicott as a fraud?

"The laws of genetics, sir, would dictate that because one-quarter of my inheritance is from Ernest Fremont, you could not possibly be my grandfather, because I would not be me."

Dr. Lockhart paused in the act of settling down in a chair that had a curious, boxy mechanism tucked under the legs. His eyes widened, and she stood close enough to see only one pupil dilate, meaning the other was glass. Then he tipped his head back and laughed, a raspy, almost breathless sound, as he dropped into the chair. With a loud *sproing*, the box pivoted up and extended, revealing itself as a mechanical footrest.

"I'm convinced. That sharp mind and wit can't be taught. It's in the blood." He tipped his head toward one of the cabinets. "Stanton, be a good lad and wait tables?" He winked. "If you wait long enough, he'll tell you this is why he decided to study law instead of going into medicine. I never let him sit still long enough to open an anatomy textbook or watch over my shoulder as I compounded medicines or performed surgery."

"I had more than enough time to read between running your errands, sir." Lewis moved around the kitchen part of the living area with enough visible ease, Ess decided nothing had changed since he had served as Dr. Lockhart's assistant. She found the entire concept curious. This impressed on her again how much time had passed. Her father had been a boy with

Lewis and had come here for some of his training. Would he also have silver threads in his beard and moustache and hair by now, if he had lived? "What the good doctor neglects to say is that he kept his official medical students so busy, compounding and bandaging and cutting—to keep them from flirting with Vivian, I might add—he needed to borrow from the law students for his everyday errands."

Dr. Lockhart chuckled and nodded, never taking his gaze off Ess. She focused on his features to avoid meeting his eyes. Or rather, eye. She supposed if she met the non-gaze of his glass eye, that would let her endure the intense scrutiny from across the oblong table, but she considered that rather rude. This close, she saw the scarring that puckered the skin around his glass eye, and the depressions that indicated bone loss. She imagined some major damage, a blow that broke bone and tore away flesh, taken in some battle. If it happened at the same time he lost his leg, then it must have been catastrophic, such as being close to the impact point of a cannonball.

"Well, Miss Odessa, they tell me you suffer some pernicious malady, possibly inflicted on you by Revisionists or Resurrectionists." Dr. Lockhart held out his hand. She gave hers into his grasp, wrist upward, earning a wink from him as he set about checking her pulse. "That's a Fremont for you, never satisfied unless they knock down the biggest, nastiest hornet's nest."

"Unintentional, I assure you," Ess said. "I was a Pinkerton until recently, and my job was to protect Egyptian artifacts from thieves. Encountering the nasty R's was entirely accidental. A by-product of the assignment, I suppose you could say."

"Nasty R's." He chuckled. "Wouldn't be surprised if that becomes a new catchphrase."

"Let's hope they are kept separate." Clytie got up to help Lewis distribute the cups and plates and the refreshments he had brought out.

One of the cabinets must have been an icebox, because the pitcher of cream had condensation on the sides and the layered cream cake was cold and firm. Clytie's words stayed in her head as Dr. Lockhart put her through a preliminary examination just sitting across the table from her, studying her skin, her pulse, her eyes, making her stick out her tongue, stroking her bared arm and cheek and down her neck. When he finished, and she was free to enjoy the refreshments, she asked what the woman had meant.

"Merely that we're hearing rumors of the Revisionists joining forces with the Resurrectionists. Or rather, more visibly aligned with them. They supported the South during the war, using their knowledge of original history to try to turn the tide of major battles." She shook her head and gazed pensively down into the remains of her coffee. "It is only by the Good Lord's mercy that history was not changed on that large a scale, at least."

"As far as we can tell," Dr. Lockhart said, punctuated with a grunt. "Took several big, frightening losses to convince the hide-bound noninterference faction that it was time to open up the forbidden history books and use them to steer history back onto its proper course. If we could."

Four students joined them in Dr. Lockhart's domain, reporting for duty as guides and assistants. Phoebe stayed with Ess and Clytie as the three lawyers headed out. They were to report to whoever was on duty in the council chamber while the doctor examined Ess. Then she would have her turn to prove she was who she claimed to be.

Dr. Lockhart carried on a running commentary as he set up his equipment for his tests, while Ess changed into a long, loose smock for the examination. She deduced early that he really didn't expect any response from her, even when his comments sounded like questions. He listened to her lungs and used multiple layers of lenses to look into her eyes and ears and down her throat. He drew blood and put it on glass slides to examine under a convoluted microscope, adding drops of different liquids to test the health of the organisms in her blood and the presence of bacteria and diseases. Ess found it fascinating, even when she only understood one out of every four words. In some ways, she felt rather as if she were in her grandmother's laboratory. Dr. Lockhart peered at her from under scowling brows when she said so, then abruptly barked laughter. Of course, she waited to say that until he gave her leave to change back into her own clothes, and Phoebe had helped her dress.

"Trying to flatter me into giving you a clean bill of health?"

"No, sir," she responded in all honesty. "Do you have any indication of what is bothering me?"

"Oh, some suspicions." He nodded and made a shooing motion. "Need to do some more studying. Might have to dose you a few times. Do you resent being experimented on?"

"It never did me any good when I was a child, so what's the use of protesting now?"

"Your father protested vehemently, from what I hear." He narrowed his eyes and focused on her for a few heartbeats, then shook his head. "Neither here nor there. Tell those eagles in their nest I'll tell them what I know when I know something worth telling. No sense in pestering me. Won't get my tests done any faster." He continued muttering as he went back to work, looking at the slides again and reaching blindly for another glass beaker of odd-colored potion.

Clytie shook her head, her expression fond, and gestured for Ess and Phoebe to follow her.

They had time to stop in Ess's guest quarters to allow her to wash and change. Ess wasn't quite sure what she should do. The clothes that had been too hot and heavy for the humidity above ground felt almost comfortable in the cool of the tunnels. However, they were still damp and sticky and felt heavier than usual. If she changed into cooler, lighter clothes, would that be wise? More importantly, would they fit with the image of an invalid? If she was too lightly dressed, she might be aided by a little unconscious shivering. She would also feel more balanced and ready for trouble, ready to move quickly. Which option was best for her?

She didn't have a chance to choose. Phoebe hadn't hung out her clothes for her, but she displayed a talent for quick assessments. The clothes that would look best without requiring ironing were Ess's lightest clothes. Phoebe provided wash water while Clytie helped Ess get out of her heavy, sweaty dress and petticoats. Between the three of them, Ess was freshened and dressed and her hair brushed into a simpler style, and ready to hurry down the passageway within twenty minutes.

The guest quarters were two levels higher than the council chambers where the most vital Originator work was done, and almost directly above them. Clytie led the way down an iron spiral staircase to the next level, then walked a dozen feet along the passageway, then down another spiral.

The now-familiar blue-tinged shimmer of light from fist-sized lumps of crystal reached out through the wide open double doors of the council chamber, as Clytie led the way through the antechamber. Ess wondered just how much of the crystal used for lighting and other purposes was necessary for the functioning of the Great Machine, and how much was extraneous material, the outer shell. If anyone ever needed to put the Machine together and make it work again, how much would have to be retrieved from locations all over the world, and members of the Originators deprived of lighting, healing tools, even the power for things like Zeus guns? Did the Originators deliberately put the disparate pieces of crystal to use to prevent the Great Machine ever being reassembled?

Maybe the lotus had been removed from its safe hiding spot within Sanctuary decades ago to keep it from attracting all the shards and fragments of crystal that were here, and putting them back together, bit by slow bit. Not to hide it from powerful people who might try to sway the lotus and its holders to serve their goals. Or maybe the lotus had the ability to touch minds, more than just for the purposes of healing. Had its guardians somehow sensed it was in danger when the first traitors infiltrated the leadership?

Such thoughts kept her busy on the walk through the antechamber and into the council chamber. It was round, set up like an amphitheater with twelve seating levels going downward to the center. The bottom level contained a wooden platform and a dozen heavy wooden chairs. The symbolism of the twelve steps and twelve chairs irritated Ess. Was this conscious or unconscious reference to the twelve Apostles? That begged the next question: Who among the leadership fancied himself the Messiah? How long had it been since any of them read their Bibles, and did they remember that all but the Apostle John had been martyred?

Five of the twelve chairs were occupied and faced the aisle of steps through the twelve levels of seating. Ess only recognized two of the five faces—two of the three Council members whose assistants had been replaced by Revisionist doppelgangers. Where was the third, Mrs. Polidory? Would she join them?

When she passed the seventh level of seating, Ess saw her three lawyers sitting on the first row of seats, facing the five members of the Council. She stumbled with the cool relief that shot through her. Phoebe and Clytie both reached out to steady her and her face heated, even as she fought a grin. That bit of clumsiness should reinforce the image of the frail victim of some nefarious biological attack.

Ess suspected she had feared, even if only subconsciously, that she would find only Endicott waiting, that Lewis and MacDonald had been waylaid before they reached the council chamber to make their report on her. Endicott would be free to warn his superiors that Ess and her grandparents suspected them, and to reveal the location of the lotus and the activities of the Blue Lotus Society.

Lewis got up to bring a chair out of the row and put it in the open area directly in front of the platform and the five leaders. Ess sat down, and Phoebe took a seat on the other side of the center aisle, in the front row. Clytie stepped up onto the platform and joined the five facing her. Ess wondered if she should have expected it. Yet shouldn't this woman who claimed to be a friend of her mother have at least warned her? Clytie's presence, welcoming her, was most likely part of the testing she would have to undergo to prove that she hadn't fooled Endicott, Lewis and MacDonald, that she was indeed the long-missing Odessa Vivian Fremont.

"For someone who has been told to expect the Spanish Inquisition," Nathanael Ogilve said from his spot in what had been the center of the group, "your smile seems somewhat out of place."

To Ess's surprise, he winked at her, making a total lie of his growl-filled voice and expression.

Chapter Seventeen

"Excuse me, sir," Ess said, "but now that the whirlwind of my arrival has settled down, it occurred to me that we could save a great deal of time by simply taking me to my family vault and letting me prove, through crystal and blood, that I am who I say I am. As I understand it, I am the last Fremont to have been presented to the lock for coding. My parents and grandparents never returned here, never had a chance to present anyone else, to allow them access, so unless someone found my missing brother and persuaded Ulysses — oh, wait, he was never coded. The chance of his blood being so close a match to either mine or my parents that he can slip past the safeguards of the crystal lock are so low, it's near impossible that he could have snuck in through some non-existent back entrance and coded some outsider to our lock."

A single pair of hands clapped slowly, with a snap-pop sound of air caught between slightly cupped palms. Graebausch stood slowly from his seat on the left end of the group. Whickham sat between him and Ogilve.

"You know a great deal, Miss Fremont, for someone who has had most of her memories and vital Originator information blocked in her mind." He took a step forward, bending forward slightly and hooking his forefingers in the slit pockets of his vest. It took some restraint on Ess's part not to recoil. He struck her as a practiced orator preparing to hold forth for hours, and likely try to harangue her into submission.

No Fremont ever submitted to deceivers, thieves, or traitors.

"I have spent eight days crossing the width of these United States and the territories, sir, with nothing to do but fill in vast gaps in my education, at the hands of three highly educated lawyers. What would you recommend I had done with my time? Embroidered? Recited poetry? I may be ill, and physical effort may tax me yet, but my mind is alert and I detest being bored or wasting valuable time. May I ask, did you take a walk or perhaps a nap while Mr. Endicott and his associates reported to you what I have been doing? I was a Pinkerton, sir. They do not employ delicate, frilly, empty-headed misses!"

Clytie muffled a chuckle behind her hand. Ogilve gripped the armrests of his throne-like chair, leaned forward, and cough-laughed. Whickham's expression indicated he had something sour, perhaps rotten, stuck in his throat. The other two gentlemen, between Clytie and Ogilve, exchanged bemused looks. Ess immediately wrote them off as harmless, neither for her nor against her. Behind her, Phoebe muffled her laughter into squeaks, while the three lawyers sounded like they were either choking or finding it hard to breathe.

Fremonts, as Graebausch must have forgotten, defended themselves by attacking. Fremonts, as her grandparents had most likely done, turned the enemy's plans and weapons into defensive tools and fortresses. The moment Ernest and Matilda were released, they would have something at hand to soundly pummel Graebausch and his associates.

Or, what was more likely — and Ess fought not to laugh as the thought occurred to her — she was the weapon, primed years ago and just needing a name and a face for the targeting function of the weapon.

For you, Granny. For you, Grandfather. She took a sharp, quick breath. *For you, Mother and Father.*

"All right then. We'll take it on faith, for now, that you are indeed Odessa Fremont and not some cleverly disguised and painted, thoroughly trained spy, sent in to infiltrate us." Graebausch took two steps forward. "But that faith will only extend for another twenty minutes, another quarter mile of walking. If you are up to it. That is, if you are truly ill."

"I verify that Miss Fremont is experiencing shortness of breath, dizziness, restriction of blood flow, upset stomach and other maladies best not mentioned in mixed company," Dr. Lockhart called from the back of the room. "What sort of walk are you proposing?"

"Knowing her grandparents and how they played with people's minds, I am sure Miss Fremont proposed the vaults specifically to stop us from going there. Let us go to the vaults, then."

Other members of the council voiced some concerns, insisting on following the set order of the meeting. Ogilve rapped his cane on the floor in noisy protest, demanding control of the meeting. Ess held herself perfectly still and tried not to cheer.

Good. Let it happen as rapidly as possible. I can't wait to see their faces when they see the vault is empty.

She caught her breath. If her dream was accurate, it was an actual memory and not something she had heard her grandparents discussing but had never done. Perhaps the dream was a result of her grandparents instructing her *how* to empty the vault, rather than a memory?

Pride goeth before the fall. Please, Lord Almighty, let it be their pride and not mine!

Ess imagined this was how condemned men felt on their way to their executions, with three members of the Council leading the way down the tunnels and ramps and spiral staircases. The other three brought up the rear, with her in the middle, leaning on Lewis' arm for support, and Endicott and MacDonald walking ahead of them. She learned different people produced different colors from their lighting crystals. The shades and tints couldn't have anything to do with the personality or strength of good or evil in their minds and hearts. Graebausch's light had a yellowish tint, while

Whickham's tended toward a pale blue, and Ogilve's had a lovely green like fresh spring grass, just like Endicott's crystal. A soothing lavender streaked over her shoulder, accompanied by a soft tapping, and she looked back once to see Dr. Lockhart coming up behind her. He winked at her.

Graebausch underestimated the length of time it took for their procession to wind its way downward and along the passageway stretching out eastward, toward the fault lines. At twenty-nine minutes and forty-three seconds from the time they left the council chamber, they reached an alcove in a long, dark corridor that curved slightly to the left, just like in Ess's dream-memories. That was encouraging. The mineral coloration seemed the same, but of course the dimensions were somewhat diminished. She had last been here when she was six years old. Everything was much larger in comparison to her back then.

Ess didn't fight the shiver that worked through her when Ogilve gestured for her to step forward and put her hand on the panel of crystal. Every bit of weakness or emotion would work in her favor in the masquerade. She hoped. Despite knowing it was coming, she still flinched at the sensation of needles swiftly piercing her palm and fingers, and pulled her hand away to look at it without thinking. She still expected to see blood. Someone snorted to her right, and someone else made a satisfied "hmph" sound. What did that prove to them? Other than that she didn't know what to expect, since she hadn't been here since infancy?

Her head ached from all the questions and possibilities and the deception she had to maintain.

Slower than in her dream, perhaps because of the many years since it was last opened, the door panel slid inward a few inches, then to the side. Ess held her breath, anticipating a gust of stale air. She felt nothing. The light crystals did not glow, not even a spark.

"What is supposed to happen now?" She glanced at Ogilve. When movement on her other side drew her attention, she turned to Graebausch.

He sniffed and gestured for her to step into the vault. Ess thought a moment, long enough for the left corner of his mouth to draw up in a sneer, then held out her hand for the light crystal in his. He took a step back. Several people behind her chuckled, but in the slightly odd acoustics of the passageway, she couldn't identify the voices. Taking a deep breath, she stepped over the threshold.

An invisible spark hit her in the forehead, just enough to sting, then spread to envelope her. Ess gasped and took a step backward, anticipating attack. Had some enemy gotten into the vault after all, and set a trap? Had her grandparents come back and put up a guard against intruders?

Light covered her in a thin film, like a soap bubble, and the sting turned to a warm, almost tickling sensation. Ess laughed, bursting with energy, feeling as refreshed as stepping out into a dewy cool morning and taking a deep breath of air tinted with mint and apple. Light burst from the crystals inset into the walls.

Her laughter turned to a gasp, only partially planned. Most of the people in the passageway behind her let out gasps and curses. The sound was echoed and punctuated by the clatter of the empty wooden shelves falling apart, as if the sound was enough to shatter them. Ess took a step back into the passageway. The lights didn't die, but a cloud of dust and fine debris from the disintegrating shelves stopped at the doorway. Stopped by whatever defensive field had been established.

"What happened?" Ess demanded, gesturing at the piles of broken boards and settling dust.

She barely stopped herself from glancing at the place in the wall where her grandmother had opened the stone and deposited that intriguing crystal whistle. Since the rest of the dream had been proven true, that meant the whistle was there, and she needed to retrieve it.

"Mr. Endicott," she continued, when Graebausch and Whickham gaped and stammered and muttered between them. "You told me my answers were here, but there's absolutely nothing! How are my memories to be awakened thoroughly, how am I to find out what happened to my grandparents, if there is nothing to be retrieved, nothing to help me?"

Ess turned a quick circle, trying to get at least a glimpse of everyone's faces, gauging their reactions. They all seemed stunned. Gauging which expressions had more panic, fury, or disappointment, as opposed to surprise, was tricky. Especially with the different tints in the light, clashing with each other's crystals as people stepped up to look into the vault or moved into shifting clusters to talk, to ask questions, to make suggestions. She stayed in the doorway, her back to it, while she watched the reactions around her.

Graebausch's expression settled back into what she assumed was his customary cynical sneer. Ess supposed anyone who spent their daily life working against what they had vowed to support would be cynical. Since they couldn't be trusted, how could they trust? He gestured for the two men who remained unnamed to move aside. He stomped up to the doorway and reached to push Ess aside, since she effectively, and deliberately, blocked the doorway into the vault.

"What are you doing, sir?" Endicott said, his tones dropping the pleasant chill in the air a few more degrees. He stepped up and caught hold of Ess's elbow, as if he expected her to lose her balance.

Graebausch glared at Ess, silently ordering her aside. She didn't quite need to fake a shiver, and let Endicott guide her a few steps to the right. The other man took two steps forward, to enter the vault.

A flash of non-light made Ess blink and flinch away. Graebausch cursed and staggered backward, almost losing his balance. He lunged forward. Another flash. This time the light seemed tinted a dark violet. He bounced backward, landing on his rump with an even louder curse. Ess covered her mouth with both hands, to muffle the laughter that wanted to burst out. She wanted to ask him why he didn't learn better the first time.

Whickham and the man he addressed as Butterfield tried the invisible door, with a little more caution than Graebausch displayed. The flash of non-light wasn't quite as strong, indicating the repelling field reacted in direct proportion to the force used against it.

"I have an idea," Dr. Lockhart said. "Knowing how Matilda's mind worked..." A charmingly roguish smile lit his face. "Clytie, would you and Odessa oblige me?"

He directed them to lock arms and walk through the doorway in step. Clytie let out a gasp, ending in a chuckle as the sting-tickle washed over them. They remained linked together as they turned around to face the others in the passageway, some with their mouths dropping open. Ess made a mental note how Graebausch, Whickham and the other unnamed man had somewhat sour expressions and were silent, even exchanging glances, while the others dove into discussing what exactly had been done to create such a discriminatory defensive field. Ess gathered that none of them knew such a barrier existed or was even possible. That led to the question of what other inventions her grandparents had come up with, and never divulged to even their allies. Or was the problem that her grandparents had trusted no one here in the passageway, the current leadership of the Originators, with such inventions?

Most of the company retired to Butterfield's workshop. Ess learned on the walk that he had also been a student of Matilda's. He specialized in adapting the crystal from the Great Machine for all sorts of uses for the Originators. His great-grandfather, he told Ess as they walked up several levels to his workshop, had theorized that crystals contained energy much like electricity, and could be harnessed like steam or combustion engines to start the laborious process of recreating all the miraculous technology of the ancestors who had come from the future. Ess found the information fascinating enough that she nearly forgot to cough, lose her balance, and pretend to be winded when they reached his workshop.

For the remainder of the day, Clytie, Dr. Lockhart, Ess, Lewis, Phoebe, Ogilve and the now-named Mr. Sinclair, sat around Butterfield's desk. They theorized and referenced dozens of hand-written journals of experiments and memories from the ancestors, and speculated on just what Matilda Fremont had done to establish the field that defended the vault. Ess wondered if any of them remembered that the vault door had been left open. Not that it mattered, since it was visibly empty and she was the only one who could walk through it. Unless of course, the vault door had been left open deliberately to allow Graebausch or Whickham or Mrs. Polidory and their assistants to attempt to penetrate the field. For all she knew, right that moment they were assaulting it with their own crystal devices. Who knew what the Revisionists had come up with using whatever pieces of crystal they had obtained over the generations?

Ess's top priority now was returning to the vault in secret to retrieve that whistle. She had to make a miraculous—but not too miraculous—recovery from her illness, so no one would be surprised if they caught her moving about without her escorts, and without losing her breath or her balance. She had been relieved when Phoebe didn't completely unpack her clothes, so the boy clothes hidden in the false bottom of her trunk remained secret. The less anyone suspected Ess was prepared for stealthy activities, the smaller the chances she would be watched and caught.

~~~~~

Dinner wasn't quite the trying situation Ess had feared. In deference to her weakened condition and the shock of finding the vault empty, Ogilve decided the reception and dinner would not go forward as planned. Ess dined with her three advisors, the Council and their assistants in a dining room that seated twenty, off the central dining area. That area held twenty long tables that seemed adequate to seat twenty each. Only a third of them seemed to be occupied as she and Phoebe walked the perimeter of the room to the smaller dining room. Ess held a pleasant expression on her face and nodded to anyone who made eye contact with her as she passed. She wondered if she looked as overwhelmed as she felt. A room, underground, lit well enough that it didn't feel like it was underground, large enough to seat four hundred people? Just how many could fit into Sanctuary at any one time? She tried to calculate how many supplies would be needed to accommodate that many people, the water, ventilation, and waste disposal, the medical facilities, and the power to excavate such a place.

Someone called Phoebe just before the two of them reached the closed door of the dining room. With a muttered apology, she hurried away, to the far corner of the dining room. Ess watched her go, wondering if any of the men in the group of nine young men and women happened to be a sweetheart, if they were Phoebe's closest friends, or just fellow students. What would it have been like if she had been brought here for training? Would this dining room be so familiar that she wouldn't be amazed by the size?

To give Phoebe some privacy, Ess continued to the dining room. She grasped the latch of the door and slowly pushed down. Angry voices penetrated the wooden panel just before the latch clicked open. Ess held her breath and debated for perhaps five seconds whether to shove the panel open and hope for a loud creak, to warn whoever was inside. Acknowledging that once a Pinkerton, always a Pinkerton, she eased the panel open slowly, praying the hinges didn't creak in inverse proportion to the speed of movement.

Three men argued, stomping over each other's words, enough she couldn't make out individual words. Until she had enough of a gap to see into the room, Ess couldn't make out the voices, either. She almost stopped
~~~~~

pushing when she recognized Endicott's warm baritone, with sharp edges.

When she could look around the door panel, she saw Graebausch and Whickham, facing down Endicott. From their postures, well-lit by brightly burning lamps hanging from four chandeliers, it was clear the two members of the Council were joined against the lawyer. Ess struggled with an odd feeling that tightened her chest. Strongest was the sense of relief that the traitors were visibly divided over something. She knew better than to stand there and try to decipher the source of their disagreement. That was just begging to be caught. Backing up, she eased the door shut and turned to face out into the dining room. Just in time. Phoebe hurried to catch up with her, followed by several of the young men and women she had gone to speak with. Ess had met none of them so far. Phoebe had just finished introductions when Lewis, MacDonald, and Clytie swept into the room. The students scattered.

The argument had ended, at least audibly, when the five entered the private dining room. Endicott stood at one of the sideboards, fixing a cup of coffee, while the other two men were seated at the far end of the long table, heads bent together, talking in low voices. Ess looked for some sign of strain in Endicott's face but didn't see a single wrinkle or drop of sweat.

If dinner was intended to be pleasant, to make up for Ess's reception in the council chamber, it failed. The discussion circled around theories and research done on memory blocking and unblocking, and speculation on what Matilda had done to Ess's memories. Then it shifted over to the empty vault, the possibility that someone else had emptied the Fremonts' vault, meaning someone had learned to circumvent the security. Several times, Graebausch or Whickham tried to broach the subject of why exactly Matilda and Ernest Fremont had emptied their own vault, and implied that Ess was part of it. Each time, someone cut them off, redirecting the conversation or trying to make a joke of the very idea that the Fremonts, the most brilliant minds among the Originators, had acted against the interests of their associates. Finally, Dr. Lockhart faced down Graebausch.

"If Matilda or Ernest took such action without notifying the leadership, then common sense says someone in power was untrustworthy." He punctuated his words with the thud of his drinking glass settled next to his plate. "Common sense says they would have warned their friends what they were doing. Common sense says if they discovered a friend was a traitor, then they wouldn't have warned that friend. We will never know the answer to that until Judgment Day. Then we can ask them what they were thinking. Until then, I see no reason for such useless, repetitive speculation and innuendo. Your only results are to distress this charming young lady who is as lost and uninformed as any of us." He nodded to Ess, who nodded back to him.

She could have sworn he winked at her. If so, what was he trying to signal her? He knew something about her grandparents' disappearance? He knew they had taken refuge in a time box? He had been warned to empty his vault and prepare for traitors to strike?

Ess's head ached, no need for playacting. She was relieved to finally be dismissed for the evening. Dr. Lockhart took charge of her, offering her his bent arm to escort her away. Her respect for him grew quickly into affection when he said nothing about the uncomfortable dinner conversation and made no reference to the empty vault. Instead, he was entirely the concerned physician, interspersed with some amusing stories about her grandparents, when they and he had been students together here at Sanctuary. He asked her about her physical symptoms, and inquired about her health history, her schedule of exercise and exertion, and what sort of physical training the Pinkertons required of her. She caught him at least six times start to say something along the lines of, "Just like your grandmother," or "That's your grandfather, exactly," always stopping himself before he finished the comparison.

Dr. Lockhart's quarters were lit in blue light from crystals embedded in the walls, and Ess was intrigued to discover that heavy cloth panels had been extended from the walls, meeting in the middle, to effectively block light from leaking upward. The panels didn't touch, but did overlap, allowing for airflow. She found it rather clever, and helped ensure security, if anyone did manage to get past the patrols surrounding the network of canyons enclosing Sanctuary's entrances.

She and Phoebe sat down at the worktable, while Dr. Lockhart went to the long rack of jars full of herbs, infusions, tisanes, powders, and pastes. This was her first chance to really talk to this young woman, near her own age. There had always been something going on, someone else requiring her attention. Dr. Lockhart laughed when Ess apologized for what could be taken as rudeness.

"There is no one among her year group of students more balanced, more commonsense, or more forgiving than Miss Stryker," he said, as he ground several ingredients together in the pestle.

"I hope that doesn't mean everyone imposes on you," Ess said, trying not to wince. Her words certainly sounded inane to her. On the other hand, she had to say something to keep from blurting her first response — to ask if Phoebe was related to the late Mr. Stryker.

Chapter Eighteen

Phoebe laughed, which was reassuring.

"Dr. Lockhart is trying to be funny. What he neglected to say is that people may try to impose on me, and they may try to play foolish tricks, but they learn rather quickly that I do not suffer fools." She fluttered her eyelashes. "Meaning if someone tries to trick me, I manage to turn it around on them."

"Vengeance is mine, saith Miss Stryker?" Ess offered.

Phoebe had a lovely, rippling laugh.

"There is something of an unpleasant tradition among our students who earn the right to come here." Dr. Lockhart paused while he eyed a trickle of some pink-tinted liquid going into a clear vessel, and then tipped the contents of the pestle in and mixed it with a glass rod. "They like to prove what they have learned, and they especially love to test their theories, their experiments and inventions on each other. Unfortunately, so much of what we focus on nowadays is defensive weaponry and devices, so..." He shrugged as he lifted the glass vessel and studied the contents.

"You have a bright future in detecting stealthy attacks from our enemies?" Ess offered.

"I would like to try my hand at being a detective," Phoebe said with a deprecating little shrug. "I think it would be fascinating, investigating, asking questions, wearing disguises, taking on false names, tricking people into making mistakes so they can be caught in their crimes."

"Perhaps you could ask your friends among the Pinkertons to take on an apprentice or two," Dr. Lockhart offered. "When our current crisis has settled down."

"Perhaps." Ess nodded slowly, trying to compose her expression into something thoughtful, and praying she didn't reveal the shudder struggling up from deep inside. What exactly did Phoebe Stryker know about August Stryker, and the time he spent as Mr. Judson, Pinkerton?

If she asked, would Allistair Fitch support her request to allow Originator students to apprentice with the famous detective agency? Or would he balk, especially when he learned the surname of one student? Ess almost laughed aloud to realize she seriously considered the idea. Did she honestly think she had any influence in the agency? She could just hear her brother teasing her that she had quite a bit of influence with Allistair.

"Here we are, your first dose." Dr. Lockhart stepped up to the table and offered her a bottle with a clamp lid. The liquid inside was a murky brownish-pinkish swirl full of specs that alternately floated and sank.

"Am I supposed to drink it, or bathe in it or put it on my face?"

Dr. Lockhart chuckled and gave her a narrow-eyed look as he shoved the bottle across the table to her. "Drink half when you go to bed, and half when you wake up, before your feet touch the floor."

"I am tempted to accuse you of taking some revenge on Granny."

Ess still had a most unpleasant taste and texture on her tongue an hour later, completely alone for the first time since she woke in San Francisco that morning. A sensation of running full-tilt remained with her, so she thought the four-poster bed vibrated a little as she sat down on it. She closed her eyes and considered just dropping backward and lying there, without taking off her robe.

The sensation of grit and bits of slightly sticky globules catching on her tongue fought against the spinning that should have sucked her downward into sleep. Ess focused on the texture of the ceiling of her room and took slow, deep breaths, willing her stomach to settle down. She concentrated hard enough that she didn't hear the first few taps on her door. When she did, and called for whoever was outside to come in, she sat up too quickly. She stumbled across the room to her basin and pitcher, expecting her stomach to empty.

When she felt a little steadier, she turned around, wiped sweat off her forehead, and found Lewis and MacDonald watching.

"I'm tempted to ask you not to get too caught up in the part you're playing." Lewis pulled a chair out from the wall and offered it to her.

"Not by choice," she said, nodding thanks as she sank into the chair. Ess felt better sitting up than she had lying down. "What's happened?"

"There was some ruckus over Mrs. Polidory not arriving as expected, and then we connected the names of the imposters with three members of the Council. Imagine our surprise to learn that all three are rumored to be an alliance unto themselves against the rest of the Council," MacDonald said.

"Do you know why Mrs. Polidory is missing?"

"Oh, we found out so very much while you were plotting with our elders." Lewis winked, but his attempt at levity didn't reach his eyes. His smile faded too quickly. He traded glances with MacDonald. "We have a number of friends who are trusted with investigations and they were willing to tell us about a report that just came in. We know what she was doing, where she was, before she vanished; both she and her assistant. Some witnesses say soldiers who appeared seemingly out of thin air snatched them. Or maybe yanked up into thin air would be more accurate."

"Ah." She didn't hide her thin, headachy smile now. Uly had promised they would follow up on the three conspirators if it didn't interfere with the *Golden Nile*'s rapid voyage west.

"That's ten you owe me." MacDonald leaned against the closed door.

"What did you two wager on this time?" Ess's headache eased a little more. Maybe later she would be worried over this tendency of such otherwise respectable lawyers to wager at the drop of a hat.

"If you had anything to do with the disappearance." He crossed his arms over his chest. "I also wagered that you are irritated with our esteemed Randall Endicott. What crime has he committed, that you don't lean on your father's closest friend any longer?"

"Fordyce Chamberlain was my father's closest friend."

"When it came to getting into scrapes, yes, but he and Randall were thicker than thieves—"

"No such phrase," she retorted.

"Something turned you against him. Maybe he hasn't noticed, with all the work he's had to do, but those of us on the sidelines." He smirked and nodded at Lewis. "Well, some of us have noticed."

"He isn't Randall Endicott," Ess whispered. "Any more than those three frauds are the people they claim to be."

Lewis swore. MacDonald slammed his fist into the wall—stone, with a thick coating of quilted material to absorb the damp and insulate against the ever-present chill. He didn't make a sound, though she could have sworn she heard bones crack in his hand.

She told them what Wallace had found and that the *Golden Nile* was on its way to Sanctuary. Ess's stomach finally settled down and her headache faded. They made plans for exchanging information, what information to look for, and tentative plans for keeping watch on Endicott, Graebausch and Whickham. They both embraced her before they slipped out of her room and returned to theirs. She choked on a bit of laughter when MacDonald threatened to tuck her into bed. Then when they were gone, she curled up in her bed and buried her face in her pillow, and she wept.

They never doubted her for a moment. She couldn't comprehend how she had been so blessed with such trusting allies.

Perhaps the Almighty had granted them to her, to make up for the traitor who stood as close as her heartbeat.

"Uly," she whispered, when her tears dried. "When are you going to get here?"

~~~~~

Morning came with aches in her head and her stomach. Ess rolled out of bed after taking her second dose, as ordered, and nearly went to her knees before she caught herself. She staggered and stumbled across the room to the privy cabinet, barely reaching it in time. Her stomach twisted and acid filled her mouth as whatever remained inside came back up. Twice while washing up, she had to sit down and catch her breath. When Phoebe knocked on the door and came in to help her dress, Ess wasn't sure if she wanted to tell her to go away or hug her in gratitude.

Her underclothes felt heavy and damp by the time they reached the
~~~~~

dining room. Phoebe led Ess to a table, told her to sit before she fell off her new, sturdy boots, and announced she would bring breakfast for both of them. Ess was grateful. For the first time since she got up, the throbbing behind her eyes didn't threaten to pop them out of her skull.

The fading ache reminded her of the efforts to meet with Carmen in her dreams. The silence confirmed her fear that the other girl hadn't managed to escape before her father's enemies took her cross, and the crystal rose in the center of it. Ess could only pray that Agent Sutter had enough information, including several sketches, to find Carmen and make sure she was safe. Thinking about those sketches gave Ess an idea. Since sketching sometimes helped her relax, she took out her sketching book from her satchel and let the images in her mind flow through her pencil.

"Do you know her?" Clytie said, interrupting just as the tightness eased in the cords in her neck.

Ess flinched, swiping the pencil across Carmen's face. That struck her as funny, but when she glanced up, her smile froze at the flicker of guilt or perhaps pain in the woman's eyes.

"Do you?" More of the aching and nausea fled away with a surge of adrenalin and a nebulous idea.

"I'm not sure." She glanced around the dining hall. The hunching of her shoulders eased a little, making Ess wonder what worried her. A glance at the empty tables around them seemed to help her relax. Sliding into the seat next to Ess, Clytie asked. "Where did you meet her?"

"She was a friend of Mother's... I think."

"Yes," Clytie whispered.

"Her name was Anna."

"Put that sketch away, Odessa. Don't let anyone see it." She reached over to close the sketchbook.

"Tell me about her. So I understand." Ess licked her lips. "I think she is part of why my parents were—"

"Hush," the woman whispered, and pressed her forefinger against Ess's lips.

"Tell me about her?" she repeated, lowering her voice.

"There's little to tell, other than that being her friend was... dangerous," the woman finished on a sigh. She tried to smile, then let out a louder sigh. "I'm not even sure Anna was her real name. For safety, no one was told the new identity fabricated for her. The name she used when she hid with us was Anna, and she was a Revisionist." Her eyes narrowed when Ess didn't respond. "You knew that?"

"Just bits and pieces. Don't tell anyone, but I've been plagued with a cascade of dreams ever since I fell ill, and I could swear they are returning memories. As if the barrier in my mind is disintegrating."

"No, I will tell no one. Keep it secret, just like your knowledge of Anna." Clytie studied her face for a moment, flickers of myriad emotions darkening and brightening her eyes. "We helped her escape the Revisionists. Over the years, there has been a steady trickle of those who have renounced the goals, the doctrines of their ancestors. Some walk away and make new lives for themselves. Others are so revolted by what their ancestors tried to do, they join us. However, there are those whom the Revisionists will not allow to leave. They know too much, or they possess valuable talents."

"Anna could hear the crystal."

"Anna could sing to the crystal. It was amazing to see. She could call up visions, images from a chunk of crystal as small as a pea, draw light and energy from it, more amazing than the kinetoscope. She could sing to the crystal and make it store the sound of her voice."

"Do you think I could sing to crystal and make it show pictures, too?"

"Possibly. But for your own safety, go slowly. There is an instability... Be careful of who you trust with your revelations and returning memories." Clytie's gaze turned distant again.

"What happened to Anna?"

"Oh—well—let's see. I last saw her before you were born. She moved from one group to another, to blur her trail, never staying anywhere long enough for anyone to remember her. She was supposed to cut all ties, and yet somehow she kept in contact with Vivian. I know that because I heard about one time when Vivian sent Edward and some of his friends racing across the country to rescue Anna. Someone among the Revisionists found her, entirely by accident, supposedly. People wondered and asked too many questions, how could Vivian have known where she was and that she needed help, from so far away? After that, Anna vanished again, and there were whispers of unpleasantness from people trying to pressure Vivian to reveal where she had gone. Your parents pulled back from many Originator contacts after that, as if they didn't trust anyone." Clytie patted the sketchbook. "Keep this hidden. Better yet, destroy the drawing. And pray that wherever she is, Anna no longer looks like herself."

"Twenty, thirty years ago? How could she?" Ess tried to smile, despite the renewed throbbing at the base of her skull. She had a feeling like something had slithered down her throat and churned through her stomach. If she understood what little she had caught from Carmen's thoughts, Anna was dead—but that meant mother and daughter looked enough alike to be dangerous.

Most definitely, Ess needed to contact Agent Sutter and emphasize the urgency of finding Carmen and bringing her to safety. Even if she didn't have the crystal rose, she could still be in great danger from the Revisionists.

Phoebe brought breakfast for all three of them, having seen Clytie sit down to talk with Ess. The three settled down for a pleasant breakfast. Phoebe saw the sketchbook and wanted to discuss technique. She wanted to apply for a position in a traveling team but had no outstanding skills in learning languages or using weapons or keeping records. Her sketching talent was above average, according to Clytie, but she felt she lacked a certain something.

Ess's stomach rebelled after the fourth bite of hotcakes. She excused herself and stumbled toward the hallway to the privy closet. At least, Ess hoped that was the way. The floor kept tipping under her feet and the wall tried to sidle out of reach when she leaned against it to regain her balance.

"What's this?" Dr. Lockhart appeared in front of her as she stumbled toward a door she found impossible to read, with sweat streaming across her face and stinging her eyes. "Another attack? Something is definitely wrong with you, lass. Come along with me." He hooked his arm through hers and nearly yanked her off her feet. "We'll figure out what's wrong and fix you up right as rain."

She stumbled along with him for a dozen steps before her stomach tried to turn inside out. Her words garbled as she tried to warn him.

"None of that here. I hate making messes I won't want to clean up, don't you?" he said with enough cheerfulness, she wanted to punch him. "Try this."

An aromatic cylinder collided with the end of her nose. Startled, Ess inhaled deeply. She could have sworn from the stinging that she must have inhaled sparks. The lining of her nose burned and the sensation shot straight up to her brain, then plummeted into her stomach with an explosion of spices, heavy on cloves and ginger. The nausea stopped as if chopped with a guillotine. Through her coughing and gasping for breath, she heard him tell someone to find Phoebe and tell her Ess was with him. Then while she was trying to clear her eyes, he set off down the passageway at a pace she wouldn't have expected from a man with a mechanical leg.

"Did I mention the research and concocting and plain old cooking Matilda and I used to do together, when we were students?"

"No—I don't think so."

"Ah. Pity. Still, a clever girl like you shouldn't have been caught out so easily. Steps here."

"Caught?" Ess focused on her feet. How did he manage to fly down those stone steps? Perhaps she hallucinated all this?

Quick enough to startle her, they came out into the open air of Dr. Lockhart's workshop. He guided her into a chair at the end of the long table with a little more force than necessary. Ess caught at the arms of the chair to stay upright and took deep breaths. The open room steadied around her.

Understanding dawned as her brain stopped spinning.

"You poisoned me?" She tried to calculate what force it would take to pick up the chair, swing it around, and knock him off his feet.

"Totally to the contrary. I really did expect better of Matilda's granddaughter." He glanced over his shoulder at her, then turned back to mixing several vials.

"What did you do to me, then?"

"Revealed the tricks you were playing. Well, to be specific, one trick. Matilda and I had some fun when we were a little younger than you, creating a potion that would mimic several unpleasant symptoms without actually forcing you to suffer the illness."

"Ah."

"Indeed. The potion I gave you last night, which you took so obediently and trustingly, and I assume you drank the rest this morning, as ordered?" He waited until she nodded, then stirred the contents of the tall tumbler and crossed back to the table. "It wasn't to cure you, but to reveal the existence of the potion you took. Now, the next question is —"

"If I should toss this in your face and run for my life?" She held out her hand for the tumbler.

"No." He stepped back, evading her reach. "The question is what you're looking for and who you don't trust, that you employ deception."

"Ah."

"Again with the understatement," he muttered, and plunked the tumbler down on the table in front of her. "It's a little late to wonder if you can trust me."

"I'm not wondering."

"Oh, to know what is occurring behind those piercing eyes." He settled in the chair and crossed his arms over his chest, as if preparing to fall asleep, slouched comfortably.

"If you weren't trustworthy, you wouldn't have told me. You tested me, and you aren't the sort of man to waste time with confrontation, when it would be wiser to poison me and blame it on someone else. Most likely one of my companions, or perhaps Phoebe."

"Phoebe?" He watched her down the potion. "Hmm, something tells me you don't need the warning I was preparing to give you, to be careful of that young lady."

Ess finished swallowing. "Because she is August Stryker's niece?"

"Now it is my turn to say 'ah.' And to wonder when you encountered said gentleman."

"Is anyone wondering why he hasn't made contact in a very long time? How long has it been since anyone has heard from him?"

"Mr. Stryker is one of those people whom you try not to think about when he is absent, except to be grateful that he is absent."

"How can he be absent if Phoebe is here to keep watch in his place?"

"Phoebe is... an unwilling accomplice."

"Then why were you about to warn me about her?"

Dr. Lockhart tipped his head back to release a half-dozen rumbling chuckles. "And to think that I came so close to being your grandfather."

"Oh, please, must we go through that again?" Ess mimicked his slouch. Truthfully, she felt so much better now the sensation was almost euphoric, compared to her misery such a short time ago. Now she wished she had finished those hotcakes.

"We need to ensure we can trust each other." He held out both his hands to her, palms up.

Ess slid her hands into his and froze as the image engraved on his left cufflink caught her attention.

"Something wrong?"

"Why do you have deer on your cufflinks?"

"Eh?" He turned his left wrist, to look at the square. "It's not a—well, yes, it's a deer, but more accurately, it's a hart. A play on words. Matilda loved to play with people's names, making up secret codes. I used to tease her that she fell in love with Ernest because the code image for Fremont was an upside down mountain, floating in mid-air."

"Did she—" Ess caught her breath. Without the distraction of that nagging headache and nausea, her mind easily assembled facts into theories and solutions. She turned his hand until she could see the lock-and-key image on the other cufflink. It and the hart were exactly like the images on the strip of paper Hilda had showed her.

"Odessa? What are you thinking?" His smile stiffened and so did his hands, gripping hers.

"Do you have the time lock?" she whispered.

"Ah." His smile warmed and he released her wrists while he sank back in his chair again. "They did manage to send the final message after all."

"Hilda got it, and chose not to share it with anyone," she said, pitching her voice soft.

"Lovely woman, Hilda. Highly intelligent. I'm surprised that rascal Giles hasn't yet persuaded her to marry him. He was always sweet on her, you know."

"Giles is dead. And no, I didn't know how he felt." Ess tried to smile. Her heart ached a little. So many small, inconsequential memories raced through her mind. No wonder Giles had dedicated himself to the household. Ess had eavesdropped the day their grandfather told Uly about Hilda's broken heart, so she knew why the housekeeper was so fiercely devoted to Matilda, then to Edward and then to her and Uly.

"When did that happen?" Dr. Lockhart softly thumped the table. "So many things they've kept hidden from us all these years."

"He was killed shortly after my grandparents vanished. We don't really have time for those details, do we?"

Chapter Nineteen

"No." Dr. Lockhart rested his hands over Ess's. "We don't. Now, do you mind telling me what is really going on, young lady?"

"Is there anywhere we can be completely certain of privacy, so we can talk?"

"That grim, eh?" A slow, sly little smile crept up one side of his face, then expanded to the other as his gaze went distant. A snort escaped him and he nodded once for punctuation. "You're still deathly ill, you know."

"Well, I do now." She shared a grin with him. He patted her cheek and gestured for her to lie down on the cot in one of the curtained alcoves off his workroom. She thought hard, while listening to him use some sort of communication system like the speaking tubes on the *Golden Nile*. He sent for Phoebe, first. Guessing she would end up in her room, Ess thought hard about who to include in the conference they would have.

Dr. Lockhart agreed with her, though she could see questions in his eyes when she requested he send for Lewis and MacDonald, but not Endicott.

"What has the man done to irritate you enough to leave him out?" he mused, as he came back to the alcove where she was quite comfortable. The fresh air made for a lovely sickroom, but she imagined it was too easy here for people to eavesdrop. "He was a good friend of your father's, you know."

"So I thought." Ess sighed and sat up. There was something very vulnerable about lying on the cot.

"You Fremonts." He shook his head. "I remember Edward having some kind of argument with Randall. They looked daggers at each other for what seemed like months. Your father dove into his work, and half the time when he saw Randall coming, he would go the other way. Finally they talked, and whatever he said..." He chuckled. "Well, Randall is a very good lawyer. Whatever he had to say, he persuaded Edward to resume their friendship."

"Yes, he's a very good lawyer." She shuddered to think of her father's reaction if he would have ever learned the truth about his good friend.

Phoebe hurtled into the doctor's workroom then, curtailing any chance of private conversation until Ess was settled in her guest quarters, in her nightgown, with a bottle of what Dr. Lockhart promised was a blood purifier that would get her back on her feet in "oh, a day or three, depending on how serious the situation reveals itself to be," said with a solemn wink.

Meaning he was giving her an excuse to hide all day, stay out of the reach of those who couldn't be trusted, and immerse herself in the manuals about the history and layout of Sanctuary, which he sent Phoebe running to fetch. Once the door of her quarters was securely closed again, Dr. Lockhart signaled Ess to silence and brought out a handful of small triangles of crystal, which he set in the corners of the room, perched above eye level. He kept them in place with small dabs of something dark and sticky-looking.

"Ernest and Matilda designed them," he told her, after a tap sent a soft shimmering through the air, visible and audible. After a few seconds, light and sound faded away, but Ess felt the soft resonance in her sinuses. "That was the moment I knew I had been utterly outpaced. He wasn't much of an inventor, more fascinated with theory, but when those two put their heads together, they came up with amazing things. I swear he surpassed his previous brilliance, just to impress her." He made a heavy sigh, but Ess had to laugh, knowing most of it was foolery. "No one outside the room can hear what we say. The vibrations create a sort of insulation against sound. Masking noise, Matilda called it."

Before Ess could ask any questions, a sharp rap on the door gave warning and the door swung open. Lewis and MacDonald stepped into the room, obeying Dr. Lockhart's simple signal of a finger pressed to his lips. They frowned at him, then at her, but obeyed in silence as he gestured for them to settle on the bench against the wall. Now they could all sit in comfort and see each other. Ess snatched up the notebook and pencil that Phoebe had brought for her and drew the three symbols that had been at the bottom of her grandparents' note. She gestured for all three men to turn around and hurried to slip out of bed and pull a robe on over her nightclothes, silently grumbling about the injustice of her figure finally showing up and inconveniencing her at the worst possible time. Then she handed the paper to Lewis and settled back down on the side of the bed.

"Are we permitted to speak now?" he said, after glancing at it and handing the paper to MacDonald.

"Sound masking devices of my grandparents' design," she said, gesturing at the small triangles. The clear crystal had curiously darkened. She wondered if the clarity and lack of color would return when they stopped blocking sound.

"Useful." He nodded to Dr. Lockhart, indicating he guessed where they came from. "What about the mysterious code? Have you unraveled it?"

"Key means lock," she said.

"Egads," MacDonald said and dropped back down onto the bench. "Of course. And that's not a deer — it's a hart." He tipped a salute to Dr. Lockhart off his eyebrow. "So that means he's perfectly safe and trustworthy?"

"One of many, fortunately, in this nest of vipers," Dr. Lockhart said. "More importantly, Matilda entrusted the time lock to me. I can only guess it had something to do with the trouble in South America. We should have a good half hour, at the least, before Phoebe manages to pry the manuals loose from the archives. I wouldn't doubt, with the snarling and sour looks

Graebausch and Whickham and their toadies have been conjuring regarding you, young Odessa, there should be some delays, some protests, and some discussion over whether you can be trusted with the information you truly do need to study."

"Still some doubts about her identity?" Lewis said.

"Among other considerations. There has been rumbling ever since Matilda and Ernest vanished, trying to persuade the loyal they feigned their disappearance so they could switch sides."

"We believe they retreated into a time bubble to save their lives, and we were given the keys, in more ways than one," Ess said with a grimace.

Quickly, the three of them shared the gist of the information the elder Fremonts had left behind, indications of traitors among them, and the news from Wallace, via Uly, that Endicott was an imposter who had taken the real Randall Endicott's place years ago.

"I retained some optimism up until now," Dr. Lockhart said when they finished, and had perhaps two minutes left of his half-hour estimate. "If Endicott is on the side of the Revisionists..." He shook his head. "We could very well be outnumbered, in intelligence and resources, if not actual workers."

"We need to find and free Ess's grandparents. The balance will swing to our side then, and we can come back and..." Lewis shook his head. "No, we cannot simply sail away, no matter how swift the *Nile* might be. We have to deal with this problem here and now, not run away and hope it doesn't grow. Our mere presence here could be the signal for the traitors to act before they lose everything."

"Indeed. While a Fremont lives, with all those secrets hidden deep in her mind, our enemies must either destroy her or turn her to support them," he said, nodding. Then his frown deepened. "*Nile*, you say?"

"Our airship. As far as Mr. Endicott knows," Ess said, "it is on its way to South America, to the spot where my grandparents' expedition vanished. However, when Uly contacted me with the information about the substitution, they chose to come here instead."

"On an airship. How soon will they arrive?"

"I will need to check with Uly."

"Not within these walls and tunnels," Lewis said. "We'll find some way to sneak you outside tonight, past the sentries."

"Check with your brother how?" Dr. Lockhart wanted to know.

"Oh, Doctor, we have amazing developments to show you," MacDonald said.

Ess played a discontented, whining invalid for those who visited her throughout the day. She kept a running tally, trying to determine which visitors were preparing for a shift in power, if they wanted to truly be her friend, or they wanted to test if she could be swayed to support either the traitors or a new group seeking power among the Originators. Someday, she hoped they would have enough distance from these troubling times to laugh about so many people who couldn't seem to understand that she was an invalid and needed rest.

Dr. Lockhart checked on her every few hours. When Ess apologized for monopolizing her time, Phoebe laughed and said she enjoyed the respite from running errands for anyone who had a claim to her feet and hands. The girl was a wealth of information, and helped Ess figure out the multiple layers of maps and connecting ladders and ramps among the tunnels, and gave her an idea of all the people who populated Sanctuary.

When Phoebe went to fetch Ess's dinner, Dr. Lockhart came with a small bundle wrapped in multiple layers of cottonwool and canvas. He had only taken two layers of padding off, much diminishing it in size, when Ess felt the first shimmering of crystal against her skin. With each layer, the resonance grew stronger, until it was audible. It became a chord.

"It's an incomplete chord," Ess murmured, as the construction rested on the blanket covering her legs. It was a mass of crystal triangles, interlocked or woven together so that visibly they all seemed to run into each other, Soft ripples of color and what she could only call non-color, non-light, moved through the room like ripples in a pond. Visible and yet somehow tangible, like a filmy curtain brushing across her skin, or a thin rivulet of warm water that passed through her and made her bones tingle.

"Chord? As in music?" Dr. Lockhart stepped back from depositing the construction on her blankets and rubbed his hands together. She imagined they itched slightly, like hers did, wanting to touch and yet fearing what energy or subliminal chords would shoot through her upon physical contact. "Yes." He settled down on the nearest visitor chair placed by her bed, and stroked his chin as he narrowed his one good eye at the mass of crystal rods. "Ernest kept insisting that music meant much more in controlling the Great Machine, all crystal, than we could understand."

"Is that—" She slid both hands under the top blanket and used it as insulation so she could pick up the object, cradled between both hands, to bring it closer to her eyes. Ess feared she would work herself into a real headache, just studying the confusing thing. There was no discernible warping or melting, and yet each bar seemed to lead into another triangle, around and around.

"Yes, the time lock." He snorted. "Matilda had great fun constructing some out of trash, bits of glassmaker's fancy, with colors woven in. She called them decoys, and convinced several of her friends who were musicians to fashion them into Aeolian harps, in a sense, so when the wind blew over them they sang." The amusement faded from his eyes.

"Decoys, as in helping to discern who was loyal and who was a traitor?" Ess guessed.

"Every single one of them vanished, over time. Some were broken. Some were designed to break as soon as they were stolen. I found two in

Stryker's workroom, shortly after your grandparents were reported missing." A heavy sigh escaped him. "I found him in my workroom countless times over the years, ostensibly waiting for me to return from some fool's errand — wild goose chase, instigated by him, no doubt. I always had the feeling something had been moved, something wasn't quite right."

"I know this will sound impertinent, especially since I still know so very little about how things are done here—"

"But you want to know why I didn't report my suspicions to someone I trusted? Why I didn't accuse Stryker or have someone investigate him? My dear child... I have been under suspicion myself over the years. You suspected me. Conditions were so precarious after your parents died, and then your grandparents vanished and... I decided it was safer to play the curmudgeon, loudly decry politics on all sides, and sit back to wait." He winked. "Wait for a messiah, perhaps? A hero from prophecy and legend."

"Hardly." She delighted in her unladylike snort, and drew her knees up under the blankets, letting the time lock slide down the slope of her legs to rest between her feet.

"How do you think it works?"

"How should I know?" Ess sighed and rested her right cheek on her upraised knee, so she could look at the enthralling, aggravating tangle of crystal triangles and look at him without much shifting or eye strain. "Granny would know."

"Matilda would tell you to stop asking questions and just use the wretched thing."

"I think she was playing games with us," she murmured, trying to relax and encourage the ephemeral thread of idea drifting up through her thoughts. "Another decoy... it's not the lock at all... but why did she call it the lock if..." She bit her lip, holding back the growl of frustration that would snap the fragile strands of the idea.

"Maybe she called it a lock just so she could point to me," Dr. Lockhart offered. "She and Ernest did love their word and symbol games and playing with people's minds, until they were like India rubber balls and go bouncing around the room."

"Like drawing a key when she meant a..." Ess sat up, and nearly forgot herself, stretching out her legs so the time lock rolled toward the edge of the mattress. She snatched at it. Tingling, hot-and-icy energy shot up her arm, swirled around her brain and then down her torso to escape out her toes, with such force she thought she should see sparks pierce the blankets.

"A what?" Dr. Lockhart prompted.

"When is a key that symbolizes a lock not a lock?" She giggled and pressed her free hand over her mouth to muffle the sound. "When it's a key. No, that's silly, but..." Ess waved her hand, brushing away the concern starting to crease his face. "It's the time key, not the lock. Hidden in plain sight like Mr. Poe's letter. The chord will complete when it's near the lock.

It's the detector for the time trap, the box Granny and Grandfather and their team are hiding in. I shouldn't doubt, when we're close enough, the two will be drawn together, just like when crystal fragments come close enough to the lotus they attract each other."

"The lotus," he whispered, and shook his head. "I should like to see it for myself one of these days. It's a legend among us, even those of us who serve here at Sanctuary all our lives."

"Well, if things happen as we fear they will, you will have no recourse but to come on board the *Golden Nile* to find shelter. I'm sure Athena will show it to you. No doubt you've been changed by your guardianship of the time lock—time key," she corrected, as she reluctantly put the construct down on the blankets again. Too much euphoria might just be bad for her. Ess feared becoming too enamored of the sensation, like some men were enamored by liquor and opium. "You've been changed by your exposure over the years, enough that you might hear the lotus, feel it working." She picked up the first layer of discarded wrapping to fold around it again.

"That would be something, wouldn't it?" He bent to help her.

"We have a theory, Uly and I, that all of us, all the Originator descendants, should be able to hear and feel crystal. We simply need to find a way to block out the disturbances, the dissonance that blocks the music."

"What have the two of you been up to?" He shook his head, his expression clearly admiration.

"We'll tell you tonight, after we show you how we've learned to communicate." Ess's spirits dropped, and she couldn't entirely blame losing contact with the construction. "The sooner we get out of here, the better. I wish... well, to be honest, I came here fearing I would have to destroy Sanctuary, depending on what level of corruption I found here."

"They told you that, did they?" Dr. Lockhart handed her the battered, fire-toughened leather sack that held the time key. "Not sure how I feel about Matilda and Ernest entrusting such perilous information to children. Well, you're not children now, but you were when they told you."

"Showed me. Locked it away in my head." She elbowed her pillows into position. "I am heartily tired of having my head used as a vault."

That earned a chuckle from him.

~~~~~

Uly knew the chances of Ess being able to sneak out of Sanctuary, to some place where she could activate the communication plate without being detected, were slim. He had still come to the room at the nose of the airship and awakened the plate at midnight his time, as agreed, and kept it open, waiting, until one in the morning, Ess's time. He did it the night she arrived in San Francisco, then the next night when she should have been established in Sanctuary, and now tonight. He wasn't sure if he should be grateful for his sister's stubbornness or curse her for it. All disaster required was for one suspicious, untrusting mind, one person who came back to
~~~~~

check on her and found her missing—or worse, followed her outside.

Still, he came to the room tonight and awakened the communication plate and prayed Ess would be smart and cautious and safe.

At ten minutes past midnight, Athena, Ford, and Theo joined him.

At twenty-two minutes past midnight, the communication plate shimmered awake. Uly gripped the sides of his chair. Lunging at the hovering plate, as if he could go through it, wouldn't do them any good. Demanding to know Ess was all right would just waste precious time. After all, she wouldn't use the plate if she wasn't safe.

When the silvery-rainbow haze cleared from the plate, a copy of that frustrating bit of image-code their grandparents had left filled it.

"Ess—"

"Solved it," his sister said, her voice subdued. The paper lowered and shrank, moving away from the plate, and now he could see her face. "It's two words." She beckoned to someone behind the plate.

Light flared and filled the plate, and there was some muttering and apologies. The light came from a lantern, held by whoever stepped into the visual range of the plate, close enough to temporarily blind all of them. When the blob of lantern light moved away, he saw an elderly gentleman, brows lowered, staring intently back at him.

"Dr. Lockhart?" Theo said.

"As I live and breathe," the man said, his frown of concentration brightening. "Theophilos! They told me you were dead. Well, that settles it, no one of any authority in this God-forsaken place can be trusted. Might as well bring it down to the depths of Sheol and save the Almighty some time."

"You told him?" Uly felt like he would choke.

"There's no time." Ess waved the paper at them. "Key also means lock, and the deer is a hart. Clock means time—"

"Dr. Lockhart has the time lock—the time key?" Athena blurted. Ford caught hold of her hand, stopping her when she started to rise from her chair.

"In a nutshell," the doctor said, nodding. "Wonderful to see you again, Athena. Ford, is that you as well? My, my, is it the final day of judgment, with so many rising from the dead?"

"No time," Ess said. "I told Mr. Lewis and Mr. MacDonald, and I saw Mr. Endicott arguing with Graebausch and Whickham just before dinner yesterday. Graebausch was exceedingly testy when I stood before the Council, so all it took was a little push and they took me to the vault."

"Was it empty?" Uly asked.

He felt Athena flinch, sitting next to him. He was glad he had made the big confession about having dreams that were returning memories, triggered by the coded songs in their grandfather's journals. No one made a sound as Ess related, as sparingly as possible, her reception, the walk to the vault, and opening it. He and Theo exchanged glances when Ess told how she had been hurried away without closing the vault again.

"When are you going to try for the whistle?" he asked.

"The dratted whistle," Dr. Lockhart said. "Of course." His bemused expression melted into something close to shock. "Don't tell me, Matilda actually found the right frequency to shatter the support posts and knock half the coastline into the ocean?"

"Not that I know of, but it should open some doors, crack some foundations," Ess said. "Uly, fill in the others on all our dreams, will you? I don't have time. We had to sneak out, and it's best if we go back inside as soon as possible. Especially if I need to sneak out again tomorrow night to confer with you. How close are you?"

"We should be within an hour of flight from you by tomorrow noon," Theo said, when the other three turned to him. "Vulcan wants to try out the steam-cart she's been tinkering with, and Heinrich and his flyers are eager to try for long-distance gliding. We don't dare get too close during the daylight, or we could raise the alarm. We might need to stop somewhere and hire horses or some other conveyance, but we'll be there after dark tomorrow."

"Good," Lewis said from somewhere outside the visual range. "The sooner this is over, the better for all."

~~~~~

Ess paused, positive she heard a footstep out of pace with the four of them as they walked down a narrow gulley. Lewis rested his hand on her shoulder and gestured to their right. Despite so much time spent in books and meetings, he had retained the sharp senses, physical fitness, and ability to move with grace and stealth that had made him such a valuable scout during the war. She nodded and tapped her ear, to indicate she had heard as well. His grimace was clear to be seen, despite the paucity of moonlight within the gully, several dozen yards from the hidden entrance to Sanctuary. He stepped ahead, leading the way, while she dropped back. Ess pressed herself against the angled rocky wall and waited, her head bowed to keep the pale skin of her face as hidden as possible.
~~~~~

Chapter Twenty

The three men were only seven or eight steps away from her when the footstep scraped on the loose debris on the floor of the gulley. A man-shape emerged from the darker shadows of the gulley bottleneck. Ess held her breath and waited, watching as he crept past her. When she could see his back, she pulled a length of cloth from her pocket. In a heartbeat, she leaped, on his back, wrapping her legs around his waist and the cloth around his face. Twisting, she knocked him off balance and turned the cloth into a gag. As he went down, she leaped free and managed to get a knee into his gut, knocking his breath out of him with a grunt-whoosh. Her three companions turned back. In moments, she and MacDonald dragged the man back around the bend in the gulley, away from any sentinels in this back area of Sanctuary.

Chances were good there were no patrols here, because very few people knew about this back entrance. Dr. Lockhart was stunned when Ess showed it to them three hours ago, using her father's map. Lewis took the lantern from Dr. Lockhart and opened the shield to let a thin line spill on the prisoner's face.

"Tumperman," MacDonald said. "The false one." He bared his teeth in a fierce grin when the prisoner's eyes widened. "Yes, we know you replaced the real man, and your features were altered with surgery. You and Sheridan and Clayton. The question is whether you were sent here to support Graebausch, Whickham and Polidory, or to have them kidnapped and replaced as well."

"He's sweating, his eyes are dilated, and I can almost see his pulse in his temples," Dr. Lockhart observed, his voice cool and even. "At an educated guess, I would say he's terrified."

"What do we do with him?"

All three men turned to Ess. So did Tumperman, after a moment.

"We can't leave him out here," Lewis said. "And I doubt there's any place in Sanctuary where we can put him for long where someone wouldn't find him or wonder why a door was locked."

"Too bad your family vault was left open," Dr. Lockhart offered. "It's soundproof. Can't remember, exactly, if anyone ever studied whether it was airtight."

The prisoner moaned. Clearly, the man was a paper-pusher and a tattletale, but not a spy, with the requisite nerve.

Dr. Lockhart's words gave Ess an idea. He was halfway right. There was no *known* place in Sanctuary where the prisoner could be held.

"In for a penny," Ess muttered. She knew her smile was nasty, if not evil. "Well, gentlemen, you've been trusted with several Fremont family secrets tonight, why not the largest?" A snort escaped her when Tumperman whimpered at "Fremont." He most likely hadn't recognized her, in her boy clothes and cap.

Dr. Lockhart chuckled when Ess led them downward, through the illusion of a pile of rubble that blocked the way. He said nothing, and neither did the other two men. MacDonald led Tumperman, his eyes covered with the cloth and Ess's cap wadded up and jammed in his mouth. His breathing grew quite labored as they walked, following curving paths downward through the bedrock. By the smoothness of the way, the path had been carved by water flowing down here. Ess shuddered at the thought of what a flood could do to this place.

Finally they stopped, within sight of a faint glow that spilled around another bend in the tunnel. According to the map Ess carried in her head, the cache of gunpowder and dynamite and the protective crystal light lay another twenty or thirty yards away. This was close enough. She rather suspected the light would draw Tumperman, once he dared to take the blindfold off. That would just make him more lost. He could wander down here in the dark for days, and he could cry out as loudly as he wanted, but no one would hear him.

"Be a good lad and stay put," she said, as she yanked her cap out of his mouth. She made a mental note to find some way to wash the cap, soaked with his saliva. Were those teeth marks? "Someone will bring you food during the day."

"Maybe," Dr. Lockhart muttered, looking far too cheerful about it.

Ess wondered if he had learned his cheerful nastiness and sharp humor from her grandmother, or he had taught that to Matilda.

The four stayed silent as they made their way back, except when Ess whispered the turnings, to help them remember when to go left or right every time the tunnel branched. The correct pathway never leveled out. Ess ached from weariness by the time they parted company with Dr. Lockhart, he to go to his quarters, and they to the level for the guest quarters. Ess grudged the time it took to wash and to put her clothes carefully away, wrapped up with a mixture of herbs Dr. Lockhart gave her to hide the scent of outdoors and the tunnel damp and stone. She couldn't fall asleep in anything but the nightshirt Phoebe had helped her put on three hours ago. With morning so close, she would likely still be asleep when Phoebe came with breakfast and wash water.

~~~~~

The next day, Ess felt as if she were being punished for spending the previous day in bed. Not only was she denied any chance to sneak away to check on Tumperman, but she didn't have a single moment of solitude. If
~~~~~

Phoebe wasn't at her side, guiding her through the maze of tunnels and levels from one meeting to another, she was responding to messages brought by assistants assigned to various researchers and scholars, asking for "just half an hour of your time." She didn't know what irritated her more: the people who thought they could break the block her grandparents put on her memories, or the ones who assumed she knew everything her grandparents had ever written or taught or discovered, and wanted to discuss them with her. Then there were the ones who insisted they were good friends of the family and wanted to benefit from that friendship.

Ess wondered how their stories would change when all the inhabitants of Sanctuary went through the testing Athena and Dr. Sylvia had proposed.

The worst part was coming to not just like but appreciate Phoebe. She managed to keep everyone sorted, kept Ess from being lost, and gave her clues how to handle the various people she met and had to endure. She stayed cheerful, despite what had to be an irritating, frustrating duty. Phoebe was a student at the Sanctuary because she had proven herself talented and intelligent, and yet she was little more than a messenger and secretary.

The only time Ess saw Phoebe's smile or the sparkle of interest and alertness fade was when someone mentioned her uncle, asking if she had heard from him. She felt some irritation on Phoebe's behalf when the same two people came back several hours later and rephrased their questions. Did they think Phoebe lied when she said she hadn't heard from Stryker in several months, and she didn't know when he planned to return to Sanctuary?

Finally evening came. In front of many witnesses, she asked Dr. Lockhart for a tonic to ease her headache. They could assume she was either not recovering as quickly as hoped, or she simply didn't want to attend the offered evening entertainments of music or billiards or cards or conversation. He escorted her to his workshop and Ess gladly sent Phoebe on her way to enjoy the evening with her friends.

"I can't decide if you like her, or you don't trust her," the doctor remarked under his breath, as he brought Ess the tonic. The time while she sat at his table and he worked on the tonic had been a welcome oasis of quiet and sitting perfectly still.

"That's the problem. I can't decide either." She took a sip.

"Drink it down all at once." He chuckled when she made a face at the bitter taste.

"Some warning would have been helpful."

"What about Phoebe don't you like?" he asked as she tipped her head back and tried to swallow without tasting.

"Her uncle." Ess coughed.

"The fact that he hasn't been in contact shouldn't count against her." His eyebrows raised and he leaned closer. "Unless you know why he has lost contact?"

"What kind of trouble would he be in if he was discovered... wearing a different name?"

"Ah." He leaned back, crossed his arms, and studied her just long enough Ess wanted to fidget. "Then you should know Phoebe does not like her uncle. In fact, I would hazard a guess that she fears him."

"Does he have some power over her?"

"I would say so. When her parents died, he became sole guardian for Phoebe and her three younger sisters. There has been some conflict between Stryker and the few remaining relatives on their mother Lavinia's side. They want to raise the girls, but he has refused to surrender them. The last I knew, he refused to tell anyone where he has sent them. He claims Lavinia was unfaithful to his younger brother, and he will not let her family influence the girls to follow in their mother's footsteps. Phoebe is strangely silent when asked. I would wager she supports her uncle so she doesn't lose her sisters altogether."

"Then we have a problem." Ess got up and poured water from a pitcher dripping with condensation. She had to get the awful taste out of her mouth. "The Pinkertons are investigating Mr. Stryker, whom they knew under another name. I will ask them to look for the girls, but..."

"But what?" Phoebe said, stepping from the shadows with a suddenness that startled Ess into dropping her cup.

"Your uncle was playing a dangerous game." Ess looked past her. "Is anyone else hiding there?"

"Not that I know of."

"How much did you hear?" Dr. Lockhart asked.

"Enough to know you don't like my uncle any more than I do." She wrapped her arms around herself, shivering a little, though the night was turning humid.

"Considering he tried to kill my brother, and the husband of a good friend—did I mention that Athena Latymer and Fordyce Chamberlain are married?" Ess muffled a snort when Dr. Lockhart wagged a finger at her. "He attacked Ford, cracked his skull on the rocks in San Francisco bay, and died the same night."

"Good," Phoebe said, her voice a rasp. "But what about—"

"We will find your sisters," she promised, and held out her hand to the younger girl.

"It isn't true, what he said about my mother."

"Of course not. Anyone who knew Lavinia is offended by the accusation," Dr. Lockhart said.

"Things he has said..." Phoebe made a little hiccupping sound, and at last gave her hand into Ess's grip. "I think sometimes he killed my parents. He was arguing with my father for weeks before the explosion, and Mother caught him ransacking Father's office, and there was some awful row about the regular couriers being changed and message bundles going astray. My sisters are all I have left. I have to spy on people and tell him what people talk about when they have meetings. And the last time he was here, he gave me strict instructions not to give any information to anyone, even the people I was supposed to report to before. It's been the most awful struggle not to be caught alone by some of them."

"Mr. Wickham, Mr. Graebausch and Mrs. Polidory, among them?" Ess guessed.

"Those are the worst. And their assistants. And then there's—"

"Write down all the names of the people you formerly reported to, would you?" Dr. Lockhart stepped back to the shelving that served as a desk and filing cabinets combined. He took several sheets of paper out of a box and offered Phoebe two sharpened pencils.

"We need to bring more people into this," Ess said, as she wiped at her eyes and settled down at the table. "Phoebe, is Clytie among those people?"

"Oh, heavens no. She despises my uncle. I think she keeps me on as one of her aides just to spite him. Every time he shows up, they have a very civil row about the course of my education and training. I think she is a little frustrated with me, because I don't dare voice my opinion when someone actually asks me what I want to do." Phoebe hiccupped once more. "I think she suspects something." She bent her head over her task and got to work diligently writing down names.

"I wouldn't doubt it," Dr. Lockhart said. "What are you planning?"

"I need to retrieve something from the vault, hidden in the walls by Granny." Ess smiled when her words earned a flinch and a partial glance from Phoebe. "Give Phoebe a general idea of what we have planned for tonight, then send her to fetch those who will stand with us, starting with Clytie."

"You can't go running about the lower levels dressed like that."

"Speaking of the lower tunnels, did anyone check on our guest at all today?"

"I believe Stanton did." He gestured at an alcove covered by a curtain. "There should be some costumes in there. You'll save time changing here, rather than going all the way back to your room."

Phoebe had filled one sheet of paper with names and was halfway through the second when Ess stepped out in a new set of sturdy boy clothes, perfect for moving through the damp and dark and rough terrain of the lower tunnels. The time key made a noticeable lump in her hip pocket. Ess reflected with a grin that wearing skirts had helped to hide quite a few things she needed to carry on her person, just to prevent untrustworthy folks from searching her personal effects while she was away from her room. Phoebe's eyes grew big and she stopped writing altogether as Dr. Stockwell dug out ammunition that fit Ess's derringer and gave her several throwing knives, and his own crystal to light the passageways.

"This will be the safest place for everyone to gather," he said. "I have several ladders, rope and wood, tucked away for emergency evacuations."

"You don't trust the engineers who stabilized this area, do you?" She muffled a chuckle.

"Man proposes and God disposes. I am never surprised when the best-laid plan suddenly develops ridiculous, obvious flaws."

Ess headed out into the darkness of the passageways, praying Uly had overestimated the time it would take for the *Nile*'s soldiers to reach Sanctuary, and they had already reached the hidden entrance. The sooner the invasion and testing of the ranks began, the sooner they could head for South America with a clear conscience and release her grandparents.

All was silent as she made her way down the last ramp into the gallery holding the vaults. Ess knew better than to trust that silence. She couldn't afford to slow her pace. She had to open the wall and retrieve the crystal whistle before she went down into the lower tunnels and met Uly and the soldiers. Despite what she had told Dr. Lockhart, it couldn't possibly be simple to operate the time key to release her grandparents. If it was important enough for her grandparents to show her the whistle and teach her the tune, and to hide it in the wall of the vault, then it was vital to the operation of the time key. Why else would she have that memory unlocked? Life, and especially her service among the Pinkertons, had taught her there was no such thing as coincidence.

Ess closed her hand around the crystal to muffle most of its glow. Even that seemed too bright, when her eyes adjusted to the deeper darkness of the long, curving passageway of the vaults. She imagined the light bouncing off the glossy blue-black and red-streaked mineral of the walls.

She slowed her steps when instinct screamed to move faster. Just three more alcoves and she would be at the opening of the vault. She could see it, still standing open. Did the emptiness convince the traitors that they had been discovered, or just frustrate them and send them on wild goose chases, perhaps even accusing each other of treachery?

She slowed more, walking on the toes of her boots. Now was the perfect time for someone to step out from around the bend in the passageway ahead of her, and shoot.

No movements, no sounds of breathing, no sense of another presence, no prickling feeling of watchful eyes. Ess paused in the opening of the vault and turned to look down the passageway in both directions. She brightened the crystal's light just a little more and looked again.

Fairly sure of having no company, but not satisfied in the least, Ess braced for the sting of the defensive field, stepped into the vault and brightened the crystal. She closed her eyes and drew up the dream memory, remembering the feel, the subliminal sound of the crystal as she followed her grandmother's command and control. A soft sigh escaped her as she opened her eyes and the crystal's light took on a purplish tinge and reached out tentacles, to brush over the wall where the opening had been made so long ago. She had a moment of doubt. After all, she was twice as tall as she had been back then. Perspective changed over time and could interfere with accuracy.

Oddly, the rock didn't vanish so much as it seemed to grow transparent. Ess wondered if she had remembered incorrectly, or perspective did indeed change, depending on the angle. She could see into the alcove. The whistle she remembered as the sole occupant had company now. Two small journals the size of her palms and several pieces of crystal, hexagonal disks with rounded edges, larger than gold dollar pieces and twice as thick. Reaching into the niche in the rock, Ess's fingers tingled and she had the oddest sensation of trying to reach through something thick, resisting movement, as if the rock had been turned to molasses. A sudden image of the rock solidifying while her hand was thrust into the illusion nearly had her leaping backward. She scooped up the disks first. Definitely no time to waste.

Thinking quickly, she unbuttoned her shirt and thrust the disks, seven in all, into the binding around her breasts. She tucked the journals inside her shirt, against her back, and jumped up and down a few times to assure herself they would stay in place. They wouldn't fall out, but shifting at an inopportune time could cause her trouble if she needed to wriggle into or out of a tight spot. Her years as a Pinkerton had taught her to expect the worst complication to happen at the most inconvenient time. Even if she couldn't prevent that trouble, she wouldn't be surprised, and had an idea of what to do to remedy the problem.

The whistle, she saved for last. She took it out of the niche in the rock and could have sworn the illusion of transparent stone resisted her even more than the first two times. Ess gave in to her shaking need to back away. She clutched the whistle in one hand and wiped her other hand on her trousers as she took two steps back. It wasn't just her imagination, she decided, when the rock lost some transparency. She looked at her hand, expecting to find it coated with some residue from passing through the illusion rock. What other wonders had her grandparents discovered and kept hidden from everyone? She reached for the crystal in her pocket, to close the niche. Or would it close on its own if she left it alone?

"Lovely night for a stroll," Endicott said.

Ess turned, nearly fumbling the crystal. It was no use hiding the whistle.

"You do remember far more than you admitted," he continued, and remained leaning against the smooth wall opposite the doorway. If they had been outside, in the moonlight, he would have looked entirely comfortable, leaning against a wall in a garden, perhaps smoking a pipe, gazing up at the stars. He had no pipe, no hat, and his hands thrust into his coat pockets gave him a sinister look, rather than casual and relaxed. Ess imagined all sorts of things in his pockets, all of them useful in attacking her.

"Knowing my grandparents, how could you doubt it?" She raised the crystal to close the niche. No sense in leaving it open, and the action could buy her a moment or two to think.

"Do you know what it does?" He stayed against the wall.

"Why did you follow me?" she said instead and watched him from the corner of her eye while the wall went solid again.

"It's time we had a talk, and you weren't in your room. Logic said to check with Dr. Lockhart first. When I saw a boy sneaking away from his workshop, logic also said that had to be you. I took a chance that you would want to investigate the vault again, just because you are a Fremont, and Fremonts always have a trick up their sleeves. I know several shortcuts, so I was here a good five minutes before you. Then it was just a matter of waiting."

"Do you think anyone has been trying to penetrate the defenses?" She discarded three plans that required running as fast as she could. If he knew shortcuts, then he could cut her off no matter which way she went. At this level, there were only so many options where she could go, and he had already proven he knew more options than she did.

"Most likely. In fact, that's part of what I came to discuss with you." He pushed off from the wall and held out a hand to her. "We need to talk, Odessa. It's time to lay all our cards on the table and be thoroughly honest with each other."

"That would imply you haven't been." She stopped just outside the vault. If the door slid shut, it would brush against her boot heels.

"No, I haven't." Endicott's weary smile faded into a touch of pain when she didn't take his outstretched hand. He let it drop to his side. "How long have you believed I am against you?"

"Are you against me?"

"Some would say that, yes." He withdrew his left hand from his pocket, stopping with his fingers still out of sight when she flinched. For a moment, the pain on his face clutched at her heart.

Ess reminded herself that he had to be an incredibly deft actor to have fooled her parents and grandparents for so long.

Chapter Twenty-One

"My grandparents never told you about this, did they?" She tucked the light crystal into her pocket, snug against the leather bag of bullets, freeing up both hands. Now was as good a time as any to find out why her grandmother had told her not to play the last three notes of the tune.

"That clever trick of hiding things within the rock itself? How many other niches are there?" He gestured into the vault, and sighed when she just shook her head. "I think we should go outside, where we can be assured of some privacy. This long talk is well overdue."

Ess fell into step beside him, ready to run the moment it looked as if he were leading her anywhere other than to the surface.

"Does it have anything to do with the argument you were having before dinner, with Mr. Graebausch and Mr. Whickham?"

"Your skills in stealth are exceeded only by your..." He sighed. "Yes, the argument decided me. I had hoped to protect you, to try one last time to persuade them to turn aside. This place should not be destroyed for the sins of the few."

"Destroyed?" Ess caught her breath, wondering what he knew or suspected. "Why would it be destroyed?"

"Why did the Almighty destroy Sodom and Gomorrah?" He offered her one of those pensive, sad smiles that used to tug on her heart when she was small. "Perhaps it is a flawed analogy, but why should Sanctuary die because of the sins of only a handful? Shouldn't the numbers of loyal, honest, honorable people outweigh the traitors, just as the vast crowds of the sinful outweighed the few good souls in Sodom and Gomorrah?"

"I doubt anything my grandparents devised will rain fire and brimstone down on this place." Ess shuddered and nearly stumbled, her mind's eye filled for a moment with the image of a vast pile of gunpowder kegs and dynamite.

What would it take to shatter the bracing beams and destroy the stability created by the ancestors?

"You're talking as if I can actually do something," Ess said.

"Your grandparents only gave me a hint of what was hidden inside your mind, but they referred to you and Uly as their avenging angels, their desperation ploy, and the deluge that would rival Noah's flood."

"How can I do anything if I don't remember?"

"You need to leave, Odessa." He caught hold of her elbow and stopped them both, just a few steps from the intersecting passageway. "While you've been playing ill and testing everyone, they've been digging through the archives and excavating unproven theories. Your grandparents built their theories of memory control on the work of others. No matter how cleverly your mind is protected, no matter how many walls Matilda built, someone will find a way to tear them down, and they won't care how much damage they do to you, as long as they get what they want."

"What do they want? Besides the time lock. Besides proof that my grandparents are still alive, safe from the traitors they identified too late." Ess tugged her arm free and backed away, out of his reach.

"Control. Power. And if they can't turn you to their cause, by persuasion or by turning you into a mindless child—"

"For what purpose?" She had to fight not to shriek.

"To control the lotus. Your bloodlines, through your mother and your father, give you the potential to use the lotus to call all the pieces of the Great Machine together."

"Do they know where the lotus is?" Ess shivered at the thought of how close the lotus was to Sanctuary, right that moment, because the *Golden Nile* had come to purge the heart of the Originators.

"No. I would never tell them that." Again, that sad smile.

Ess bit the inside of her cheek to keep from demanding, *How can I trust you, when you aren't even you?*

She extended her arm, opening her clenched fist to reveal the crystal slide whistle. Endicott offered her a confused, weary little smile. When he reached out his hand, perhaps thinking she offered it to him, she snatched it back out of reach. She raised it to her lips. He opened his mouth in protest.

The first note slid out, just as piercing as in her dream, instantly penetrating the rock around them. He froze, eyes widening, and Ess knew he felt the resonance sink into the bedrock.

"Please—" He paused, swallowed. "Ess, we won't be able to go out." He pressed his fingers against the bones around his ears as she continued to play, each note hanging on in the air, combining with the ones that followed. "Everyone will hear."

Good, she thought, and kept playing. She felt no pain, nothing but a great unfurling of some unplayed chord deep in her chest, resonating out to her bones.

Ess came to the end of the simple little tune and nearly paused before the last three notes.

One long note slid into place, held for a six-count.

The bedrock shook around them.

Ess staggered backwards and Endicott went to his knees with a strangled shout. In trying to regain her balance, the flute slipped from her lips.

The note continued, all the other notes dying away. Now pain reverberated in her skull. Ess pressed her fists against the side of her head, until the long note itself died.

"The deluge," she whispered, and her mouth tasted sour, as if she had vomited.

Her grandparents had put the power to destroy Sanctuary into her hands, with a simple child's tune and a slide whistle.

Endicott stayed on his knees, his forehead resting on his crossed arms. Ess smelled blood, hot against the cool stone scent of the passageway. She struggled to her feet and hesitated before stuffing the whistle into her other pocket. When she turned to look at him, he had raised his head. Blood trickled from one nostril.

"Odessa—"

"Stay away from me."

Then she ran.

Ess knew the path she needed to get from the vaults to the hidden entrance where Uly and the soldiers should be waiting, and she grudged every turn, every ladder she had to clamber up or down to another level. The closer she got to the habitation levels, the clearer grew the sounds of panic and emergency teams and security guards. She ran in darkness, refusing to bring out the crystal and make herself visible, and trusted to her gut instinct to lead her down the dark tunnels, holding the map in her head and counting her steps from each turn.

Voices came to her from the left, if she could trust the echoes. Ess slowed her steps. Her boots sounded too loud, no matter how lightly she tried to run. She reached into her right pocket and curved her fingers around the whistle. If she had to, could she play the song and knock her opponents lightless before they shot her? Would she be asking for trouble if she stopped here and played?

"Don't ask for trouble," she whispered, hearing her grandfather in the back of her mind. Ess pressed against the curving wall of the tunnel and crouched down as she saw a dim yellowish-green light reflected on the tunnel wall, indicating an intersection of two passages. At least she was right where she calculated, while running in the dark.

The men sounded more worried than frightened. Ess listened to them cross the passage where she waited, just out of reach of the light they carried. She saw their silhouettes—four men, carrying boxes or bags slung over their shoulders. None of them seemed to be armed. Their voices and the light quickly died, and she waited until all sound vanished before she continued down the passageway crossing theirs and took the next ladder down a level. From that point, the sounds of alarm and people trying to find out what had happened faded to nothing. These tunnels had been built in anticipation of large numbers in the far future. Ess wondered if anyone ever explored these tunnels, other than her father and his inquisitive, adventuresome friends. Would anyone guess she had come down here?

More importantly, when the teams looking for damage and injuries from the quake found Endicott, what would he tell them? Would anyone think to look for her down here? Or would he claim he didn't know what had happened, and then confer with the other traitors before acting?

One thing was certain: as soon as she let Uly and the *Nile*'s soldiers in, they needed to go directly to Clytie and Ogilve, hurry them away to safety, and then convince them of the true situation as quickly as possible. If Endicott revealed what she had done, if anyone guessed that she was involved, and if anyone looked for her and couldn't find her where they expected, they would hunt for Phoebe. She had promised to protect her new friend's sisters and expanded that promise to protect her as well.

Finally, she reached a depth and distance where she felt safe to call up light. Ess slowed enough to pull out the crystal without dropping it.

"Who goes there?" a man shouted, when the light in the crystal was little more than a pinprick.

Ess shoved her hand back in her pocket. Light erupted from the intersecting tunnel she was about to cross. She stumbled, trying to reverse her momentum. The light coming at her was red-tinted. Holding her breath, she felt for her derringer tucked under her coat at her waist. The crystal clutched in her palm subsided back to darkness.

"What did you see?" another man asked, his voice echoing slightly, coming up the passageway from behind the first.

She recognized Whickham's voice. What was he doing down here?

Looking for Tumperman? Or was there something down here the traitors didn't want found?

Ess saw her shadow, soft, lost in other shadows, stretching out in front of her.

Someone was coming up behind her with a light. Any moment now--

"What's that?" A man stepped out into the passageway only ten feet away from her. "Albert? Is that you?"

Ess snatched the crystal out of her pocket in one hand, and the derringer in the other. She threw all her force of will into the crystal, igniting it into brilliance as the man in front of her threw up his hand to shield his eyes. A man shouted from behind her as Ess lunged forward, running straight at the first man. Stretching back her other arm, she fired blindly at the man coming up behind her.

Then she was past the intersection and three men shouting so their voices echoed off the tunnel walls. She shoved the crystal back into her pocket, willing it into darkness and she ran, as fast as she could. She stumbled, slammed her right shoulder into the wall, and bounced off with a yelp. The noise of shouts and more gunshots behind her multiplied in echoes, aching in her ears. Gasping, Ess ran blindly, praying that she hadn't gotten herself lost.

The man coming up behind her, or at least the man Whickham expected, was named Albert. Was that Graebausch's first name? If so, what were they doing down here, rather than sending their assistants?

Ess had to slow to catch her breath and stop slamming into one wall and stumbling against the other, back and forth in some crazy giant's game. She hoped she would live long enough to laugh about it someday. Her shoulders felt numb from the repeated blows. Willing her breathing to slow, she kept walking and listened until she fancied she could hear her own blood fizzing in her veins.

No footsteps behind her. No hints of light.

If they weren't hunting her, why not? Did they think she couldn't go anywhere? Did they expect her to eventually turn around and come past them again?

That was exactly what would happen, but she would come with several dozen soldiers.

What if Whickham and Graebausch decided not to wait for her to return? There had to be a good reason why they would ignore the threat, especially if they didn't know who had run past and shot at them. What were they up to that they didn't chase her? Something dangerous to them? Or were they so sure of themselves, they didn't care?

Was there an ambush waiting for her down here? Ess paused and leaned back against the wall. Her shirt felt wet enough to stick to her skin. She was working herself into a panic and didn't like how it felt at all. Yet she had to consider such possibilities. What if one of them, or one of their underlings, had come down here and discovered where Tumperman had been stashed for safekeeping? What if they had released him, they knew she was involved—and Lewis and MacDonald? Were they going after them, while someone waited for her?

"Please..." Ess swallowed, irritated by how dry her mouth felt, while sweat plastered her clothes to her skin. "Please, Almighty... don't let us stumble now."

She listened for echoes and walked softly, brushing one hand against the wall until she reached an opening. Pausing, she took deep breaths through her nose. Did the air smell fresher, indicating an opening ahead that led outside?

A moan came out of the darkness ahead of her. Ess felt for the wall and followed it as the passageway opened into a wide room. Counting her steps, she nearly cried out when her foot caught on a gutter cut into the stone. She kept moving, going around the spot where Tumperman—if that was him, and not someone sitting in ambush—was still tied to a pillar of rock, sitting on several layers of blankets. Beyond him was one more tunnel, leading to a stone slab hidden behind a wall of brush. Uly should be waiting for her there with the soldiers. Ess moved as silently as she could, trying not to breathe and alert Tumperman she was there. After sitting in the darkness all day, with only the light brought by visitors who came to check on him and bring him food and water, there was no telling how close to panic he might be. If he started yelling, could he summon the lungpower to lead rescuers to him?

She wasn't ashamed of the damp in her eyes when she found the opening of the tunnel. Ess pulled out the crystal, ready to light it, just enough to guide her feet, and find the stone slab and the handholds for moving it along the groove in the rock.

She stumbled to a stop when she saw moonlight filtering through the screen of brambles and brush. The stone slab had been moved aside.

Silently praying, she took a few more steps, then brought out her derringer.

"Uly?" Her voice cracked.

"Here." Her brother dove through the brambles and brush with a loud crackling, and in a few steps caught her up tight against his chest. Ess clung to him and pressed her face against his jacket, the dark material harsh and comfortingly thick.

Too soon, she had to push away enough to speak. Time was of the essence.

Theo led the *Nile* soldiers approaching the front gates, while Uly and his team headed down into the tunnels with her. Ess missed his presence, as she appraised Uly and his men of the situation. She was sure he would find something amusing in the earthquake she had caused with the whistle her grandmother had left for her.

In rapid order, one man was dispatched to gather up Tumperman and take him outside for the support troops to handle. Ess offered her light crystal to Lynden, who was to lead the way up through the tunnels. He had memorized the drawings she had made of all the tunnels. The big, dusky-skinned man gave her a gentle smile and gestured for her to put it back in her pocket.

"Heinrich is walking on the clouds," Uly said with a chuckle. He tugged on the goggles hanging around his neck. "He finally discovered the compound he's been seeking for the last twenty years, to allow us to see in the dark."

"How useful are those things if someone flashes light in your eyes?" Ess countered. She wasn't mollified when several soldiers chuckled in response to her concerns. She kept her derringer at the ready, to fill the gap while the soldiers tore off their goggles to deal with enemies carrying lights.

No one waited at the intersection where she had shot at Graebausch. Ess couldn't decide if that was a good sign, or bad. They headed to Dr. Lockhart's workshop, because Uly wanted to take advantage of the emergency exit possibilities. They could set up the ladders the doctor said were ready, to evacuate any innocent parties if fighting broke out in the tunnels.

Clytie and Phoebe weren't waiting. Dr. Lockhart didn't have to say anything. As soon as Ess led the way into his domain, she looked at his worried expression, and she knew.

"Two are faster and harder to catch," Uly said, as soon as Ess told him. He rapped out orders to Lynden, caught hold of her hand, and they ran. He led the way, proving he had memorized all the maps just as she had.

Ess rapped once as soon as they reached Clytie's quarters, then pushed on the door. It swung open—it hadn't been locked. She only needed one look around the front room. A toppled chair, a desk with papers strewn across it and onto the floor, and a dark smear on the tight-woven carpeting told her all she needed to know. Clytie's absence was almost an afterthought.

"Where did they go?" Ess whispered, as she and Uly stepped out into the passageway.

"Depends on who took them, and why," Uly said. "She's a member of the Council. Is she worth kidnapping? Holding her for ransom? Maybe dangerous information?"

"The vaults." Ess couldn't explain what gut instinct told her. Fortunately, Uly didn't argue with her.

Even more fortunately, Sheridan, Whickham's assistant, was so intent on subduing Clytie in front of the massive double-wide doorway of the Council vault, he didn't notice Uly and Ess coming upon them. Uly drew his Zeus gun before Ess could take her third step away from him, intending to leap on the two struggling figures. Her right arm felt slightly singed, but it was well worth the price of seeing the weasel-faced man crumple, and for Clytie to fall awkwardly on him, so her elbow jabbed him hard in his considerable belly. Clytie caught enough of the by-blow of the Zeus gun that she wobbled and her knees threatened to fold. Ess pulled her to her feet and looped the woman's arm around her shoulder to hurry her away, leaving Uly to deal with Sheridan.

"Ess." He paused in dragging the limp man by his heels. "Is that our vault?" He gestured with his chin at the open door, barely visible in the dim glow of Sheridan's fallen crystal, a good thirty paces further down the passageway. "How do you close it?"

She didn't feel the least bit ashamed at the gleeful thought of Sheridan's reaction when he woke and found himself locked inside the vault. Ess settled Clytie to the floor, reasoning it would take less effort and time to come back for her.

"Are the vaults airtight?" she asked.

Clytie blinked a few times, then nodded, frowning.

"There should be enough air for him to last until someone comes back for him," Uly said. He snorted and pulled Sheridan through the opening. "If he doesn't waste it yelling and panicking."

Ess hesitated a moment, wondering how she could code Uly to the crystal panel. There wasn't time, and yet she didn't want to have to come back here and let the odious man out. He had stared at her far too long, the few times she had the misfortune to encounter him.

"Put your hand on it," she said, and caught hold of Uly's hand to press it flat on the panel when he hesitated.

To her satisfaction, the panel lit blue-green and the door slid closed.

"Huh. What do you know about that?" her brother muttered, then they shared a grin and sprinted together down the passageway to retrieve Clytie.

By this time, she had regained enough of her senses to resist a little, when they bent to haul her to her feet. Then her eyes widened and Ess knew the woman recognized her, despite smears of dirt on her face and her hair tucked up under her cap.

"This is my brother, Uly. Trust us." Ess looped her arm through Clytie's and the three hurried down the passageway, with Uly taking point, his Zeus gun ready. "What did he want from you?"

"My hand, my blood." Clytie gasped a little, but she seemed steadier with every step they took. "It takes four members of the Council to open the vault with our most dangerous records. They wanted the lists of our division leaders and their aliases, and the locations of our safe houses." She shuddered once, but Ess suspected that was more fury than fear or residue from the Zeus gun. "I knew he planned on killing me, once he got what he wanted. Why would he tell me what they wanted, if he was going to let me live? That quake... triggered something, I suppose."

"It made the rats frantic to abandon ship before it went down." Uly spread his arms, blocking them as they reached another intersection of passageways. Ess stopped and he went forward a few steps. When he nodded, they continued forward.

Chapter Twenty-Two

"What is that thing?" Clytie asked, gesturing with a now-steady hand at the Zeus gun.

"Athena Latymer's division has a large number of inventors. And soldiers," Ess added. "The short story is that we've uncovered treachery in the higher levels, and we're here to sort things out."

"Knowing you Fremonts..." A gasping little sound escaped Clytie, turning into a chuckle. "You wouldn't have anything to do with that quake, would you? Your father and his troublemaker friends were constantly exploring the unused tunnels and lower reaches. For all I know, they rigged the braces to collapse like telescopes at need."

"The quake was quite by accident, and as near as I can determine, that was entirely Granny's doing."

"Ah. Good. Even better. We have enough hide-bound fools who couldn't decipher what to do with Matilda."

"If it takes four, where are the other Council members?"

"Hopefully, too busy to make their rendezvous," Uly said.

Three times, they crossed paths with groups of Sanctuary workers, each time ducking into a doorway of a meeting room or hurrying to cross the intersecting passageway to stay out of their sight. Clytie recovered enough to walk on her own. The fourth time, a group of men, all carrying guns, came upon them so suddenly that disaster nearly caught them. She opened the door to a room sealed with a crystal panel in the wall and they hid just in time. A team of *Nile* soldiers intersected them just one turn away from Dr. Lockhart's workshop. A crystal button in Uly's collar flashed green, and a voice called out from the darkness ahead of them before Ess could ask what that meant. Uly responded in what sounded like Russian, and light flooded the passageway.

"All it does is let us know if other troops are nearby," Uly said, when Ess pointed at it. He nodded to the two men standing on either side of the passageway as the three of them hurried past.

Clytie gasped as they stepped out into the brightly lit and now somewhat crowded open area of Dr. Lockhart's workshop. More than a dozen of the thin black cables ubiquitous to the *Golden Nile* hung down through the opening in the rock overhead. Ess nearly cheered at the sight of friends from the ship sliding down, armed and armored. Theo stood at the central worktable with Dr. Lockhart, conferring over maps of the various levels of Sanctuary. That meant his soldiers had made it in through the main gates. Clusters of people Ess could barely recognize stood together, watching the soldiers working, or staring upwards as a familiar blue light spilled downward, growing stronger with each heartbeat.

"Phoebe." Clytie gestured at the groups of students and teachers and workers who took care of the daily needs of Sanctuary. "I sent her to check on Nathanael, just before that brute burst in on me."

"Nathanael?" Ess asked.

"Nathanael Ogilve," Dr. Lockhart said, stepping over and holding out a hand to Clytie. "You look somewhat worse for wear."

Clytie didn't answer, her eyes widening and her head tipping back as she watched the largest of the landing baskets from the *Golden Nile* come down through the opening. It was a tight fit and brought down vines and a few small shrubs and some dirt with it. Ess supposed that after tonight, maintaining the secrecy of Sanctuary would be a moot point. No matter who the traitors were allied with, and how many of them had infiltrated this centuries-old stronghold, it would have to be abandoned.

Polly, head of the *Nile*'s soldiers, swung her legs over the side of the basket, followed by four of Dr. Sylvia's trainees and Vulcan, with five of her top assistants. Vulcan laughed, a sharp bark of sound, hugged Clytie briefly, and hurried past her, waving a two-foot-long rod of crystal wrapped in bands of several different colors of metal. All her assistants were armed with similar rods in one hand, Zeus guns in the other.

"What are they doing?" Clytie asked, watching the newcomers disperse while several soldiers urged a large group of Sanctuary folk into the basket.

"There's no telling what sort of booby traps and spoilsport tactics the traitors will have ready against the day they are discovered," Theo said, stepping over to join them. "It's better to track everything down, especially anything made with crystal, and make sure nothing is carried away."

"If the rats do manage to escape the ship," Uly added. "Who is Phoebe?"

"Stryker's niece, who happens to loathe him," Ess said, and gestured for him to follow her. "Where would Mr. Ogilve be?"

"He likes to take a stroll through the conservatory before bed," Clytie said.

"I like Phoebe already," Uly remarked, as they loped in matched step down the passageway. Ess could only spare him a grin.

Twice they had to slow and press against the side of the passageway as pairs of *Nile* soldiers led groups of students and workers toward either the main gates or Dr. Lockhart's workshop, both designated as evacuation points. Both times, several men were unconscious, carried by others in their group, everyone looking somewhat shocked. Ess supposed it would take some time before those people could be convinced that the people who had stormed into their safe underground world and knocked some of them unconscious were in fact their allies.

The smell of blood greeted them as they reached the double doors of the conservatory, which hung open less than a foot. Soft, green-tinted light filtered through the opening, and Ess saw dark smears on the worn-smooth stone floor. She took care to step around them and reached for the door panel on the right. The smell of green growing things spilled out on air thick and sweet with humidity. The high domed roof was lined with threads of crystal that had been taught to mimic the cycle of light outside. A large section of crystal light far to the right matched the progress of the moon across the night sky, and speckles of light matched the stars.

Enough light remained to show Ogilve lying on his back, eyes wide in death, sprawled where he had fallen. Missing a hand.

"He was a friend of Grandfather's," Ess said, fighting the urge to shriek. She wasn't sure if it would be fury or fear or something incomprehensible. She only knew a heavy churning threatened to fill her chest and explode out of her if she didn't do something soon.

"He can wait." Uly gestured back through the open doors with the Zeus. "Whoever took his hand took Phoebe."

They took care to avoid the blood smears. Ess pulled the lighting crystal out of her pocket. It revealed the blood trail to give them an idea where the killer had gone.

Another hundred yards or so ahead of them lay an area called the Crossroads, where five tunnels intersected, and spiral staircases led upward and downward, effectively connecting all the inhabited levels. It was as close to a throughway as Sanctuary had, but none of the staircases touched all the levels or led all the way to the surface. Ess imagined the killer dragging Phoebe up a staircase to one of the levels that did have access to the surface, an emergency exit shielded from sight, and easily escaping capture. Her emotions affected the crystal, expanding the light so it seemed to race ahead of them.

A shape lay in a heap on the floor at the base of one of the metal staircases. Ess choked on a shout and nearly swung at Uly when her brother grabbed hold of her arm and skidded to a stop. She stumbled and tried to tear free. Then she saw the dim blue light, and the legs of the man hurrying, stumbling down the staircase to their level. Ess shoved the crystal into her pocket and covered her mouth with her hand to soften the sounds of her gasps for breath. Without the stronger light, her eyes adjusted enough to make out details of the man as he emerged into view. She and Uly took slow, quiet steps forward, watching as he hurried over to the form lying on the floor. He stumbled once, then went to his knees and bent over the shape.

Phoebe lay on the floor, on her side, her face revealed as the man rolled her onto her back.

The man was Endicott.

Ess reached for Uly's Zeus gun. He whipped it up and shot Endicott.

Uly confiscated Endicott's light crystal and searched the man's clothes while Ess checked Phoebe for injuries. Other than a darkening bruise on her temple and some blood in her hair, behind her left ear, she seemed otherwise uninjured. Uly tugged a flask from one of the three pouches hanging from his belt. Ess sniffed at the contents. Whisky and some potent herbs, one of Dr. Sylvia's restorative tonics. She tipped a few drops into Phoebe's mouth, after pressing on the sides of her lips to open them. Then she held the mouth of the flask under the girl's nose. In moments, Phoebe choked and her eyes fluttered. She moaned and pressed a hand to her injured head and tried to twist out of Ess's arms, to curl into a fetal ball.

"What do we do with him?" Uly settled down in a crouch, putting himself between Endicott and the girls.

"My mistake was leaving him free the last time." Ess fought back a shudder. The only options to halt Endicott the last time she encountered him were to either shoot him or continue playing the slide whistle until he suffered more damage than a bloody nose. One note of the forbidden three had made Sanctuary shake and caused panic. What would two do? The bottom line was that she couldn't make herself kill the man, despite knowing he had played a game of friendship all these years.

"What happened?" Phoebe said, her eyes fluttering and full of tears. "Who attacked us?"

"Who are 'us'?" Uly asked.

"Me and Mr. Endicott. He rescued me from Mr. Graebausch and Mr. Whickham." Her throat worked a moment. "They were—they wanted—I don't know what they wanted, but they threatened to cut my hand off if I didn't come along, and hurt Miss Reul." She continued staring at Endicott. "Is she all right?"

"She's safe now," Ess said.

"As safe as any of us can be," Uly muttered. He shifted to one side, to get a better look at Endicott. "He rescued you?"

"He killed Mr. Whickham, and Mr. Graebausch was in a fury. A spitting, swearing fury." Awe put some color back into Phoebe's cheeks. "I thought his head was about to burst like an enormous blood blister. He threatened all sorts of things, said he knew Mr. Endicott's secrets, he could destroy him, there was nowhere he could run to hide, that he was a traitor." She swallowed hard, a shudder rippling through her. Ess guessed she had a bout of nausea, and handed her the flask to sip. Phoebe made a face at the taste but got down a mouthful.

"What did he say about me?" Ess said, studying Endicott. She knew it was ridiculous for the three of them to huddle here and talk, when they should get moving, back to safety in numbers. Or was it four of them? They couldn't leave Endicott here, to recover and move about freely for a second time. What if Phoebe wasn't mistaken, and he had indeed rescued her, rather than playing twisted mind games?

"Nothing. They were all arguing about my uncle, how he had kept them in the dark too long, and he had most likely sent you to get them out of the way, so he could finally sit on the Council. They seemed to think that your grandparents didn't block your memories, but my uncle did something to your mind while you were working with the Pinkertons. They were rather upset, something about giving him too long of a leash and he had gotten too big for his britches and hadn't followed through on his promises to make the Pinkertons their tool." Phoebe pressed her fists to her temples. "I didn't tell them that he was dead. They didn't ask me any questions at all. They just kept dragging me down the tunnels, arguing and blaming each other for losing control of my uncle, and every time I fell or slowed down, they threatened to cut off my hand."

"They wanted something in her family vault," Uly said.

"Do you think we should go see?" Ess said.

Echoes of shouts and blue flashes of light reflected off a distant passageway wall where it curved. Reason enough to move on. Ess helped Phoebe to her feet. Movement would help drive the rest of her nausea away. Uly slung Endicott over his shoulder and gave Ess his Zeus gun. They set off, out of the Crossroads and heading toward Dr. Lockhart's workshop. Phoebe took one more sip of the restorative and put the flask away, her legs steady again. Then she told them how Endicott had rescued her.

He came running after them when Graebausch and Whickham took Phoebe down an access tunnel to the expansion area. Ess exchanged flattened grins with Uly when Phoebe explained this was a section of Sanctuary where tunnels had been dug for future use, but had lain abandoned and unexplored for generations. They were strictly off-limits, she said with a muffled little giggle, which meant that adventurous students challenged each other to go in with nothing but a candle. They would make maps of what they remembered, once they got out, and compare them, and give names to the chambers and twists and turns and ramps they found. A favorite pastime was to make plans for extravagant living quarters, when they were all powerful leaders among the Originators.

Endicott had caught up with Phoebe and her captors after the first turn going downward into the expansion area. He told them Sanctuary had been surrounded by men in uniform, and the quake a short time before had been from a series of cannon shots at the base of the cliffs. Ess flinched at that blatant lie. Yet if he lied to his co-conspirators, rather than telling them she had caused the quake with the crystal slide whistle... maybe that argument she overheard the night of the welcoming dinner meant something entirely different from what she inferred? Now her head hurt enough she pitied Phoebe more.

At that point, Whickham had started shouting about Graebausch selling them out, that the leaders would have all their heads, that he had double-crossed their superiors for the last time. Graebausch shoved Phoebe into Whickham's arms and told him to see what her uncle had been hiding from them all these years. He said something Phoebe didn't quite catch, but she inferred he hoped her uncle's long silence and lack of cooperation meant he was dead. Whickham shoved Phoebe back at Graebausch and said it was a waste of time, he wasn't going to be burdened with a stupid girl, and they should kill her and cut off her hand and save time.

"I screamed," Phoebe said, her blush apparent even in the greenish light of the crystal. "Wouldn't you have at that point?"

"Would have done a lot more." Uly paused to grunt and adjust Endicott hanging over his shoulder. "Swear up a storm and kick someone into singing soprano."

Phoebe giggled, blushing even darker. "I did take a swing at him. Mr. Graebausch shoved me against the wall." She lightly brushed her fingertips over the bruise on her temple. "The next thing I knew, Mr. Endicott shot Mr. Whickham. He had a knife. It was huge. Mr. Graebausch swore at him. I thought my hair would burst into flames. Then he grabbed hold of me and held me in front of him, and there was Mr. Endicott pointing the gun at him—well, at both of us, actually. Then Mr. Whickham staggered into us, swinging his gun around like a club and he hit me, and Mr. Graebausch swore at him and pushed him and I quite saw stars. Then the next thing I knew, Mr. Whickham was lying there, bleeding terribly and he was so still..." She shuddered. "Mr. Graebausch ran the other way and I suppose I fainted." She frowned at Mr. Endicott. "What happened to him? He was rescuing me—wasn't he?"

"Everything is very complicated right now," Ess said.

"Granny's schemes and gizmos are complicated," Uly said. "This is... I don't know what this is."

"Granny?" Phoebe said.

"This is my brother, Ulysses. He and our soldiers are taking control of Sanctuary because we've discovered a... well, a plot, to put it simply. As far as we can tell, Revisionists have infiltrated us, and Sanctuary isn't safe anymore."

"They want the lotus," she said. "That has to be it. When Miss Reul had me assist her during Council meetings, I heard several arguments about the lotus, how it needed to be taken out of storage and used. It was meant for more, or at least could be used for more, than simply reassembling the Great Machine. Several members of the Council insisted it could be used as a weapon, and it should be." She shuddered as they came around the final bend in the tunnel. The warm, welcoming light from Dr. Lockhart's workshop and the sounds of activity reached out to meet them. "Mr. Ogilve was most adamant that not only would the lotus not be used for such a thing, but he would make sure it was taken out of the vault and handed over to a trustworthy guardian, and he would go to his grave with the secret before he would let younger folk with no grasp of the solemnity of their responsibility let themselves be panicked into foolish actions." She shrugged, then winced when the movement seemed to aggravate her head wound. "Miss Reul often asked me to witness such meetings, she said my memory for exact words and even inflections was very useful."

"Very useful indeed. Too bad we can't copy her brain into the crystal to record things for us," Uly said, with a wink for Phoebe.

Then they stepped into the light and the chaos of evacuating the residents of Sanctuary. Ess wondered how many of those being herded out of their quarters and hauled upward in the *Nile*'s basket were innocents and how many were traitors, perhaps new recruits to the Revisionist cause, perhaps not even aware they were being suborned. Thanks to the many tunes and the herbal potions her grandparents had left behind, every mind would be opened and explored and tested. She didn't want to think about what they would have to do with the proven traitors. Ess was content to deal with the present crisis and let matters of justice and punishment fall into wiser hands than hers.

Clytie called Phoebe's name and pushed her way through the lines of people waiting for their turn to go up in the basket, and groups of people being brought in, escorted by *Nile* soldiers. Ess knew there were less than two hundred people resident in Sanctuary, according to what Phoebe had told her. Why did it seem like there were that many present or trying to come into Dr. Lockhart's workshop? Shouldn't several basket loads of evacuees have already gone up?

"Where is Nathanael?" Clytie said, reaching for Phoebe to grasp her shoulders. When the girl could only shake her head, she turned to Ess. She must have seen the truth in her face, because hers crumpled in sorrow before Ess could say anything.

Then to Ess's horror, she saw Athena coming through the crowded room toward them. She traversed the crowd to meet her, passing Uly as he put Mr. Endicott down on a stack of crates and duffels someone had tossed to one side.

"You can't stay down here," Ess said, grasping the woman's arms above her elbows. "They killed Mr. Ogilve, most likely trying to get hold of the lotus. He's been resisting a group trying to bring it out of storage to turn into a weapon. They cut off his hand, and they were going to use Clytie to get into the vault."

"It takes four members of the Council to open the Council vault," Athena said. "Where are the others?"

"Whickham is dead. Mr. Endicott killed him, to rescue Phoebe. Graebausch ran down into the unused tunnels. He could find his way out. Athena, you must go back up, where you'll be safe. Have Phoebe tell you what they were talking about when they were kidnapping her. Stryker had something in his family vault that they wanted to get at, and it sounds like he's been playing triple traitor, playing different sides against each other. They haven't heard from him in months, maybe a year."

"Very interesting." Athena's eyes went distant for a moment. "I don't suppose I can talk you into coming topside and being safe too, can I?"

"Not a chance." Ess gasped a little when Athena pulled her into a short, tight embrace, then released her. Uly called for her and she turned to find him, as Athena called for Clytie and Phoebe and gestured at the basket just coming down for another load.

Endicott had regained consciousness. He was sitting up, holding his head with one hand and sipping at one of Uly's flasks with the other. He held up a hand to stop her before she could even think of something to say.

"I know you don't trust me," he said.

"I have the feeling they have even less reason to trust you."

"Do you want proof that you can trust me?"

"That would be greatly appreciated," Uly said, turning slightly to watch the evacuation activity around them.

"I know the song you played." Endicott nodded, glancing down at her pocket. Ess clenched her fist to keep from sliding that hand in to be sure of the whistle. "You played one of the three notes that shouldn't be played except as a last resort."

"How does knowing about the song prove you're on our side, for the moment?" her brother retorted.

"I know what Ess played. I was there when Matilda and Ernest deciphered the instructions and warnings in the language of the ancestors." Endicott shrugged. "I was there when Edward found it."

"That just means you deceived our father," Ess said.

"Your father knew what I was."

Chapter Twenty-Three

The words, spoken so quietly, echoed through Ess's chest like a shout. Endicott gestured at the worktable a few steps away, where paper and an inkwell waited.

"I know where Graebausch is going. There is a cache of weapons, specifically barrels of gunpowder and dynamite preserved in wax. It's a spoilsport tactic, to seal up the main entrance and the central living quarters, but leave them access to the stores, the archives, the vaults."

"But if they don't know about the secret entrance—or do they?" Uly said.

"Not that I'm aware of." Endicott met their gazes in turn, until Uly and Ess turned to each other. They only took a few seconds to come to silent agreement.

"Show me." Uly stepped over to the table and picked up a sheaf of papers.

While Endicott sketched, another basket load went up to the *Golden Nile*. Uly picked a half-dozen soldiers. He took the first map, to get to the secret cache of explosives, and picked two teams to guard the entrance and the Crossroads, to catch Graebausch, if they couldn't stop him at the cache. Two soldiers stayed with Ess and Endicott, while he finished sketching the second map, and marked where the passageways intersected with the unused portions of Sanctuary and led elsewhere. Their job was to go to one of the bracing support chambers, to make sure Graebausch didn't start there placing the explosives.

"What is all this?" Ess pointed at the far right edge of the sketch. "That's not in any of the maps or any of the descriptions my parents and grandparents left."

"The Revisionists have been digging their own nest for two generations, with the goal of getting into the vault and taking the lotus."

"You were helping them do that?"

"That was outside my responsibilities."

"Why should I trust you, that you aren't leading me into a trap?"

"I promised your grandparents I would look after you."

Ess believed him. She just wished she knew where "look after you" stopped and gave way to his loyalty to the Revisionist cause.

Thanks to Ess's study of the secret passages and where tunnels and staircases intersected, they cut at least twenty minutes of traveling time, even at a near-running pace, from their journey to the deepest chambers of

Sanctuary. There were six chambers where the stabilizer columns had been installed, using the technology and scientific and engineering knowledge of the ancestors. They checked the most crucial two first—if an explosion large enough took place in them, the stabilizers would collapse or simply crack, and the portion of Sanctuary above them would be destroyed. Ess left one guard in each chamber, to make sure Graebausch or his underlings didn't get in there and set the explosives. She went on with Endicott to check the others. All empty, with thick layers of dust, and watermarks—oddly contradictory and a little frightening—showing where there had been flooding a few years ago.

"How long were you spying for the Revisionists?" Ess asked, and crossed her fingers in the pocket holding the whistle. She knew it was a childish gesture, but she felt a little too young, childish right now, with so many things twisting and turning around her.

"I was substituted for the real Randall Endicott when he was twenty and I was eighteen. He came to the attention of my father's people when he fell ill and spent nearly four months in a convalescent home. What made him especially attractive was that his family all died of the same illness, and they had been so long out of touch with the leadership there was literally no one alive who could speak for or against a young man who claimed to be Randall Endicott. I had a strong enough resemblance to his parents that there was no need to subject me to the altering surgery that others had to endure, to take the place of others here."

"Did you kill—"

"The original?" He shook his head, as they stepped into the sixth and final chamber. "He spent nearly four months struggling to live, then died without any clue what was about to be done with his identity. I was put in his place, subjected to various tortures to make me lose weight, make me look haggard and pale, so when some officials showed up to take custody of the sole survivor, no one questioned me. The doctors' records testified that I had suffered brain fever and loss of memory, which covered any mistakes I made. I was brought here, put under Dr. Lockhart's care to finish my recovery, and began the rounds of testing and assessments, to determine my talents, what I could do to serve the cause. Thank the Almighty, your father was a student here, and he was bored. His investigations into the archives, to unsolved mysteries and tragedies changed my life."

He leaned back against the wall and tipped his head back, to study the massive pillars of the stabilizers.

"I know enough about the layout of the serpents' nest to know that this entire complex must be destroyed if we want to wipe out the serpents." He tipped his head slightly to the right and offered her a flat little smile. "What does that have to do with what I'm telling you? Your father unearthed the clues to the whistle and the specific song, with the long-lasting harmonics. We searched the records for years while we were students here, and every chance we had to return. He trusted me with the knowledge, because only someone who knew the perfidy of the Revisionists had the right to decide when it was necessary to make the ultimate sacrifice and destroy them."

"You always scold anyone who skips around in the story. Please tell it from beginning to end." Ess barely restrained herself from showing him the Zeus gun Uly had made sure to give her.

"A story that takes far too long. The important detail is that Edward was investigating a mystery and tragedy surrounding the Endicott family. One Reginald, two years younger than the firstborn, Randall, had been kidnapped when he was perhaps three years old. The trail of the kidnappers was literally wiped from the face of the Earth. No body was ever found, no demand for ransom. Some people said the search to discover what happened to his son drove Reeves Endicott quite mad, so he requested the isolated post in the mountains of India where his family eventually died. Edward found a sketch of young Reginald, and a listing of his birthmarks and several scars from childish mishaps. Including a coin-sized burn on the heel of his hand. He and Randall were playing with pennies and made the mistake of putting several in the fireplace and leaving them in too long." He held out his hand.

That was unnecessary. Ess had always wondered about the perfectly round scar that she had seen so many times since childhood.

"Edward had suspected me early on in our acquaintance. Investigating the Endicott family, he found this mystery, this hole that I fell neatly into." He shrugged and offered her a slight widening of his flat smile. "It didn't take long to convince me to change allegiance, and to work with him in investigating and poisoning the efforts of the Revisionists."

"I want to believe you, but I hope you understand that I can't... quite," she finally admitted, after several moments of deep thought, while her hand tightened on the grip of the Zeus gun.

"I would worry if you did believe me without any proof." He gave her a shallow bow in salute. "That doesn't matter right now, Odessa. What does matter is that you found the whistle, and you need to destroy this entire place. Graebausch has been feeding the Revisionists crystal. As fast as the agents searching the ancient sites find it, he feeds it to the agents hiding in the tunnels with access to Sanctuary. That quake you caused pushed them to jump beyond the plan, to try to get into the vault, to throw aside years of caution and preparation."

"What do they want besides the lotus?"

"The secret records, the books with the names and locations and aliases and the missions of all the Originator divisions. So they can hunt our people down one by one. They'll go in with all the countersigns and knowing the names of those in charge, and when everyone is relaxed and smiling, murder them all. Or worse, they'll use that information to make Originator divisions into Revisionists without anyone knowing or even guessing, until it's too late."

Ess shuddered, thinking of Ogilve, dead and missing a hand, and the words of the man threatening to cut off Clytie's hand if she wouldn't help him open the Council vault.

"Destroy this place with just the whistle?" she said instead of the dozens of questions pressing against her tongue to be released. "I admit, one note did shake this place, but there were no aftershocks, no real destruction. Other than panic."

"Down this far, in the same chamber with the stabilizer? It will crumple like melting wax with the first note."

"How do you know?"

"Edward told me so, and that's good enough for me."

"Just stand here and play until the chamber falls down around me?"

The need to move grew strong enough to ache. Ess knew it was foolish bravado, but she stepped further into the chamber instead of out the door, as everything within her clamored to do. Reaching out one hand, she leaned against the nearest stabilizer column. It was wider around than three of her, reached up to the ceiling that lay beyond the globe of light from the crystal, and extended down through the rock under her feet. This close, the rock looked glossy and yet uneven, as if it had been melted and started to flow in waves, then stopped, frozen in place. Just imagining all the power it took to put these ten stabilizer columns in place in this room alone, and melt the rock to penetrate untold depths made her a little breathless. Or maybe it was the pressure of all the rock overhead, and having to make the decision to destroy all this. Yet if Endicott was correct, and the Revisionist access tunnels were so close by, they needed to be destroyed, didn't they? She needed to deny them another chance to get into the vaults. They had killed Ogilve, they had tried to kill Clytie. Who knew how many other leaders they had killed and replaced or else suborned all these years? Their goal was ultimately the lotus, and through it control of the Great Machine, and time itself. Everything her ancestors had done down through the centuries would be wasted. How many times would the chase have to be repeated through history?

"Ess?" Endicott took a step toward her and held out a hand. His expression was the concerned, warm one she had known since childhood.

She was dithering, trying to avoid having to make the decision that her father seemed to have assigned her, and her grandparents had approved. Otherwise why would her grandmother have taught her that particular tune, and shown her where the whistle was hidden?

"I believe you," she said.

He closed his eyes and bowed his head and his shoulders shook. When he raised his head again, he opened his mouth, and a gunshot reverberated through the room with ear-piercing echoes.

Ess leaped at him, shoving them both to the ground and behind the pillar. A dark shape stood in the opening of the chamber. They rolled, and she felt the light crystal still clenched in her hand. That was stupid — give the enemy light to aim at them? She threw it with all her might, and for an elongated moment she saw the astonishment on Graebausch's face as it tore through the air, to hit him directly between the eyes.

The scent of blood choked her and fire streaked up her arm. She felt it hot and wet, then heard Endicott's gasp as he shuddered. Silently apologizing, she pressed her bloody hand over his mouth to quiet him.

More gunshots filled the chamber, drowning out the soft sounds they both made. She found the bleeding hole high in his shoulder. It didn't seem to pump, so an artery hadn't been hit, but there was so much blood. They crouched behind the pillar and he struggled to sit up. She couldn't tell if the stinging in her biceps was just from a graze, or a deeper wound. Her shirt and coat were torn and scorched by the bullet.

The echoes and reverberations of gunfire grew louder. Ess didn't dare look out from behind their shelter to see if Graebausch had come into the room, coming closer. She nearly cried out in panic when she realized she had dropped the Zeus gun in the first flurry of action, getting out of the line of fire. She found it, and tried to envision just how she was going to get to her feet, step out, and aim at Graebausch without being able to see him. She could shoot and use the light from the Zeus gun help her spot him, but the converse was that she would give Graebausch light to see her.

It was the best — the only — plan she had. Muttering a prayer for divine help, she pulled her legs under herself and leaned against the column to get to her feet. Endicott caught hold of her uninjured arm and pulled her closer to him. He had to speak four times, before she could hear him over the ear-shattering echoes. Any moment now, one of those bullets was going to ricochet just right and one of them was going to get hit. Just how many guns and bullets did Graebausch have?

"Play," Endicott said.

Ess shuddered and she stared into the darkness that hid his face from her. She had been wrong. They did have another option, another plan.

The tremors began after the tenth note. Her fingers fumbled, sliding the whistle to the next note. Last time, she hadn't felt anything until she reached the first of the three forbidden notes. Ess continued playing, speculating on a cumulative effect. Did proximity to the stabilizing columns get a quicker response?

The notes came louder, purer, drowning out the sounds of gunfire. Light spilled through the darkness behind her closed eyes.

"Enough." Endicott closed his bloody hand around hers and tugged the whistle away from her lips.

Ess resisted for a moment, opening her eyes, and was stunned to see light shimmering from the whistle. That hadn't happened before either.

Providing light for their enemy to aim at wasn't wise, was it?

He wasn't shooting at them.

"Ess?" Uly's voice echoed from the high ceiling and the columns. Light streamed into the chamber as the light from the whistle faded.

He came around the column and dropped to his knees, reaching out for her. Uly looked pale, and it couldn't all be blamed on the greenish tinge to the light from the crystal in his hand. Then Ess understood. Uly and his soldiers had heard the gunfire and came running and drove Graebausch away.

Naturally, he was all for going into the Revisionist tunnels and chasing Graebausch down. Despite his gunshot wound and looking even greener than Uly, Endicott had the strength of voice and persuasive power to stop that. There were at least one hundred Revisionists in the nest at any time, and they would spill into Sanctuary the moment Graebausch reached them. Uly demanded Endicott show them the Revisionist entrances, to catch them as they tried to come in.

"Catch the rats as they run for their lives," Endicott insisted, holding Ess captive with the intensity of his gaze.

She had to agree.

"Show them the exits," she said, getting to her feet. She opened her hand, showing Uly the slide whistle, streaked with blood and still glowing faintly. "I'll stay here and play through to the end."

"It will take more than just this room." Endicott pointed straight up. "Edward calculated you will need to play in the areas on each level, along the dividing line between the nest and Sanctuary. It starts here, though." He glanced at Uly, who scowled at both of them. "I should stay with you. Edward would want it. Just in case."

"I trust you." She took a step back. "Show them the exits and help them catch the rats. Uly, don't argue with me. This has to be done. Better that no one has Sanctuary, than take the chance the Revisionists get what we've stored here."

For once, her brother kept his mouth shut. Ess shuddered and fought to stand perfectly still as they created a makeshift bandage for Endicott's injured shoulder, and a sling fashioned from his belt. One of the soldiers retrieved her light crystal. She had to put her Zeus gun in her pocket to keep the light alive with one hand, and clutch the slide whistle tight with the other. When they were gone, and the last reflected flicker of light from their crystals had faded, she put the crystal in her pocket and waited for it to fade. She stood in complete darkness for a count of twenty.

Then she played. The trembling in the rock began softly, whispering the notes back to her through the soles of her feet. Ess tried not to listen, concentrating on the notes, the placement of the slide as she played, and the route to get to the same spot directly above her on the next level.

She played until the first of the three forbidden notes. The rock under her shrieked and groaned and heaved like the thick rolls of the sea when the turbulence began in the depths. Listening to her gut instinct, she stopped there. Clutching the whistle in one hand, she pulled out the Zeus gun with the other. The light remained in the whistle, swirling in streaks of purple and blue and crimson. She ran, her steps faltering for a few heartbeats when she saw answering swirls in the glass barrel of the Zeus gun. Ess grinned into the darkness, envisioning the weapon coming to life and firing without her pulling the trigger. That might come in handy, if Graebaush managed to reach his "rats" and send them into Sanctuary before Uly and his soldiers got to the outside entrances and engaged them.

The trembling in the rock remained, though quieting. She got to the next level up, gasping for breath so she had to stop and catch it before she could play. Her pulse pounded loudly enough she feared she wouldn't hear if anyone came upon her in the darkness. Between the lights filling the whistle and the Zeus gun, she was an easy enough target. She just hoped the swirling colors would confuse someone long enough she would have warning.

"Please, Almighty..." she whispered, swallowed hard, took a deep breath, and shoved the gun back in her pocket. With both hands free, she raised the flute and began the song from the beginning.

The trembling grew stronger with the first note, proving she hadn't imagined it. Ess closed her eyes, trying to feel through her feet and through her backside pressed against the wall behind her. She needed the bracing, as the floor rose, rippling in a way that solid rock should not, without being a good thousand degrees hotter. Ess faltered a moment as her imagination took over, showing her lava bursting up from the depths, melting each level in turn like a dried honeycomb sinking into a candle maker's melting pot. Yet the air and stone around her felt cool.

The air felt cool, because there was a breeze, where Ess knew no breeze could blow. Four notes from the next stopping point, she nearly faltered, and her imagination showed her air moving through Sanctuary, prompted by the movement of rock like enormous, stiff bellows. She prayed everyone had been found and evacuated, and no one had resisted or ignored orders.

Stopping at the second of the three forbidden notes, Ess clutched the whistle, drew her Zeus gun, and ran. This time the trembling in the ground remained steady, vibrating in her bones. She heard the sweet notes in her sinus bones, trilling through the song, so she half-feared the whistle played itself while she ran. A gasping giggle escaped her as a snort, with her mouth clenched tight shut, as she imagined the song playing to the conclusion, to the final, third forbidden note, before she reached the last spot where she needed to play. What would happen then? Would all the levels collapse like a massive fortress of playing cards struck by an errant gust? For all she knew, she had become the whistle.

Granny, you and I are going to have a very long, serious talk when I find you. Since I cannot scold Papa for all the ridiculous responsibility he put on me, you will have to stand in his place. I can't imagine he did any of this without your input and approval, and most likely your guidance.

Ess listened for shouts of panic, for screams, as she reached the spot she calculated was directly above the crucial chamber. She heard nothing but the groaning and grumbling of the tunnels of Sanctuary. In the swirling light of Zeus gun and whistle, the shifting and swaying of the walls, the rippling of the floor and ceiling could be blamed on the movement of the light. The feeling of rising and falling, solid through the soles of her boots, could be blamed on imagination, perhaps a little blood loss. Maybe she had hit her head on the column when she took down Endicott?

"Ninny," she muttered, and went to her knees to be a little steadier. Ess leaned against the wall beside her, but it rippled too much to bear. Her imagination painted a picture of a very large creature awakening from a deep sleep, its skin rippling like a horse trying to shudder away annoying flies. That was not a good image to carry in her head, as she could be likened to the fly, annoying the solid rock creature with the simple childish tune on her whistle.

Zeus gun in her pocket, she paused to listen one last time for footsteps, for shouts, for any indication of movement, other than the rock. Ess grimaced, knowing she wasted time from sheer nervousness. Taking a deep breath, she kept her eyes open and played. The ripples in the stone around her grew more pronounced. That wasn't lava trying to boil up from the depths, but the very fabric of the bedrock rippling, shifting, coming undone, melting without heat, becoming supple like leather. A shudder almost tore the breath from her lungs as she envisioned clearly what would happen the moment she reached that final note. Trying to maintain circular breathing, in through her nose and out through her mouth, trying to keep the music going without break, Ess struggled up to her feet and turned, aiming for the shortest passage that would get her out of here.

The final forbidden note arrived and she elected for breath control and as long a note as possible, rather than volume. One heartbeat. Two. Three. Four. Five.

Empty air appeared beneath her boots. Ess yelped and rock slammed into her soles. She stumbled, scrabbling against the wall for balance. Another yelp as her hand came open involuntarily and the whistle rose up in the air. She snatched at it as the rock dropped again. Ess ran, staggering, envisioning each successive layer of tunnels collapsing into the one below, like a massive stack of nesting cups.

Chapter Twenty-Four

"Stupid. Stupid. Stupid," she snarled at herself as she ran for Dr. Lockhart's workshop. While it was the nearest exit, closest to the surface, with no tunnels underneath it, what guarantee did she have that any of the ropes and ladders would still be in place when she got there?

Tears streaked her face and she was gasping, her legs threatening to fold under her, but she didn't care. The weight of her heritage and her destiny crashed into her, generating fury that gave her the energy to run when fear would have paralyzed her. She rounded a corner and didn't slow, slamming into a wall when the shifting rock tried to tip sideways and throw her off her feet. Ess rebounded and kept running, and a quiet portion of her mind kept a tally of the bruises she would find in the morning.

If she lived until morning.

Light met her eyes as she rounded the final turn in the intersections. Torchlight, warm and golden and flickering. Ess silently vowed: No more tunnels. No more underground warrens, like massive anthills. Humans weren't meant by their Creator to live that way.

The breeze that touched her face now wasn't scented with rock, but with green growing things. It wasn't pumped by the unnatural movement of rock, but the forces that created the weather. She tasted sand and wood and water in the breeze as she dashed down the last short slope, into the wide open gallery of Dr. Lockhart's workshop. A swift glance showed a few cabinets and shelves knocked over, and a small fire where a lantern had fallen and oil spilled, but very little damage.

Ess saw nothing but the rope ladder hanging down from the nearest lip of the crevice overhead. Wiping at her face with her sleeve, she slowed her pace going down the steps to the open air seating that had once been so pleasant, but was now all chaos from the evacuation. She leaped over several overturned benches, some dropped crates, broken plates, spilled books and papers, and reached for the ladder. Her legs ached so she nearly fell. Fine, then she would pull herself up by her arms.

"I don't care that you're past twenty," Uly shouted, leaning over the side and grabbing hold of both sides of the ladder. "When I get you up here—" One hard yank, pulling the ladder up nearly a foot. Theo joined him and they pulled in unison. "I'm swatting your backside—" Another yank. "Until you can't sit for a week."

Ess grinned, her chest aching with the need to breathe, combatting the need to laugh. She crouched on the thick rope of the ladder rung and held on tight and let them pull her up to safety. She told herself the crashing and thunderous echoes were her breathing and the rattling of her heart in her ears, and not generations of excavation collapsing in on itself, burying people's homes, the accumulated inventions and archives of her ancestors, taking it all out of the reach of enemies and allies alike. Her father had theorized this would be necessary. Her grandparents had given her the responsibility. Only time and future generations could judge if she had chosen wisely.

When Uly and Theo got her above ground, she could barely keep herself upright, much less walk. They joined arms and created a seat and hurried her away from the trembling lip of the crevice. As Ess regained her breath, she heard people shouting, a few cries of panic, some cursing, but mostly the sounds of authority keeping people under control, directing them into some semblance of order.

"Did you get them?" she was finally able to say, when they put her down on a blanket in the shelter of a stand of trees that smelled of apples ripening. The ground seemed to hum underneath her, but that was a vast improvement from rocking and heaving and grinding.

"Maybe not all." Theo stepped away but stayed in her line of sight.

Ess saw sunrise spilling through the trees and over the tops of the ridges on her right.

"Enough," Uly growled, and dropped to his knees next to her. He pulled her up tight against him and they clung together until she thought her heart had finally slowed to a normal pace. The only reason she didn't cry was because she didn't think she had any spare moisture left in her body. Uly cried, big, manly, furious tears, and that was enough for both of them.

Theo brought a canteen over and waited until she could reach for it without her arm wobbling like it would break off. "By 'enough,' he means a large enough number, we should have some people with useful information."

"You didn't catch Graebausch?" Ess guessed.

"Let's hope he's one of those stupid enough to stay and get flattened," Uly said.

~~~~~

Ess was glad to return to her cabin on the *Golden Nile*, wash, and collapse for more than a day. She woke up and ate as if she hadn't eaten in three days, then curled up on the couch in the parlor and slept until hunger woke her again. Panic took her for two seconds, when she woke to find Dr. Sylvia bending over her and Dr. Lockhart seated on the end of the couch at her feet, but then she saw the lack of worry on either doctor's face. Ess reasoned she wasn't about to die but had simply drained herself. Their theory was that something in her genetic structure fed the crystal and gave it the power to complete its task of collapsing Sanctuary, literally draining
~~~~~

her. Ess tried not to grumble when she had to endure the gorge-and-hibernate cycle for another day.

While she slept, a camp of sorts was set up on the ground, in among the canyons leading up to Sanctuary, where the ground was stable and the *Nile*'s soldiers could monitor all activity. No one would say it outright, but the residents of Sanctuary were in effect prisoners, everyone under suspicion of treachery until they could be proven otherwise. Fortunately, they had the means to do that, effectively and quickly. Ess and Uly had translated dozens of songs from Edward and Ernest and Matilda's journals. Between those songs, the teas Matilda had devised, and the crystal-guiding abilities in Athena, Clytie, and Vulcan, they searched the minds and memories of everyone who had been evacuated from Sanctuary and the Revisionist nest.

Endicott insisted on being the first to be examined. Lewis and MacDonald stayed right there in the tent being used for the examinations, keeping watch, their faces somber. Ess watched them melt a little as they learned the whole story. Yes, he had begun as a traitor, sent in by the man who claimed to be his father. Once he learned the truth of his parentage and history and the injustice perpetrated against him and his true family, Endicott had immersed himself wholeheartedly in protecting the Originators. With Edward Fremont, he had helped to root out nearly twenty Revisionist infiltrators before Edward and Vivian died. Ernest and Matilda had agreed with Endicott that his position had become precarious, and they preferred that he take on a watchman's role, rather than actively fighting their enemies. He had enjoyed his work all these years, simply being a lawyer, watching over the legal matters of people he considered his friends.

When the examination finished, Lewis and MacDonald shook his hand and clapped him on the back, and then kept him company as he slept off the nausea and after-effects of Matilda's mind-opening potions.

Once Endicott was cleared, his testimony for or against various people in high positions helped to streamline the process of verifying who was loyal, who had turned traitor, and who was an infiltrator, substituted for the original person. Ess spent most of each day in the examination tent, helping to mix the herbs and brew the potions and then playing her flute. She was glad to leave the questioning and judgment to others. The last few days, having to decide and judge and act and carry the weight of her discoveries had been exhausting.

Uly brought her news of the work being done to ensure the Revisionists who had survived the collapse of their nest didn't escape. Neither of them were quite sure how to feel, when prisoners were questioned and tallied, and they determined that nearly eighty Revisionists had been trapped in the collapsed tunnels. Many people were found smothered in the dust or crushed just yards away from escape. Mr. Graebausch and several of his people had managed to get to Sanctuary's stables and steal several horses. The good news was that they had been forced to abandon trunks, crates, and sacks of records, equipment, and supplies they had stolen from Sanctuary.

Word would spread as swiftly as possible to all Originator connections and divisions and support stations that Graebausch and his followers were traitors and enemies. However, chances were good that despite the darkness of the cloudy night, despite the panic and other "distractions" at the time, he would have seen the *Golden Nile* hovering over the far end of Sanctuary and evacuating people via the baskets. It was only a matter of time before he gained enough information to identify the airship.

"It might be wise to send the *Nile* overseas for some time," Clytie said, when that information and assessment came before the emergency Council. They met every night in the parlor of the *Golden Nile*, to go over the discoveries and reports of each day's work. "A world tour might be wise, spreading the news from nation to nation that our secrecy and divisions must end."

"Tightening the circle and closing the ranks," Ford offered, looking up from the piles of paperwork and maps that he and Theo examined every night. While they weren't officially part of the Council, they were always present as leaders of the defensive forces. As Vulcan said several days before, the end of the secrecy and keeping the right hand ignorant of the left hand's activities had to start somewhere.

Everyone agreed with Clytie's assessment and suggestion, even if somewhat reluctantly. MacDonald tried to joke that the lovely airship tower he wanted to build in Cleveland would be wasted if the *Golden Nile* wasn't going to dock there. That led to a more pleasant discussion, dealing with ideas to build an entire fleet of airships for the Originators, for both courier and supply transport purposes, and to ensure greater security. A headquarters was needed, no matter what changes were made in the structure of their organization. It only made sense to put it in a growing city at the hub of industrial growth, with access to every possible mode of transportation. The plan for a modest office building with one airship docking tower would have to be expanded upwards and downwards as well as outwards. It would accommodate several airships at a time and have docks on the Cuyahoga River for access to the lakes for shipping, as well as the railroads.

By the time the last resident of Sanctuary had been examined and either identified as a Revisionist plant or cleared as loyal, the plans for the tower in Cleveland had solidified. Endicott, Lewis and MacDonald gathered up a team to go east with them and begin the preliminary work. They would travel on the *Golden Nile*, which needed to make some repairs and regather supplies for the trip south. Ess hated the delay, even knowing it was necessary. Gathering the latest news from diplomatic sources was vital for their safety, to ensure that territories and governments that were previously friendly to United States citizens hadn't changed their minds and declared war while the crew of the *Nile* was busy elsewhere, making it dangerous to fly over them.

Some of her impatience eased when she realized she would have time to contact Agent Sutter and ask about any progress in the hunt for Carmen. She was encouraged when the Council agreed that finding Anna's daughter and ensuring her safety was vital. Only slightly less important was determining what had happened to the crystal rose that matched the one Ess now wore around her neck.

Captain Astrid pushed the engines of the *Nile*, heading east. Ess and Uly kept busy during the trip with Vulcan, Dr. Lockhart and Dr. Sylvia, studying Edward, Ernest, and Matilda's journals for any last shreds of information about the time key. For amusement, they theorized ways to bypass the necessary blood link for operating the communication plates. Dr. Lockhart was fascinated with the plates and declared that finding a way to expand the blood-crystal-music link was now his personal challenge. There had to be some way to code more people into each plate, so that communication between multiple points became possible. Instantaneous communication, vocal as well as visual, would help with the security challenges in the years ahead of them. With the collapse of Sanctuary and the discovery and destruction of the Revisionist nest literally under their noses, their enemies would be scrambling to regroup and exact revenge.

Uly confided to Ess that he would almost welcome some Revisionist attacks. They would be honest and open, and he had some confidence he could handle that kind of trouble. The puzzle of untangling how the time key worked made his head hurt, almost as much as the anticipated long-range effort of contacting every Originator division and outpost around the world. Ess understood exactly how he felt, even though she had very little experience in dealing with the far-flung network of Originators. Diving into the problems of the time key and the communication plates was an escape for her, and despite the headaches, almost pleasurable. Uly scowled when she told him that and threatened to swat her. Then they laughed together.

When they reached Cleveland, there was little time for a reunion with Hilda and the others. Ess was pleased to see that in the short time she had been gone, the family retainers had finished negotiations for and bought the buildings on both sides of Hilda's, and were expanding operations, offering shelter for more children, more trades training, and they intended to turn two entire floors in the left-hand building into a charity medical facility. With great upheaval in the structure of any city as it expanded in size and technology and industrialization moved in, the way of life for too many people had to be rewritten. Some were unable to cope and were swept up in the current of change and tossed about. Others didn't even try to swim or find a way to stay afloat. All needed some help. Thomas, Waldo, Bridget, Peggety, and Hilda couldn't help everyone who would soon be in need, but they could reach out to the most vulnerable.

Ess expressed her concerns once again to the trio of lawyers, the day they disembarked from the *Golden Nile*. Endicott assured her he would make it his personal quest that every family and business displaced by their massive building project would receive assistance in relocating and creating a new life that was better than, not just equal to, what they had before.

That reassurance helped to ease the sting of hearing from Agent Sutter that he had made no progress in finding Carmen. There were over two dozen known camp meeting organizations operating across the country. That number didn't count the smaller teams supported by individual churches rather than missionary societies. He promised her he would find Carmen, and she trusted him.

Then, with the *Golden Nile* physically ready for the challenges of the voyage south, and with all the diplomatic channels cleared, all the latest political tides accounted for, at last it was time to search for the time box and those who waited inside it.

~~~~~

Hours before they passed the southernmost point of the Yucatan Peninsula, the time key lit up. Ess was holding it. Brooding over it, Uly claimed later, but without too much force, because he could be accused of the same thing. She wouldn't have noticed the soft ripples of purple and indigo in the core of the interlocking triangles if she hadn't been turning it over and over in her hands, half-mesmerizing herself with trying to follow the bars with her eyes and fingers. She nearly let out a shout, then confusion strangled the sound before it reached her throat. They were hundreds of miles north of the place where her grandparents' archeological camp had been, so what was the irritating device doing? More importantly, what had it detected? Something crystal, most likely. What were they supposed to do about it?

Ess had been in the lower forward compartment, where she could see out over the landscape ahead of them. The illusion of moving slightly faster, getting closer to her grandparents before anyone else, had been comforting only for the first day of the voyage. She continued to come there during breaks in her studies just because she could be sure of some solitude. The compartment was noticeably chilly, compared to the rest of the ship, but she didn't mind. When the time key lit up, she waited a few minutes for it to lose the light or do something else. When the light remained steady, softly shifting through the colors, she got up and hurried down the passageway to Athena's office. Everyone in the room also saw the colors.

However, the light faded after another twenty minutes. Everyone agreed the time key was reacting to crystal, somewhere on the ground below the ship. The light faded because they had moved out of range of whatever was down there. Chances were good it was a large amount of crystal, close to the surface, or highly charged with energy. The discussion
~~~~~

over dinner that night was enjoyable, full of speculation and friendly arguments about theories and what experiments in the past had proven.

In the end, they could do nothing about the deposit of crystal, whatever it was, however strong it was, other than chart the location on Captain Astrid's navigational maps. Those who were most sensitive to the key agreed to take charge of it in shifts, so that next time it reacted, they could accurately record the location. Someday, they would have the resources to come back and search on the ground for that crystal. Not now, though. Until they could be more secure, until they were sure the Revisionists couldn't track their movements and spy on them, they didn't dare take the time to stop. Besides, they were heading into politically volatile territory. Even if Revisionists weren't nearby, there were other forces that might try to shoot them out of the sky if they lingered, or even slowed the airship.

Over the next three days, the time key reacted eight more times. Ess, Athena, Uly, and Dr. Lockhart were in possession of the device when it awoke. They took careful notes of the colors, the speed of color shifts, and several times the soft humming or chiming sounds it gave off. There was no telling what the sounds and colors indicated until someone found the crystal the key sensed.

The time key sang when they were an hour of flight at top speed from the elder Fremonts' former archeological dig site. Uly had it in his guardianship, and came running to Dr. Sylvia's office, where she, Dr. Lockhart, Athena, and Ess discussed altering some of the mind-opening potions Matilda had devised. The two physicians were of the opinion that a thorough understanding of the effects of the potions would help them devise counteragents, for defensive purposes.

All four of them felt the subliminal humming in the air before they heard Uly's boots pounding on the deck. Moments later, he burst through the door, one arm extended to push aside all barriers while he cradled the time key against his chest. He skidded to a stop several steps from the long worktable as the song became audible.

"Well," Athena said, breaking the slightly stunned silence, while the light radiating from the time key shimmered between white and gold, "I think that's a very good sign."

Uly whooped and tossed the time key to Ess. She swallowed down a furious shriek as she leaped to her feet and held out both hands. Scalding curses caught in her throat. She nearly dropped the time key as the energy buzzed through her fingers like thousands of tiny, icy, oddly pleasurable needles.

He sobered quickly, when Athena gave him the duty of organizing the teams of soldiers who would go down to scout out the terrain, guard the rescue team, and watch for any reaction from nearby military or native tribes. The plan of attack had been discussed multiple times, and everyone on board the *Golden Nile* had a chance to offer suggestions and volunteer their specific skills to the effort. While they could hope their arrival would attract no attention, or at least no negative reaction, wisdom said to plan for the worst possible reception from the locals and any military that might be nearby. They had to come into the area at full speed and locate the spot where the camp had been. The drop-line teams would go down first and ensure the safety of the searchers.

Hopefully, the time key not only would unlock the time box that had held the archeological team all these years, but lead the searchers to it.

"Is it too much to ask it to attract the time box to us?" Ess said, as she came into the bay with an estimated twenty minutes until descent time. She wore the flexible armor Vulcan had devised on the trip south.

In the chill air of the bay, with sharp gusts of wind piercing the seams, it felt comfortably warm. Ess didn't look forward to the weight and heat in the jungle three hundred feet or so below them. The armor looked like jackets and gauntlets and leggings of particularly thick, heavy, dark leather. Vulcan had infused it with threads of metal, requiring tin snips as thick as her arm to cut the resulting material.

"That's an idea," Ford said, raising his voice to be heard above the roar of the wind. "Athena lectures me constantly on my need to learn to ask for what I want, instead of just getting up and going after it myself."

"I suppose good table manners can apply when dealing with gifts from the Almighty," Theo said. He winked at Ess and beckoned her over to the security railing, to attach her safety rope next to his.

Ess had the time key in a leather satchel securely strung across her chest. A fine netting of tough fibers enclosed the crystal device and was tied to the netting sewn to the inside of the satchel, to ensure it couldn't be dropped and lost during a rapid retreat, if they came under attack. She pressed both hands over the closed satchel. Through the thick leather, she felt the increased humming of the crystal device, even though she couldn't hear it. If she opened the flap, the light coming from the time key might just have grown bright enough to be blinding. Another reason for keeping it in the satchel until absolutely necessary. She had a sudden vision of the light attracting angry military forces and unfriendly locals like a lighthouse.

Chapter Twenty-Five

Ess prayed, asking the Almighty for guidance, for a quick, efficient search, for the knowledge of what to do to find and then open the time box. She prayed for mercy and grace in this rescue mission, and for safety for everyone who had volunteered to put their lives on the line to retrieve Matilda and Ernest Fremont. Then, despite feeling it was slightly blasphemous, she asked the time key itself to cooperate and lead them.

Who could be sure that the substance from the future didn't have some kind of intelligence or awareness? One of her grandfather's journals had provided fascinating reading. Ernest had gathered up all the stories of thinking machines that managed the future world, handling the growing of food and medical treatment and communication. Where was the line that divided a machine that appeared able to think from a machine that had become self-aware and able to decide for itself? How much information had to be stored in a thinking machine, or perhaps an incredibly complex device made of crystal, to bring it to self-awareness? Could the time key be one of those devices, or just poised on the verge of awareness? Ess reasoned that wisdom required she use politeness. Just in case.

Despite being ready, despite watching Uly and his team as they prepared their drop lines and Captain Astrid's lieutenant counting down the altitude as the *Nile* dropped, Ess still gasped and flinched as the bay doors opened and a gush of air roared through the bay. After the first chill blast, the scent of jungle and the humidity from far below swirled through the bay. Uly turned to her and saluted, a tip of his first two fingers off his right eyebrow, then he and his team gave a shout and a hard shove on the basket, sending it dropping instantly out of sight. Ess listened to the scream of the cord going through the block-and-tackle arrangement, counting in her mind for the first drop, then the second. In her mind's eye, she saw Uly and his men tip backward off their perches on the outside of the basket, dropping headfirst, with only their harnesses and the thin, incredibly strong black cord to keep them from hurtling to their deaths on the jungle floor.

A bell rang through the bay. The *Golden Nile* reversed engines and turned to stay above the spot where the basket dropped, effectively anchored to the jungle clearing.

Ess focused on the open square in the bay floor, silently counting, one hand gripping the safety line, the other clutching the satchel and the time key inside it.

"Go." Theo nudged her, and Ess saw the last sparkles of a flare rising up through the opening in the bay floor.

Grinning, feeling foolish and glad of it, Ess headed for the basket waiting for her team. She wanted to unclip the safety line and run, but she knew better. Uly and Theo had both lectured her on proper procedures before allowing her within twenty feet of the drop basket. She climbed in, detached the safety line from her belt, then clipped her belt to the lines inside the basket. Theo winked at her and took his place facing her, on the outside of the basket. The other dozen in their team climbed in or took their places on the outside in a matter of seconds. The silent countdown in her head got to fifteen and Ess gripped the rim of the basket hard, throwing all her weight backward.

An exhilarated shriek escaped her, despite her resolution to be silent as the basket tipped and for an eternal heartbeat, she thought they were stuck. Ess met Theo's grin, then they were falling. She managed to hold back the other shriek of utter terror as her feet left the floor of the basket. Uly had warned her — she wished he had only been teasing — she wished she hadn't convinced herself he was teasing.

She couldn't breathe, couldn't feel her heartbeat, and her time sense utterly escaped her. How could Uly do this again and again, and not only do it, but outside the basket, and then go headfirst?

Her brother was the bravest man on the face of the Earth.

Theo shouted. The wind and speed of their descent tore the words away before Ess could make them out. He gripped her hand on the rim at the same moment the basket jolted, hitting the point where the brakes caught the cord, slowing the descent.

Amazing, the comforting feel of gravity pulling her toward the ground again with something solid under her feet. Ess finally got her lungs to work and raised her head to meet Theo's eyes. He winked at her and squeezed her hand.

When she could finally look over the edge of the basket, she saw the ground rushing up toward her. Ess remembered to bend her knees to bounce as the basket landed. She chose to take the empty sensation in her chest as exhilaration and grabbed the side to unclip the safety line, swing her legs over, and climb out immediately. Before her legs locked permanently, and her hands refused to let go of the basket.

Her ears popped and she muffled a yelp. The worst part was the sensation of something breaking loose between her ears and trying to slide down her throat.

A muffled chiming filled her newly cleared ears. Ess turned around, dropping into a crouch, her face heating as she realized she was the source of the sound. More accurately, the time key was the culprit. She dug into the satchel and brought it out, still wrapped in the netting.

"Can you make it shut up?" Theo barked, settling into position with his back to her, Zeus gun drawn.

"We're clear," Uly called, coming into the clearing with his own Zeus at ready. "Whatever you did..." He beckoned, eyes wide, his mouth twisted in that odd expression that meant he wanted to grin but wasn't sure he should. Without waiting to see if they obeyed, he left the clearing.

Ess ran to catch up with him. The time key's light shifted from solid gold to a rainbow that shifted at dizzying speed. The chimes changed.

"It's the 'Find Me,' song," she blurted, and nearly ran into Uly when he skidded to a stop. She leaned to the right to look around him.

A swirl of light matching the time key churned in the air about shoulder-height above a wide, barren patch of ground. It looked like a mixture of clay and damp soil, reminding her of every spring when Hilda would have Thomas and Giles clear some ground behind the house, so she could mix in the compost that had been fermenting all winter and then lay out her kitchen garden.

It looked scraped clean of all plant life.

What could do that, out here in the jungle?

"My guess is, the time box," Uly said, when Ess repeated her question aloud.

They both had to shout, as the chimes grew loud enough to threaten to become painful.

"Grandfather tried to teach me about time travel theory. Of course, he treated it like a story, a faerie tale, but... what if the time box is kind of frozen in time? The journey from that moment to now is faster than the fastest train. That's enough energy to kill all the plants in the area." Uly shrugged.

"Be careful Grandfather doesn't hear you handling scientific theory like that. He'll insist you stop being a soldier and theorize with him."

"That's cruel." He grinned and stepped to one side, keeping his feet safely away from the bare ground. Ess copied him, imagining what could happen to a body when the time box reached the present moment and tried to occupy the same space. "So what do we do now?"

"Do something before we're surrounded." Theo stepped into the clearing with them. He let out a low, appreciative whistle.

Ess knew if she didn't act, she might paralyze herself with questions. Untangling the time key from the net, she pulled it completely out of the satchel and took a step closer to the swirl of light.

"It's growing, isn't it?" Theo gestured for the soldiers who had followed him to spread out, surrounding the clearing, standing in the jungle growth and facing outward.

"It was a handful, just before we signaled you," Uly said. They stayed where they were as Ess took another step closer, holding out the time key. "As soon as the basket dropped, it started growing."

"Let's hope that's another good—" Ess yelped as the crystal construction leaped from her hand.

It spun, so the edges smoothed and rounded and looked like a top diving straight into the middle of the swirling light of the time box. Light erupted, unfolding like a massive rose blossoming.

Ess smelled blood, gunpowder, and the mud and crushed green scent of the jungle.

The light faded, turning into more than twenty people and assorted baggage, crouching down together, with Matilda Fremont standing at their head, and Ernest behind her, bracing her with his hands on her shoulders. Everyone showed signs of hurried flight through the jungle, smears of mud and blood, torn clothes, and several people on the ground, propped up against the legs of others, with makeshift bandages on their wounds. The time key spun to a stop in a loose-woven basket of crystal. Everyone in the group looked around, blinking as if waking from a dream.

Ess wondered if the jungle clearing had changed noticeably since the light surrounded them. Shouts rose up from the rest of the soldiers, coming filtered and somehow surreal through the thick, humid greenery around them.

"Sorry—that means we have company coming," Theo said, stepping forward and holding out a hand to the cluster of battered time travelers. "We need to leave. Quickly."

Everyone in the group turned almost as one person and stared at the other three in the clearing with them. Matilda wobbled a little as she tried to take a step forward. She blinked rapidly. Ernest dug his spectacles out of his coat pocket and slid his other arm around her waist, to support her.

"Granny?" Ess absolutely refused to cry, but she couldn't seem to keep the wobble from her voice and the hot wet from her eyes.

"Merciful Lord." Ernest chuckled. "She's all grown up."

"That's ten dollars you owe me," Matilda said.

"Granny, you didn't!" Uly slung his arm around Ess's shoulders and shook her. "They wagered on how long they would have to wait!"

"Common sense." Her voice cracked a little and she looked down at the quiescent time lock and crystal basket. "Well done, my dears."

Then she fainted.

<div align="center">~~~~~</div>

Matilda Fremont was not the fainting type. The strain of controlling the time box, the shock of being held suspended in one moment of time and then being yanked forward almost eight years, combined with the effort of controlling the crystal energy, had drained her. She displayed the fortitude she was famous for by reviving before everyone had moved to the clearing where the baskets waited to haul the first load up to the airship. Naturally, she wanted to wait for the second basket to go upward, so she could watch the process from the ground.

Everyone in the archeological party suffered the same effects, and Ess worried a little when her grandparents didn't protest how Dr. Sylvia and Dr. Lockhart bundled everyone off to medical for thorough examinations.

196

She expected Matilda to insist on hearing a condensed report of everything that had happened, first to the Originators, then to their family, then events in world history, before allowing herself to be examined. Ess and Uly spent an anxious half hour, waiting for the first examination to be finished. Then they were allowed into the recovery room to sit with Ernest and Matilda while Athena and Captain Astrid and Ford took turns with the reports they had prepared. After all, they had been trained by Ernest and Matilda and knew even better than their relieved grandchildren what to expect.

By the time they reached the conclusion of the massive effort to rid Sanctuary of the Revisionist infiltration, the elder Fremonts had reacted well to the tonic Dr. Lockhart had devised on the trip south. Ernest joked that the noxious taste was partly in revenge for him stealing Matilda from the doctor so many years ago. Ess was astonished to see her grandmother blush.

Every member of the party had come through the experience with very little negative effects. The worst damage had been caused by the bullets from the attack that came out of nowhere in the early morning hours. Some were still reacting to the strain of the headlong flight through the jungle, away from their burning campsite, and the tension of waiting for the attackers to catch up with them while Matilda struggled to activate the time box.

The archeological party was released from medical, other than one man with a broken arm and two who Dr. Sylvia wanted to retain for continued observation, because they had lost so much blood. Ess and Uly hurried on ahead to the large cabin assigned to their grandparents. They turned on the lights and put out towels and soap and clean changes of clothing, retrieved from Matilda and Ernest's own possessions in storage. They were finished with the chore and paced a few times in the sitting room of the cabin, waiting, until they heard Ford's voice. Of course, he and Athena were still bringing the elder Fremonts up-to-date on events. Ernest laughed and he sounded so normal, Ess again had a hard time holding back tears.

"Ulysses." Matilda beckoned for him the moment she stepped through the door, with Ernest right behind her. When she spread her arms, he hesitated, eyes widening. "Young man—"

"Sorry, Granny. I really expect you to box my ears," he said, voice strained with more emotions than laughter, as he stepped into her embrace.

"That will likely come later." She squeezed him tight.

Ess shuddered, wondering how much longer these odd feelings of not-quite-right would last. Uly was so much taller than Matilda, and the last time their entire family had been together, he had been only an inch or too taller than her, just able to look Ernest in the eye. Now he towered over them both.

"Thank you, for helping bring two of my favorite pupils together." She sighed loudly as she released him. "At long last. The only couple more oblivious to how perfectly suited they were for each other were your own parents."

"Well, the whole effort to find Ford and bring him back to the land of the living is an adventure in itself. Have they told you about Mr. Stryker?" he said, stepping back.

"I have the terrible suspicion it will take the entire journey back north before we hear all the details," Ernest said.

"That can wait," Matilda said. She turned to Ess. "My little girl, all grown up." Her eyes glistened and Ess was horrified when her grandmother sniffed, just once. "I suppose I should thank the Good Lord I was spared all the battles and arguments, but... well, I must admit I was looking forward to them at the same time. Oh, mercy, am I such a harridan, child?" She spread her arms.

"I think that is our cue to leave." Ford laughed, and Ess saw that Athena had already retreated out into the hall.

"I think she fears hurting you, dear," Ernest said. "Or perhaps the opposite."

"Curse my reputation. I am most definitely not made of granite," Matilda said on a sigh.

"Granny..." Ess finally unlocked her legs and stumbled the last few steps to hold her.

Matilda shuddered, but at least her sobs were silent. She let Ess and Ernest guide her down onto the divan set against the wall and they clung together for several long moments, just long enough for Ess to release some of the aching longing and a bit of jealousy that Uly got the first real hug.

"That's better," Matilda said, when Ess slid out of her reach enough to kneel on the floor, but still allow them to hold each other's hands. "I am so sorry, my dear, for the incredible burden we had to put on you. Both of you," she said, lifting her head to include Uly. "I know already you did splendidly."

"We tore Sanctuary to pieces," Uly muttered. "How can that be splendid?"

"It needed doing," Ernest said, settling down on the divan beside Matilda. "I must admit to being relieved that I was not the one to have to make that dread decision. Bad enough we will spend so much time looking backward, just to catch up with the rest of you. To have to look back over that particular bit of history and wonder if I chose wisely, if the timing was handled correctly... my dear, we are not as young as we used to be. Time to put the burden on younger shoulders." He nodded for punctuation and winked first at Ess, then Uly.

"Ford mentioned something about rebuilding in Cleveland. I suppose that will be home now," Matilda said.

"Not for a long time." Uly grunted as he dragged an easy chair over to settle down for what Ess suspected would be a long talk. Much as she would prefer making sure her grandparents had a chance to wash up and change their clothes and take a long nap, she knew the discussion couldn't be avoided. "It's already been decided that you two need to take a long voyage around the world. After the battles we fought and all the poison and sickness within the ranks we've uncovered, you two are the most well-known and visible of all the elder Originators. We need you to go to each of our strongholds in Europe and Asia and Africa, to confer with the leaders there, assure them that they are safe, and come to some consensus on new policies and practices going forward." He sat back, raising his hands slightly. "That is the decision of the remnants of the Council. I am just the messenger."

"Harm not the messenger, eh?" Ernest said.

"You're among the few that everyone can trust," Ess offered. "Your miraculous return from the dead will be a rallying point and raise all our spirits."

"A trip around the world." He nodded, lips pursed, eyes going distant as he caught hold of Matilda's hand and interwove their fingers. "After what we've been through, that could be... relaxing."

"On the *Golden Nile*," Uly added.

"That changes everything," Matilda said, exchanging a smile with Ernest. "Like bringing our hotel with us. No need to pack and unpack, no worry about adequate accommodations, clean linens, and healthy water."

"As if you ever worried about such things," her husband muttered. "Most scandalous woman of her generation, quite as comfortable slogging through knee-deep mud and speed-loading pistols as she was sitting in a parlor with royalty."

"Will you be with us?" she said, wrinkling up her nose at him. "I imagine you have your duties, things you need to do, but there is so much catching up to do."

"We're not sure," Ess said, squeezing her grandmother's hand a little tighter. "While you are strengthening our people and closing the ranks, we have several tasks just as vital. First, I need to find Anna's daughter."

"Her daughter?" Ernest said.

"We have a link, a bond, when we wear the crystal roses. Her mother is dead, and Carmen seems to be in some distress. I need to find her."

"The other mission is just as vital as finding Carmen," Uly said. "What happens when we have enough pieces of the Great Machine to assemble it? We need to find a place where it will be safe for all the ages to come, where no one can get to it, no matter how deep treachery runs through our ranks."

The End

About the Author

On the road to publication, Michelle fell into fandom in college and has 40+ stories in various SF and fantasy universes. She has a bunch of useless degrees in theater, English, film/communication, and writing. Even worse, she has over 100 books and novellas with multiple small presses, in science fiction and fantasy, YA, suspense, women's fiction, and sub-genres of romance.

Her official launch into publishing came with winning first place in the Writers of the Future contest in 1990. She was a finalist in the EPIC Awards competition multiple times, winning with *Lorien* in 2006 and *The Meruk Episodes, I-V,* in 2010, and was a finalist in the Realm Awards competition, in conjunction with the Realm Makers convention.

Her training includes the Institute for Children's Literature; proofreading at an advertising agency; and working at a community newspaper. She is a tea snob and freelance edits for a living (MichelleLevigne@gmail.com for info/rates), but only enough to give her time to write. Her newest crime against the literary world is to be co-managing editor at Mt. Zion Ridge Press and launching the publishing co-op, Ye Olde Dragon Books. Be afraid … be very afraid.

And please check out her newest venture: Ye Olde Dragon's Library, the storytelling podcast. Each week, listeners are invited to join Michelle on her blog to ask questions and give feedback and suggestions. Interspersed between the chapters will be interviews with authors of fantastical fiction. Listen to the podcast on your favorite podcast app or listen on the website: www.YeOldeDragonBooks.com, and click on the Ye Olde Dragon's Library link. Then go to her blog to interact: www.MichelleLevigne.blogspot.com

www.Mlevigne.com
www.MichelleLevigne.blogspot.com

www.YeOldeDragonBooks.com
www.MtZionRidgePress.com

Look for Michelle's Goodreads groups:
Guardians of Neighborlee
Voyages of the AFV Defender

NEWSLETTER:
Want to learn about upcoming books, book launch parties, inside information, and cover reveals?
Go to Michelle's website or blog to sign up.

Thanks for reading!
If you enjoyed this book, would you help Michelle by posting a review on Goodreads?

Are you a member of Book Bub? If so, please follow Michelle on Book Bub, and you'll get alerts when new books are coming out.

As a way of saying thanks, Michelle invites you to the Goodies page on her website. It will change regularly, offering you a free short story, a sample audiobook chapter, sneak peeks at new cover art, inside information on discounts and new release dates, etc.

Please go to: Mlevigne.com/good-stuff.html

Also by Michelle L. Levigne

Guardians of the Time Stream: 4-book Steampunk series
The Match Girls: Humorous inspirational romance series starting with **A Match (Not) Made in Heaven**
Sarai's Journey: A 2-book biblical fiction series
Tabor Heights: 18-book inspirational small town romance series.
Quarry Hall: 11-book women's fiction/suspense series
For Sale: Wedding Dress. Never Used: inspirational romance
Crooked Creek: Fun Fables About Critters and Kids: Children's short stories.

Do Yourself a Favor: Tips and Quips on the Writing Life. A book of writing advice.

To Eternity (and beyond): *Writing Spec Fic Good for Your Soul.* A book defending speculative fiction.

Killing His Alter-Ego: contemporary romance/suspense, taking place in fandom.

The Commonwealth Universe: SF series, 25 books and growing

The Hunt: 5-book YA fantasy series

Faxinor: Fantasy series, 4 books and growing

Wildvine: Fantasy series, 14 books when all released

Neighborlee: Humorous fantasy series

Zygradon: 5-book Arthurian fantasy series

AFV Defender: SF adventure series

Young Defenders: Middle Grade SF series, spin-off of *AFV Defender*

Magic to Spare: Fantasy series

Book & Mug Mysteries: cozy mystery series

Quest for the Crescent Moon: fantasy series

Steward's World: fantasy series reboot and expansion

The Enchanted Castle Archives: fantasy series